Friends Like Us

By the same author

Place of Reeds
Black Mulberries

About the author

Caitlin Davies is the author of the highly-acclaimed memoir *Place of Reeds*, an account of her twelve eventful years in Botswana. She now lives in London, and writes education features for the *Independent*.

Friends Like Us

CAITLIN DAVIES

POCKET
BOOKS

LONDON • SYDNEY • NEW YORK • TORONTO

First published in Great Britain by Pocket Books, 2009
An imprint of Simon & Schuster UK
A CBS COMPANY

1 3 5 7 9 10 8 6 4 2

Simon & Schuster UK Ltd
1st Floor, 222 Gray's Inn Road
London WC1X 8HB

www.simonsays.co.uk

Simon & Schuster Australia
Sydney

A CIP catalogue record for this book
is available from the British Library

ISBN 978-1-41652-255-3

Typeset by M Rules
Printed by CPI Cox & Wyman, Reading, Berkshire RG1 8EX

To the women I've been lucky
enough to know since school. And to Buncle,
with love and without whom . . .

Portugal 1989

Chapter One

BEL

Shit. It's happening again. Why is it happening again? It's been ages since I did this, why is it starting again? I've put the film in the side pocket of my suitcase, I've seen my fingers zip it shut, I know it's in there, safe. But I have to check it again, I have to make sure, I have to feel the shape of the hard black canister as it bulges against the pocket.

At least I'm alone; at least there's no one in the house but me. The silence is startling. When I go into Ashley's room I can't even hear the sound of my own bare feet on the tiled floor. Ashley's got the best bedroom, but then she would; it's white and cool and uncluttered and smells of vanilla, just like her. The cover on her bed is so smooth it's like she never even slept here last night. There's a small wooden table with a mirror on top and she's arranged all her creams and potions in a row. She's left her bracelets here as well, in a pile of silver and gold.

I walk through the room and step onto the balcony. Outside, down in the garden, the fig trees aren't moving. The almond trees are still. All around the trees are square little stones like crumbly biscuits. In the mornings I water the trees with a hosepipe like a white snake, but it's late afternoon now

3

and they are thirsty. I can hear the air buzzing. Down by the cliffs the dragonflies are mating.

Did I shut the door downstairs? If I shut it then I'll be able to hear Ashley coming back. Why isn't she back yet? The others will be back soon too; it'll only take them twenty minutes to get up the cliff. I stood there, on the top of the cliff, just ten minutes ago and I felt on top of the world.

I'm sure I shut the door; I can see myself closing it tight, see the way the handle went down in my hand. But what if I didn't? What if I didn't shut it properly enough? And what if the film's not there, safe in the side pocket of my suitcase? Sometimes I don't know how to know whether I know something or not.

I go back into my room and put my suitcase, my brother Joe's cast-off, on the bed and unzip the side pocket. It's like a bag, this pocket, like Mum's old string shopping bag. I check the film again, feel the canister. I zip the pocket shut and pat it. Then I pat it twice more to make it three. Three used to be one of my numbers. Three still feels safe.

I wish I'd never taken the picture. I just came up to finish the film because I was bored of taking pictures on the beach: Loreen holding half a watermelon on her head so the pips got caught in her hair, Karen pulling that face where she sucks in half her mouth. And Ashley had gone; she'd disappeared with the German boys from the bar. It's always the same when we meet boys. Loreen sees them first, decides in an instant which one she fancies, which one she'll marry and have kids with, but the boys always radiate to Ashley, even though out of all of us she's already got a boyfriend. And she's slept with him, Loreen told me.

4

'Why are you going back?' Loreen asked. 'Why don't you stay with us?' She was sitting on a towel in her new Top Shop bikini, peeling back the wrapper on a Cornetto, licking at the swirly jam topping. We were in the same spot we'd been going down to every morning. The beach is long and wide and at one end it weaves around a little peninsula, the sand disappearing between hunks of jagged rock and then sprinkling out again. The spot we like is up against the cliff which has pitted holes like open mouths; it's where the rocks form a pool and the water is warmer.

'I'm just going back to the house,' I told Loreen, 'that's all.' But Loreen can never understand why I would want to be alone, because she doesn't even like going to the loo on her own. At school she still moves her desk so it's next to mine. When we walk down the street she links arms. When I stay the night she squishes the beds together so we can talk without raising our voices and waking her mum.

'Can't you wait for us?' Karen asked, and she looked at me as if I was up to something. She was sitting in front of Loreen, cross-legged on the sand. She put down her book. Everywhere she goes she reads; it doesn't matter what's going on around her she can still read. Only she doesn't read a book, she eats it. She opens it up and she holds it right up near her face and she stays like that, turning the pages, until she's full and the book eaten. That's why she's so good at school. That's why I get her to do my English homework.

'No,' I told Karen. 'I'm going to go up and finish my film. I'll see you back at the house.' Sometimes even when I'm settled, even when I'm happy with what I'm doing, then I just have the urge to move on. I picked up my rucksack, my

5

brother Joe's old rucksack, and I thought I was putting it on carefully but Karen heard the clang as I lifted it onto my back.

'You took that bottle!'

'What bottle?' asked Loreen, scrunching up the wrapper of her Cornetto.

'The one at the bar,' said Karen. 'The one that was on the table where the German boys were.'

I laughed, caught out.

'Did you pay for it?' Karen asked.

I shrugged. If someone was stupid enough to leave a bottle of vodka on a table then what was I going to do?

'They'll have seen you,' warned Karen, putting her book face-down on the sand. Her hair was matted; she'd only just been swimming, going far out as she always does until Loreen worries she won't get back.

'What's it about?' I asked, nodding at the book, distracting her from the fact I stole the bottle because I knew she was going to tell me off.

'Well,' said Karen, 'it's about this American bloke, Nick, who rents a house in Long Island where all these really rich people live. His neighbour is called Gatsby . . .'

'I've heard of him,' said Loreen. 'Didn't we do that book in English?'

'No,' said Karen. 'We were going to but we never did.' Her eyes were bright now and she was holding the book in both hands because Karen wants to go and live in America, that's why she's always reading American books, even when we don't have to. 'Anyway,' she said, 'Gatsby lives in this mansion and has these wild parties with all these celebrated people . . .'

'What does that mean?' asked Loreen.

'That's what he calls them,' said Karen. 'Celebrated people, you know, famous. And everyone gossips about Gatsby because they don't know who he really is or how he made all his money. Nick, his neighbour, has this cousin, Daisy, who's married. One day Nick, he's the one telling the story, gets an invitation to one of the parties and it turns out Gatsby knew Daisy before and has never stopped loving her and all these parties are really just a way to impress her . . .'

'Aah,' said Loreen, because she's soppy.

'So he wants Nick to help arrange a reunion with Daisy. And that's as far as I've got.'

'Sounds boring,' I said. I don't like the books Karen likes, I like detective books. I like books where you have to find out who did it.

'Not really,' said Karen. 'Because it's about how messed up these rich people are and how everyone wants to know about Gatsby because he's such a mystery figure.'

'It still sounds boring.'

'Well it's not.' Karen put the book down again but she was smiling because she doesn't care whether or not someone likes something she likes. 'And I still think you should take the bottle back.' She said it like it was the right thing to do and that she knew I knew it was the right thing to do and once I thought about it I would admit this too. It's the same way Mum talks. But it isn't the way Loreen's mum talks. If I could choose one of our mums I wouldn't choose Karen's because her mum never listens to her, and I wouldn't choose Ashley's because her mum is always in a panic. I would choose Loreen's. I would swap my mum for Loreen's mum

Dudu any day. Loreen's mum is always smiling and saying, 'yes my dear'. Even when she's telling Loreen off, she's smiling. Loreen's mum talks about 'where I come from in Africa' and 'people back home' and she makes me feel there is a bigger world than the one we're in.

But if I had to choose one of our fathers I don't know who I'd choose. Loreen's father died when she was a baby, Karen's father is too grumpy, and Ashley's father gives me the creeps.

I stood there, still with the rucksack on my back, while Loreen got a magazine out of her beach bag. 'Stay with us and let's read this,' she said, and I could see she had a copy of *My Guy*. Loreen still likes that crap. She and Karen like answering all the questionnaires and reading the problem pages, like they've been doing since they were thirteen. 'Listen to this!' laughed Loreen. 'I used to masturbate when I was younger and now the lips around my vagina are very swollen and stick out. I'm worried I'll never be able to have sex properly.'

'Go on,' said Karen, frowning.

'OK, at a disco I met this fella and we had a great evening together and I didn't let him go any further than putting his arm around me. But next day I heard some other boys saying he was only after what he could get. Should I see him again?' Loreen looked up, to see what me and Karen thought about this, and then she saw Ashley. 'Look, she's with the dark-haired one.'

We all looked down the beach, past the bar where we'd been sitting earlier. The bar is like a shack, its walls are wooden and painted green. Half is built over the beach; the rest is built on stone. Inside there are octopuses turned inside out hanging from the ceiling, and Loreen says that's why she's going to become a vegetarian.

Along the beach I saw the man who comes every day to sell doughnuts from a wicker basket. I saw him stop and bend down on the sand by a family with three small children, and I could see him open the basket and take out the doughnuts, all filled with cream. And I could see Ashley in her cut-off jeans and red and white bikini top walking slowly past the doughnut man, along the shoreline with three boys. Two were behind her and the third, the dark-haired boy wearing blue and white Bermuda shorts, was right next to her. Ashley's legs, against the bleached denim of her jeans, shone. She waved; she could see us watching her. Her yellow hair was wet and slick and reached her shoulders.

'She looks like the girl in the Tampax advert,' said Loreen, enviously.

The tide was coming in. In the morning I'd walked around the rock pools and got some great reflections. Now the pools were submerged and gone. A Portuguese family next to us started to pack up: a yellow umbrella with white frills round the edge, a hamper, a big red Thermos, towels with pictures of leaping dolphins, two inflatable rings, one with the head of a duck. Along the shoreline people's bodies were becoming shadows in the afternoon light, almost as black as the hunk of rock that stood alone in the water, separate from the cliff and the beach and everything else.

I watched Ashley and I watched the sudden explosions of silver over the sea and saw it was sparkling. The night before

I'd come down when the sand was grey and cold and smooth like a London pavement after rain, and the sea was dark like metal, and I'd watched the fishing boats go out. I'd watched until the swinging lights of the boats became almost too small to see.

'Has she got a love bite?' Loreen said, putting on a t-shirt before the boys reached us. 'Oh my God, I think she's got a love bite!'

'Gross,' said Karen. 'How can you see from here?'

'What if Steve sees it?' Loreen asked excitedly. 'Oh my God, what would he say if Ashley came back from Portugal with a love bite? Would we tell him?'

Karen and me looked at each other; we couldn't believe Ashley was serious about Steve anyway. She only likes him because he's eighteen and in a band. She met him outside the school gates; he's got black spiky hair and skinny legs and plays the drums. His band is crap.

Loreen stood up and started putting on her shorts. 'He's got very close-together eyes,' she said, watching the dark-haired boy. 'And very thin lips.'

'And that's bad?' asked Karen.

'Eyes that are close together aren't good,' said Loreen, and I knew she'd got this from one of her magazines. 'It means he's mean and you can't trust him.' But I knew she was only saying this about the dark-haired boy because that was the one she'd fancied. He was the one I had liked as well, even though I knew there was no point.

'I'm going to the bar,' Karen said. She pulled a dress over her head and got up.

'Why?' I asked.

'That's for me to know and you to find out.'

Loreen sighed and settled herself on her towel with *My Guy*.

'Where did you go with them?' I asked Ashley when she'd come back and the boys had gone.

She looked up; she was busy spreading sun cream along her legs, smoothing it in from her ankles up to her thighs. 'Just having a walk,' she said, and she threw down the sun cream, lay back on the sand, put on her sunglasses, and just like that she looked glamorous.

'Just having a walk, oh yeah!' said Loreen.

'What, with all three of them?' I asked.

'You could have come,' Ashley said.

I couldn't see her face. I was sitting down by her legs and I could just see the skin of her stomach golden from the sun.

'What?' She put her head up; she could tell Loreen and me were staring at her. 'What? You think I got off with one of them?' Ashley did that thing where her cheeks tighten and her eyes go narrow and she looks beautiful and scary at the same time. 'Oh come on! Are you saying I got off with one of them?'

'Maybe,' Loreen giggled. She took a battered white paper bag of sweets out of her beach bag and offered them around. 'Mmm, lemon bon bons,' she said, 'mmm mmmm mmmm. Who wants the pear drops?'

'So you think I'm going to cheat on Steve?' asked Ashley. 'Is that what you think?'

I looked at Ashley. I couldn't see any sign of a love bite; Loreen was making it up.

11

'Because I wouldn't,' said Ashley. 'I wouldn't cheat on Steve because it would be morally wrong.'

I laughed. Only Ashley would use a word like morally. If Ashley says something is wrong then we don't do it, and if Ashley agrees to something, we do it, even if other people would say it was wrong, like nicking earrings from Top Shop. Like putting a pair of Top Shop trousers over our own and running off with them. That was what we'd done the Saturday before we left, the four of us standing on the escalator into Top Shop on Oxford Street and seeing ourselves all glittery in the mirrors.

'Would you cheat on someone? Would you?' Ashley sat up properly now, brushing sand off her legs. 'So are you saying you think it's OK to cheat on someone?'

I was going to answer, when Loreen nudged me with her foot. Then I remembered about Ashley's father. So now Ashley's going to know what it's like not to have a dad around, just like me and Loreen.

'Anyway,' said Ashley, 'he fancies Loreen.'

'Who does?' asked Karen, coming back to where we sat.

'You know the German boys?' asked Ashley. 'The dark-haired one fancies Loreen.'

'Really?' Loreen beamed and put a lemon bon bon in her mouth. 'What did he say?'

'He said,' Ashley started picking sand out from between her toes. 'He said, "mine's the tall one".'

'How do you know he said that?' asked Karen, sitting down.

'I've been doing German for three years, haven't I?'

'But you're taller than me,' said Loreen.

'Yes, but he didn't mean me,' said Ashley.

I looked at her. She was lying.

'Are you sure?' asked Loreen, and she started picking at the skin round her fingers, all excited. 'Did he really say that? Oh my God, it's the last day of the holiday! Do you know where they're staying?'

It was good to leave the beach and get away and be alone. I spent ages on the way up the cliff trying to photograph two dragonflies. They were stuck together, mating, their green and yellow bodies trembling, wings spinning. I waited a long time to get them; I stood so still I could have been frozen. Then I kept on going up the cliff, staying as near the edge as I could get because I like the feeling that I could fall. I could see the sand down at the shore and the ripple of the crashing waves like the end of a long tiered skirt.

I went up, past purple flowers and huge cactuses, their pale green arms lined with little white spikes. The cactuses had faded brown markings where someone had written on them, slashes and lines like the hieroglyphics we did in history. Some of the cactuses had shot out trees of their own, long hard stems with little rigid clumps at the end. They were not pretty like the almond trees I could see further up at the top of the cliff. The almond trees looked as if they were dancing, their thin stems stretched out in crazy patterns heavy with nuts in soft green casings.

I went further and stopped under a fig tree, big like a bush with wide hairy leaves sheltering purple fruits as fat as little balloons, as if the tree had been busy blowing them up. I stopped to take a picture and to finish the film. I wanted to

13

fill the viewfinder with the purple figs, to zoom in and focus right on the white sap that would spill out when I pulled a fig down from the branch. This is my very first SLR, it's a grown-up camera. Dad gave it to me for my birthday. He likes to give me something I can't say no to.

I turned away from the tree for a moment because I could see two people coming up from the beach, walking up the cliff path from the green-roofed bar. I swung the camera round, using it as a telescope, refocusing so I could see what they were doing. The girl was laughing. I couldn't hear her but I could see she was laughing from the way she moved her head. The boy put his arm round her shoulders. They disappeared for a moment, behind a wall of cliff, and when they appeared again they were much nearer. I could see the boy's black hair was wet and I could see the blue and white pattern on his Bermuda shorts. They stopped, leaning their bodies against the sandy wall of the cliff as if they were hiding from someone. Then all of a sudden the boy moved in front of the girl and slid a hand into the top of her bikini and I could see how white her skin was beneath. I watched, riveted, as the boy pushed his other hand between the girl's thighs and the girl put her head back and I saw it was Ashley.

I took a picture. I had the camera right there; it was what I was doing.

I thought about three weeks ago at school. Mr Jefferies had shown us a film of a man filming his own murder. The man was a cameraman; he was in a war zone, filming a war. But because he was behind a camera he thought he was protected. Until he filmed the bullet that shot him in the head.

14

Chapter Two

I stood on the patio of the house, out of breath. Had she seen me? She couldn't have or she would have said something, shouted out. Why did I feel I had done something wrong? Why did Ashley always make me feel like I'd done something wrong when it was Ashley who had done something wrong? From the edge of the patio I could just see the sea below the garden, beyond the cliff, glistening like it was burning up.

Behind me was the house; the white walls bright against the blue of the sky, the tiles on the roof as orange as fruit. The house is joined to three others; it has a little turret on the top and long, thin windows. Across the back is a bougainvillea tree; the shadows of its pink flowers splattered against the wall.

I crossed the patio, passed the two plastic loungers with shiny blue covers, and quickly slid open the glass door. In the living room the air was still and smelt of coffee and new plastic shower curtains. Loreen and Karen had left their things all over the floor: nail varnish, custard cakes, a jar of Nutella, another of Loreen's girly magazines, open to a picture of Bros. Someone has drawn a willy on Matt Goss. Loreen loves Bros, but not as much as she used to love Simon Le Bon. At home she still has a poster of Simon Le Bon on the inside of her bedroom door. Sometimes she talks to him, tells him her problems and asks for advice. But I'd rather be Simon Le Bon than talk to him.

I went up the stairs to the kitchen, my camera still tight in my hand. The kitchen is on a floor of its own. When we'd first arrived it looked as if it had never been used before, although there must have been people before us, and people before them. It's full of empty cupboards and there's a big gas bottle chained to the floor. I opened the fridge and looked inside, pretending that I wasn't clutching and unclutching my camera. I had to get rid of the film. I was wasting time.

I opened a bottle of Sumol, twisting off the metal cap with my teeth, and I drank it and pretended Ashley's parents' holiday home was mine. I pretended that I owned it, that I was an adult, a famous photographer with an array of funny friends and my own drinks cabinet. Ashley doesn't know how lucky she is.

I went up the stairs, past the toilet that's also on a floor of its own. The walls are covered with big white tiles and next to the toilet is a bidet which Ashley uses to wash the sand off her feet. There is a square light switch on the wall and I like the way it flips so easily off and on, and I like the way the toilet has a flush on the top not a chain to pull. I went up the rest of the stairs to my room. I got the smallest room, the one at the top of the house, the one without a balcony. From my window I can see the front of the house and the door we never use, big and thick and wooden like a prison. Attached to the door are two ceramic tiles with the house number painted in blue.

If Ashley had had a choice she maybe wouldn't have

invited me to Portugal at all. Her dad said she could have three friends, so she chose Loreen and Karen. But I know Loreen would have said I had to come too. And then Ashley gave me the money, because otherwise I couldn't have come. Now I owe her, and she knows that. If she hadn't given me the money I wouldn't be here.

I walked up the stairs, brushing against the white wall that is bumpy to the touch as if it is a face with spots. I like the feeling when it grazes my skin. My bedroom doesn't look like it did when we arrived. Then my bed was all newly made with matching cover and headboard and pillow so it looked like a tightly wrapped Quality Street. Now it looks like a gerbil's nest, like the gerbil we had at primary school that had seven babies and ate them all.

'Bel!' I can hear Loreen calling from downstairs. 'Bel!' She always calls me like this, like she thinks I've gone missing.

I'm on my bed. I've rewound the film. I've snapped it out of the camera and I've put it in the canister and I've stuffed it into the side pocket of my suitcase. If Ashley did see me taking the picture, she'll kill me. She said the dark-haired boy in the Bermuda shorts fancied Loreen and she was lying. I knew that and now I have proof. She said she'd never cheat on Steve and now she has.

When I come down they are all in the living room. There is no sign of any boy. I can't tell if anything has happened, if they've all come up together or not. I don't go all the way down, I go into the kitchen first and fill a glass with water and it comes out of the tap in a frothy spurt. I turn the tap off with my right hand, then check it with my left, and then do it again with my right to make it three. This is it, it's happening again.

'What are you doing?' Karen is next to me; I didn't hear her come up.

'How do you mean?' I turn my back against the sink.

'Is there something wrong with the tap?'

'No.' I drink my water and go down into the living room.

Karen is making spaghetti sauce. She pierces a giant red tomato with a fork and holds it over the gas flame. Nothing happens, but then the skin starts to split and it shrinks apart and there's soft wet flesh underneath. It's like watching a cine film and the film gets stuck and starts burning up the screen. Karen holds six tomatoes over the flame one after another and then she peels them and makes a sauce. She puts the sauce and the spaghetti in a thick brown earthenware pot that smells like nail varnish. It's so heavy she has to carry it with two hands.

We eat outside, insects flying around the paraffin lamp on the table which is covered with tiles of yellow and blue flowers. Karen brings out bread rolls that look like conch shells bursting out of themselves. Then she brings out more green bottles of beer and a plate of chocolate umbrellas, cold and from the fridge, with curved little plastic handles at the end, small enough to hang on a finger.

I don't care about anything else now; I don't care about Ashley lying or if the film is safe in my suitcase. I want to stay here, in the foreignness, in the night that is still warm, and wait until the sun comes up and never go to bed and never get on the plane tomorrow and never go back to England.

'I can't believe this is our last night,' says Karen. 'This

could be the last time we're all on holiday together.'

'Will it?' Loreen is peeling flakes of skin off Karen's back and she stops and looks worried. 'We should have gone to find those German boys, shouldn't we, Ashley? It's our last night, why did we have to meet them on our last night?'

Ashley puts her head down and doesn't answer. She's painting her nails.

'It won't be the last time we're together anyway, will it?' Loreen asks. 'We can come again next year, can't we?'

'We'll be doing A-levels then, and then we'll go to uni,' says Karen.

'But we'll all go to the same uni, won't we?' asks Loreen, because she wants us all to stay together.

'I'm not,' I say. 'I'm not going to uni.'

Loreen goes into the house and comes out with the bottle of vodka and a razor. 'Where did that come from?' asks Ashley when Loreen puts the vodka bottle down on the tile-covered table.

'Bel took it from the bar,' Karen says.

I glare at her.

'What, you *nicked* it?' says Ashley. 'When did you nick it?'

'Oh, I think you were busy,' I smile. 'With the boys. Although not the dark-haired one, obviously.' I drink back a glass of vodka. Then I push the glass across the table, waiting to hear Ashley's response.

'Your neck is really red,' she says.

I touch it, annoyed at Ashley bringing attention to my sunburn. Ashley never burns.

'Anyway,' she says, 'I thought you went off to take photos . . . not steal something from the bar.'

19

I ignore her. She's got it wrong anyway. I took the bottle way before I took the pictures, she just didn't notice, that's all.

'Come on, girls!' says Loreen, because she doesn't like it when we argue. She picks up the razor and shows it to us.

'What?' I ask. 'What's that for? You just did your legs this morning.'

'I've got this idea . . .' Loreen holds the razor between her fingers, slides out the blade. 'What we do is, we can be blood sisters. Come on! Ashley? Karen? Bel?'

'Fuck off,' I say, but quietly because I love Loreen.

'What do you want us to do?' asks Ashley, and Loreen looks pleased. If Ashley agrees, we'll all do it.

'We each cut ourselves, just a little bit on the thumb, just enough to get some blood, then we put our thumbs together and . . .'

'Gross,' says Karen.

'No,' says Loreen insistently. 'It's like a pact or something, that will keep us all together.'

I look at her; she must have got this from one of her magazines, but I put my thumb out straight away. We've known each other since the first day of primary school but we won't stay together, and it doesn't matter whether we do.

'What does the pact mean anyway?' asks Karen.

'It means we never tell,' says Ashley, and she is the first to draw blood and my thumb is the first she goes to touch.

LONDON 2005

Chapter Three

DUDU

I am sitting in my kitchen on this lovely Sunday morning and I am thinking of when the girls were little and the very first day they started infants' school. That is a day I can see in my mind as clear as anything, and I can turn it like a fortune-teller's ball, seeing it from different sides. I can see the girls in their short dresses and ribbed white socks pulled up past the knees, see their smooth young faces all washed and ready. At least my little Loreen's face was all washed and ready, I wasn't so sure about some of the others, for the English are not exactly known for their cleanliness. It was an autumn day, a time of year when the seasons change in this part of the world, and we were outside the open double wooden gates of the school. There was no CCTV in those days and no inter-com. Parents and visitors were free to come and go as they pleased, not like today when I collect my grandson, my little Dwaine, and I am made to feel I have to prove he is mine. I remember a warm smell coming from the school kitchen, a soft, hot smell of mashed potato and a sweet, thick smell of custard, and from where I stood I could see inside: the cooks with their white hats, the fridge as large as a wardrobe, the giant pans upon a row of metal trolleys. In those days school kitchens were busy places, now they are simply where they warm up ready-made meals.

Further along from the kitchen I could see into a classroom and I hoped that this would be where my little Loreen would be for then, as it was positioned so near to the road, I would be able to peep in and see her as I came home from work. Inside the classroom were radiators on either side, like sheets of white corrugated iron, in the middle were tables with cartons of crayons, and on the back wall was a row of blue, paint-splattered aprons hanging by their string necks on child-sized pegs. Above the aprons was a display about the weather, little paper symbols showing what it had been yesterday, what it was expected to be today, what it could be tomorrow. For in England the weather is always something to talk about and children are educated about this from an early age. It is not that the English are interested in the weather as such, although it can change violently from day to day, but a discussion about the weather enables people to talk to each other. The English consider themselves to be very private people and the weather provides them with the opportunity to share opinions and most of all to agree. Isn't it cold? Lovely and sunny, isn't it? Oh I hope it isn't going to rain again, don't you?

That day the girls started infants' school, we parents were shown into the playground where boys with their pudding-bowl haircuts and cardigans were throwing themselves down a metal slide. A man was sweeping up red and yellow leaves into a plastic container, but by then I had grown used to seeing white people doing menial work and I didn't pay him too much attention. All over the concrete playground were

24

groups of children, two girls attempting a cartwheel, others with a skipping rope calling out the names of colours and making wiggly patterns on the ground, some just standing up against the wall next to two wooden buckets of red geraniums. And as I stood there with the other parents I wondered that the children weren't afraid, for the school around them was so large, the thick brick buildings towering over them where they ran around like stick figures in the playground. But if the children in the playground were not afraid, I certainly was, and I held my little Loreen's hand a little too hard at first. I didn't know what we were to do, I didn't know what the procedure would be and what part I would play. I felt Loreen's little hand in mine and I worried that she would feel my worry, that I would infect her with it at the very moment when she needed to think her mother knew what she was doing. What I knew was that this was the day when I was supposed to let my child go.

After we were shown into the playground a lady came out and rang a bell and the older children, the children who had already started school, lined up, none of them able to keep still, heads turned this way, feet the other. That is why I love watching children, they don't keep still. Even when a child is sitting down, he can still be moving, like my little grandson Dwaine who will suddenly put a leg up in the air while in the middle of reading a book.

I looked around at the other mothers in the playground, at their very short dresses and their platform shoes. Some of the mothers held a child in their arms, others stood protectively behind them, some stood a little apart. And then the headmistress came into the playground, a tall lady with a sharp nose and very straight hair which she repeatedly wrapped back around her ears like a fastidious housewife adjusting a troublesome curtain. On her face she wore a pair of black-rimmed glasses, around her neck was a single string of pearls, and as she came closer I could see her red lipstick had bled slightly into the lines around her mouth. She smiled at us and told us to leave our children without a fuss, explaining that it would be better that way.

So I nudged Loreen forward so she would join the line; I had to show her that it was OK for her to leave me. Only I didn't think it was OK for her to leave me and I wondered why people in England sent their children to school so young. In Africa a child plays, that is what I did during my childhood in my home village of Manyana. I played with sticks and stones and sand, I played singing games and clapping games with my sisters and with the other children, I played by the river and I played with the goats at the cattlepost. And while we played, all around us the adults worked. I can see my mother even now, digging earth in the rocky bush, bent straight from the waist hacking at the ground with a metal tool, or kneeling on the floor of the compound applying cow dung in sweeping lines, or fashioning a pot out of clay to store water in. My mother would work round and round the pot, pulling it up as if it were skin, until she reached the lip and the clay became thin. Sometimes I was allowed to help shape the mouth of a clay pot and I took my work seriously, just as she did, although when I was finished my mother had to make the mouth all over again. Then I would take a small amount of clay and a small container of water and build myself my own miniature house and pots while my mother continued with her work.

Some days we children ran through the bush to the rock paintings, for our home village Manyana was already well known for these paintings, which were to be found at the base of Kolobeng Hill in an area of overhanging rock. We children knew these paintings well: the three giraffe, yellow against the ochre of the rock, the spindly brown antelope, the squat black rhinoceros, the single delicate gemsbok. It was not only the rock paintings that fascinated us, it was the stories the elders told us, like the cave where Kgosi Sechele's first wife Mma Sechele had been hidden from the invading Boers. Other days we children clambered up Dimawe Hill, and if my father were with us then he would sit on a rock and play his penny whistle and tell us of the fighting days.

That was my childhood, but I was in England now and things would be different for my child. I was beginning my nurse's training and my little Loreen had to go to school and I had to get used to the way people did things in England. I had been in England for some years by then, but I still hadn't got used to the way people treated their children, always encouraging them towards this thing they called independence, pushing them away as soon as they could. Yet who is to say that independence should be so sought after, that people wouldn't be better off teaching their children to think of community and family and how we link together rather than how to stand independently apart.

I stood in the playground and again I looked around at the other parents so I could see how I should be behaving. I saw a father making a great deal of fuss over his child, bending down to stroke her hair, informing her about something they would do later in the day. There were not many fathers in the

27

playground – he may have been the only father in the play-ground – because in those days it was mainly the women who took and collected their children from school. His hair was brown and curly, something like a sheep, and he wore jeans that were wide at the bottom and very tight up at the top around his private parts. But although the father was making a fuss, his little girl wasn't concerned at all; she joined the line, a bright white Alice band in her hair, without which she would have been an unremarkable-looking child, except for her eyes that were too large for her face so that she had the look of a baby animal about her. That was how Ashley looked back then.

Although I had nudged Loreen into the queue, she would-n't look ahead; her neck kept on turning, looking back at me. She wouldn't say anything, she wouldn't leave the line. She was the only black child in the line; she didn't want any more attention brought her way.

Behind my little Loreen and Ashley in her white Alice band were two other girls I noticed that day. The first had black hair cut straight across her forehead and a serious little face, and I could see her staring at something just behind me and I turned a little to see the girl's mother and another child. The child was smaller than her sister, I could see they had to be sisters, and she was crying. She was standing in front of her mother and running her arms up her mother's dress, dragging on it, clawing on it. And she was screaming, 'I want to go with Karen! I want to go with Karen!' I looked at Karen standing there in the line with my little Loreen and I saw her clench a book against her belly, her face staring determinedly in front of her as if afraid she

28

would be called out of the line, that her little sister would ruin her first day.

Behind Karen there was another girl I noticed and that was Bel. She was such a small girl and there was something a little ruffled about her, and I could see even from a distance there were crusts of sleep in the corners of her eyes and a stain, perhaps of egg yolk, on her dungarees. She was standing with a woman whom I took to be her mother and they were arguing about something, I could see.

'My hair's not right,' I heard Bel say.

'What do you mean, not right?' asked her mother, bending down.

Bel pulled quite violently at her two plaits, she really pulled at them, several times on one plait and then several times on the other, and inbetween tugging on her plaits she was rubbing on her nose like there was something in there she needed to get out.

'Stop it!' hissed her mother.

But little Bel wouldn't stop, she had taken the bands out of her hair now and it was all loose upon her shoulders and still she was tugging at it, saying, 'It's not right!'

'Stop it!' hissed her mother again. 'People are *looking*!'

Bel did stop then, and her mother seemed to see an opportunity and she hugged her daughter quickly, then she waved and went on her way.

With her mother gone, Bel seemed happier and she began chattering with the other children in the line, chattering with any child who would answer her back. She wasn't actually standing in the line herself; she was near the front standing parallel to the others and every now and again she made a move as if to work her way into the line. I could see she was aiming for something, that there appeared to be a particular position she wanted to reach but was unable to. I saw a lady teacher watching the line; I saw that she was considering telling Bel to stop all her chattering and get into place, because the English like their lines to remain orderly. They do not like it if someone pushes in, although they will not say so, they will just look at you and perhaps murmur something low enough that you can feel their disapproval but not hear their words. Bel saw the lady teacher approach, but I could see she couldn't have cared less and that made me want to laugh and to give her a good hard squeeze. I always wanted to give Bel a good hard squeeze; she looked like she needed one.

And then suddenly Ashley, standing at the front of the line, her white Alice band all clean and shining in her hair, began to shout out. 'Miss!' she called. 'She's pushing in! That girl there.' And Ashley stopped and turned and inspected the queue behind her and pointed at Bel. 'Miss! She pushed in. It isn't fair.'

I watched, surprised at this little girl who cared so much about the orderliness of the line and who displayed such a noisy conviction that she knew what was and was not fair. The headmistress came over then, and she looked at Bel and after a minute or two Bel gave in and walked away towards the back of the line. I saw my little Loreen and Karen watching this and I wondered what they were thinking, and if they thought it was wrong of Ashley to pick on Bel when there were plenty of other children trying to push in. And that was when Bel began to bleed. She stood there at the back of the line with blood drip drip dripping down from her nose until Ashley saw and shouted, 'Ugh! Miss! Now she's *bleeding*!' The blood fell in perfect circles onto the grey cement of the playground, darkening as it fell, and Bel stood there motionless watching it, and it struck me as quite remarkable, the way she stood there not asking for help.

Chapter Four

It is getting warm today and still I am sitting in my kitchen on this lovely Sunday morning, when my clever little kitty cat comes in. I put out some milk for her and she drinks it in a delicate fashion as I sit down to listen to the radio. They are talking about the man they call Piano Man, a young man who was found some few months ago wandering a seaside town in a soaking wet suit who refused to say where he came from. I remember this story, for when the hospital people gave the man some paper and asked him to write where he was from, all he did was draw a big grand piano. When I first heard this I couldn't understand, because how would you not want to say where you come from and why would you want to forget?

I certainly cannot forget where I come from and I have always been careful to teach my little Loreen about where she comes from, for while England might be her home, her heritage is Africa.

I put the kettle on for my tea and I think of the day I arrived in England and how my husband and I walked along the Thames Embankment early in the morning, peacefully arm in arm. He wanted to show me London, for although he had never been to the city before he knew all about it from his studies at Fort Hare. He knew its history and its buildings, its churches and its monuments, and he was excited to see the things that he had read about for so long. He looked so handsome in his white shirt and black suit jacket, his closely shorn hair, his lopsided way of smiling so that he rested his chin a little to one side and drew up his cheeks and smiled at me next to him, my arm in his. He was so happy that he had come to a place where he had wanted to come for so many years, for right from that first day I met him, at the family wedding in South Africa, he had told me his ambition was to study theology in England. But before we even spoke I had noticed him, because the way he sat across the aisle from me in that old stone church, with his face upturned and his eyes closed, made me think I had never before seen such a peaceful man.

My husband had a very particular way of speaking, which came from his studies at Fort Hare, and that was how he managed to rent the bed-sitter where we lived when my little Loreen was born. The landlady had thought he was a white from the way he spoke on the telephone – it was a way of speaking that used to be called proper English – and she had given him the room, then and there on the telephone, and then when she met us in person she had seemed unable to withdraw her offer, even though she clearly wanted to. She had a very funny habit of taking a duster and wiping the knob of the front door each time my husband or I had touched it. My husband behaved as if he was above noticing such things. 'Rise above it,' he would say to me. 'Rise above it.' But it made me furious, especially when she would mutter just under her breath, 'I know my rights!'

It was a small, dull room that we rented, with dusty curtains and a spitting gas stove. It was not particularly clean either; the only clean thing about that house was the toilet, and the landlady kept that toilet locked and kept the key around her neck so that we were to behave like children and request permission to use it. But still, we were happy there, with our little baby Loreen, until the morning came when my husband boarded the tube to Moorgate. And there he was on February 28, 1975, on the 8.37am tube train from Drayton Park that failed to stop. At the moment it happened I was doing something inconsequential, dusting his books in our room perhaps, soaking tea leaves in the pot, rinsing my little Loreen's clothes. I should have known before I was told, I should have felt something, a thunderbolt should have struck me down in that room, the heavens should have exploded, God should have called down to me, I should have felt it in my very flesh and bones. And yet I didn't, I had no fore-warning, I was just doing whatever inconsequential thing I was doing.

It was my landlady who first told me the news, for that was the day she chose to invite me, quite unexpectedly, into her rooms to watch her television. I suppose she was so horrified by what she was seeing on the television that she wanted someone to share the horror with her, and so I stood there, my little Loreen on my hip, watching as well. I had wondered, of course, why my husband had not yet come home, why he hadn't rung as he would normally do if he were delayed, and yet I had not been alarmed at all until I saw the news. And there on the television I watched as a young man with long black hair explained what he had witnessed down in the underground that was as hot as a mine that day. I can see that man's face even now, he was so very normal-looking except

34

for one thing: a long gash that ran across his forehead like a bolt of lightning, and it was clear by the look on his face that he had no idea it was even there. He had been standing on the Moorgate platform, he explained, when the tube train arrived, and he could see that it wasn't slowing down, and that was it, smash. Those were his words: 'that was it, smash'. At first the television people said a dozen or so people had been injured, but then the first of the dead were brought to the surface and the police carried the bodies covered with red cloths into the waiting ambulances. I continued to stand there in my landlady's room, watching the television, as a police-man walked around shouting through a red megaphone, asking people to donate blood to the injured, as firemen in their sparkly silver buttons went back underground to help, and as reporters surrounded eyewitnesses and politely held out their long, thin microphones. And as I watched the tele-vision news I felt my blood turn to ice and I knew at last what had happened.

And then later the police came to my bed-sit room, for they had found some papers in my husband's jacket that had indicated where he lived. And what I wanted to know was why had my husband been in one of the three front carriages that had been crushed together as the tube train hit the tunnel, and not in one of the back three carriages that had remained intact on the Moorgate platform? What had he heard and what had he seen? What had he felt on the moment of impact? That last question was the one that haunted me most of all, for although the police said he died instantly, I couldn't believe that it was possible for any living being to die instantly, within a single instant. So I made up a

35

little story for myself: my husband was tired when he got on the tube train, I decided, for the night before he hadn't slept well, and so he had got on a little wearily, settled on his seat, a newspaper under one arm, a packet of biscuits in his pocket that he had bought on the way, the kind he liked that came in packets of three with hard little crystals of sugar on top, and then as the tube train set off he had he sat back and closed his eyes, the way I had seen him do that first time I saw him at the small stone church in South Africa, to rest a little before his final stop.

Forty-three people died on that tube and one of them was my husband. I waited so many years to be able to say that my husband died in a tube train crash. To say it like it is a fact, like 'today is the coldest day since records began' or 'now it is eleven am and I am having my tea', and not something that tore my world apart. And however hard I tried I could find no reason for it, there was no reason for his sudden death, there was not even a reason for the crash. There was nothing wrong with the train, nor with the signalling equipment or the track, the driver was sober, experienced and conscientious, and yet for some reason the brakes had not been applied.

Afterwards, although I could have returned to Botswana and to my home village of Manyana, I felt that I owed it to my husband to stay. It was a question of pride; my husband had only been in England some few years, he had not finished his studies, indeed he had just signed up for some more, and he had always wanted to come to England. So even though he was gone, dead and buried in a strange country, I decided that my baby and me would stay.

After Loreen's father died, I found a better landlady, a German lady named Adelaide who had come to England as a refugee and who had a better understanding and a better sympathy for other people. Her name, she told me, meant noble and serene, and she was both. A tall woman with a back so straight it was as if her backbone were made of iron, she had a cheerful face and a ready smile. One evening I was sitting in Adelaide's front room having bathed my little Loreen and put her in her pyjamas. This was the time when Adelaide liked to bring out the newspaper that one of her other lodgers would bring her each evening, and lay it on the table to read. And while she read the paper she often invited me in to sit with her. I recall the news that day, for that was the day Buckingham Palace announced that Princess Margaret was to separate from her husband Lord Snowdon after sixteen years of marriage. The newspaper said Lord Snowdon was desperately sad, that the Queen was also very sad, and I even felt a little sad myself too as I looked at the pictures of the formerly happy couple and their children. There was something strangely soothing about looking at the photographs and reading about the news and wondering about another person's life, because it meant that, for those few moments at least, I wasn't worried and saddened about my own.

'See here, Dudu,' said Adelaide, speaking in the direct way that she had. 'Are you still planning to take that bus journey tomorrow?'

'Yes,' I said, for I was planning a journey to the country-side the next day.

'You're a Taurus, aren't you? It says here, "If travelling, do follow all safety precautions." That doesn't sound good, does it?'

I sat up then. 'Who says that?'

'Here,' said Adelaide. 'It's your stars for the weekend,' and she pointed to the page before her. 'Katina and the stars. Your birthday is May, yes? So then your star sign is Taurus.' Adelaide could see I didn't know what she was talking about and she got out a pen and began to draw all over the newspaper. 'There are twelve signs of the Zodiac, yes? Each sign is like a sector of the sky ruled by different stars. So, astrologers look at the interaction of the planets and at your star sign and they can tell you about yourself.'

'You mean I shouldn't travel tomorrow, is that what it says?'

'No, no,' Adelaide laughed. 'The stars don't tell you what to do, they just help you to think before you act.'

'Oh.' I thought what my husband would have said, how he had always said the English were a crazily superstitious people, and this star sign business sounded like superstition to me. Who was it that was looking at the planets and the stars and putting advice in the newspaper like this? But I was also intrigued and I thought I understood now why my kindly landlady, a refugee from her homeland, read her newspaper so carefully every evening: she was wanting to see what would happen next.

'I would have guessed you were a Taurus even before you told me your birthday was May,' said Adelaide. 'It's an earth sign, yes? And the symbol is a bull. A typical Taurean doesn't let other people get too close and they are able to switch off to the world around them, just as you do. A Taurean is a seeker of stability.'

I sat down opposite her; stunned at the way she had described my character and outlook on life.

'So according to the weekend forecast for Taurus,' continued Adelaide, 'there are some exciting undercurrents which keep you very much on tiptoe. However, if travelling, do follow all safety precautions, this is not the time for bold gambits.'

The moment I saw that horoscope, the moment Adelaide read it out to me, I knew it was a sign that I shouldn't go. And I cancelled my journey and I never did go into the countryside that weekend with my little Loreen, and I felt great relief that there was something I could read every day that would tell me whether or not I should do something.

At once I got Adelaide to work out my little Loreen's star sign, which was Pisces. Those born under the sign of Pisces, Adelaide explained to me, were imaginative and sensitive, compassionate and kind. A Pisces person would help you when you were down, and the symbol for this sign, as Adelaide drew it on the newspaper for me, was two little fish swimming in opposite directions. This meant, said Adelaide, that a person born under the sign of Pisces could also be weak-willed and easily led.

It was then that I started to read our horoscopes on a daily basis, because while I couldn't protect Loreen from the past, while I couldn't protect her from losing her father, I could try and protect her from what might come. And the horoscopes then were full of warnings, warnings that once I had read I felt I could not afford to ignore. *Avoid hasty action or you will have cause for repentance. Keep your temper under control and do not make unreasonable demands on other people. Aim at getting the necessary jobs done today. This is a day for planning rather than action, cut down the gadding about.*

How I read those horoscopes then, how I believed they could warn me of bad things to come. And I will never forget how I had read my little Loreen's horoscope the evening before her first day of infants' school, when she stood in the playground with Ashley and Karen and Bel, the girl who bled all over the playground, and this is what it had said: *Your future is uncertain but the friends you meet tomorrow will be friends for life.*

Chapter Five

LOREEN

Hi Simon, ha! It's been a long time since I talked to you. Mr Simon Le Bon, just look at you with that spiky hairdo! Those are some highlights you have there, Simon. Very nice. That must have taken ages to get right. And oh, your blue eyes! How I used to love your blue eyes. This poster I've just found is really old, but those eyes of yours are still so blue and those lips of yours are still so red, and they're all pursed up like a little boy's.

That's some jacket you're wearing, Simon, white and thigh-length over a black t-shirt and baggy trousers, and a scarf tossed so casually round your neck. God, what a poser you were, you and the rest of the Fab Five, but I loved you anyway. We would have been good together, Simon, a Pisces and a Scorpio, that's what I thought. Two little fishes and a scorpion. Quite a sexy sign, Scorpio. Exciting, powerful, passionate . . . I knew everything about you, Simon. I knew your birthday, I knew you'd once been a milkman's assistant, I knew you got your legs from your gran, I knew you never got the girls when you were a boy because you were too shy, and of course I knew you were married to Yasmin. But that didn't matter; I thought there was still hope for me.

Remember how you used to run around the stage in your shiny plastic trousers, Simon, tossing back your hair – that was when you had longer hair – and shaking that tambourine? And remember when you used to wear that thick white scarf in your hair, tied tight around your head and the rest hanging down one side? Oh my God, that was on the 'Girls on Film' video, the one they banned on the BBC, the one that started with John Taylor having his makeup done, when you wore all white except for black boots and you did that little shoulder wiggle you used to do. I loved that. There was a woman in a black negligee and I think they cut the bit where she mounted a long white pole and began to pull her crotch along it, so that in the end they could show it on the BBC. That's a bit sad, Simon, isn't it? I really thought you were being controversial because you made a video with a load of women in negligees.

Anyway, just look at you in this poster here. Why oh why are you standing like that, with your right hip raised, your left hand sliding down your leg? Are you supposed to be dancing? No wonder the others laughed at me. I was a Durannie and I had you on the inside of my bedroom door, didn't I, Simon? I would shut the door and look into your blue eyes. I would tell you if someone was bitching about me, if the girls had left me out, if I didn't feel clever enough, good enough, if I was worried about exams or homework, if I hadn't been picked for the swimming team and Karen had.

It's pretty funny that Mum's kept you all these years. The moment I told her I was moving, that I'd got the three-bedroom flat in Holly Lodge, then out she came with all these boxes she's been keeping. I love this flat. I love the way the outside of these mansion blocks have beams so there is a cottage feel about the place, even though it's so huge; in my block alone there are at least sixty flats. My neighbour told me this used to be private land and then they built the mansions as bed-sits for single women working in the City. It still has a bed-sit feel about it, even though most of it has been converted into family flats. The kitchen is tiny and the front room is pretty small, but there's a balcony which I'm going to start growing things on because I've always wanted to do that.

The walk is a killer; going downhill in the mornings is fine, but coming back up after a day's work with the boys and with my marking isn't fun. But it's good we've moved in July because there's less than two weeks before school breaks for the summer. I can't believe someone would swap this flat for my place, and most of all I can't believe the boys get a bedroom each. So we're in Highgate now, Simon. Very posh. But I know what Mum thinks, she thinks there's room enough for her in here as well.

Oh God, what am I doing, Simon, going through these boxes and talking to you on a Monday morning? I'm not ready and nor are the boys. Anthony's probably gone back to sleep. It's PE today and I bet he doesn't have his stuff ready. Dwaine is ready, I think. But he's such a dreamer. 'Brush your teeth,' I'll tell him. Then I come into the front room and he's still there with his cereal. 'Dwaine! Brush your teeth.' 'Yes, Mum,' he says, 'sorry, Mum.' Then I hustle him into the bathroom. Half an hour later I find him running a toy car up and down the bottom of the bath. 'Brush your teeth, Dwaine, remember?' 'Yes, Mum, sorry, Mum.' Last night it took me an

43

hour to get him away from the TV because he was watching his favourite pop star, Donny Green. I don't think much of Donny Green myself; he's not half as seductive as you were, Simon.

I was going to think about what to wear on Thursday; if it stays hot like this then it will have to be something light. That's why I opened this wardrobe, that's when I started going through the boxes and found you, Simon, rolled up with a map of the world Mum gave me. Mum was always giving me maps of the world. 'And this,' she would say, pointing down to the bottom of Africa, the fat bit just before the tip, 'is where you come from, Loreen.' There was a time when that excited me, and a time when it bored me to tears.

Mum's going to baby-sit on Thursday and I'll have to clean the place up before she comes otherwise she'll start on the kitchen and work her way through the entire flat. I hope the boys will be good. What do you reckon, Simon? Will they play up and will Mum say, 'In Africa a child would never be allowed to behave like that . . .'

Mum's probably right. Would an African child demand a mobile phone like Anthony did last week? Would an African child draw a big willy on a piece of paper and give it to his teacher? Because that's what Dwaine has done, apparently, so his teacher tells me. And would an African child come snuggling up to me on the sofa and say, like Dwaine did yesterday, 'Mum, can we talk about s-e-x?' He spells it out like that because he thinks it's too rude a word to actually say.

I thought of cancelling Thursday night. I haven't slept properly for weeks worrying about the Ofsted inspection, even though it's not until after the summer. It's not the best time, with a new headmaster as well. He's given us a 'briefing paper' on how he sees the school moving forward. I've got it right here on my bedside table. I fell asleep reading it last night. Then I picked it up and tried to start reading it again this morning. Then I gave up. Our new headmaster has spent the entire opening paragraph talking about the need for successfully embedded change. He wants to know if the core values he sets out resonate with our views. The briefing paper is twenty-four pages long. So I'll put it in my bag to read later. I'll need to show him I've read it, we all will.

The new headmaster doesn't seem too bothered about the Ofsted, but then he doesn't actually teach, does he? He's not the head of the history department; he doesn't know what it's like to get the jitters because after nearly ten years of teaching some Ofsted inspector is sitting at the back of my class scribbling down notes. I'm just glad I've got Barbara as a deputy. 'Right. Let's kick some ass!' she says every morning, then she punches the air with her fist and off she goes.

But while I thought about cancelling Thursday because I'm just so tired, I can't wait to see Bel and Ashley because I haven't seen them together for ages. It's taken forever to find an evening when they're both free. Ashley is really hard to pin down at the moment. I bet she has a new boyfriend because she's always hard to pin down when she has a new boyfriend. You know what, Simon, when Karen comes over from California then we'll all be together again, all four of us, and I can't wait because it's been so long since we were all together.

I bet Ashley's not wondering what to wear on Thursday. I

bet Bel's not fussing either, she'll just wear what she always wears, jeans and a t-shirt. But I can't make up my mind; it's a big thing for me, going out. Do you think Ashley is with anyone at the moment, Simon? Maybe I should do what Barbara suggested and join a dating site so I could be going out with someone too. I haven't been on my computer for ages, not since I joined Friends Reunited. OK, Simon, I'll tell you everything that happens on Thursday, but right now I'm rolling you up and putting you back in here.

Chapter Six

BEL

Shit, the computer's down. It's Tuesday lunchtime and I'm the only one in the office. Does everyone arrange their lunch break so they won't have to take it with me? I have to find a middle way, between the girls who think a job like this will get them somewhere and the girls who don't give a shit but are likely to move on. Right now I just hate this job and if I have to listen to one more what-I-did-last-night story I'll scream. This morning Jodie told us all about her date. That's what she called him, My Date. Like he was a day in a month she'd picked out at random. My Date this, and My Date that. And I thought, how long since I had sex? Last New Year's Eve, for fuck's sake. And I'm stuck in an office with Jodie the serial dater.

My mobile rings and I can't find it. Unlike Jodie, I don't have a handbag that I can keep on diving into and pulling things out like an endlessly replenished magician's bag of tricks. Need a pen? She has one in her bag. Lippy? A tissue? She has one in her bag. A tampon? Some multivitamins? A hairbrush? A mini bottle of Coke? A sports bra? She has them all in her bag.

I find my mobile on the chair, answer it. 'Hi hon, it's

Loreen!' Loreen always starts conversations like this. She always says 'hi hon' and then she says her name with a giggle like she's surprised by herself. She's been doing the same things for nearly twenty years. But today I'm annoyed that Loreen always has to sound so cheerful. I don't know how she got to be head of department when she's so nice to everyone.

'Hi Loreen.' It's a good job no one else is in the office; we're not supposed to take private calls.

'Are we still meeting on Thursday?' Loreen asks. She always likes to double check things. She likes making an arrangement and then checking several times that it's still in place.

'Yup,' I say, looking down at the credit card bills and the notebook I've been laying out on my office desk. My desk's in a mess. I pick up a picture of Dwaine that Loreen gave me, which has fallen face-down, and I prop it up. He had it done at school and it makes me think of when we were kids, because although Dwaine doesn't really look much like Loreen, they still take school photos the way they used to, posing the kid at a table, hands awkwardly holding a book. Then they sell it to you in a grey hardback frame with two bands of gilt around the edge. I told Loreen not to pay for it; I told her I'd take a better picture myself.

'Guess what?' asks Loreen.

'What?'

'Karen's coming back! I just got a letter from her. She won't be able to come on Thursday because she's coming back first thing that morning, but isn't it exciting?'

'Yeah, that's great,' I say. I can't get quite as excited as

Loreen. I never can. It's like she can do enough excitement for both of us. It will be good to see Karen, but I'm not going to lose sleep over it. I've seen her twice since she went to California and I'm quite happy to be out of touch for a year and then hook back together again. But Loreen wants more, she wants us all together; she has always been the one who holds us all together.

'Ashley still coming on Thursday?' I ask.

'She said she was,' says Loreen.

'Great,' I say. I stop myself from saying that Ashley hardly ever does what she says she's going to do. If I say that, Loreen will only defend her. Still, Loreen's happy we're meeting up. I just wish she'd choose where we're going and not leave it to Ashley.

I put the phone down and stand up. I can't stand this feeling of confinement, of being in the same place day after day, hour after hour, except when Clive sends me out on the sort of errand a work placement kid could do. The one good thing about this office is the window opposite my desk. If I stand up I can see the park in the middle of the square, or at least I can see the tips of the trees in the park. This is not the pretty side of the square, the side where pigeons sit on the balconies with their heads tucked in like grey stones, where the buildings look old and quietly grand even if they're just offices inside. When I walk along the square in the morning I like to look inside, at the 80s furniture, shelves of old-fashioned hardbacked files, little desk fans, clocks on the wall that never seem to be working. Every morning I read the sign for the Institute for the Study of the Americas and the plaque that says a founder of Pakistan once lived here. And Dickens lived in this square as well; Karen wrote to tell me that when I first started. I've been here two years. It's too long. I don't know how I ended up in an office job anyway.

I go over to the window and look out. I like to go into the park on extremes. Days that are the hottest ever, or days when the trees have all turned red, or days when the snow suddenly falls and stays. Every time I open a newspaper I see a picture like this. If it's hot then there's a picture of people at the seaside, if it's snowing then there's a sentimental picture of a kid on a toboggan. I could easily take pictures like this, I just don't know who to sell them to.

I've seen the park in every season now. I've been inside and inspected the monuments and trees, the memorial to conscientious objectors made of a grey rock so perfectly wrinkled it looks like cloth, the tiny little sweetgum tree planted by some Camden mayor, and the cherry tree that was placed in memory of the victims of Hiroshima. I like that Hiroshima tree; it's thirty years old and very simple. A single trunk and five sturdy branches. I like to stand and look at it before I leave by the sign that says it is prohibited to sell or exhibit any written material in the park. What sort of rule is that?

'Hiya!' says Jodie. She comes into the office, chucks her handbag down, throws her cardigan over the back of her chair. It's too hot to have a cardigan on today. Jodie must have had Mr Kipling's for lunch, she looks very perky. She looks about twenty years old, which she is. I can't remember being twenty years old.

'Did I miss anything?' asks Jodie.

I look at her. Like what? What could she possibly have

missed? I go back to my notebook. I'm trying to list my direct debits. Then what I spend on food. Then rent. Then what I get paid. Then the fact we've only just started the month. I need to find somewhere else to live, but where? At least a housing association is cheap, relatively speaking. But then they couldn't charge much for the place I'm in, considering the back of the house is propped up with bits of wood the size of railway sleepers, that when it rains my bedroom walls are wet to the touch, that the front wall is going to fall down any day soon. The house is going to be sold, we keep on being told this, we're ready to be rehoused, but it never happens. Shit. Clive will be back soon too. And he will stand there, crotch forward, hands on his hips, and ask to see what I've been doing all morning. It's not my fault the computer's down.

Jodie clip clops across the office floor in her high heels to the water cooler, gets herself a glass and goes back to her desk. Lunch hour is over and I'm supposed to be getting back to work as well but office life makes me feel like a kid; I'm told when to come and when to leave, I don't even have a choice who I sit next to, and so I do all the time-wasting exercises I used to do at school. I go to the toilet. I have a wee when I don't really need one, when I can happily go the entire day without one. I look in the mirror. I pick a spot. Why am I still getting spots at my age? Aren't spots supposed to be a teenage thing? I'm thirty-two, for fuck's sake. I check the lily plant for dead leaves. There was a time when I would have checked the lily plant quite a few times. I would have checked the window lock as well, closed, opened and reclosed the cabinet on the wall, stroked the blue hand towel three times with one hand and three times with another. But that hasn't happened for years.

I go to the toilet. Three minutes wasted and I'm back in my chair. I'll give myself half an hour and then go make tea. That should take up ten minutes, longer if there's anyone else in the kitchen area.

'Hi!' Jodie is on the phone. She sounds excited. 'It's Jason,' she says to me, her hand over the receiver.

I nod, trying to summon enthusiasm. Jason is one of the directors. He's doing a youth programme on an estate in south London. Why am I still researching programmes like these? I'm not impressed by people like Jason, especially when they're up their own arses. He thinks he's avant-garde when really he's just establishment. And I don't like establishment.

'She's *so* gorgeous, isn't she?' sighs Jodie. She's put down the phone; she's looking at a paper now. 'I actually love her hair like that.'

I walk reluctantly across the office, which is all open plan so you can't get away with doing anything without someone seeing. 'Who?' I ask. 'Who's so gorgeous?' I don't care, but even stupid conversations can waste time.

'Kate Moss,' says Jodie, like I should know. I look over Jodie's shoulder. She's staring at a red top Sunday paper. It's the *Sunday Post*. My dad used to read the *Sunday Post*. He said he got it for the sports results, but Mum used to call it the *Sunday Poke*. There's a photo of a woman in a white bra on the top right-hand corner of the front cover. Right the way across her breasts it says: *Moss a mess?* Jodie starts humming to herself as she opens up the paper. She pauses at two

52

photos of blonde women in golden dresses, so big they're almost life-sized. Then she stops at a double-page spread. The paper says Kate Moss has been spotted looking pale, gaunt and stumbling. I wait while Jodie reads the story. The paragraphs are tiny, there're no long words, but it takes her a while. At last Jodie turns the page and stares at a series of grainy photos of some bloke in a clinch with a half-naked woman.

'Who's that?' I ask.

Jodie groans. 'From *Coronation Street*,' she says. 'That's his ex.' She points at a photo of the man and his ex, which the paper has imaginatively torn in two. Jodie turns the page and I read another headline: *Her non-stop lust wore me out*.

'Who's that?' I ask.

Jodie groans again. I'm really starting to annoy her. 'Makosi,' she says. 'From *Big Brother*.'

'Oh right,' I say. I've heard of *Big Brother* but I've never watched it because I don't have a TV. My housemates do, both of them have one in their bedrooms, but when the TV in our front room broke down no one replaced it. I've told Jodie this. The first time I told her she looked at me as if I'd said I always go out without my knickers on. She just can't understand why I wouldn't want a TV. *How*, said Jodie, *can you work for a TV production company and not own a TV?*

I bend a little further over Jodie's shoulder, start reading about the curvy cardiac nurse who lives in an exotic world of threesomes, lipstick lesbianism and quickies round the back of the local takeaway. 'She had it coming to her really, didn't she?' says Jodie. 'She never should have said she was a virgin. Fuck me!' She's turned the page again and she's looking at a

53

picture of a young man with messy blond hair. He looks like he's on holiday, the background isn't in focus but it could be a beach. He's only wearing trunks and he's got a small tattoo on his naked shoulder, perhaps a bird. He's got sunglasses on so it's hard to see what his expression is or where he's looking, but he's definitely not paying much attention to the bare-breasted woman on his left who is wearing nothing but a red thong. Jodie smoothes down the page with both hands, her fingers flattening the creases. 'Fuck me,' she says again, 'I've never seen Donny Green like this.'

'And who's she?' I ask, pointing at the woman.

'Just some bimbo,' Jodie says nastily. 'He could do better than that. He could have anyone he wanted, but *she* looks like a right tart, doesn't she? It says here he's bought a new house. Where's that? Notting Hill? It looks nice, doesn't it?' I straighten up, bored by the people in the paper just like I get bored watching people on TV.

'Doing anything nice over the weekend?' I ask. Jodie doesn't need any encouragement, she tells me which pub she's going to, how many drinks she'll have there, where she'll move on next, what club she's going to, how she's on the guest list, how she's going shopping to Wood Green on Sunday . . .

'What about you?' she asks at last. 'Doing anything good this week?'

'I'm seeing some old friends on Thursday,' I say.

Jodie yawns, inspects her nails. 'Good for you,' she says, and I realise with a bit of a shock that I'm being patronised by a twenty-year-old. 'Oh I love this song,' says Jodie, and she turns up the volume on the radio that is always on the shelf above her desk. She wriggles her shoulders. 'I just love Jay B,' she says.

I look at her in disbelief. Jay B is the prick Ashley went out with for ten minutes all those years ago. I think about telling her this, but Jodie's back on the phone to Jason again. I think about this evening, how I'm going to Mum's. She says she's got an old friend coming round. She sounded guilty on the phone, so I assume it's a man. She never calls my brothers to meet them, only me. I go back to my desk and look at my accounts again. I'm maxed on five credit cards. I won't be able to buy another camera for a very long time. I thought the pub taking two of my prints would help, but they still owe me. That was a month ago when I got one of those urges to do something with my life. I went around the area, taking black and white pictures on a misty early morning: dog walkers in the park, a queue outside the Church of Living God, a man stacking oranges outside a greengrocer. Then I printed them out, framed them and went from pub to pub with them in my hands. The Canbury Arms took two, but when I went in there last week they hadn't even put them up. Perhaps they don't like them after all. Shit.

Chapter Seven

'You were wearing that last time.' Mum opens the door and stands on the steps. There's something about her block of flats that makes me think of the old elephant house at London Zoo. The steps up to Mum's flat are shrouded with a brick wall and the brick wall is blackened as if there's recently been a fire, which there probably has. 'Weren't you?' asks Mum. 'Wearing that last time.'

Why does she think it necessary to wear different clothes all the time? I squeeze past her at the doorway and get into the hall. 'Smells nice in here,' I offer. Mum's hallway is always dark; she never puts the light on in here.

'You've put on a bit of weight,' says Mum from behind.

You wish, I think. I've seen she's wearing her gym clothes and I've seen they're very tight. For some reason, Mum would like me to battle with my weight the way she does.

'Joe and Rich were here yesterday,' she says.

That's unusual. It's not like my brothers to pay a social call. 'What's for dinner?'

'A roast.' Mum leads the way into the kitchen where the glass on the back window is all steamed up because she hasn't opened it. The window sill is full of plants, all trying to grow their way towards the light, their leaves flattened against the glass. I don't know why she doesn't put them outside. 'Roast beef, with all the trimmings,' says Mum. 'You are staying to eat, aren't you? I wonder if I should do peas with this.'

'I thought you didn't like beef?' I say.

'It's his favourite,' says Mum.

'Who? Oh, your gentleman caller?' I sit down at the table which is wedged with cardboard under one leg. A spider plant hanging in a wire basket from the ceiling tickles my hair; Mum's spider plants could take over the world they multiply so fast.

'He's an old friend, Bel. An old friend of your father's.'

I snort. 'So, what, you're suddenly just back in touch?'

'Well it was very funny actually.' Mum sits down, puts her hands flat out on the table. 'I was just sorting out the rubbish because that silly bitch next door knocked it over again and I've said to her that . . .'

'And?'

'And.' Mum looks at me sharply, she wants to tell the whole story. 'Glen was driving past and for some reason he slows down when he passes my Audi, which as you know I've had for a good bloody twenty years, and he looks to the right and he recognises the car and so he slows right down and,' Mum takes a breath, 'and here we are!'

'Glen? I don't remember a Glen.' I wonder why her story has ended so abruptly. If Glen is one of Dad's old drinking buddies, then Mum wouldn't want anything to do with him.

'Your memory,' says Mum, standing up again, 'isn't great. I blame the drugs. I think I will do peas, they'll only take a couple of minutes. There's the door, you answer it.'

'What does he do then, this Glen?' I get up, ignoring

57

Mum's reference to drugs, and take an apple from the bowl on the table.

'He's a pap,' says Mum.

'He's a what?' I bite on the apple and it's very soft and sweet.

'You know, a paparazzi. For the *Sunday Poke*.'

'Are you *kidding*?' I think of Jodie in the office, the way she was poring over the *Sunday Post* this afternoon. She's going to love this.

The man on the doorstep is a surprise. He has bushy white hair and thick white eyebrows, and his eyes are a strange glittery grey. He's got a big black pair of sunglasses that he's pushed on top of his head. He's quite chunky, but in a firm sort of way. He looks ten years younger than Mum. There's something about him that makes me think of a jazz musician; I can picture him on a smoky stage holding a saxophone. I was expecting a man in a dirty brown mac.

'Bell!' he laughs and shakes my hand. He has a deep voice and his hand is big with rough, calloused fingers. 'Long time!'

'Glen,' I say, glad I've remembered his name.

'You probably don't remember me.'

I shift from foot to foot.

'Alright if I come in?'

I laugh because it must look like I'm blocking him from the flat. I move to one side and watch him walk down Mum's hallway. He's been here before, I think, he knows exactly where this hallway leads. So she hasn't just met up with him, they must have been seeing each other for a while.

'These yours?' Glen stops by a row of prints on the wall. There are three photos of Mum. I put them in one long

58

frame because they are like a story, three frames in the story of Mum. I took these years ago at art school when we were studying Cindy Sherman; I loved the way she took photos of herself dressed up like a black and white movie star. You could see what she was dressed up to be, but you still had to guess what was going on. I tried to do the same with Mum, posed her like a leading lady in a 1950s film still, but she's put them in the hall where no one really sees them because she doesn't like them. She's not much into photos on the wall. She didn't like the way I plastered my walls with photos as a kid. I didn't have posters of pop stars and boy bands like Loreen or Ashley; I didn't want Simon Le Bon or Spandau Ballet staring down at me, it was my own pics I put up.

Everywhere I went I took pictures, I used to photograph everything: my family, my friends, my neighbours, my street, I just never stopped taking pictures. I got really hooked the day Mr Jefferies taught me in the school darkroom, a narrow room with enlargers on one side, black metal boxes on stands that made me think of the dentist's, and two sinks on the other side, with rubber hoses on the taps. I remember a collection of glass bottles, a big black stopwatch and a whole row of white plastic processing trays. I can still see that first sheet of paper, when I knew it had been exposed but it was still blank. Mr Jefferies showed me how to soak it in the developer, dip it in the stop bath, put it in the fixer and the wash, and finally hang it up with a clothes peg to dry. Best of all was that moment when the image first appeared, when that piece of blank paper magically changed, when the black and the greys seeped into view and grew stronger until they

59

merged into something familiar, into the picture I'd taken, captured just like that.

'Yes, they're mine,' I say, because Glen is still standing next to me in the hallway, waiting for an answer. I look at the pictures of Mum, the series of three, and I think there is something about a photograph that lets you remember something like nothing else can, whether it's something bad or something good, it lets you remember. These pics of Mum in the hall, they let me remember when she was the age I am now, when I could still persuade her to pose, when she was still happy with the way she looked.

'Interested in portraiture?' asks Glen.

'I used to be,' I say, 'but I think it's landscape I like best now.'

'Quite impressive,' says Glen, and he strokes the bottom corner of the frame with two fingers. 'Nice shallow depth of field in this one.'

I'm a bit taken aback because I think he's actually admiring them in a genuine way and I feel embarrassed all of a sudden and so I lead the way into the kitchen where Mum is stirring something with great concentration on the stove. It can't be the peas, they don't need stirring that much.

'Hello darling,' says Glen.

Darling? To my amazement, Mum blushes. I wait, is Glen going to go over and give her a kiss? He does and Mum blushes again. Then she waves him away. 'Go and have a drink in there with Bel.' She says it like it's the right thing to do.

We go into the front room and Glen sits down on Mum's fake leather armchair and gives me a big smile. There is something different about the room, or perhaps it's lots of things. Then I see Glen is sitting right under Mum's old Green Lady picture, the picture that used to give me the creeps as a kid. When did she dig that out and put it up again? I haven't seen that print for years. I used to like the dress the girl's wearing, all the golden bits around her neck, and I liked the way her hands were hidden in her sleeves, but the face, painted in that sickly green, was scary. I remember the way the Green Lady stared at me, especially when I was about to get found out for something. I sit down on Mum's blue sofa that's covered in white dog hairs even though her last dog died two years ago. 'So,' I say, 'Mum says you're a pap.'

'Not exactly, darling, not exactly.' Glen laughs. He settles on the armchair, puts one arm along the back. 'The paparazzi, and that's the plural term, work for agencies. I'm a press photographer, to use the proper term. I don't have to bash someone out the way to get a picture.'

'So what's the singular term?'

'The singular?' asks Glen, and he looks pleased that I'm asking. 'The singular is paparazzo, darling, it means mosquito. Ever seen *La Dolce Vita*? The Fellini film? No? Well that's where we really get the term paparazzo because there's a character, see, a news photographer called Paparazzo. Fellini based him on a real-life snapper, an Italian called Secchiaroli. The story goes . . .' Glen lowers his voice, 'the story goes that one evening Secchiaroli and some other snappers were having a stroll through Rome when they saw the ex King of Egypt sitting at a café with two women, neither of whom was his wife. So one of the snappers took a picture. The

61

King lost it, started flipping over the table, and there was Secchiaroli's picture just waiting for him. That, you could say, was when the paparazzi began, because the idea of this game is to get someone famous doing something they shouldn't be doing, a famous somebody doing something a nobody would do. But the thing with *him*, darling, unlike today, his snaps were good, very artistic.' Glen coughs, clears his throat; perhaps he thinks he's been talking too much. 'So, Bel, what are you up to these days?'

I shrug; I don't really want to go into *what I'm up to these days*. The room feels too hot all of a sudden. The carpet's too thick; the Green Lady is looking at me. I'm feeling claustrophobic. But then that might be all the junk in the room. Now I see what else is new, apart from the Green Lady: there are monkeys everywhere. Mum has always collected; she starts up new collections all the time. Last year it was sheep: clay sheep, toy sheep, sheep magnets, sheep on cups and towels and saucers, black-faced sheep and blue-faced sheep, sheep with shaggy brown hair and sheep with thick white curls like a fake Santa's beard, anything at all as long as it was a sheep. In the toilet she has a series of sheep portraits, four long sheep faces with slanted eyes and erect ears. But now I can see Mum has moved onto monkeys. On the hatch that leads into the kitchen are a line of them: a white fluffy monkey with a brown face, a brown hand-knitted monkey with a pink face, a big one dressed in a tartan jacket with a red hat and a pair of cymbals in its hand. Then I see a new lamp in the corner of the room, two monkeys sitting under a palm tree. Then I see a statue on the TV, three monkeys squatting on top of each other.

The top one has his hands over his ears, the middle one has his hands over his eyes, and the bottom one has his mouth covered.

Mum puts her head through the hatch. 'Bel, do you see my new monkeys?'

'Yes, Mum.'

'Hear no evil, see no evil, speak no evil,' says Mum, flicking a dishcloth in the direction of the TV.

'Yes,' I say, 'I get it.'

Glen looks at the monkeys as well. 'There is sometimes a fourth one,' he says thoughtfully.

Mum has disappeared back into the kitchen so I say, 'Really?'

'Yeah,' says Glen. 'The fourth one has his tummy covered, or just has his hands crossed in front of him.'

'And what's that supposed to show?'

'*Do* no evil,' says Glen. 'It's what's known as a pictorial maxim.'

'Is it?'

'Yeah. The three wise monkeys, that's the Japanese phrase, but that's a shortened version of the original which was from China. There're different ways of interpreting it, aren't there?' Glen leans forward in the chair. He wants to engage me; I can see that he wants me to be interested too. 'If you don't see evil, Bel, then does it therefore not exist? Does it mean if we don't see, hear or talk evil then we'll be spared it? Or does it mean that we're ignoring evil, turning a blind eye to it, refusing to acknowledge immorality perhaps?' Glen laughs all of a sudden. 'The fourth one should really be a monkey with a camera!'

Chapter Eight

'So, Bel,' says Glen, and he leans back in Mum's armchair again, 'you always loved your photography, making any money from your snaps?'

'Not really,' I say. That sounds nice and casual. What I really mean is, not a fucking penny. I wonder if Mum's told him about the pub taking two of my prints.

'I always remember you with a camera as a kid,' says Glen. 'You used to go round with one of those mass-produced plastic things that took roll film, and what about that Pentax SLR your dad gave you when you were what, sixteen?'

How does he know this? I still don't remember Glen from my childhood. Was he really Dad's friend and was that before or after Dad walked out? And would that have been the first time Dad walked out, when I was five, or would it be the time he walked out when I was twelve and never came back? I think of the plastic camera and how I used to save up my pocket money to buy a cube of flashes. There were four; you used one up and then snapped the other in place. 'Yeah, I've still got that SLR.'

'And didn't you go to art school?' Glen asks.

'Yeah, I did a foundation.' How does he know this as well? I think about art school and about the students, the ones who'd saved up for years to get onto the course and who were so serious. One man spent a month building a loom; he had some tapestry idea and he worked all the hours there were, he even tried to sleep in the college. Then one morning he came in and the whole thing had collapsed and he went crazy, sat on the floor and howled. I think of the rich kids in the photography class who would photograph a tree and then blow it up eight times, which cost a fortune to frame. It was only a tree blown up large but they got great grades. After a year I just couldn't handle the arty farty nonsense any more. But the college darkroom, I missed that.

'Does it pay well?,' I ask Glen. 'Working for the *Sunday Post*?' If he can question me, I think, then I can question him. Isn't this why Mum's got me round here this evening, to get to know her gentleman caller?

'The *Sunday Poke*?' Glen smiles and stands up. He takes a pouch of rolling tobacco and a packet of blue rizlas out of his trouser pocket and sits down again. I watch as he separates a rizla from the packet and pulls it out. Then he starts laughing and the half-made cigarette shakes in his hand. His laugh is high, like a girl's; it's a real giggle. I watch while he steadies his cigarette and then while he licks the whole thing together.

'To be honest with you, Bel, being a pap used to pay very well. I mean, if a picture tells a thousand words, why not pay me a thousand for it? Or ten thousand come to that. Does it pay well working for the *Sunday Poke*? You haven't noticed my Armani suit?' He pulls on the lapels of his jacket, a thinly striped black and white affair that I now see is quite snazzy, just like him, and then he pushes up the jacket sleeves and I see how his arms are sprinkled with white hairs that make me think of Father Christmas. 'And the Merc outside?' I laugh

65

because I saw his car when he arrived. When I opened the door I saw a bashed-up little white van. He seems to know this because he holds his cigarette between his fingers and points it at me. 'Oh you can laugh at my van, darling, but you don't want to drive around in anything too showy in this game. The idea is not to draw attention to yourself.' He smiles in a satisfied way and puts the cigarette in his mouth. Then he takes out a chunky silver lighter from his jacket pocket and lights it. 'But the thing is, Bel, to be honest with you, I've been in this game too long.' He inhales his cigarette and he looks tired now, his expression has changed. 'I'll give it another year and that's it, because I've had enough. It's time to retire, darling.' He looks around for an ashtray, finds one on top of the TV next to the monkey statue, and gets up to take it. Then he turns to me and smiles. 'Although, Bel, there's no such thing as a retired pap. Old photographers never die, darling, we just go out of focus.'

'Bel needs money,' says Mum, appearing suddenly at the doorway. I wonder if she's been listening. We weren't talking about money anyway. 'Bel always needs money.'

I laugh like it's funny. I don't think she knows how much I do. Mum's got a bottle of screw-top white wine in her hand and two glasses. She hands one to Glen and pours him a drink. 'You could get her some work, Glen?' she asks.

'No,' I say at once. Is this why she asked me round? Is she trying to get me another job, just like she got me the office job, because a friend of a friend knew a neighbour of a neighbour who knew someone who . . .

'Glen just loves his photography,' Mum says. 'He even named his son Canon, didn't you, Glen?'

I stare at Glen. He named his *kid* Canon?

'She could do it,' says Mum, pressing on, handing me a glass, pouring me a drink, 'couldn't she, Glen?'

'Any muppet with a ten mega pixel could do it,' says Glen. 'At least they think they can,' he adds, looking pissed off.

'How did you get into it?' I lean forward. For a second I see myself as a pap, stalking the famous, hiding behind trees, doing car chases. It might be fun. Fucking better than working in an office for film producers up their own arses.

'How did I get into it?' asks Glen. 'That was thirty years ago, darling. Like you, I loved my photography, I couldn't afford a college course or anything, but I fancied myself as a bit of a news hound. So, one day, I wrote a cheeky letter to the pictures desk on my local paper. They never replied, so I wrote again. I wrote four times. I was a cheeky bastard back then.'

'Unlike now,' says Mum.

'Unlike now,' laughs Glen. 'Then, see, I started sending in snaps, finding my own stories. I said, don't even pay me. In the end the bloke on the desk got so fed up he rang me up and called me in. After that I joined an agency for a few years, there was more money in that, see, and then the *Sunday Post*.'

I laugh. The *Sunday Post* is crap. I know because I've just spent half the afternoon looking at it over Jodie's shoulder.

'Oh I know,' says Glen. 'Work for the *Poke* and you expect to be mocked, but people forget that the *Sunday Post*, and I'm not referring to the Scottish *Post*, is the only British newspaper to have always supported a Labour government. Yeah, it has,' he nods his head, although I haven't contradicted him.

'It's not the oldest Sunday paper, that's the *News of the World*, that goes back to 1843, and it's the *News of the World*, the *Screws*, see, that started the whole celeb scoop thing, but both the *Poke* and the *Screws* were aimed at the newly literate working class,' Glen adopts a posh nasal voice, 'like myself, darling.' He smiles and drinks his wine, puffs on his cigarette, sees it's gone out and lights it again. 'The *News of the World* started the celeb scoops, the *Express* started the whole gossip thing, but what the *Sunday Post* did was to combine the two. But, most of all,' he points his cigarette at me, 'it added pics. That was the paper that really thought a photograph could tell a story. That was the first newspaper to devote the whole of a front page to just one single snap.' Glen stops and looks sentimental, like he's talking about someone he used to love. Then he realises his cigarette has gone out again and he relights it. 'I was a snapper on the *Post* for years, darling. I only left after my wife died. Then I realised it was the only thing keeping me going and I went back to them. Sad, isn't it?' Glen laughs, to lighten the mood, then he sighs. 'Yeah, an awful lot of people hate the paps these days, whereas before, tell someone you were a pap and they'd find it funny. That all changed when Lady Di died, see, then people wanted someone to blame and they blamed the paps. They forget it was them who bought all the pictures of her. And they forget that the paps wouldn't have been outside the right door to her hotel in Paris that night if they hadn't been tipped off, and who do you think would have done that? Most tip-offs, Bel, are inside jobs, they come from someone very, very close to the celeb in question or . . .' Glen smiles at me, 'they come from the celeb themselves. Fergie and the toe-sucking job?

Now how do you think the paps knew exactly where she would be and with whom and doing what? And don't forget, it was the paps at the scene of the Lady Di crash who started giving first aid; they were the ones who rang for an ambulance. But the public wanted someone to blame and so . . .' He stops and sips his wine and watches me, waiting for another question.

'Can you really make ten grand from a picture?' I ask.

Glen nods. 'A couple of years ago, I got a snap of Posh Spice.'

'Who?' I ask, because I know this will drive Mum mad.

'Posh Spice!' snaps Mum. 'From the Spice Girls, for God's sake!'

Glen nods. 'I snapped her at her local Tesco, see? She was buying some supersaver-brand toilet paper and you could see it through the bag. Bingo! Sold for ten grand.'

'Ten grand?' says Mum. She's so excited she's almost shouting.

'As I said, the idea of the game is to "catch" a celeb doing something a normal person would do, see, like buy cheap bog roll. No one wants to see a normal person doing this, no one wants to see a normal person in tears, say, or walking down the street, or having a barney, or buying bog roll, but a *somebody* in tears or walking down the street or having a barney or buying bog roll, we all want to see that.'

'Are you allowed to do that?' asks Mum, like she's just thought of something. 'Take pictures of someone just doing their shopping in Tesco?'

Glen shrugs. 'It's a public place, darling, there's no law against taking a photograph, or not yet there isn't. If you were using a telephoto lens to take a photo of Posh in her living room, well someone in their living room, or even their back garden, might expect to be private, mightn't they? But in a shop? That's different. And Posh knows the paps follow her, she knows what she's doing when she goes into Tesco and buys supersaver bog roll. "Look at me; I might have more money than you'll ever see in your life but here I am buying this. So I'm not Posh Spice, see, I'm Normal Spice. Now go out and buy my record."' Glen laughs, then he looks serious. 'These privacy laws things change all the time, though. Look at what happened with Naomi Campbell last year.'

'Who?' I ask.

'Naomi Campbell,' says Mum through gritted teeth, 'the super model.'

'That's right,' nods Glen, and he smiles at me because he can see I know who he's talking about. 'She sued the *Mirror* when it published snaps of her coming out of a Narcotics Anonymous meeting, said it was an invasion of her privacy, even though she was in a public place. Well, she didn't actually sue for invasion of privacy because you can't do that, but she sued for breach of confidentiality under the Data Protection Act. First she won in the High Court, that was overturned by the Appeal Court, then the Law Lords agreed with her. So she won; the snap was in a public place but the actual photograph was of a private nature.'

'But why would someone pay you ten grand?' I ask. 'For a picture of someone buying bog roll?'

'Because like I've just said, darling, other people want to see it! Because people will buy a magazine if Posh is on the cover, whatever she's doing. It doesn't matter what, she's a celeb. Think about it, Bel, we're a nation of gossips.' He lowers his voice again, like he's about to share something intimate. 'Most of what people talk about in this country is who is doing what with who, whether they're in the pub, chatting on the bus or having a natter over a garden wall. No one likes a nosy parker, of course, but we do like our gossip. So who can we gossip about, who can we all join in and gossip about? Celebs! And you can't have a good gossip in a paper if there's no snap, can you? That's where the paps come in.'

Mum nods, refills Glen's glass, although he's only drunk half of it.

'The pap who took the Daniella Westbrook photo?' asks Glen.

'Who?' I ask, and this time I mean it.

'Daniella Westbrook!' snaps Mum. 'From *EastEnders*, for God's sake!'

'Mum,' I say, 'you know I don't have a TV.'

'Good for you, girl,' laughs Glen.

'Well you should get one,' says Mum.

'Why?' I ask.

'Anyway,' says Glen, 'the pap who took that snap, the one where Daniella was leaving the Soap Awards, showing all the coke had eaten away the inside of her nose so she only had one nostril? From what I heard, there was a real bun fight that night and this pap crouched down and he got that shot of her nose. He was on his knees, apparently, because the only space was down between people's legs, and he was shooting up and he didn't even realise what he had until he was going through the snaps later. Everyone else had known

71

about the coke, but that was the first public snap. He bought a house with that.'

'He didn't!' says Mum.

Glen enjoys our looks of wonder. 'Poor girl.' He shakes his head. 'Everyone made a lot of money off her. Mind you, she went on to make a TV show about it, didn't she?'

My phone beeps. For a second I can't think what's making that noise. I'd forgotten where I was, I was so busy listening to Glen. I take out my phone; there's a message from Loreen. I look up to see Mum's watching.

'Anyone nice?' she asks. She's trying to sound casual but she's already heading my way, she's going to try and read the text over my shoulder.

'Loreen,' I say, and close the phone. That will disappoint Mum, she's hoping it's a man. But if it was a man I wouldn't tell her. 'We're meeting up on Thursday, me and her and Ashley. Karen's coming back too, she says.'

'Really?' says Mum. 'These are her old school friends,' she tells Glen. 'I can't believe the four of them still keep in touch.'

I shrug. I don't know why Mum is making it out to be so odd.

'Your brothers hardly have any friends from their school days, let alone primary school.'

No, I think, well they wouldn't, would they?

'And what's Loreen up to these days?' asks Mum. 'How are those boys of hers?'

'Fine,' I say.

'She still struggling along on her own?'

'She's still struggling along on her own.'

'And what about Karen,' Mum asks, 'she still in California?'

'Yeah.'

'Nice,' nods Glen.

'And Ashley,' says Mum, 'she did well for herself, didn't she? She's an interior designer,' she tells Glen, 'she has her own company. Bel could have done some work for her. Have you asked her, Bel, if she has anything you could . . .'

'No!' I say.

'Well,' says Mum, 'what were you saying, Glen? About how much money you can make from being a pap?'

Glen sighs. 'Yeah, I was saying you can make a lot of money in this game, but that wasn't what got me into it. The *Post* was a campaigning paper to begin with, see, and that appealed to me then, I liked being a part of that. Plus there was some glamour in the old days, because back then it was stars, I mean real stars, people who were untouchable, unreachable, people you only saw all dolled up at a première. Now it's the same old scruffy celebs and anyone can be one: diet doctors, chefs, home decorators, muppets off reality TV shows.' Glen looks disgusted. He inspects his roll-up and sees it's gone out again. 'Television brings these celebs right into our houses, see, so we don't have to go to the cinema any more, and it makes us feel we know them, makes us feel we want to know all about them, so that we know they're as messed up as we are, only more so.'

'Who were you doing today?' asks Mum.

'Kate Moss,' says Glen, and his sunglasses fall suddenly forward over his eyes.

I think about telling Jodie this tomorrow, that I met a real-life pap who works for the *Sunday Post* and takes pictures of

Kate Moss. I don't want to go to work tomorrow. Or the day after that. Mum goes off to the kitchen and I look at Glen; he's still got his sunglasses over his eyes and he's quiet now, I can't see what he might be thinking. So I get up, start nosing round the room, inspect the remains of Mum's sheep collection on the mantelpiece above the gas fire. She must have got rid of a lot of her sheep to make way for the monkeys. I pick up a wooden sheep, the size of a brick, and it makes a thump when I put it down again.

'Wooah!' Glen says.

I look round, he's pushing his sunglasses up from his eyes and he seems startled. 'How long was I out for?' he asks.

I stare at him, was he asleep?

'Just having a little snap.' He rubs his eyes and yawns.

'A snap?'

'A snap,' Glen smiles. 'A small nap. I've just done eighteen hours on the trot, darling. Do you know what time Kate got in this morning? Five am. You know, Bel,' he leans forward, looking serious now, 'you should never give up on a passion in life, it's the only thing worth pursuing. If you've got a passion, then to be honest with you don't give up on it. Your mum's right, it's a shame to waste a talent.'

And I think, a talent? Mum said I have a talent?

Chapter Nine

KAREN

If we met now, I wonder, would we all be friends? It sort of like spooks me this question, especially now on the plane home when I'm encased in the darkness, suspended somewhere between the end of one continent and the beginning of another. I've been thinking about the four of us ever since the idea for this sabbatical came together, because we were as close as anything when I left England, me and Bel and Loreen and Ashley. I guess I've always taken our friendship for granted, because we've known each other so long, and although over the years I haven't been desperate for it like Loreen sometimes has, or careless with it like Bel sometimes has, it's still always been important to me. But hell, I've no idea what Ashley thinks of our friendship any more; of the four of us it's Ashley who has been least in touch.

In eight hours I'll be back in England and my sabbatical will begin. I pick up my book; I've been waiting to read it in the peace of the plane. It's not what I should be reading, it has nothing to do with my research at all, this is reading for pure pleasure. That night I left for America, when my good-byes had been said and my bags all packed, I stayed up reading until four am because I was so excited to be beginning a new life that I had to do something to keep myself calm. I read on the plane all the way to California as well, I read through the meal and through the film, and when people put those diddy little eyeshades on and the cabin lights were dimmed I read then too. And every now and again I stopped and put the book down and thought, where am I now, am I flying over Indiana or Kansas or Nebraska, is it Colorado down there or Utah or Nevada? And then I went back to my book, just as I do now, only now there is a diddy little screen in front of me that shows exactly where I am, how fast the plane is going, how high we are, how many hours have gone and how many hours there are left. But I don't want to look at the screen, I would rather read. I take out my glasses – the light in the plane is too dim to read without them – and although I still feel a bit of a bozo wearing glasses I try to make myself comfortable. It's too simple to say reading is escapism, and there's nothing in particular I need to escape from right now, except obviously the whole situation with Stella, but there are times when it feels good for my mind to be in another place, to be facing different dilemmas from the ones I normally do.

What was it the immigration guy said when I landed at Frisco Airport in the Fall of '93? 'What have you come to study?' And I said, 'American literature', and he laughed and stretched his fingers out on the counter top and said, 'I didn't know we had any literature!' And I picked up my suitcase so heavy with books: the *Complete Poems of Emily Dickinson*, Whitman's *Song of Myself*, Plath's *The Bell Jar*, Fitzgerald's *Tender is the Night*, Faulkner's *As I Lay Dying*,

Hawthorne's *The Scarlet Letter*. I loved Dickinson the best, I loved the way her poems could be so easy to read and so difficult to understand; they were romantic in a terrible sort of way, and so was I.

That evening I arrived I took the Amtrak train from Frisco, the first time I'd ever seen a double-decker train, and it slid in its air-conditioned fineness into Martinez, Suisun and then Davis. The train guard put a little blue box out on the platform for me to step on to, and as he did he said, 'There you go ma'am', like I was a character from a Henry James novel and not a fresh-faced twenty-year-old just escaped from London. I watched the aluminium glory of the train leave in a shimmer of white, red and blue and then I looked along the empty platform, at the curved terracotta archways of the station building and the weak light from an old-fashioned street lamp. I couldn't believe I'd got here, that I was in America, because it was where I had wanted to be since I was sixteen. That was why I had chosen American Studies for my undergraduate degree: it meant I could get away.

The Davis train station was empty that night and I walked through, the only soul in the place. Then I stood for a second to look at my map and to plot my way to the apartment complex where I'd be staying, and when I looked up, after folding my map away, I saw an apparition: a double-decker London bus. I saw, from the corner of my eye, as the red bulk of the bus turned a corner and was gone, and I watched after it, wondering what a London bus could be doing here in California and whether I'd really seen it or not. I didn't know then that this was how some students got to campus every day.

There was something very silent, very new and clean about the town of Davis then, built so snugly between two freeways, Interstate 80 and Highway 113. The very word 'freeway' sounded so exciting to me, it didn't sound dull and old-fashioned like 'motorway'. I could see from the map that the town of Davis was set out like a grid: the streets with numbers went in one direction – 1st Street, 2nd Street, 3rd Street – and the streets with letters went another – J Street, K Street, L Street. Even someone as useless at directions as Loreen would have found it hard to get lost in Davis. Every road was named and every road was a street, there were no crescents or lanes or mews or terraces, just streets. When I'd first looked at the map, when I was preparing to leave England, I'd wondered if the town planners hadn't had the goddam imagination to come up with actual names for the streets they'd designed, but as I left the station that evening and followed the signs on little poles at the corner of each road I thought there was something democratic about it, that no one street sounded any different, any better or worse, than the next. And as I walked I looked constantly around, though the streets were empty of people, I looked at the smooth grey sidewalks, the yellow fire hydrants I'd only seen in movies, the neatly positioned garbage cans, a house made from wooden slats the colour of milky coffee. I tried to pin-point what was different about the air that made me feel lifted, because in London, walking on a hot, dark night, I would have felt stifled, but here I felt light. And that's when I first realised, I could be a different person in California, with no mother, no sister, no friends, no background, nothing anyone else knew about me at all.

78

I found the apartment complex on J Street, a two-storey outfit set back from the road, nearly obscured by a row of palm trees with trunks like shaggy candyfloss. I found a key under the mat outside apartment 16, as the orientation people said I would, and I opened the door and came in, walking quietly, not knowing who else was there. The living room was large with closed white drapes on the windows like an attorney's office, and on the floor was a pyramid made from empty Budweiser cans. I walked along a short, dark corridor and saw three doors, one of which was wide open, so I took it to be mine and I got into bed fully dressed and fell asleep.

The next morning I drew back the drapes in my room and I saw a diddy little swimming pool right in the middle of the apartment complex. A goddam swimming pool! How could I not have noticed it the night before? I thought I'd died and gone to heaven. The day was new, the sky was blue, the sun was out, I was in California and I had a swimming pool outside my door! I couldn't wait to get into it. I even walked out of the apartment with just my towel and bathing suit, all my usual self-consciousness blown away; the sort of thing Ashley would have done, walk around in nothing but her bathing suit, not cover herself like me or Loreen would do. The pool was small, perhaps ten strokes a length, but when I lay on my back, star-shaped in the middle, I saw only sky.

I came back from my swim to find a guy right by the door of apartment 16, wearing a plaid shirt and a jacket the colour of puke.

'Yo!' he said cheerfully. 'I'm Bud, you're Karen, my English roomie? I heard you coming in last night.' He said it with a look that made me feel uncomfortable standing there in just my bathing suit. 'So Karen, you're from England, hey? Cool. I have a cousin over there in London, Kennington Street?'

When I didn't answer Bud went and sat down on the big white recliner, though it had looked like he was on his way out. He kicked at the footpad so that the recliner tipped up and then he lay there prone. 'Help yourself to a soda,' he said, nodding towards the kitchen. 'But the moose meat is mine.'

'Sorry?' My voice sounded flat and affronted. I wanted to sound cool and hip and fun now that I was in California, but I sounded like boring old Karen again.

'That package of meat in the fridge,' said Bud, 'it's moose and it's mine, I just got it from Mom. She likes to send me care packages. Ever since her and Pop split and he ran off with her girlfriend it's like I'm her little boy again.' I looked at him, unnerved. I'd just met him and he was already telling me all about himself. Then I saw he was tapping a small ceramic pipe into an ashtray that was balanced on top of two empty pizza boxes. 'You smoke?' he asked.

I shook my head; Bel would laugh when I wrote and told her this.

Bud took out a lighter, lit the pipe, the weed glowed red and he took a breath and held it. 'You sleep OK?' he asked, smoke whooshing out of his nose.

'Yes thank you.'

'*Yes thank you*,' Bud repeated, laughing. 'I just love the way you guys speak!'

I left the apartment and set off for campus and my orientation. In my hand I held a folder filled with all the information

I needed: my passport and my photo ID, my 1:20 form, a housing request form, a medical form that asked me for a sample of my stool. I crossed the road from the apartment complex, heading west, looking around and thinking perhaps Davis had been built only a few minutes ago; everything was so new. And everywhere there were bikes, gleaming bikes ridden by sun-tanned blond students all wearing t-shirts and shorts as if it were some sort of uniform. As I got closer to the campus the bikes increased; there were bicycle lanes and circles for bikes and traffic signals for bikes, and later I discovered there were bike police who could ticket you for cycling under the influence. Davis was a place on two wheels.

The grass on which I walked was cut so close and so neat it was like an ornamental park, not a university, and as I headed towards Mrak Hall I had the feeling I was approaching something impressive like the Taj Mahal. After the paperwork was done I made my way to the Quad, passing Shields Library, a space-age building of blue and grey that looked like something medical or corporate, not like a library at all. And then I saw the campus bookstore and went in and it was huge inside like a big, bright food hall and the Californian sun seemed to bounce off the books, to make them come alive, to make them call out to me to buy them. I knew I was supposed to go to my orientation and I knew I might be late but I began to walk, dazed, down rack after rack of books: shiny hardbacks with spotless spines that had yet to be cracked, paperback novels with colourful covers that looked freshly printed like they'd just come off a production line, textbooks with scientific diagrams on the front. I saw students with wire shopping baskets, adding book after book as if they were vegetables, a couple of zucchini here, a sweet potato there, checking off a list in their hand until the baskets grew so heavy they had to put them down on the bookshop floor and nudge them along with a foot. I stood waiting in the checkout line, the walls adorned with Davis clothes as if we were expected to become part of one big soccer team: sweatshirts with hoods and UCD on the front, sweat pants with UCD down the side, shorts with UCD along the thigh and UCD t-shirts in every shade of grey. And it was then I saw Jen, standing watching me at the checkout line in her grey sweats and her hair cut spiky on the top like David Bowie.

'Hi,' she said as I left the checkout line. 'I'm Jen! You new around here?'

I blushed, said that I was, felt embarrassed that I stood out so much that I didn't fit in with the Californian crowd.

'I'm just standing here,' said Jen, 'letting people know about Women's Studies one oh one.'

I smiled politely. I had paid for my two books, I needed to go to my orientation.

'Can I give you this?' she asked, and she handed me an orange flyer and I took it because I wanted to know what a Women's Studies class was and because most of all I wanted to know if it would be full of women.

Chapter Ten

'Is this the Women's Studies class?' I asked a red-haired woman waiting outside a closed door in a corridor that echoed with the sounds of students, their sneakers squeaking on the floor, their hands opening lockers, their cries of 'Yo!' and 'Dude!'

'I think so,' said the red-haired woman, who seemed as uncertain as me.

I looked through a glass window in the middle of the door at a lecture hall packed with students and I thought perhaps I should sign up for something else. But I had all the Lit classes I needed, I had kept the orange flyer Jen had given me, and I was free to choose other courses now as well.

'Hey!' the red-haired woman said suddenly. 'Are you from *England*?'

I nodded, smiled, looked again through the glass window of the door at the bunch of students inside.

'Wow!' said the woman. 'That is *cool.*'

I smiled again, thinking it impossible that anyone, ever, would think I was cool. My little sister Romana was cool; if she were here then everyone would think her cool, but never me. I had always been the dull one in my family, the reliable one who happily took second place, the one who did her homework and her recorder practice, who wrote her Christmas and birthday thank-you cards, who gave visiting relatives an obliging kiss goodbye.

'I just *love* your accent,' said the woman with the red hair waiting outside the closed door.

'Thank you,' I said, and with a burst of confidence I pushed open the door to the lecture hall. Inside it was nothing like the classes I was used to at uni, held in small, cold tutors' rooms with out-of-date calendars on the wall and tea-stained mugs on the desk. Instead this room was full of students and shiny new desks and chairs and light was pouring in from the windows that ran along one wall as if the room had enjoyed a sudden power surge. Then I saw a woman perched on top of a table, wearing a multi-coloured skirt. Her hair was grey and woven into two meaty plaits and she waved as I came in, the red-haired woman behind me, and then she clapped her hands at all the students milling about the room and called out, 'OK, everyone, I want all you guys moving the tables and chairs, I want this place in a circle!' For a second I panicked and wanted to leave, I didn't like the attention I had suddenly received, I didn't want anyone looking at me, and I didn't want to sit in a circle; I wanted the protection of having the back of someone else in front of me. But I was too far into the room now; I would have had to push to get out.

When at last all the tables and chairs were in a circle the woman perched on the table implored us to sit. 'Welcome,' she said, flicking one long plait over her shoulder and then the other. 'This is probably the first Women's Studies class for a lot of you guys so let me give an idea of what it's all about. Some people ask why Women's Studies is necessary, they want to know what we study in here . . .' A couple of the students laughed, conspiratorially. And then I saw her, I saw Jen sitting on a chair just to the left of the professor. She wore a white shirt and green pants and she was tapping a pen up and down on a pile of folders which sat in her lap. When Jen smiled at me I looked around to see if she was smiling at everyone in this way or if it was only me. And I thought, please let it be at me. 'So,' said the professor still sitting on the table, 'let me begin by saying that there is a need for Women's Studies because this country of ours is the most racist, sexist, homophobic country on earth.'

Two men sitting at the far side of the circle got up in disgust, scraping back their chairs and walking out. Two women nearby them clapped. And I just sat there with my mouth open because I was twenty years old and I'd never heard anyone in authority talk this way before. So I stayed in the room and I signed up for Women's Studies 101 and that same day I found a new apartment, south of Interstate 80 near the railroad tracks on a short dirt road. It was smaller than the apartment the university had found for me, but at least I wouldn't have to live with Bud, and there was an air of impermanence about the place because the apartments looked like mobile homes, as if they had just this moment been set on the ground and could easily be picked up and moved someplace new again. That evening I stood at the back of the apartment where the field and the railroad tracks were, and I listened to Amtrak going by and I wondered where the passengers inside were going and I wondered where I would be going the next time I got on an Amtrak train.

In the morning I walked along to Richards Boulevard, passing the stores that told me I was in California now: a

Mexican restaurant, a gas station which stayed open all night, a takeaway joint called Murder Burger because the burgers were so good they were to die for. I went into town and opened a checking account at Wells Fargo, and on my cheques was a picture of a stagecoach pulled by horses and I thought the people in the picture were setting off on an adventure, just like me. I had no friends or family with me now, no little sister to steal the limelight, no overanxious mother, no father who lived and breathed only for his work. I was Karen with the cool accent and I was in California now.

It wasn't until the second quarter, when I was midway through my second Women's Studies class, that I gathered the nerve to approach Jen. I was walking home one afternoon, past one of Davis' numerous coffee shops, when I saw her sitting alone under a big Bud Light umbrella drinking iced coffee. I could see she was marking something; she had a pile of journals on her table and a pencil in her hand. I took a deep breath and I dared myself to cross the road. She was alone, but I thought that at any moment a friend or a student might appear and the moment would be gone because Jen was popular; I hardly ever saw her alone.

'Hi,' I said a little shyly, standing on the sidewalk.

Jen looked up, and as she did I felt that she had known I was there all along. Her hair was longer than when we'd first met and her fringe was pushed away from her forehead with a large pair of brown sunglasses. 'How are you liking class?' she called out, waving that I should come over. 'I loved what you wrote about the education system in the UK last week.'

'Thanks,' I said. I felt embarrassed then, not by the essay

I'd written on education, but by the journal we were required to write each week and hand in to the teaching assistants like Jen to read. It was to be a personal journal, we were to put down our thoughts as the class progressed, and while the American students had no problem with this, I did. I could see what the professor meant when she said the personal was political, that personal problems were political problems too, but I would have far preferred to keep the personal to myself. I felt that Jen knew too much about me now, because she read my journal each week, and now that I was with her and thinking this I blushed. 'I'm having a pool party later,' she said, closing the journal she'd been writing in, putting the eraser tip of the pencil into her mouth and then tapping it softly up and down between her lips. 'We'd love it if you came.'

I smiled that I would love it too, but I wondered what she meant by 'we'.

That evening I set off for Jen's house, just near the Davis Food Coop on the corner of 6th and G. The Food Coop was my favourite place in Davis then. I'd never seen a store like it before: aisles full of bulk bins stuffed to the brim with granola; rolled oats with nuts and honey the colour of autumn leaves that you helped yourself to with a metal scoop and then tumbled noisily into brown paper bags. There were smaller bins too, of carob-coated raisins, toasted almonds, dried red squares of cranberries. And along the aisles were foods I'd never seen before like cartons of soy milk, like corn chips that you couldn't stop eating once you'd begun, like bottles of maple syrup, like freshly made blueberry bran muffins. I stood there that evening wondering what to buy to bring to the pool party, wondering what was normal to bring to a pool party, until finally I chose two watermelons which I paid for and put under my arms like green and white basketballs.

Jen's house was old by Davis standards, built of yellow slatted wood with a porch on the front and gables up near the attic. I came up the steps, but although the front door was open it was secured with a mosquito screen fastened from the inside and I stood there wondering how to get in. Then I heard the sound of a guitar being played from somewhere out back and I walked round the side of the house to find a huge garden still filled with sunlight and with a pool on one side and an area of grass on the other. I could see perhaps ten people at the party; I hadn't yet got used to the idea that when a Californian said they were having a party that didn't mean there would be many people there.

There were three women sitting with their bare feet dangling in the pool, drinking light frothy beer from plastic cups, and another group of women sitting cross-legged on the grass, eating burritos and salad from paper plates. All round the garden was a wooden fence, and branches from the trees in the neighbouring gardens hung over the fence, making the garden feel tranquil and enclosed. Then I saw that just beside the pool was a Jacuzzi, like a sunken paddling pool with bubbles erupting in clusters in the pale green water.

As night fell some of the women left the party, but others began to take off their clothes and one by one they slid into the Jacuzzi like mermaids returning to the sea. Jen got in last. I had hardly spoken to her all evening, but she held her arms up by the side of the tub and her breasts were translucent in the light of the moon and she looked at me and smiled and for the second time since I'd arrived in Davis I thought I'd died and gone to goddam heaven.

I was only meant to be at Davis a year and after that I was supposed to return to England and my degree, but that was the moment when I knew I would stay if I could, because no one knew me here and I could do as I pleased. If someone invited me skiing, hiking in Yosemite, visiting the wine groves of Napa, then I could say yes. There was no Loreen, Ashley or Bel there to say, but Karen you don't know how to ski, you hate hiking, I thought you didn't like wine? And if I was invited to take my clothes off and get into a Jacuzzi with a bunch of naked women and water that bubbled like gas against my thighs then I could do that too.

Chapter Eleven

DUDU

I am sitting in my kitchen on this lovely Wednesday lunchtime and I am thinking of when the girls were young and the day that Ashley had her seventh birthday party. That is a day that stands out in my mind, a hot July day like today, when it was too humid to sleep properly at night and I had spent a long time listening to the radio. School had closed for the holidays and we walked there, my little Loreen and me, over Hampstead Heath. We passed by the fairground and I told Loreen that I would take her there after the party, because I knew in one of the caravans parked near the car park there was a fortune-teller and that was a treat I was saving for myself.

Loreen was all dressed up that day: I had braided her hair and put her in a little cheesecloth dress, for it was the first birthday party she had been invited to. She was excited because she thought there would be a certain boy at the party, a boy named Christopher Collins whom she had said was her boyfriend. I didn't want her thinking of boys as boyfriends, but she had set her heart on this Christopher Collins, a boy with the face of a pumpkin who, as I had observed in the playground, had an aggressive streak. I hadn't told her what

Ashley's father had told me before school closed for the summer, that Christopher Collins had already had his seventh birthday party and my little Loreen hadn't been invited. I felt pained for her, even though she knew nothing of this.

The front door of Ashley's parents' house in Hampstead was nicely decorated that day with very large colourful balloons and a banner that had been hung from the vine of the wisteria tree in the front garden. Loreen clasped my hand and I nudged her forward so that she could ring the bell herself. The door was opened by Ashley's mother who wore a plastic-looking apron on which were painted two large pink breasts. The English have such a cartoonish approach to body parts and I averted my eyes from the painted-on breasts, embarrassed for Ashley's mother although she herself showed no signs of shame.

'Come in!' she said. 'We're totally behind schedule, come in!'

My little Loreen squirmed on the steps and I just knew I was going to have to go in to the party with her. So I hung my handbag where I was shown, on a tall wooden hat stand in the hall, and then we went down a small flight of steps and into a very large, very light room where everything seemed to be made from metal and glass. I thought two or perhaps three rooms had been knocked together, it was so very big. Along the length of one wall was a table, or perhaps two tables put together, and it was covered with a tablecloth and party food. There were cold little wrinkled sausages forced onto pale sharp toothpicks, several varieties of crisps, round bumpy biscuits with thick icing in pink and yellow and orange, large cartons of juice and big bottles of fizzy drinks, a bowl of my little Loreen's favourite sweets, hard lollipops that you could whistle on before you ate, sandwiches without any crusts and fairy cakes with little wings on top. I had not seen such a display of food for many years; it was as if a wedding party were expected.

'Our first guests!' said Ashley's father, bounding into the room like a dog released from a kennel. 'Ashley!' he shouted. 'Ashley! Your friend is here!' He wore jeans which looked as if they had been dripped with bleach, and on each side of his face he had very thin sideburns as if he had something growing on his skin, which I suppose he did. I could see he had come from a room at the back of the house, and this I assumed was his office for he had told me one day at the school gates that he worked from home. He had mentioned a patient he had had that day and so I thought he was a doctor of some sort. I looked around the party room and at a wall of shelves at the far end; in the middle of the lowest shelf was a book placed so centrally it was hard not to see, a very worn copy of *The Joy of Sex*. Quickly I looked away from the bookshelf and towards a tall wooden cabinet in the corner of the room which had a clock face on top, and I saw that we were a little early and wished we were not.

Then Ashley appeared in the room with her hair in two bunches and fairy clips on either side. 'Hello,' she said to my little Loreen. 'Have you brought a present for me?'

Her father laughed as if she had said something very clever.

I nudged Loreen and she handed over her parcel, inside of which was a Sindy doll she had chosen herself. I had wanted to buy Ashley a cloth doll, because it was soft and could be

92

cuddled and was cheaper, but Loreen had been very insistent. She wanted a Sindy doll in a striped cotton dress with a red ribbon as a belt and sharp little red shoes, a doll whose body was made of vinyl so hard that if you tapped your fingernails upon her face it sounded like rain on a tin roof. Ashley took the parcel from my little Loreen, tore off the paper, carelessly letting the wrapping fall to the floor as if she was someone used to being cleaned up after. 'Oh,' she said, holding up the doll, 'I've already got three of these.'

Then there was a knock on the door and the other children arrived. I moved further into the room as Karen and her little sister Romana and their mother came in. Karen held her arms tightly by her side, trying to loosen the grip of her little sister who was pulling on her. Karen's hair was freshly brushed and it formed a straight line over her forehead, hiding the frown lines which I knew were under it, for Karen was a little girl who took most things quite seriously, even a birthday party.

'Bye, Mum,' she said, and she braced herself to join the others.

'Ashley is there,' I told her, nodding towards the table with all the food.

'Thank you,' said Karen for she was a very polite little girl, always ready with a please and thank you.

But the moment Karen set off into the room her sister Romana began to shriek, 'I want to stay! I want to stay!'

'No!' said Karen, quietly but desperately. 'It's my party not yours.'

She stepped into the room and at once her sister Romana followed. 'No!' Karen said again, but her mother came in behind the two of them and she patted her youngest daughter on the head. 'OK, OK, Romana, you can stay.' Then she looked at me and said, 'It's just too much trouble, isn't it?' I knew Karen's mother a little by then, enough to speak with briefly at the school gates in the morning, and I knew that for some reason she was very protective about Romana. I had heard her saying that Karen was the strong one in the family, and that had puzzled me for anyone could see Romana was a very tough little child indeed. At once Romana stopped shrieking, her face went from tears to a smile like the sun sliding out from behind a cloud, so that anyone could see the tears had never been real, and I saw Karen give her mother a look that was utterly defeated.

'Would you mind?' asked Ashley's father, handing me a packet of balloons. 'We wanted them all round the room and we just haven't had the time.'

I smiled agreeably and I took the packet and I selected one of the balloons and I thought, why do they expect me to be the one to do this? And as I thought this the other parents all began to dissolve away, leaving their children to be independent at the birthday party, and I was the one left helping. It was just like at the hospital; if there was a job that no one else wanted to do, if a patient needed a bed bath or a bedpan needed cleaning, then for sure I was the one who was going to have to do it. Rise above it, I could hear my husband saying in my head, rise above it.

I looked around the room and I saw Bel had arrived. 'Bye, love!' her mother yelled, waving, still waving even though her back was turned and she was halfway out the front door.

'Bye, Mum,' said Bel, and she gave a series of shrugs with

her shoulders like she wanted to loosen her muscles. A moment later she was standing close to my little Loreen and the two girls were inspecting something on the table, Bel still shrugging her shoulders quickly up and down. I saw Karen standing with her present in her hand, and I saw Ashley in the middle of all the children, her arms held wide, singing, 'Happy birthday to me! Happy birthday to *me*!'

Then Ashley's father told the children they were going to play musical chairs and he set out a row of twelve chairs in the middle of the room. The girls, for they were all girls, there were no boys at the party, took a chair each and sat primly, waiting. Ashley's father explained they would have to walk around the chairs and when the music stopped they would have to sit down on one. But, he explained, each time he would take a chair away. I listened, puzzled at the cruelty of the game. There had been no birthday parties during my childhood in Africa and I was unprepared for how the English conducted these things.

The music started and Ashley's father bopped along. Then he stopped the music and the girls ran for the chairs. Again the music started, stopped, and a chair was removed. The girl who found herself without a chair started crying, but already the music had started again and I could see that the ritual would continue without her. I watched and I knew what was going to happen, I knew my little Loreen wouldn't fight enough for a chair, that she would soon get knocked out. I knew that Karen would let her little sister Romana get a chair if there was a choice between the two of them and then be knocked out herself as well. And I knew that Bel and Ashley would be the ones who remained because that is how it was, those two little girls always facing up to each other like a pair of bulls.

Ashley's father started the music and we all stood around the edge of the room, watching. Bel moved slowly, she was not shrugging her shoulders now, instead her arms were stiff by her side and she refused to move more than an inch from the one remaining chair. I laughed to see her determination; she was a very determined little girl. But Ashley had a cooler approach, for Ashley knew that her father was in charge, that it was her birthday party, and that he would stop the music just when it was needed so that she would win and get the chair, which he did. It was a small thing, a very small thing, but I wondered if my little Loreen and the other girls had realised what I had realised, and if so what conclusions they would draw.

It was a very tiring party, Ashley's birthday party when she turned seven, but I had promised my little Loreen that I would take her to the fairground on Hampstead Heath afterwards and so I did. I had saved my money to ensure she had a good time. First she rode on a carousel, and then on the bumper cars, then she dipped for plastic ducks and won a doll that was very small and badly made and hardly worth winning at all. It was only after an hour or more that I bought her candyfloss and went to the fortune-teller.

I had always wanted to go to a fortune-teller; the moment I had discovered there was such a thing I had wanted to go to one. It was my kindly German landlady Adelaide who first told me about fortune-tellers of course, just as she had first told me about horoscopes that evening as we sat in her front room when Loreen was still small. Adelaide had told me about a lodger of hers who had gone to a fortune-teller and had been told everything that would happen to her. And I wondered then if there really were people who could tell your future and how did they do this and what would they say of mine? If a person knew what was in their future then they could perhaps stop a bad thing before it happened, and if it was a good thing in their future then they could reassure themselves of what would come next in their life.

So I led my little Loreen to the caravan belonging to the fortune-teller at the Hampstead Heath fair. The outside of the caravan was decorated with twinkly stars and pictures of famous people whose fortunes the fortune-teller had told. Inside, the fortune-teller was a lady and she sat in front of a table on which were three shiny balls all in a row. She looked up and I caught a flash of red lipstick and thick, drawn-on eyebrows. The fortune-teller motioned me forward so I seated myself opposite her, my little Loreen with her candyfloss next to me. I hadn't wanted to take her in with me, but I couldn't very well leave her outside. Now that I was nearer I could see the fortune-teller was quite an elderly lady, and on her head she had a brightly coloured scarf, like one of my aunties back home in Africa would wear, and this reassured me and made me feel more comfortable. I handed over the money and the fortune-teller took my hand a little reluctantly, I thought. She held it with two fingers just touching each side of my palm and I could feel the skin on her fingers was warm.

'You come from a hot place,' said the fortune-teller, speaking very slowly as if I were hard of hearing, enunciating every word. 'Is . . . that . . . right?'

'Yes,' I said, and my hand quivered a little because I wanted to take it back and fold it in my lap.

'Wish for two things,' said the fortune-teller briskly, and she took away one finger and picked at something between her teeth. 'Then tell me one of them.'

I wished that I hadn't brought my little Loreen into the caravan with me. She didn't appear to be listening, she was too busy with her candyfloss, but how could I speak of the things I really wished for in front of my child?

'Happiness,' I said at last.

'Happiness,' said the fortune-teller. 'You have had heartache.'

I nodded, unable to speak.

'You have recently lost someone.'

Still I found it difficult to speak for I hadn't thought we would talk about the past, I thought she would tell me about the future, but at last I said, 'Yes.'

The fortune-teller let go of my hand. 'You will recover from your grief. I see two loves in your life. There is another love here waiting for you. An older man.'

An older man? All of a sudden I felt hopeful.

'Is she your only child?' The fortune-teller looked at Loreen.

'Yes,' I said, and I felt a tightening in my throat.

'You will have another, a boy for her.'

And Loreen heard this, she swivelled her face to mine and smiled as if I had just told her that this year she could have a birthday party after all.

I waited while the fortune-teller took up my hand, again with just the edges of her fingers, and she traced a fingernail along the lines without coming into contact with my skin. 'I see fame,' she said suddenly and she sounded surprised.

'Fame?' I asked, and I was surprised as well.

'Yes. Well I never, that's very strange,' said the fortune-teller, and I realised then that her voice had changed, that until now she had been speaking in a voice she had assumed for her role as fortune-teller, but that now she was speaking as she normally did, as if she were chatting with a friend in the street. 'Someone is going to be very, very famous indeed,' she said, and then the lady fortune-teller studied my little Loreen, still sitting there, her lips sticky from the candyfloss, as if she couldn't quite believe what she was seeing.

Chapter Twelve

A few months after the birthday party when Ashley turned seven, when school had reopened after the summer holiday, my little Loreen announced that she wanted to have her friend for tea. Ashley was the first school friend Loreen had invited home and so she was very excited about it, although it meant simply that Ashley was under our care for two hours or so. Today they call such visits play dates, as if they were business arrangements.

The first problem started when I went to pick them up from school, which as I recall was a Wednesday like today. I stood outside the gates, standing on my own, for although Karen's mother sometimes spoke to me, as did Ashley's father, the other parents tended to stand in their own carefully drawn groups. These groups arranged themselves largely along lines of class; and as a foreigner, and as an African foreigner, my class was simple: I was second-class. The only way I could join a group of any class was if I were to be directly asked about something, and the only thing I was ever directly asked about, of course, was the weather. So occasionally a friendlier mother might say, 'Isn't it freezing today?' and then I could say that yes, it was. After I had been asked a question about the heat or the cold, the rain or the sun, and I had agreed with the person asking the question then I could, briefly, be included in the group and could even, perhaps, move on to other topics. I could, for example, admire an item that another mother was wearing, or comment on a baby they had in a buggy, or complain about how much something had cost at a shop. And this was the way it went on, for years and years, so that I might see the same mother every single morning yet still the conversation never progressed much further than a discussion about the weather, never becoming anything that could approach intimacy.

That day I was collecting my little Loreen and her friend Ashley, no one asked me anything about the weather, and so I stood there alone, waiting for the moment when the children were released from their last lesson of the day and would come running along the tunnel that led to the playground. At once my little Loreen came hurtling towards me, dragging Ashley by the hand, urging her to come. Usually when I picked Loreen up from school she came out into the playground walking slowly, a dreamy look on her face, an expression of being a little stunned by whatever she had been taught at school that day. Today, however, she could barely contain herself.

'Hello, Ashley,' I said with a smile. 'You're coming to our house today, we're very happy to have you.'

'Am I?' said Ashley, pushing impatiently on a clip in her hair. 'Daddy didn't tell me.'

I looked at the child, seeing a faint orange mark on the corner of her mouth and wondering what she had eaten for lunch, for this was a child whose skin was so white that even a carrot would stain her. 'Yes, you're coming, my dear,' I soothed, but I was soothing Loreen more than Ashley for my daughter's face was utterly crestfallen at the idea that her friend might not come. 'I discussed this with your father only yesterday.'

'OK,' said Ashley. 'But you have to tell my teacher.'

I was a little annoyed at being directed what to do by a seven-year-old, but I took each girl by the hand and went to find their teacher. I had until then regarded Miss Pond as a lovely young lady, very nicely turned out, kind but with just the right amount of sternness.

'Miss Pond,' I said. 'Ashley is coming with us today.'

Miss Pond looked at me, frowned, waved away a child that was calling for attention. 'Ashley is going with you?' She blinked her blue eyes worriedly.

'Yes. Her father and I arranged it.'

'Is that OK?' Miss Pond asked, only she wasn't asking me she was asking Ashley and still her eyes looked worried. She was so worried-looking in fact that she put one hand on Ashley's shoulder as if to protect her from something.

'Yes,' I said again. 'Loreen and Ashley are friends and . . .'

'They do play together,' said Miss Pond thoughtfully. 'Although of course they are in different streams. Your Loreen is a very well-behaved pupil,' she smiled at me, suddenly, so that her lips opened into a gap-toothed mouth. 'She will never be as clever as Ashley, but that's to be expected, isn't it?'

I stared at Miss Pond, utterly speechless. How could she possibly say such a thing and how could she possibly say it in front of the children? 'Come along then!' I said to the girls. 'Or we will be late.' There was nothing we would be late for, but I was very annoyed now and I marched out of that playground with the two girls by my side. I didn't know if my little Loreen had heard what Miss Pond had said, and at that moment I didn't want to find out, but I had seen a look in Ashley's eyes that suggested she had. In what way was Ashley cleverer than my little Loreen and what did Miss Pond mean that 'it was to be expected'? I should have challenged her, I thought, I should have stood there and asked her what she meant, but I hadn't. I took several deep breaths as we left the school and then, as we reached the end of the road and were about to cross, we heard shouting behind us.

'Loreen! Ashley!'

We turned to see little Bel running up behind us, her face flushed. 'Wait for me!' she shouted.

'Ugh!' said Ashley as Bel came nearer.

'What is it?' I asked, and I thought for a moment that the child had trodden in dog mess, for the English love their dogs and they allow them to do their business right there on the pavement, and the problem has not got better over the years, only worse.

'She wet herself,' said Ashley as Bel caught up with us. I looked at the poor girl and saw she had a cardigan wrapped around her tummy and that it was hanging down at the back. It was a hot day and so I knew the cardigan had been added by someone, a teacher perhaps, to hide the fact Bel had wet herself.

'Never mind,' I said. 'Accidents happen.'

At the word 'accident' my little Loreen brightened up. 'My mum's a nurse!' she said proudly.

Bel stood for a second looking at my little Loreen and

Ashley and then she came and stood before me, her face upturned, and she said with a plaintiveness that tugged at my heart, 'Loreen's mum,' for that was what she always called me, 'Loreen's mum, I wish we were born knowing everything and didn't have to go to school and learn every day.'

I gave little Bel a good hard squeeze and breathed in her little seven-year-old smell.

'Can't I come with you?' she asked, and beside me I heard Ashley snigger.

'I'm afraid not, not today,' I said. 'Look, your mother is there, see, she's by the gates looking for you.'

When we arrived at our house Ashley began commenting at once. There was something blunt about the child; she didn't think before she spoke, as if she had never been taught to do so, and I thought that if this was cleverness then I was glad my little Loreen was not clever.

'Why are there so many doors here?' said Ashley after I had let us in and we stood inside the shared hall below a sign that warned against hawkers and spitting.

'Because there are many flats in this house,' I told her. 'And this is the door to our flat.'

'Don't you have a whole house?' asked Ashley.

'No,' I said, unlocking the door, 'we have a flat.'

'We have a whole house,' Ashley said, following Loreen and me into the hallway.

'Yes, I've seen your house,' I replied.

'Then if you don't have a whole house, don't you have a garden?' asked Ashley.

'No.' I smiled reassuringly at my little Loreen because her

104

face looked worried; she had never thought to ask *why* we didn't have a house, *why* we didn't have a garden.

'We have a garden,' said Ashley.

'That's nice,' I said again. I had seen her garden, as big as a field, on the day of her birthday party in the summer.

'Do you have a car?' asked Ashley.

'No,' I said a little sharply as Ashley opened her mouth to tell us she had one, and I told myself it was not right to take against a little child. Rise above it, I could hear my husband saying in my head, rise above it. 'Hey, *mosetsana yo, o rata dipotso*,' I muttered to myself. 'Loreen, why don't you take Ashley to your room?'

'What's that funny language your mum's speaking?' Ashley asked Loreen as if I wasn't there and couldn't hear her.

'It is not a funny language,' I said, and I bent down towards her very close and I smiled. 'I am speaking Setswana, the language of my people.'

'My mum speaks African,' said Loreen.

'Woo woo woo!' went Ashley, cupping both hands to her mouth.

My little Loreen stared at her. 'What are you doing?'

'I'm speaking African too,' said Ashley.

'No, my dear,' I said to her, still smiling although my face felt stiff, 'you are not. You are playing a game while I am speaking Setswana, the language of my people in Botswana. There are many, many languages in Africa and Setswana is one of them. Loreen can speak it too.'

Ashley stared at my little Loreen with her baby animal eyes and said, 'Really?'

Next to me I felt my daughter shrink a little and for a

105

dreadful moment I thought that she was about to deny knowing her parents' language. 'Yes,' I said, before she had a chance to say anything, 'Loreen can speak it too,' although this was not entirely true. When Loreen was a baby I had spoken Setswana to her all the time, but then around the time she started school I began to do this less and less and now, while she understood what I said, she could not speak it so freely herself. 'And what languages can you speak, my dear?' I asked Ashley. Rise above it, rise above it, I could hear my husband saying in my head and I shushed him.

'English,' said Ashley at once.

'Yes,' I said a little triumphantly, 'we all speak English, but do you speak any other languages?'

Ashley frowned.

'Well,' I said nicely as if the conversation was well and truly finished.

'But,' said Ashley, 'Daddy says I might start French.'

I led the girls into the kitchen where I had some food prepared for them. I had planned and worried about this, wondering what Loreen's friend would eat, about what an English child would have. In the end I had made some small sandwiches, like I had seen at Ashley's birthday party, and I had bought two doughnuts with jam in the middle which were Loreen's favourites. But the girls weren't interested in the food; they ran at once to Loreen's room and left me alone in the kitchen and I cluttered around making tea and feeling out of sorts, while from Loreen's room I could hear whispering and the occasional giggle. After a while I went to Loreen's room to call them. I opened the door, which was not easy as the girls had put something behind it,

106

cushions perhaps, and there I saw my little Loreen under her quilt on the bed with Ashley on top of her, her legs set wide apart, her little thin body bouncing rhythmically up and down.

'What are you doing?' I asked, my heart racing at this unexpected sight.

Loreen immediately hid herself under the quilt but Ashley turned to me as cool as anything and said, 'Loreen wanted to play mummies and daddies.'

'Well you both must be very thirsty,' I said, as if everything were quite normal. 'Come into the kitchen and I will give you some squash.'

I went into the kitchen, my heart still racing, and when Loreen came in she avoided my eyes and instead she sat down with her friend Ashley at our table and she would not stop giggling. I wondered why my little Loreen had wanted to play mummies and daddies and where she had got such an idea and who she could have seen doing this thing I had seen her doing on the bed just now.

It was not long after that Ashley's father came to pick his daughter up, wearing a Hawaiian shirt that almost hurt my eyes to look at, seeing as it was so busy with pink flowers and white flowers and blue sky and rolling white waves. 'Darling!' he called as he came into my flat. 'Ashley! Darling!'

Ashley came bursting out of the kitchen shouting, 'Daddy!' and he picked her up and clasped her in his arms and my little Loreen and I stood in the doorway with little else to do but watch. 'I'm a little late, I'm afraid,' he said to me. 'My last patient was . . . a tad upset today. And did you have a lovely time?' he asked his daughter.

'It was OK,' said Ashley with a coolness that made me flinch. 'But I'm really hungry.'

I was about to protest, to say tea had been offered, sandwiches and doughnuts with jam in the middle, but Ashley's father just smiled. I smiled back at him, wondering whether I should tell him what the girls had been doing in Loreen's room. I knew, without question, that it was Ashley who had initiated this game, and I thought that if I did not tell her father then perhaps he would find out another way and that my little Loreen would be seen as the instigator when she was not. But I couldn't very well tell him there and then.

'I was wondering,' Ashley's father said as he helped his daughter on with her jacket, 'whether to take the girls to Harrods.'

'Yippee!' shouted Ashley.

'Hurrah!' shouted my little Loreen, although she had no idea what Harrods was.

'Once we're nearer Christmas, I could take them to have their pictures taken with the monkey,' said Ashley's father.

'The monkey?' I asked.

'Every Christmas Harrods has a monkey in its children's section. The children love it, don't you, darling?'

'Well,' I said, because I didn't know what else to say.

'But I bet you've already met plenty of monkeys, haven't you?' Ashley's father said to Loreen. 'Coming from Africa!' And he laughed and the pink and white flowers on his shirt quivered.

'Not at all,' I said, not because it wasn't true but because I had a sudden impulse that I did not want to agree with

Ashley's father. If Ashley thought talking African meant cupping her hands to her mouth and making ape noises then who, I thought, had taught her that?

I have had my lunch and now I put the radio on and I find them talking again about Piano Man, the man found wandering in the seaside town with his clothes soaking wet and unable or unwilling to say where he was from. I have not heard any more news about him since the discussion on the radio on Sunday. They are yet to find out who he is, although all sorts of people have been claiming him as their own. A woman in Denmark said Piano Man was her husband who had been missing for some months. She said although Piano Man had lost twenty kilos and bleached his hair, she could see in his eyes that it was him. Now, however, this does not appear to be the case, and yesterday, the radio tells me, some students from Norway, where he is also suspected to be from, have identified him as an exchange student from Ireland.

I listen to the radio for a while and ponder the fate of Piano Man. Then I open the back door of my kitchen and rattle a box of dried food and at once I hear a rustling and a leaf shaking sound as my clever little kitty cat throws herself through the latticework of the wooden fence around my garden. She slinks into the kitchen and I can see her body is low on the ground and that she has something in her mouth, the wing of a bird perhaps, for it looks grey and feathery. But then I see it's not a wing at all, it's a torn piece of material, perhaps from a sock, but my little kitty cat carries it in with great seriousness as if she has been out hunting on the plains of Africa all night and now needs to return her prey to her lair and hide it.

I put a crumpet in the toaster and I sit down to wait because my leg is troubling me today. I wait until the crumpet is hot and then I drip a teaspoon of honey on the top and watch it soak into the holes. I lift it to my mouth and the taste reminds me of the fat cakes we used to eat back in Africa when I was still a girl playing in the compound of my home village Manyana. I will take some crumpets with me tomorrow, I think, when I collect my little grandson Dwaine from school and make them for his tea.

As I think about tomorrow and the evening I will spend looking after my grandsons because my Loreen is going to meet her friends, I think, as I often do, that it is unnatural that a mother and daughter live apart. I think of my home village of Manyana, the way each compound was self-contained behind a low mud wall and yet joined to the neighbouring compounds with a pathway so that a person could cross from one threshold to another with ease if they so chose and if they were welcome. I think of our compound which held three generations of our family, each in their own house but within a shared yard. There were times we came together and times we came apart, times when the men would sit hunched up on the sand in one area of the compound, one perhaps on a crate or a chair, while the children would be gathered around the fire in another area of the compound, and the women would be on their own, busy, perhaps, with food preparation or laying out corn for threshing. But at the end of the day, we all came together, we all slept in the same place and woke with the same sun, and I wonder how it is that my little Loreen has her own family that does not include me.

Chapter Thirteen

LOREEN

Hi Gene, ha! I didn't know you were in here as well! You're looking hot in your skintight white leggings, so tight I can see the muscles on your bum. Very nice. But what on earth did those leggings look like from the front, with your goolies on show? And to think they showed that on kids TV! I'd pay to see a pop star like Donny Green wearing something like that now.

Gene Anthony Ray, that's a name that rolls off the tongue. Here you are as Leroy on the back of the *Fame* annual; I got that for Christmas one year. God, I loved that programme. 'Fame hurts and here's where you start paying for it.' No, it must have been, 'Fame costs and here's where you start paying.' Bel used to mime that along with Debbie Allen as she stamped that stick of hers on the studio floor.

Oh my God, remember your audition episode, Gene, when you had to get a place at the New York School for Performing Arts? There you were, naked but for tiny black shorts, with your corn-row hair and bulging biceps, and everyone in the hall looked at you and thought, 'Who *is* this guy?' God, you were handsome. I can't believe you're not alive any more. I wanted so much to live in *Fame*. I sat so near the TV I could have climbed right inside. The moment the theme tune started – *Fame! I'm going to live forever! Fame! Remember my name!* – then the adrenaline started and I was glued to the screen. Everything was happy in *Fame*, in a sparkly, sexy, leotards and leggings, American sort of way. The kids worked hard and then they made it. That's the sort of teacher I wanted to be, like Debbie Allen. I wanted to get the toughest class and transform them. *'Fame! I'm going to live forever! Baby remember my name.'*

There's a cast photo here on the front of the annual. I think I need glasses, the whole thing looks a bit blurry today, but look at you, Gene, in a red shirt opened down your chest and calf-coloured pants. That's what they call them in America, pants. Very nice. You've got the little white girl with the shiny Brady Bunch sort of face sitting in front of you; both your arms are resting over her shoulders. I think your hand and hers are touching. I always wondered if you were going out. But Karen said you were gay. She said it was completely obvious you were gay, although Karen was always far too grown up to watch *Fame* the way I did. I fancied myself as the mixed race girl; at least there was a mixed race girl, although I can't remember much about what she did. That was the thing about you, Gene, you were black and how many black stars did I ever have on my bedroom wall?

I chuck the *Fame* annual back in the wardrobe, along with my Simon Le Bon poster and the map of the world Mum gave me. The boys are asleep, finally. It's almost midnight and I should go to bed as well but instead I sit down at my computer. First I look to see if anyone new has joined my old school list on Friends Reunited, then I search for the Internet dating site Barbara told me about. Here it is. It's got a big purple love heart and a man and a woman gazing into each other's eyes and it says you get your money back if you don't find true love in three months. I can't resist.

I start to fill in a profile. I put that I'm a woman looking for a man aged between thirty and forty-five, because I wouldn't want to meet anyone much younger or older than that. I come up with a username and a password. I put in my marital status, my height, my ethnicity, my email, my date of birth, my post code, my hair colour. I put in my astrological sign. Then I click that it's all done and I sit back to wait and see what happens next.

It's quiet in the flat. Anthony is snoring is his room. I can see the orange glow of Dwaine's giraffe-shaped nightlight where it lights up the carpet in the hallway. Then I glance back at the screen to see twelve men's faces looking at me. My eyes light on Jim, he's thirty and works in finance. He has a bit of a playboy look about him, like Omar Sharif. He says he spends his summers racing old cars and his winters skiing, so he wouldn't want someone as badly off as me. I look at Sean, he's forty-one and works in the media. He looks a bit more serious, his face is half in shadow, he's got a black jacket on, and there seems to be a pool behind him. But when I look at his profile it says, 'Hello there! I describe myself as bright and articulate' and he sounds too confident for me.

I dismiss James from Bethnal Green who is doing something weird with his eyebrows, like he's been practising this expression in the mirror and thinks it looks sexy. And I dismiss Lucus who has a woolly hat on and looks like he's on speed. He describes himself as 'a bit of a Duracell bunny as

I'm always on the go!' Then I look at Mark69; he looks nice and normal. He's thirty-seven, mixed race, works in IT. He lists pesto among his likes and the *Daily Mail* among his dislikes. Then I read his profile: 'I am looking for a soul mate, a lover and a friend.' I feel a quick burst of excitement because this is what I want, a soul mate, a lover and a friend. I sit and stare at this; I look at his photo again. Then I add Mark69 to my favourites. Now I have to write a personal statement, I have to say who I am and what I'm looking for. But what should I write, Gene? It's nearly one in the morning. What would sound good? I'll have to add a photo as well, because it says profiles with photos get more replies, but which photo should I use, Gene?

It's Thursday morning, the start of my busiest day, and I must get the boys to their school breakfast club; I must get myself to school. I see a piece of paper on the wardrobe floor folded into a triangle and I pick it up. It's a snap dragon, a game we used to play as kids where you folded a piece of paper and then slipped your fingers into the folds and asked a friend to choose a colour, then a number, and then you opened it up and it said something silly like: *You are beautiful* or *You smell*. I'm amazed Mum has kept this as well; this piece of paper must be twenty years old. I fold it so the names of four colours are written on the outside and I slip my fingers in the folds and choose green. Then I open it to the eight numbers written inside and I choose six. Then I lift the flap and read: *U take it up the bum*. I'm shocked, it's not a snap dragon we made at school, it's one I took off one of my Year Sevens last week. I flatten out the paper and read everything written on

114

the inside flaps: *U come from Kurgistan. Yr mum is a Dike. U r buff. U had shit for breakfast. U give head.* This is what the Year Sevens write nowadays. I screw up the snap dragon and throw it in the bin and get my things together.

God, I've still got the head's briefing paper in my handbag, and I still haven't read it. I stopped at the point where he began talking about open communication and the change process. I've tucked the latest exclusion room bulletin inside the briefing paper. It lists a whole page of students and the reason for their exclusion: disruptive behaviour, truancy, fighting, abusive to a member of staff, abusive to another pupil, health and safety. There are twenty-two from Year Nine and most are in my form: 9Kudumane. I wonder how many will be in the exclusion room for the Ofsted inspection, and if they're not in there then maybe the new head will do what the last one did and just tell the troublemakers not to come in the day of the inspection.

I put my phone in my bag and see there's a message. Bel hasn't answered my text about what time we're meeting tonight, but Ashley has sent me one: *8pm at the front bar.* That's it, that's all she says. She hasn't said hi, she hasn't even put a kiss at the end of the message. And even if Ashley says eight, Bel will still be late.

The boys are fighting in Anthony's room; I can hear their shouts and a thud as a chair bangs against the wall. This is their idea of fun, this is what they really love doing and it's the only thing I can't do with them because I just don't know how. It's always been like this, even when Anthony was small, I just can't do the fighting thing. When their dad turns up for his once a year visit they jump on him like he's a rubber ring.

But I can't, I don't know how to fight with them and I can't give them a good rough and tumble anyway, when I also have to get them up and dressed and fed and washed and ready for school.

I know I'm supposed to be going but I decide to check my emails just in case anyone has contacted me from the dating site since last night. Has Mark69 seen that I put him on my favourites and will that make him contact me? But my inbox is empty, no one has contacted me. Should I have put that I'm a single parent?

'Dwaine!' I shout as I head down the hall. 'Anthony! Stop fighting!'

'Yes, Mum, sorry, Mum!' Dwaine calls back. I pick up one of his toy cars he's left on the floor.

'Come on! Let's go!' I shout again. If I don't shout they won't move from Anthony's room.

'Mum,' says Dwaine, rushing out to me. 'You know what we were talking about the other day?'

'Hmm?'

'You know,' his voice is low, urgent. 'About S-E-X?'

'Yes?'

'Well I don't want to talk about it any more.'

'OK, babe,' I say, 'that's fine.' I'm looking for my handbag again, where have I put it? If we don't leave now we're all going to be late. Anthony leaves the flat first, hurtles along the corridor and then takes the stairs two by two and each time he lands on a step it echoes like a slap.

'There's a letter for you!' he shouts as he disappears down the stairs. I stop in the doorway, see a white card on the carpet with my name and address on the front. But there's no stamp, so it hasn't actually been posted. I turn it over; it's an official card of some kind, like the type a gas meter reader might leave, but there's a handwritten scrawl: 'Came for our appointment today, please contact me on above office number to rearrange.' What's this person talking about? I didn't have any appointment with anyone, no one has rung my buzzer this morning, and how could I have an appointment anyway when I'm at work all day?

'Anthony!' I shout. I can't see him and I can't hear him. I hope he hasn't run right the way down the stairs and out onto the street. 'Mum!' Dwaine tugs on me, he wants us to run after his brother, but I'm still standing in the hallway looking at the card. A door opens along the corridor, I hear a sudden burst of music and then the door closes again, and I'm still standing here staring at the card in my hands because now I've seen it's from social services, it's a card from a child protection officer.

Chapter Fourteen

BEL

Shit. I never thought I'd be staring through my camera at something like this.

'Bel!' Jodie screams from somewhere behind me. 'What if there's another one?'

I'm right at the window. But whatever Jodie says I lean forward. The window is wide open and I look out and it's like a tornado has blown through Tavistock Square. One minute everything was normal, one minute Jodie was telling me not to go by tube because of a power surge, and now look at it.

I was supposed to be going to deliver a tape for Clive, but instead I was standing at the window fiddling with my digital, wasting time by deleting old pictures. I was here just as it happened. I heard the explosion, saw a flash, watched as glass split the air and rained down like mad confetti. I saw the roof of the bus lift lazily forward, almost in slow motion. I thought it was a building, not the bus at first, when the bricks flew into the air.

Now there are shards of white debris on the street, all mixed up with the white lines of the road and the white lines of the zebra crossing. The front of the bus faces me, the side wrenched off at a right angle. The seats on the top deck look so blue, so strange, like pools in a desert. I can't believe there are people standing there, I can't believe anyone is alive. There's a row of cars next to the bus, one appears to have the bus roof right on its bonnet.

The number 30 to Hackney Wick. How many times have I been on that bus? How come I'm not on that bus now? I hear people screaming but the screams are muted.

I can see everything from here. But I'm also far enough away that it's like I'm watching it outside myself. I can't decide whether I'm part of it or not and it's strange that I even have the time to think this. Everything, in the past few minutes, has changed. I take a picture and then another. It's what I was doing, the camera was in my hands. There is a tree to my left, its overhanging branches just framing the scene below. The leaves of the tree look prickly, although I know they're not. The tree branches are waving, like something underwater in a fish tank, and as I take another picture I feel oddly safe and disconnected from everything happening in the street below.

'Oh my God,' says Jodie, still behind me. 'What's going on?'

I don't answer, I've no idea. I can smell the explosion now. I put the camera down and my heart feels jerky.

'We've got to evacuate, Bel, he says we've got to get out!'

I turn round and there's a security guard in the office, gesturing at me. I give one last look out the window. There are huddles of people around the bus now. How can this be happening outside our window? I can just see the park in the middle of the square, the dappled sunlight on the lime green lawn. The security guard has his hand on my arm. I don't want to go down. It's better up here.

Then we all rush down the stairs and there's a feeling that everyone in the building is rushing, eyes too panicked to acknowledge each other as we hurtle down. I see a man from one of the offices upstairs and his shirt is undone and I wonder why. I see a woman I've seen many times in the lift before and for a moment I can't work out why her face is so familiar. She's running down the stairs and her hair is all over the place, she is not where she usually is and it makes me feel disorientated. I hear someone talking about a suicide bomber. How can that be?

'Not the lift!' yells the security man hoarsely as we pass two men in suits waiting, strangely still, by the lift door. 'Don't use the lift!'

We get outside and now I'm down here it doesn't look as static as it did from up at the window. Instead there is a craziness in the air. The world is full of wreckage. People are moving quickly but slowly too, like they don't know what they're doing. I see a woman crouched down in the middle of the road as if she's looking for something and I don't want to know what she could be looking for. I see a man with blood on his face, but only on one side like a child in the middle of dressing up for Halloween.

'In there!' shouts the security man, pointing to a building near the British Medical Association, a building as pretty as a sandcastle. I wonder who this man is and how he knows where we should and shouldn't go. I wonder why we're all doing what he says when he can't know any more than us. We run and reach the door he's showing us and rush in. But at once there's a man in a blue uniform standing there. 'Out!' he yells, and we all run out again and Jodie stumbles and sobs and everywhere there is noise, screams and yells and car horns and sirens. It's like I've had earplugs in and now I've taken them out.

On the street a woman in a blue hospital coat and hat is running alongside a trolley and there's a figure on the trolley, all covered up. The traffic is all piled up opposite the bus, a fireman is running. The air is hot, not just the hotness of a sunny day in July, but a feeling we're all breathing hard and the air is squeezing us in. Everything around us is still normal, the sun, the birds, the trees. But what is in front of us is not normal at all. I don't know what I can do to help.

I have the urge to escape, to whoosh up in the air and be gone. I want to still be standing at the window, annoyed with Clive, deleting pictures on my digital. Then I see a woman, an elderly woman in a sari, and she is being supported on both sides by two young men. She holds onto them and they hold onto her and I take a picture as she leaves because my camera is here, it's still in my hands. A little girl comes running out of another building on the square and she runs in front of the cordon the police are hurriedly putting up around the bus and she throws herself into a woman's arms. It's her mother, she looks just like the girl, they even have the same colour top and the same sort of hairstyle, and something is shining in their hair: it's glass. I hear people talking about bombs on the tube, I hear someone say al-Qaeda, I hear a man ask how many people have been killed, I hear a woman say no buses are running. I start to walk. I can't do anything, so I just start to walk. I walk to Gower Street and then to Tottenham Court Road. A bomb just went off and I don't know what to do. As I walk I'm counting my footsteps in groups of three.

'Look at the state of you!' says Mum when she opens the door. 'I've been calling you all morning!'

'Phones aren't working,' I say. All the way here I've been passing people desperately trying to use their mobile phones. 'The networks are down.'

'You OK, girl?' Glen comes out into the hallway from the living room.

'Yeah, fine.' I'm surprised to see him here.

'I just popped in for a second,' says Glen, 'to make sure your mum was OK.'

I stare at him. There are sweat patches under his arms.

'You sit down,' he says, following me into the front room, 'and have a cup of tea.'

I sit down, quite gratefully, as Mum goes off to make tea. 'Your brother Joe was supposed to be on that King's Cross tube,' she shouts through the hatch from the kitchen. 'Sharon next door, her youngest was sick this morning, otherwise she would have been on it too.'

I sink down in the chair. This is how it's going to be, everyone is going to have a story of how they almost got killed. Perhaps I almost got killed. What do you do when you almost got killed? And what about the people who are actually dead? The people who were going to work, the commuters on the tubes? The people who had had breakfast, or not had breakfast, the people who were late or who were early, the people who were thinking about a quarrel the night before or looking forward to seeing a friend at lunch, the people who were going to get married, who were on the way to a hospital appointment. And what about the people who did this, what conviction did they have to do this, what made them want to do this, and are they still out there now? Is another bomb going to go off, and if not now then when? I want to do something but I don't know what. I stand up and lean against Mum's mantelpiece, hard so the corner presses into me.

'So you were right in Tavistock Square?' asks Glen. He isn't sitting down either, he's still standing.

'It's where I work.'

'Close shave,' he says. 'Reminds me of the IRA, 1982, when the bomb went off in Hyde Park, I was right there. Nail bomb. Two soldiers dead. Seven horses. And 1993, the Bishopsgate bomb, I was there too.'

Mum comes back in and hands me a mug of tea. 'Thank God you're OK,' she says. I look down and see she is wearing slippers that have furry monkey heads on the front. 'Shouldn't you be getting back to work?' she asks Glen.

'I just wanted to check the news,' he says, and he seems edgy. Of course, I think, he works for a newspaper, he must be taking photos. When Mum leaves the room he looks at me and asks, 'Take any snaps?'

How does he know this? I realise my fingers are shaking as I take out my digital. I feel guilty that I even took any pics and I don't want anyone to know this, but Glen does. He takes the camera and sits down on Mum's sofa and he begins to go through the pictures, stopping at one or two. I sit down next to him, on the arm of the sofa, looking over his shoulder. It's like we're looking at something that happened years ago, a bomb scene in another place. Not Tavistock Square a few hours ago, not in the middle of London where I work. Glen feels very solid next to me; this is the way I used to sit with Dad when he went over my school reports, before he walked out for the second time.

'I don't even know why I took them,' I say as Glen continues looking at the pictures. He's not looking at them in a frivolous way, he's going through them carefully and he's frowning and not talking. 'I mean,' I say, 'I just started doing it. I was right at the window when it happened. I wasn't even supposed to be there, I had this tape I was supposed to be delivering. I was just wasting time, mucking around by the window . . .' I want to say more but I don't know what. Everything in the room is too normal. The Green Lady is staring at me like she's going to be sick.

'That's OK,' Glen soothes. 'You've not got time to think about taking a snap. The picture is there now, in a second it won't be. You just reacted with your instinct. The Bishopsgate bomb, I lost a friend in that. He was a *News of the World* staffer and he was apparently so intent on getting a snap he managed to get through the police cordon as they were evacuating the area. When the bomb went off he was right near the truck. Taking that snap killed him.'

I pick up my mug and drink my tea. Mum's put in far too much milk. But I feel better now I've showed someone my pictures.

'This is a good one,' says Glen. He's stopped at the picture of the woman with the sari. 'But you couldn't sell it. You could sell this one though.' He shows me the picture of the girl embracing her mother. 'And this, very good.' He's looking at the one I took from the window, the one with the shattered bus below, with the tree branches framing the left-hand corner.

'I don't want to sell them,' I say. 'That's not why I took them.'

'Of course not, darling. Still . . .' Glen hands me back my camera. He seems to be waiting for me to say something. 'Have you seen the news?' He gestures to the TV. I hadn't even noticed it was on. I see a picture of the bus in Tavistock Square, the roof gone, the blue seats on the top deck still there. I feel oddly reassured, like this is proof of what happened, that I haven't just made it up. I see police in yellow jackets, firemen in brown. 'BBC had that picture less than forty-five minutes after the explosion,' says Glen.

'Really? How did they get that?'

'Someone sent it in, darling. That one,' Glen points at another image on the TV, 'will be front page tomorrow. We're all out there today, every snapper there is, but it's the public who are sending in the snaps.'

We watch the TV reporter, she looks flustered. Words are running along the bottom of the screen, the same words over and over again. This is breaking news, but there is nothing new to add. Then a few more images flash up on the screen. 'Someone's done that on their mobile,' says Glen as we look at a grainy image, the dark inside of a tube carriage. I don't want to watch, the people are moving dreamily, their legs and shoulders blurred, almost like they're dancing. They are totally trapped and it's so very dark in the carriage and this must be just after the bomb went off.

125

Suddenly Glen puts on his jacket, starts putting things in the pockets: a lens cap, his mobile, a small notebook. He hauls a camera bag onto his shoulder. He seems to have forgotten I'm here, he's moving quickly, his face intent. Then he looks round and asks, 'You doing anything right now?'

I shake my head. I'm supposed to be meeting Loreen and Ashley, but that's not until this evening.

Glen nods, smiles. 'Want to come with me, girl?'

Chapter Fifteen

KAREN

I wonder, if I met Jen now would I still leap into bed with her the way I did that night of the pool party when she slipped into the Jacuzzi full of women, naked as mermaids, and smiled at me? I was perhaps a bit too grateful back then, a bit too eager for someone to want me and desire me and to see me not as the Karen I had been in England, the serious one, the responsible one, but as the Karen I thought I had become, the Karen in California, the cool one with the accent everyone just loved.

Jen seemed to see me like that; she'd singled me out that very first time we met at the campus bookstore, she'd smiled at me that day of my first Women's Studies class, she'd waved me over at the coffee shop when I'd almost been too shy to approach, and then she'd invited me over to her pool party. But if Jen appeared now, on this plane suspended in the darkness flying back to England, would I fall for her the way I did then?

The in-flight entertainment has just started, there's plenty of time to think. I've got an aisle seat and the food and drink has been served so I can stretch out my legs as we hum along, leaving one continent, heading to another. The woman next to me has an inflatable ring around her neck, soft and grey like moleskin, and she's fast asleep. I can see one of the flight attendants down by the toilet and she's sitting down, putting a tray of food on a fold-out shelf, about to peel off the tin-foil that covers the chicken we had earlier, its flesh as white as soap. The flight attendant leans forward and pulls at a curtain so she's obscured from view and I guess she wants to be private because I can't see her any more. The plane is silent but for the faint sound of the movie coming through the head-sets of the people in front of me and the people behind. This is a perfect place and a perfect time to think.

That night of the pool party, Jen didn't even wait until all the people had left, she just got out of the Jacuzzi, butt naked, and said, 'Karen, my room's back there.' She put a towel around herself, a green towel with little tassels at the corners, and together we went through the house and still I could hear the sounds of the other women outside, someone had a guitar and she was playing a Tracy Chapman song about driving all night in a car and it was a mournful song full of longing.

Jen's room was large and it jutted out of the side of the house like a garage or an extension so that one window looked onto the garden and the other onto the street out front. It was a very white room: fresh white walls on which nothing hung, a single soft white circular rug on the floor next to a double white futon. I'd never slept on a futon before and when Jen sat me down on it, it felt strangely hard beneath me, and then she knelt down and she put her hands around my face and she began to kiss me. Her lips were warm, and they grew softer the more she kissed, as she took my top lip between her lips, and I wanted to say, don't do that, I'll fall in love with you if you do that. It seemed so intimate the way she held my face and kissed me; the way I could feel her hands cool and a little wet still on either side of my cheeks. It was more intimate even than when she took off her towel and reached out to unzip the side of my dress. It was like she knew that this was the way my dress opened, like she had already observed, earlier in the evening perhaps, that my dress had a zip at the side. I wondered for a moment at how smoothly she pulled down the zip, how she took the edge of the dress where it lay against my shoulders and pulled it up and over my head.

'I've been wanting to do this for a long time,' Jen said, sitting back on her heels and looking at me as I sat there on her futon. I could feel something digging into me and I looked down and saw there were large white buttons on the futon and that I must be sitting on one. I shifted slightly and Jen rose up and she put her hands around my back and in one movement she had unclipped my bra and thrown it on the floor. Then she put her hands against me and I felt my heart racing and my body seemed to be made of electricity so that each time she touched it I shocked. Everything was heightened, the feeling of where the button of the futon had been beneath me, the way my bra lay soft and frozen on the floor, the way Jen's mouth felt so hot. I turned for a moment, looking towards the window where I could see the night outside and hear the sounds of splashing and the woman still playing the Tracy Chapman song on the guitar.

'Please don't stop,' I heard myself saying when I hadn't known I was thinking this, when I hadn't told my mouth to say this at all.

129

When I woke it was hot in the room and there were odd shadows; the light from a car passing suddenly outside swept the floor like it was searching for something and was gone. Jen was asleep, her body turned away from me, and she held the corner of the thin white sheet in one hand. Her neck looked sweet, a graceful curve against the sheet, her body still when only a few hours earlier it hadn't stopped moving. I lay there for some time, until the room began to lighten, until I could hear the rustle of the palm trees in the garden and a plane overhead.

Still Jen didn't wake, so I moved myself closer, slotting my body under the sheet next to hers and I kissed her neck where there was a light sheen of sweat. I had woken up and gone to heaven, but Jen was still asleep. She had to be tired, I thought, so I got up from the futon and as I did I caught sight of myself in a mirror that I hadn't noticed the night before, and for the first time in my life I thought I looked beautiful and I loved myself. I didn't want to hide anything about myself; there was nothing about me I didn't like because Jen had wanted me, she had wanted every single part of me. Then I got dressed and I looked through the window and saw the debris of the party outside, two paper plates floating like white Frisbees on the surface of the pool, a pair of sandals left on the grass, green beer bottles on the step by the Jacuzzi.

I walked through the silent house and left through the front door and made my way back to my apartment along the empty Davis streets. I had a class to go to and an assignment to complete and it didn't matter that Jen was asleep because I knew she would ring me later and that we would seek each other out. I was happy, so happy I was singing to myself because my life had changed and although I didn't know her yet, I loved everything about her and I couldn't wait to know her even more. I got back to my apartment and everything seemed different, brighter and clearer and more alive, and I did my assignment and I went to my class and all the time I was thinking about Jen.

But then she didn't call. She didn't call that day, or that night, or the next. I didn't know her number to call – I tried and failed to get it from the campus switchboard – but I knew she had mine because it was written on the inside page of my journal, the Women's Studies journal that Jen had been reading, reading all about me. When still she didn't call, I began to scan the students on campus looking for her – every person who came past on a bike, every student in every corridor and in every class – fighting a rising sense of panic, the panic of rejection. She wasn't even at my Women's Studies class and I felt naked sitting there, one woman in one chair in a big wide circle, like everyone knew what had happened, like everyone was waiting, just like me, for Jen to appear.

On the third day I went to Jen's house with a bag of soft, warm blueberry muffins I'd bought at the Davis Food Coop, blueberries so dark it was as if the muffins were stained with ink. I would pretend to be just walking by, I had decided. She would see me from the window and call me in. We were lovers now, she couldn't turn me away, and I was eaten up by the romance of it all. But the house looked empty, the screen door was closed and no lights were on. I was relieved then; she had gone away, that was why she hadn't called. Perhaps someone in her family had fallen ill and she'd had to go away;

perhaps she herself had fallen ill and that was why she wasn't in class.

But still the days went on without a call and I couldn't understand it, I had nothing to compare it to, I'd never given so much of myself to anyone before. I went to swim in the campus pool, but my legs felt sluggish and my arms could barely propel my body through the water, and as I swam I wondered what had happened and what I had done to make it all go wrong. And then I went to the Davis Whole Earth Day and I walked for an hour or so around the Quad, walking slowly because it was so hot that day that the trees seemed to be laden with it. I found some shade under a white awning and looked half-heartedly at booths selling friendship bracelets, tiny glasswork animals, candles smelling of patchouli oil. And then I saw her, I saw Jen by the food stall. She was half on her bike and half off, standing just to the left of a giant silver papier mâché mushroom cloud that stood on the edge of the sidewalk like a plastic explosion. Jen saw me and she waved, so I quickly put down the candle I'd been fingering, overjoyed to see her, feeling already the warmth of her lips, the strength of her arms, and the moment I did this she got back on her bike and rode off.

I stopped where I was, halfway towards her. I thought perhaps she was turning the bike around, that she would turn and cycle back to me if I just waited on this one spot. But she rode away and I didn't know what I had done wrong.

A man in front of me laughs, a sudden yelp, at something he finds funny in the film and it startles me because I'd forgotten where I was. I want to get up but a woman comes down the aisle with the duty free trolley and I'm trapped in my seat thinking of Jen and of the sense of humiliation I felt, a humiliation so intense that it was as if my body had been burnt. She hadn't wanted me, I was just a conquest to her, a naive, romantic English girl that she had seen at the campus bookstore one day. And I was humiliated that I had already told people about her, that I had already written to Loreen and to Bel and told them I had fallen, at last, in love.

I could have left UC Davis then, but instead I wanted to stay because I'd found a new life and I didn't want to go back to the old. I made frantic transatlantic phone calls back to my tutor in England and I petitioned professors and filled in forms and declarations and, at last, I managed to stay. I transferred my credits and extended my visa, I got an evening job in the bookstore to help pay my out-of-state fees and I became a staff assistant in the English department, and during all that time I held my heart close to me and made sure it wouldn't get broken again.

Chapter Sixteen

Bel came by Amtrak that summer of '95, the summer I graduated from UC Davis, and when the train shimmered into the station I was the only one standing on the platform and Bel was the only one getting off. I saw a guard putting down a little blue step, just as a guard had once done for me, but Bel ignored the step, she just jumped off the train and down onto the platform. On her back she had a big green rucksack, and I waited for a second while she looked around – she hadn't seen me, I was standing at the other end of the platform under the palm trees – and I wondered what I would think of her if I hadn't known her for most of my life, if I was seeing her for the first time.

Bel was wearing tight jeans, torn on both knees, and a white t-shirt. Her hair was short and parts of it were dyed red and it looked like she hadn't brushed it in a while. But she looked fit, tanned and fit, and I saw the way she looked around the station, as if she was ready for anything, and all at once I felt I was sixteen again and we were still at school and Bel was going to suggest doing something reckless and I was going to have to say no.

Bel waved. 'Karen!' she yelled, and she came running, the rucksack bouncing on her back. We looked at each other and laughed.

'How was your trip?' I asked. 'You get here OK?' I felt

awkward for a second because I could hear the lilt in my voice, like I wasn't a Californian but I was trying to be one.

'God, this is dinky,' Bel said, looking around at the curved terracotta archways of the station behind her. 'And it's so fucking *clean*! Where do you live then?'

'Just a few minutes' walk,' I said, and I waited while she took a bottle of water out of her rucksack and opened the lid with her teeth. 'How long did it take you to get here?' I asked. Bel had written to tell me that if she took a package on a plane to New York then her flight from London would be free, she just had to deliver it somewhere then she'd make her way to Frisco with the money she'd saved.

'Oh, just a few days.' Bel put her water bottle back in her rucksack. 'I hitched most of the way.'

'You did? Who are you, Jack Kerouac?'

'Yeah,' she laughed, and she looked at me as if daring me to tell her off. But I wasn't going to, because Bel was the first of my friends to visit me and I was grateful for that.

'So what was in the package you brought on the plane to New York?'

Bel shrugged.

'You don't know?' I said, leading her into the Davis station building where it was cool and quiet, where only one traveller was waiting at the booth to buy a ticket and to set off on a journey someplace.

'Nope,' said Bel, stopping to pick up a bunch of flyers and Amtrak timetables from the counter top.

'But what if it was drugs or something?' I asked, and I felt annoyed that I sounded so concerned but was unable to stop myself. 'Bel! You could have got to New York and been arrested. Didn't you open it and look?'

Bel folded the timetables and stuffed them in the back pocket of her jeans. Then she laughed, because things like this had never bothered her. 'Which way?' she asked as we came out to the front of the station. 'Shit, guess what, Karen? I haven't told you. Loreen's pregnant.'

I pulled a face, the one I used to pull to make the others laugh, but I felt hurt that Bel knew Loreen was pregnant and I didn't, like we were kids again and the girls hadn't told me something.

'Yeah, I know,' said Bel, 'rather her than me.'

We looked at each other and smiled, because neither Bel nor me had ever wanted kids.

'Shit,' she said, 'just imagine, she's going to have to carry that thing for nine months, and then squeeze it out, and then have dirty nappies and all that stuff.'

'But who's the father?' I stopped suddenly on the sidewalk.

Bel grimaced. 'It's some bloke she met through a lonely-hearts ad. Which way now?'

We got to my apartment, a smart complex off J Street where I'd moved after my lease had expired on the apartment south of the railroad tracks. It wasn't mine; for the last six months I'd been house-sitting for an associate professor in the English department.

'Shit, this is nice,' said Bel, and she threw her rucksack on the floor. 'Got enough books, Karen?' she asked, walking over to the shelves in the living room and running her fingers along the spines as if counting. I wondered, as she finished with my books and moved over to my desk, if Bel still had that habit where she used to touch things over and over again. 'I didn't know you'd kept that,' she said, looking at a picture over my desk and sounding pleased. It was a self-portrait Bel had sent me when she was still at art school, and I had liked pausing from my studies and staring up at it. It was black and white, very simple, just Bel in a room. She was wearing a black-and-white-striped jumper and holding a black box-shaped camera in both hands, holding it up like someone had put it in her hands and told her to. Her face didn't seem to know what her hands were doing and the expression in her eyes was miles away. It was a very Bel expression, focused, almost blank with intensity. 'Hmm,' Bel said, squinting her eyes critically at the photograph and then heading across the room and towards the open door that led onto the balcony. Then she turned back towards me. 'Have your mum and dad been out to see you?'

'No,' I said, going into the kitchen area and opening the fridge. I had made our lunch earlier, a rice and red bean salad, some artichoke hearts in lime juice. 'Mum was coming over for graduation,' I said, 'but my sister had a crisis.'

Bel smiled in sympathy; she knew my little sister always had a crisis. 'What's all this?' she asked, pointing at the boxes which lay on the floor and which I was about to pack.

'I'm leaving,' I told her. 'Hopefully I'm going to Stanford for my PhD.' And I was a little hurt when Bel didn't respond to this, and then annoyed with myself for expecting Stanford to mean anything to her.

'I thought you liked it here?' she asked.

'I do, but if I do a PhD someplace else then I can come back and get a post here.'

Bel picked her rucksack up off the floor and took out a camera. 'Wow, Karen,' she called as she stepped out onto the balcony, 'you've got a fucking swimming pool down here, I didn't know you had a swimming pool!'

I smiled and came out. 'So how is everyone? I can't believe Loreen is pregnant. You've got to tell me more about the guy, I don't even know anything about him!'

'I haven't met him,' said Bel.

'Why not?'

'Because,' Bel squinted into her camera, 'he's a wanker. And I don't think he's going to stay with her.' Then she held up her camera and began taking pictures of the pool below as if the story was finished, because that was how Bel was, she never wanted to pick apart anyone's emotions, she didn't overanalyse a situation the way I did.

'And how about Ashley?' I asked. 'I haven't heard from Ashley for ages, she hasn't written for months.'

But Bel didn't answer, she just leaned further over the balcony, photographing the pool below, leaning so far over that I wanted to pull her back. 'Oh Ashley's too busy for us,' she said at last. 'She's doing her arty farty design degree and she's got her rock star boyfriend. Do you remember Steve?' Bel held the camera, focusing on me.

'Don't!' I said, ducking out of the way, but Bel kept the camera in front of her face so I could only see one eye.

'You remember Steve? That boyfriend she had when we went to Portugal? The one she met outside the school gates that wore those really tight trousers and thought he was God's gift? Well, this one is just like him, only he's semi-famous.'

'What's his name?'

'Oh Karen, you won't have heard of him.'

I felt a prickle of annoyance that Bel thought I wouldn't have heard of someone.

'His name,' smiled Bel, 'is Jay B.'

'OK,' I said. Bel was right, I hadn't heard of him.

'And he's a complete prick.'

The first movie of the flight has finally ended, the duty free trolley has been packed away and the second movie is starting now. I get up and walk down the aisle, a little stiff and unsteady after sitting still for so long. The washroom is small and metallic and I feel cut off from everything and everyone in here. I flush the toilet and hear the dry whoosh of paper. I wipe the basin because the person before me has left it stained with liquid soap, and I put the soap bottle back where it should be and I look in the mirror and see a woman with odd-coloured skin and when she raises her eyebrows there are two lines on her forehead that stay there when she lowers her eyebrows again. I wonder where those lines have come from, I don't remember them the last time I looked in a mirror, when I left Davis, when I was in the bathroom checking that everything was clean and ordered for my house-sitter. I wonder if these two lines have developed since I've been on the plane.

I return to my seat and strap myself in. I pick up my book and I want to read but I can't because now that I've been thinking of when I left Davis, when Bel came to visit, I've started thinking of when I returned and when I first heard of Stella Givenchy.

Chapter Seventeen

It was the fall of 2000 when I came back to Davis from Stanford, on tenure track now with a post as assistant professor and a new house I'd rented just near where Jen used to live. Jen had left, I heard, a couple of years earlier; she'd moved to San Diego. I tried my best not to think of her when I returned, to not half expect her to come cycling towards me one day and to confess that she loved me after all. I had been careful during my time at Stanford not to give myself away again, and I had left my lovers before they could tire and leave me.

I settled quickly back into life in Davis, a place that had barely changed in the intervening years. I was assigned a small office in the American Studies department, which lay across the corridor from my favourite colleague, Macey Bloom. I liked Macey, because if I looked and sounded like an academic, she did not, even though it wouldn't be long before she would become a fully tenured professor. Macey Bloom wore tops as if they were dresses, pink and white gingham baby doll type tops with frilly half-sleeves. And she wore shades whatever the weather, huge brown-lensed shades that covered half her face. Macey Bloom's specialisation was the American landscape, but her real specialisation, her real passion, was rabbits. There was one in particular, Wilamena, that she liked to take on walks around campus, holding the rabbit by a pink ribbon fastened onto a harness. Wilamena was the size of a small cat, she had a face like a goddam arse, and inside her ears the skin was pink with bulging veins.

It was Macey who first told me about Stella Givenchy. 'You'll love her,' she said one lunchtime as she stood at the doorway to my office, munching on a handful of carrots that she carried with her wherever she went, in case her bunny Wilamena needed a snack. 'She'll be in the office down the hall. You guys will sure get on. A girlfriend taught with her in Connecticut, I hear she's pretty wild.'

I looked up from my PC. Spring quarter had just started and I was doing everything I could to turn my PhD into a book because I knew, as every other would-be professor knew, that I must publish or perish. But right now I was supposed to be finishing off a book review, a book about the real Ezra Pound that I wasn't interested in enough to write. 'When's she coming?' I asked, to be polite.

But Macey Bloom didn't answer, she had run back across the corridor to her office. 'Hold it, bunny!' I heard her shout, and I sighed because that meant she'd brought Wilamena to work again. The department chair, the newly appointed Professor Greer, a tall, thin East Coast man with liver spots on his hands like the markings on a Dalmatian dog, had said she was not to bring Wilamena to work any more, but sometimes Macey Bloom sneaked the rabbit in. She said rabbits were friendly and easy to love, but I didn't like the way Wilamena would hop into my office and scratch at the grey metal legs of my Formica desk. Professor Greer knew she did this, he knew Macey brought her bunny in, but he took his role as department chair seriously; he was, he thought, there to coordinate the democratic process, not to tell people what they could and could not do.

'She's due next month,' Macey said, coming back to my doorway after shutting her office door. Then she pointed to the clock that hung on the wall behind my desk and I saw I had class starting in ten minutes.

I left my office and walked quickly to Hart Hall, passing Frat boys with flicked fringes and arms thick below their sport shirts. 'Dude!' said one Frat boy to another, giving a high five, standing at the entrance to Hart Hall so I was forced to go round him. I thought about stopping him and asking, did he know dude was originally used in reference to a goddam horse's penis? I sighed as I entered the lecture hall, a row of faces watching me, students opening up their yellow, lined legal pads. I knew I had a reputation already; I was the tough English prof, the one who failed you without a second thought. I didn't like this class, it was too big. Last week I had taught a Dickinson poem:

'Hope' is the thing with feathers —
That perches in the soul —

The students had had no idea what I was talking about. I put my notes on the lectern in front of me and began to read, although I knew many of the students would just buy someone else's notes later on. And as I read to the students, as I watched a handful writing notes on their legal pads, I was wondering what Macey Bloom had meant when she'd said our new colleague Stella Givenchy was wild.

*

The first time I met Stella Givenchy was at the American Studies end-of-quarter potluck at Professor Greer's house, when my colleagues and I were expected to come along and bring a dish to share. I was one of the last to arrive; I'd had a late afternoon class that day and then I'd rushed back to my apartment to shower and change and fetch the chickpea salad I'd made the evening before. I didn't really want to go to the potluck, I didn't want to make small talk about who was up for tenure, about who was publishing what, about what everyone's plans were for Spring break, but I'd told Professor Greer I would go, so I went.

'Hey Karen!' called out Macey Bloom as I stepped onto the porch of Professor Greer's house. She was standing at the door, her rabbit Wilamena on a pink ribbon by her side, welcoming people in.

'Hey Macey,' I said, offering up my Tupperware.

'You go right inside with that,' said Macey. 'And put it in the kitchen for me. I'm glad someone brought something good to eat. Professor Greer has made his famous nut roast,' and Macey mimed putting two fingers down her throat.

Professor Greer had one of the oldest houses in Davis, and as I went in with my potluck salad I heard the floorboards creak beneath my feet. I saw Professor Greer through an open door and I waved, indicating that I was heading to the kitchen with my Tupperware.

And when I walked into the kitchen, there was Stella Givenchy. She was standing at the counter in the middle of the room eating tortilla chips from a big yellow bowl. She seemed utterly relaxed, as if this were her home, her kitchen,

143

her tortilla chips. And she was enjoying the chips, placing them slowly, individually, into her mouth, one after another after another. I didn't take in what she was wearing at first, only a sense of colour, a sense that she was wearing something red and something orange and that there was something flowing about it all.

'Hi,' I said, feeling very conscious of myself as I tried to find a space on the counter for my potluck food. I felt awkward, like my body had just lost colour, like nothing in myself fitted together properly any more.

Stella looked up and I took in a round face with deep-set eyes and ginger highlighted hair. 'Hi,' she said, only slowly, drawing the simple word out like she wanted to hear it, think about it, test the sound of it.

'Oh you've met!' Macey Bloom came hurrying into the kitchen, tugging Wilamena on the lead behind her. 'I wanted to be the one to introduce you guys. Well, I'll go ahead anyway. This is Stella Givenchy, our new Gothic expert,' said Macey. 'Have you tried my guacamole with that?' she asked Stella. 'Hold it, bunny!' she snapped as Wilamena began to strain against the ribbon. 'And this is Karen, our specialist in Modern American women's poetry. You guys are going to love each other!'

I smiled, blinked, felt under pressure.

Stella smiled as well. 'Karen,' she said, and she said it in such a way that it was as if I'd never heard my name said this way before. Then Stella Givenchy dipped a tortilla chip into the guacamole that Macey Bloom had pushed in front of her and she scooped up the avocado and tipped the chip into her mouth. 'Cool rabbit,' she said as Macey

Bloom led Wilamena out of the kitchen, as the rabbit hopped and stopped, sniffed and hopped again. 'Very *Alice in Wonderland.*'

Stella picked up a wine glass from the counter and I could see fresh traces of deep red lipstick where her lips had touched the rim.

'It's not supposed to be in here,' I said. 'Professor Greer doesn't like Macey bringing it into his kitchen.' I frowned at myself, I didn't want to sound so disapproving; Stella Givenchy would think I was so staid and goddam boring.

But Stella beamed at me as if I'd made a joke. 'I had one when I was young,' she said, sipping from her wine glass. 'For months and months we were like, Mom, *please* can we have a rabbit, we'll look after it, we promise, *please.* You know what kids can be like when they get something they want into their head? And we were very persuasive, my little sister and me.'

And I thought, she has a little sister too, we have something in common.

Stella took another chip, scooped it in the guacamole, and continued, 'Then Mom got this rabbit from a wildlife awareness centre and that was the thing, if we tried playing with it, if we even bent forward like this . . .' I watched as Stella Givenchy bent forward over the counter in Professor Greer's kitchen, 'it just bit us. That bozo of a bunny sure as hell hated us!'

I laughed, my body felt a little freer and I moved a little closer.

'Dogs too,' said Stella. 'My little sister and me always wanted a dog, we were like, Mom, please, *please* can we have one. But what my little bozo of a sister really *really* wanted was a horse. I mean she loved them so much she thought she *was* a horse . . .'

I smiled, watching Stella as she talked; she seemed like someone who had no trouble talking, she just opened her mouth and it all came out.

'I don't like horses much,' she continued, 'they're a bit too muscular, there's nothing soft, nothing to hold onto, they're just so sort of . . . *masculine*. And masculine's not my thing, really.'

Stella stopped talking then and she smiled very directly at me and she kept eye contact while she sipped her wine and I wondered for an incredible, fleeting second whether she was flirting with me. And I wondered if the ginger highlights in her hair were natural or if they were dyed, and I pictured Stella bending over a basin dying her hair, like she had bent over the kitchen counter top just now, only wearing a towel around her body, fresh from a bath.

'Ah, here's my wife,' said a man coming into the kitchen, and I turned towards him, blushing furiously. I saw he had a beard which was in the process of going grey, and the flecks of white and brown on his chin made me think of a porcupine. I looked at Stella, was she his wife? Was this jerk her husband? Did she have a husband? Macey Bloom hadn't told me that.

'We were talking about horses,' said Stella, and she sounded dreamy, like she wasn't really in the room with us any more.

'Uhu,' said the man, looking from me to Stella like he was trying to track something. Then he came further into the

146

room, heading for the counter where Stella stood and said, 'How about getting me a drink, *prof*?'

'Well of course,' Stella replied, not moving, not showing any sign of fetching her husband a drink and instead picking up her glass and sipping on her wine again.

'Nick Givenchy,' said the man, turning away from the counter just before he reached it, as if all along he had been intending to come on over and grasp my hand. 'You must be . . .?'

'Karen,' I said, and I returned his shake with a firm hand and I could feel Stella watching me.

'Oh you're the one from England,' Nick Givenchy said, and although he was smiling his eyes were heavy with suspicion. 'We heard there was an English prof in the department. Stella was quite excited about that, weren't you, honey?'

'Originally,' I said. 'Originally I'm from England.' And I smiled politely at the two of them. I liked the sound of that – 'originally' – it made me sound as if I had an interesting past. Eight years earlier anyone would have known I was English, now people weren't so sure.

'And now you're a true blue Californian,' said Nick Givenchy.

'Not quite,' I said.

Stella laughed and we both looked at her. 'Why is it,' she said thoughtfully, 'that you Brits find us Yanks so annoying . . . and we find you so charming?'

We're going to land. All night long I've been on this plane thinking in the dark while people around me slept, but now

147

breakfast has been served, a soft skinless tomato lying wetly on scrambled egg, and the trays taken away again. Now the flight attendants are serving us hot damp towels wrapped up like sushi so we can clean our hands. In an hour perhaps I will be out of the airport and back in London and tomorrow, perhaps, or the day after I will see Bel and Ashley and Loreen again and I won't see Stella at all. Nick Givenchy will have her all to himself.

I can feel the plane sinking through the air, down it goes and down some more and my ears begin to fill up with the pressure and any minute now the pain's going to start and it won't stop until we land. I put my hands to my ears and press in tight, it feels like my brain is filling with water and I'm plugging my ears so it won't leak out. From outside every window all I can see is white. Then suddenly the white clears and there are flat fields and trees and buildings and closer and closer we come to the ground. I can feel the wheels coming down and then the plane hits the runway and lifts and hits it again.

And now we've stopped but there is something real odd going on because they're not opening any of the doors. The plane has come to a complete stop, the seatbelt lights are off, people are standing in the aisle all ready with their bags, but they haven't opened any of the goddam doors. I see four flight attendants at the end of the aisle, huddled together, talking urgently. My neighbour, the woman who slept the whole way with her neck on the inflatable ring the colour of moleskin, looks anxious. Then the cell on her lap springs into life and she holds it in her hand to read a message and she gives a sharp intake of breath. I wonder what

148

has made her look so alarmed and I bend my head forward so I can see past her and out of the window, and I wonder what's happened while we've been on this plane because outside on the tarmac there are goddam cops all over the place.

Chapter Eighteen

DUDU

I am sitting in my Loreen's kitchen on this hot sticky evening with my daughter's radio turned down low. I cannot bear to watch the television in the front room and I have not let my little grandsons watch it either, for I do not want them to see the news. I do not want them to see the injured people, those with bandages on their heads and those wrapped up in coats of tinfoil, and the young woman with long black hair who doesn't know she has soot all over her face. I do not want them to hear the panic in the policeman's voice as he shouts at people to move away, or to hear the young man whose voice breaks when he says he does not know if his sister is alive or dead. And I do not want to think of that evening so many years ago when I stood in my landlady's room and watched the news the day my husband died. I am wondering how Loreen can go out on an evening like this when they are looking for the bombers and when the radio tells me that London is on a state of high alert. 'But Mum!' she said. 'Bel's there waiting for me.'

My little grandson Dwaine is asleep but it took a long time for him to fall asleep this evening for he questioned me a long time about what happened today and why his school is closed tomorrow. There was a sign about this posted on the gates when I went to pick him up this afternoon, a sign that said due to the terrorist attacks schools would close tomorrow. A lot of parents were at the gates this afternoon, far more than there normally are, and they were all very anxious, especially when one child came running out to where we parents stood and he shouted 'I'm a suicide bomber!' and he laughed and skipped as if it were a game.

It seemed that just about every parent was on one mobile phone or another this afternoon. I don't know what it is with these mobile phones, but people don't talk to each other any more, now they are all talking into their mobile phones and subjecting us to the details of their everyday lives. If people have a need for this constant sort of conversation, while on the bus, while walking down a street, while in a shop, while waiting outside a school's gates, then why don't they turn off the phone and talk to people around them? I have seen parents with their children and the children are asking them something and the parent is unable to answer because he or she is on a mobile phone. But of course there was a reason this afternoon because people's mobile phones had not been working and everyone was afraid and wanting to know that their loved ones were safe and not killed or injured by the bombs.

There were two teachers posted at either side of the school gates and they looked us over worriedly as we waited to get our children, as if suspicious that we could be a bomber too. And a woman in a black hijab was pulled to one side and questioned as to who she was picking up, when she is Amina's mother and she picks up her daughter in the

151

same place at the same time every day, and if I know this, because Amina is in the same class as my little grandson Dwaine, then the teachers must too. Yet today they are treating her not as a mother come to collect her child but as someone who might have a bomb beneath her clothes.

I will think of something nice, I tell myself, I will think of my Loreen when she was little, when she was about the age my grandson Anthony is now, I will think of her on her last day of primary school. The girls were still so little then, only of course they did not think of themselves as little, they thought they were big and they could not wait to be bigger still. For that is how children are, always hurtling towards their future. I can recall the smell of that day; it was a smell of dry straw like the straw used to line the cage of the classroom gerbil, and it came from the rafters high up at the top of the school hall. The hall was crowded, it had been a dismal summer and outside the streets were wet and so inside everything seemed bright and cheerful. I had arrived early for I knew the place would soon fill up and I wanted a good view of the leavers' assembly and last day at primary school. As I came in I saw my child at once; there she sat with her girlfriends all in a row, Karen, Bel, my little Loreen and Ashley. Karen still had the same severe hairstyle she had had since she was five, and she sat there not moving, except for once or twice when she looked along the row as if to check that everyone was in their place, that no one was doing anything they shouldn't be. Next to her, Bel was picking away at her t-shirt, shifting around, chattering away as she always did, ducking her head when the lady teacher looked her way. And next to Bel sat my little Loreen, trying to remain composed even though she was very excited about the leavers' assembly and about starting big school. And then came Ashley. It was clear that of the four of them, Ashley had changed the most during her time at primary school, for she had become a brighter version of her younger self and everything about her had become more clearly defined. Her hair was the luscious colour of a golden sunflower now and her eyes, while still large, looked less like the eyes of a baby animal and more like the eyes of a girl who was on her way to adulthood. She had begun to draw people to her, for there was something about Ashley that made the younger children look at her with admiration, and many of the parents too.

I sat myself in one of the small orange plastic chairs that had been set out for parents, but which were designed for small child bottoms. I had sat in the hall many times and I knew that this was the last time I would do this and so I concentrated hard on everything around me. I had sat here for class assemblies and for harvest festivals, when the children brought in fruits and vegetables and canned food and set them all along the windowsills. One year I had seen Bel sneak a grape from the windowsill and pop it brazenly into her mouth and I had seen Karen urge Bel to give it back, and instead Bel had just taken another grape and popped that into her mouth as well.

I had sat in the hall for the nativity plays at Christmas too, which they don't do at schools any more, and I remember the year Ashley was chosen to play the Virgin Mary and she wore a blue dress and head scarf and sat in the centre of the stage. She did look pretty, she had been chosen because she looked pretty rather than for any acting ability, and her father had stood up on a chair at the back to film her. Bel played a wise man and made the audience laugh with her line, Karen was a shepherd with only a few words to say, and my little Loreen was a tree. They made the poor child be a tree! I had known they would not let my little Loreen be the Virgin Mary because they wanted someone white for that, but a tree, how could they make a child be a tree?

That afternoon the girls came round for tea and I sat them at our kitchen table and I looked at each of them and I smiled to see how they were growing. They were overexcited that day and my little Loreen still had a stain of tears on her face for some of the children at the leavers' assembly had begun crying and that had set her off as well for she always was a sensitive child. She had handed me her school report and I had filed it away in a box where I kept her special things and then we had sat in the kitchen for I had bought the girls some little cakes and some vanilla ice cream and we were making a party of that day. 'Now,' I said, when they had eaten some of the cakes and the ice cream, 'let me ask you something, my dears, what do you think you will all be when you grow up?'

'A scientist,' said Ashley at once.

The other girls looked at her, they seemed startled by the idea.

'I will either be a scientist or a lawyer,' continued Ashley. 'I'm excellent at maths and my daddy says a scientist would be a very good career move. My daddy says he is a bit of a scientist himself because my daddy is a *psychoanalyst* and he . . .'

'And what about you, Bel?' I asked, for although I knew by now what Ashley's father did, I did not quite understand it for people did not go to psychoanalysts so much in those days.

'Dunno,' said Bel, and she picked up her bowl and began to lick the ice cream from the bottom. I could see she did it in a certain way, that she gave the bowl a series of short licks, then paused, then she gave it some more short licks again as if everything that she did had to be balanced by doing the same thing again. Then she saw that I was observing this and quickly she put the bowl down.

'Would you like to be an artist?' I asked, for Bel had a very clever way about her when she drew. It was the only time I saw her sit still, when she was drawing, and she always framed what she drew, making big thick lines with which to contain her people or her houses or her animals. I had even seen her draw frames on pieces of paper and then put nothing inside them at all.

'Bel wants to marry Christopher Collins,' laughed Ashley, and I thought she was annoyed that I had interrupted her when she wanted to talk about what her daddy wanted her to be, and she was taking this annoyance out on Bel.

'Christopher Collins!' said Karen. 'Gross!'

'Yuk!' said my little Loreen in agreement, only I could see her eyes were bright now at the idea of Christopher Collins, the pumpkin-faced boy that she had loved since she was seven.

'I think I'll be a punk,' said Bel.

I laughed and Bel scowled at me which made me laugh all the more. I wanted to give her a hug as she sat there at my

155

table, but she was too old now to want hugs. And there was something skittery about her as well which made me think she was more anxious about starting big school than anyone perhaps knew. 'And what about you, Karen?' I asked. 'What will you be? A librarian perhaps?'

Karen put her finger in her bowl and wiped it softly round the edge. 'Are you saying that because I like books?'

I nodded.

'I don't want to be a librarian,' Karen sighed, and it was a sigh that made her seem much older than she was. 'I want to go to America.'

'You haven't asked me, Mum!' said Loreen, cross that I was giving the other little girls more attention than her. 'I'm going to get married and have lots of babies . . .'

'Gross,' said Karen.

'Yuk,' said Bel.

'And maybe I'll be a teacher too, like Mrs Greenrod.'

'Yes, that's good,' I said, only inside I couldn't help it, I was thinking of that day when the fortune-teller at the Hampstead Heath fair had said my little Loreen would be famous, and still I was waiting to see what she might be famous for. If she were famous, I thought, then she would have all the things I was not able to give her, like new dolls and clothes and birthday parties and holidays abroad. And I felt a little ashamed that I thought this, for my late husband would have frowned at these thoughts and would have said what I knew myself, that neither money nor fame buys happiness.

'I've got a camera!' said Bel all of a sudden, getting down from the table. 'It's my brother's and he said I could use it today, so everyone line up because I'm going to take a photo.'

So the other girls got down from the table while Bel went to fetch her camera and then they stood in front of my kitchen window. 'That's no good,' said Bel, 'because of the light,' and I smiled to see Bel so serious about taking a picture. Then she went and stood herself in front of the window and got her friends to line up before her on the other side of the table. Ashley positioned herself between Karen and my little Loreen and she put her arms around her two friends and she tossed her yellow hair and she began to sing, '*Like a virgin! Touched for the very first time!*', and she laughed as she sang and she thrust her weight, such as it was, from one hip to the other.

'Not of me,' I said as Bel finished taking a photograph of her friends and turned her camera towards me. 'My dear,' I said again, 'not of me.'

'My mum said no!' said Loreen.

'But why?' asked Bel, still standing there with the camera in her hands.

'Well . . .' I began, but I couldn't think of a simple enough way to explain myself, and because an African child would never have said, 'But why?' once an elder had told them not to do something. But then I saw little Bel looking at me, saw the way she looked so very disappointed, and I thought it would be a small thing to agree. 'Very well, then,' I said, and I stood there very still with my arms folded, waiting.

'Smile!' said Bel.

But I didn't smile because where I came from a photograph is a serious business and I wasn't prepared or dressed appropriately; I was just in my kitchen still with my apron around my waist.

'Please, Mum,' said Loreen, 'smile.'

So then I did and just as Bel was about to take another photograph the doorbell rang, and Ashley asked, 'Is it my dad?' Then she shouted out 'Daddy!' as I went downstairs and let her father in. He came quickly up the stairs behind me and into the kitchen and he bent down and held his arms out although it had been only some few hours since he'd been at the leavers' assembly and seen his daughter last.

'Hello girls,' said Ashley's father, straightening up and looking at the others. He was such a tall man, especially so in a little kitchen like ours, that I wanted to implore him to sit before I felt impelled to stand up too. 'How very lovely you all look.'

I smiled, they did look lovely, the way they sat around my kitchen table having their tea. It was only now that Ashley's father was here that things didn't hold together as well as they had, and he seemed to sense this for it was making him even louder than he normally was.

'You Africans certainly know how to party!' said Ashley's father.

I looked round the room; it seemed to me we were having a very English time of it, sitting round the table with our cakes and ice cream, and I wanted to ask him, what did he know of Africans and how we like to party? Rise above it, I could hear my husband's voice, rise above it.

'Yuk!' cried Ashley suddenly and she pointed at Bel. 'You've got an ice cream beard!'

Bel frowned and wiped at her chin and then she got down from her place at the table and went past Ashley's father to fetch something from the hall. 'I got a prize,' she said, coming back and holding out a piece of yellow card. I took the card and I held it up before me and, although I already knew what it said for I'd been there at the leavers' assembly, I read it out loud: 'Most Improved Student, Bel Lavender.'

'Well done,' I said, and I took a risk and put out my arm to hug her, and for a second her bony young body slipped in right under my arm.

'What's this?' Ashley's father said, and his voice was falsely jovial as if he were joining in a children's game. 'Got a prize, Bel?'

'Yes,' Bel said, and quickly she took back the card.

'Were there prizes at the assembly?' Ashley's father asked me a little accusingly, as if I had kept something from him.

'Yes, it was just after you left.'

'Oh,' Ashley's father frowned. 'What sort of prizes?'

'Oh,' I said carelessly, 'for music, for attendance, for acting . . .'

'I got a certificate for swimming,' said Karen.

'Well done!' boomed Ashley's father. 'And where's yours, darling?' He turned to Ashley. 'Let me look in your bag, where's your bag? Bring it in here!'

Ashley went and got her school bag and brought it in and I got up to clear the table because I knew she didn't have a prize and I didn't want to see this when her father found out, for Ashley's father was a man who did not accept the not so clever. His child, surely, must have won a prize; it would be an insult to him if she had not. So Ashley's father rifled through his daughter's bag, bringing out a library book, a notebook, some shiny red stickers in the shape of hearts, a bracelet made from coloured beads, a folder, a pencil case, until finally Ashley said, 'I didn't get a prize, Daddy.'

'But I did,' said Bel. She had sat back down at the table again and she was holding her certificate in one hand and with the other she was eating the remains of the ice cream straight from the tub.

'Yes, well,' said Ashley's father. 'Sometimes, Bel, people get a prize because they need that sort of encouragement.'

Bel stared at Ashley's father and she knew, I thought, what his implication was, and so she decided the best response would be nothing, to just sit and stare until Ashley's father grew irritated and leaned his hands down on the table and said, 'Ashley! Time to go!'

I hear a murmur from Dwaine's room and I walk slowly along the hall for my leg is paining me today. I don't have the energy I used to have and on nights like this I fear my thread is running out, that the reel is almost empty. I pass Anthony's room and I see him sitting there on his bed, cross-legged, his face bent over one of these computer games children like so much. He looks up and sees me and gives a half smile. I hope Dwaine hasn't woken because he is afraid of the bombs, and I don't know what I can do to reassure him if he has. I stand at the open door to Dwaine's bedroom. He has a nightlight shaped like a squat giraffe near his bed, because like a lot of children in England he is afraid of the dark, and I stand here and think that in Africa a child would never sleep like this, all alone in a big room afraid of the dark. I remain at Dwaine's doorway and wait until my eyes can pick out the shape of him in his bed and until I see his shoulders rising ever so slightly up and down so that I know he is alive and breathing.

And I think of the day he was born, and then the day his brother Anthony was born, the day I had my first grandchild: a wet, cold day when the pavements were covered with sludge from the snow the night before. I was at work, I had just started my night shift, when a colleague told me my Loreen had been admitted, and how I ran to the maternity wing, how I flew there as fast as I could! And there I found my child in a wheelchair, her face so full of anticipation that I knew the real work had not begun and I couldn't bear to tell her that it would be some hours yet, perhaps a whole night, perhaps another day before her child would be born. But by the time my shift was over, that little Anthony had already arrived, delivered like a football out of his mother, so fast I had never known a labour so fast. I helped to arrange a separate room for my Loreen then, a room on the corner of the ward that looked out onto the street below and at the snow that had started to fall again, and I stayed with her and made sure she had everything she needed. I even let Bel in early the next morning, although I wasn't supposed to, for visiting hours were not for some hours yet, but when I saw Bel's face up against the glass of the door begging me to let her in, I did.

Loreen sat up on the bed then, her little baby boy Anthony asleep against her, and Bel sat down beside her. 'Shit, Loreen,' she whispered, and the two of them put their heads together to inspect that baby and they looked at him with such wonder and touched and patted him so carefully as if he would break, and I thought, where is the father? The father should be the one doing this.

Perhaps Dwaine was sleeptalking, I think, as still I stand in his doorway watching. And I want to lie down with my little grandson the way I used to lie with my little Loreen after her father died, nice and close and able to save or protect her from anything, for one thing I know and that is it is a child's mother who will always catch a knife at the sharp end.

Chapter Nineteen

LOREEN

Oh my God, London's so weird this evening. Everyone's really nervous, I'm really nervous. We're supposed to act as normal, so they've been telling us on the news, but one minute they're saying 'stay where you are, don't travel into central London', and the next minute we're being told not to be frightened of going about our business as normal. But what is normal? Is going out for a drink with two old friends normal?

When Bel rang this evening I couldn't believe she still wanted to go, I thought she was just ringing to tell me she was safe, because I'd been terrified about her all day knowing she was in Tavistock Square. I was just running Dwaine's bath, he'd already stripped off and was waiting there on the bath mat, ready to get in, a toy car in one hand, when Mum came in and handed me the phone. 'We can't go out tonight,' I told Bel, 'I mean, God, I've been looking forward to this evening for ages, but we can't go now, what if there's another . . .?' I didn't want to say 'bomb' in front of Dwaine, but he sensed I was not saying something and he stared at me, clutching his toy car.

'Listen, Loreen,' said Bel, 'there are cops everywhere. I've been all over the place this afternoon. I'm in town now, on the way to the bar to see you. London is crawling with cops, this is the safest time to go anywhere. Come on, Loreen, you were the one who set this up. I'm only going so I can see you.'

'But I can't leave the boys,' I said, looking at Dwaine, still standing there naked, all ready for his bath. I could see he was clenching in his bottom lip the way he does before he cries. 'Don't worry, don't worry,' I told him, 'I'm not going out.'

And then Dwaine dropped his toy car and began to howl. 'But I *want* you to go out, Mum! 'Cos I want Nan to look after me and give me crumpets! You promised!'

And so here I am in Soho, walking quickly past a newspaper hoarding saying, 'Terrorists attack London – many dead'. I clutch my mobile in my hand, in case the boys or Mum want to call. Bel will already be at the bar and I don't want her to have to wait for me, and Ashley will be there by now too. The streets aren't nearly as crowded as they'd normally be, but all the bars and cafés on this road have opened their windows and set out tables on the pavement as if they're expecting a big crowd. I'm trying to remember the name of the bar Ashley gave me, I was sure she said it was on this street, but I've been walking so quickly without really looking that now I'm feeling lost. Everything feels really hazy tonight. I look around and then I see the bar, it's just behind me on the corner of two roads, and now I can see Bel at a table so far on the edge of the pavement it's almost on the road. The bar has three brown awnings and on the wall above there are lights that give out a strange blue glow. I rush over, shouting, 'Bel!' and feeling so relieved I'm not lost after all.

'Shit, this must be the first time ever I've been on time and you're late!' Bel laughs. She's sitting near a blackboard which has been set on the pavement but doesn't have anything written on it, and she has her hands on two metal-framed seats she must be keeping for Ashley and me.

'Isn't she here then?' I ask.

'Nope.' Bel scrapes back one of the chairs, waits for me to sit down. But I feel too weird to sit and instead I look around at the other people outside the bar. This is the most crowded bar in the whole street, it's like people want company tonight so they're only choosing a bar where other people are. It feels like everyone is trying to act too normal, talking a bit too loudly, laughing a bit too freely. Nearly everyone has a mobile in their hands or on their tables and a group of people on our right have their necks craned, looking at a TV I can just see inside the bar. Oh my God, this isn't right, I should be back home with my boys.

'What are you drinking?' asks Bel. 'Vodka and tonic?'

'Yeah, I guess so. I don't know. How can you be so calm? I feel really weird leaving the boys at home.'

'Shit, Loreen, they'll be fine,' says Bel. 'Sit down, taste this.'

She hands me her drink and I sit down with it, take a sip. 'So what was it like?' I ask. 'In Tavistock Square?'

'Have you been watching the news?'

I nod.

'It was like a nightmare.' Bel's eyes flick to mine and then to the people sitting outside the bar. 'London's mad tonight, isn't it? I've been all over the place and everywhere you go there's this sort of feeling that . . .'

'Why have you been all over the place?'

165

Bel shrugs and stands. She gets some money out of her jeans pocket. 'Keep that chair for Ashley while I get the drinks. On the other hand, don't bother, I don't think she's coming.'

'She'll be here,' I say. 'She said she would and she works in Soho, doesn't she?'

'No idea,' says Bel. 'Text her and ask if she's on her way. I don't like it around here.' Bel is gone for a long time, so I text Ashley and I ring Mum and I watch the people on the street, everyone is walking so calmly it's like some slow-moving dance scene. Then I see Ashley coming down the other side of the road and I smile and am about to wave when I see it's not Ashley after all. I start to feel worried now; what if something really has gone wrong and she can't make it, what if she's trapped somewhere, what if she hasn't got my message, what if she was on one of the tubes?

'So,' Bel says, coming back with the drinks. 'She still hasn't turned up?' Bel's annoyed now and I know that any minute she's going to suggest we move on and go somewhere else.

'She's probably got held up,' I tell her. 'Let's wait a bit longer. Maybe it's something to do with her girls.'

'Or maybe,' says Bel, 'she just can't be arsed.'

It's only eleven but I'm home already because I can't bear being out any later than this. I walked home so fast I'm sweating. As I come up the stairs I take out my phone and check it in case there's a message from Ashley and I missed it, but there isn't. I check my voice mail and there are no new messages on that either. I get into the flat and it's eerily quiet. I put my head into Anthony's room, he's fast asleep, the sheet

166

is a crumpled ball at the end of the bed; he's on his back with both knees raised up. This is the way he used to sleep as a baby and he looks so very beautiful that I want to wake him up and tell him I love him. I tip toe into his room and put my hands on his knees and push them ever so slightly and at once his legs fold down. I close Anthony's door and then I peep into Dwaine's room and see Mum has got into bed with him. I don't know how they can both be asleep on his little bed but I won't wake her, she may as well stay here now, although in the morning she'll complain that her cat will be hungry.

It's still so very quiet in the flat and I feel too awake to sleep. I go into the kitchen and turn the radio off; Mum has obviously had it on all evening because it's hot to the touch. I go into my room and close the door and take my dress off and put it away in my wardrobe when I would usually just throw it on the floor. I don't know why I'm hanging it up tonight. I look down, something odd has happened to this wardrobe, then I realise Mum has cleaned it up. She's hung up a whole load of clothes, she's picked things up off the floor, the posters and the *Fame* annual I'd been looking at, and she's piled all the things back into the boxes she gave me. I pick up the *Fame* annual and underneath is a wad of papers held together with a big red elastic band that's gone soft and sticky with age. It's a pile of old school reports, thin pieces of paper with 'Inner London Education Authority' printed along the top. I hold them, listen to the silence in my flat, wonder what I can do tonight if I'm not going to sleep. Then I sit down on the floor and lean up against my bed to read the reports. The first one says July 1984, that must have been my last year of primary school, what we used to call Fourth Year. I was so nervous leaving primary school, but so happy we were all going to the same secondary, me and Bel and Karen and Ashley. Why didn't she turn up tonight? I feel so disappointed, stupidly disappointed, but there must be a reason, something must have gone wrong. But if something had gone wrong then wouldn't I know by now? I look over at my bedside table where my phone is, why hasn't she rung?

I look at the first section of my old school report where it says 'General Personality Sketch' and I read 'Loreen is a popular girl with many friends who shows great potential . . .' Ha! I was not. I wasn't ever popular at primary school. Who wrote this? They're lying. It's signed Anne Greenrod. Oh my God, Mrs Greenrod! I haven't thought about Mrs Greenrod for years. She was our class teacher and I loved her so much that sometimes when I talked to her the word 'Mum' just slipped out of my mouth. I push my back up against the bed and close my eyes and think of Mrs Greenrod. She wore jackets with big fat shoulder pads and she looked like someone off *Dallas*. She was the first teacher I'd ever had who thought I was capable of more than what I was doing.

It was in the last year of primary school that Mrs Greenrod made the announcement: she was getting married, she was leaving, and a big wail went up in the classroom because she was abandoning us. But even though she left, Karen suggested we visit her because she was in love with her too. I hadn't known you could visit teachers in their own homes; I thought teachers didn't really exist except when they were in school, but Karen said we could and she even got Mrs Greenrod's address from the school office.

Mrs Greenrod lived in south London. Karen got us there on three different buses, and her house must have been new because the moment we walked in there was a feeling of new carpet and new walls and new lights. She made us tea; she had gone to some effort to get chocolate éclairs and other things all set properly out on the big shiny dining room table. But Mrs Greenrod wasn't the way she'd been in the classroom. She had slippers on and her hair was a mess and she kept on apologising for things: that she wasn't dressed, that the baby was crying, that we'd had to come such a long way. And then she stood in her sterile living room and said to us, 'Don't get married, girls,' and I couldn't stand it, I loved Mrs Greenrod and I wanted her to love being married because that's why she'd left us. And I wanted to get married too; I wanted to get married and have kids and live in a cottage with roses on the wall.

Here's the second section in the report: 'Loreen has done excellent work in Art, Drama and Games.' I did? I don't remember ever being good at games, I hated games. I hated rounders when the sides were picked and no one ever wanted me. I turn to the next report: 'Her attitude to all aspects of school life leaves a bit to be desired and she can be an ill-mannered child.' That's not me! I feel furious in my own defence. I was always a well-mannered girl; I bent over backwards to be a well-mannered girl. I'm frowning really hard reading the rest of the report and then I see it's not mine, it's Bel Lavender's report. How did this get in with my stuff? Did Bel give it to me? Maybe she thought it was funny and she gave it to me to keep, or maybe she gave it to me to hide from her mum. I'm confused because wasn't that the year Bel got a prize in the leavers' assembly? I look at the report again; it's not 1984 this one, it's 1983.

I get up; I've got pins and needles from sitting on my bedroom floor for so long. I hear an ambulance outside and then a police car and I go to the window and look out. In the mansion block opposite I can see other people doing the same. It's way past midnight but there are lights on all over the place and figures at windows looking out. I feel so alone, even though the boys are here and Mum is here, I still feel so alone. I turn on my computer and take down a bag of sweets I bought yesterday and hid in my room from Dwaine. On the table by my computer is the head's briefing paper and the card from the child protection officer. Oh my God, I'd forgotten about this, I forgot to even tell Bel about this. Then I hear a ping and I look at my screen; there are six messages in my inbox. Someone is offering me a longer penis; another says my bank account details need to be amended. Then I see it, 'Loreen, you have a message from Mark69!' It's a message from the dating site. That's the man who likes pesto, the man in IT, the man who is looking for a soul mate, the one I added to my favourites. What is he doing sending me a message on a night like tonight?

Chapter Twenty

BEL

Shit, if this new credit card bounces I'm not going to be able to get the flashgun, let alone the digital SLR. Just take it, I will the woman behind the counter at Jessops, just take the card and give me the goods. Glen's taking me with him again and when I asked what equipment you need if you want to be in this game, he said a digital SLR, a couple of lenses, some camera cards, a card reader, and a powerful flash, not a Mickey Mouse one. So that's what I'm doing, standing here in Jessops first thing on a Saturday morning. I've just been to PC World to look at laptops too, but for now Glen's lent me an old one of his. I watch while the Jessops woman packs up the goods. The lens alone is 700 quid. I'm taking a risk, I'm taking a really big risk.

But going out with Glen, the day of the bombs last month, gave me something to do. It made me feel I'd find things out, that I wasn't just sitting around being scared like everyone else. By the time I met up with Loreen that evening I was so hyped I couldn't stay still. I wanted to move on again but she wanted to wait for Ashley and so we did. We sat outside that poncy Soho bar for two hours, Loreen endlessly checking her phone in case there was a message, worrying, convinced something had gone wrong, and Ashley never showed.

In the last month Glen's rung twice on a Saturday morning and I've gone out on a shift with him. All we did the first time was sit in the van. Glen was on a watch, that's what he calls it. So we had coffee, read the papers, had a chat. He plugged in his mini TV and watched the cricket. Nothing happened. We went for lunch, had a trawl round some charity shops. Then it was back in the van. I couldn't believe someone got paid to lounge around like that. The second time Glen called it was more exciting.

'Alright, Bel?' he said, finding me still in bed, still half asleep. 'I'm on Madonna this morning, would you care to join me?'

I sat up, laughed. Loreen used to love Madonna and so did Ashley. They used to love that song 'Like a Virgin' and they used to love the way she wore her bra, like Superman wore his knickers, on top of her clothes instead of underneath. I wasn't doing anything that morning anyway, so I met Glen at Mum's house and he drove us to a gym where a handful of other photographers were already waiting around on the pavement. There were fans too, a group of young girls standing there giggling. We parked and Glen joined the other photographers; he seemed to know them all. Then a sleek black car pulled up and a man in a grey suit and black shades got out. The giggling girls surged forward at once, but the man held out his hands, herded them back a few steps, and obediently they lined themselves up, arms folded, heads peering towards the car, as if royalty were coming. I thought something was going to happen then but the man just returned to the car and stood stiffly by the back door. Then suddenly he opened it and out stepped Madonna. I couldn't help it, I actually felt excited. I saw a flash of a black and white sleeveless top and sinewy arms as she marched from the car and across the pavement. On her head she had a baseball cap, pulled down low, but not too low, I could still see her face. The girls on the pavement began to clap, a couple held out their mobile phones with shaky hands, trying to get a picture, and Glen moved like greased lightning; he seemed to have known the exact moment Madonna would get out, the exact direction she would take across the street and he was right there, several steps in front of her, running backwards taking snaps. It only took Madonna a few seconds to pass the clapping girls and the handful of photographers and disappear down railing-lined steps to a basement and that was it, she was gone.

The photographers relaxed, Glen inspected the snaps he'd taken, and I stood there wishing I had a camera with me too, because I wanted to do what he'd just done. I didn't want to be watching, I wanted to be in there snapping away as well.

'How did you know when she was going to get out the car?' I asked as Glen lit his cigarette.

He shrugged. 'If a car pulls up then it's obvious, isn't it, someone's going to get out, so you just think which door they'll use, and anticipate where they're going to go when they do. That's what this is all about, Bel, anticipating what will happen next.'

'Is that it then?' I asked as a couple of the other photographers strolled off down the road.

'Nah,' said Glen. 'Now we have to wait for her to come

out again. The desk hasn't said to follow her, although they might yet.'

And that's when I asked him, what do you need to be in this game? What would I need if I wanted to be a pap?

Now it's Saturday morning, I have all my new gear and I'm ready to go out with Glen again. I get to Mum's and see him parked at the end of the street in his scruffy white van. If I didn't know better I'd think he was a bit of an elderly man having a read of a paper and drinking Costa coffee. But this is what he does when he's on a watch. Glen sees me in his rear-view mirror and opens the passenger door.

'Morning!' he says. He's eating a McDonald's breakfast burger.

'Hiya.' I get in the van. It's like a nest inside: plastic bags, takeaway cartons, old newspapers, chocolate wrappers, camera bags, giant empty water bottles, a set of steps, faded pouches of tobacco, loose pages from an A to Z, a pair of socks. Glen calls it his living room on wheels. 'What are we on today?' I ask cheekily, as if we always work together like this, but then if Glen takes any snaps, maybe I can too.

'Macca,' says Glen, polishing off the burger. He sees I don't know what he's on about so he says, 'Paul McCartney.'

I nod. I might tease Mum by pretending not to know who certain celebs are but I know who Paul McCartney is. Still, half the people Glen talks about I've never heard of and so since the Madonna job I've started reading the tabloids, the Sunday papers, *OK!* and *Hello!* and anything else Glen leaves in his van or at Mum's. He calls it R&D: research and development. 'Where does he live?' I ask.

174

'St John's Wood. Nice area. Traffic's not too bad, it'll take us less than an hour.'

'What's the story?' I push away at some of the stuff on the floor so I can get my feet down.

'There's no story, darling,' Glen smiles. 'As far as I know. Desk just said, go to Macca's, so I thought you might like to come along, see. I could do with the company, to tell you the truth, Bel. If Macca doesn't work out they'll probably send us to Kate Moss. Her and that nutter Pete Doherty are getting married, *allegedly*.' Glen says this in a tone of mock importance. 'What time is it? Eight? Kate will just have got in from a night out. Won't be a sign of her till at least three o'clock this afternoon. So we might end up just doing the St John's Wood circuit. It's August, darling, silly season, an even sillier season than the normal season at the *Sunday Post*, and most of the people we cover are on their hols now. What it is, darling,' Glen starts the van and looks in his rear-view mirror, 'is there doesn't have to be a story with Macca because Macca is Macca. He's a national treasure. Get a snap of him, make something up about why he's wearing shorts or why he's growing a beard, and there's your story, see. Same with Kate Moss. You can pap her talking on her mobile or eating an ice cream and it will still make edition.'

I laugh and put my seatbelt on. I'm learning things, I'm learning that if you're a snapper then all you want is to make edition.

We drive to St John's Wood and Glen points at the tube station. 'That's the only underground in London that has no letters from the word "mackerel".'

'Really?' I stare at the station as we pass, start thinking of other tube stations and whether they have letters from mackerel. Tottenham Court Road does, so does Gower Street, so does Oxford Circus.

'Mind you,' Glen says. 'There are hundreds of other words that fit the bill too, not just mackerel.'

I look at him and he laughs. He's winding me up.

'Nice area,' he says, slowing down. 'It's always been a desirable area, St John's Wood, one of the first to have villa-style housing, not the usual long terrace buildings.' I sit back and listen; Glen's like a taxi driver, he likes to point out the sights, tell me what he knows. 'Here we are then. Quite a few paps here today.' He parks the van and shows me where Paul McCartney lives. The house is pretty normal-looking for the area, a rather old grand building looming up behind a brick wall, with big double brown wooden doors at the front. Glen nods at a small blue Polo on the other side of the road. '*Express* man, Sam, public school, still wet behind the ears, but a nice bloke. Down there, two guys from the *Mirror* in the Hillman. Strictly speaking, they're not paps, just like we're not paps either, darling, and they won't appreciate it if you call them a pap.' He looks at me so I nod. 'The *Express* man is a staffer, like me. The *Mirror* men are freelancers.' He parks the van and looks around. 'Can't see any journos. But we're going to be here a while, darling. If you ask me this is the hardest part of the job, sitting on your arse for ten hours at a go.'

He hands me last week's *Sunday Post* and I flip through it. I don't really look at the stories; I couldn't care less about who's shagging who, the stories are too silly for anyone to take seriously, but I look at the photos.

176

'Crossword?' asks Glen as he sees me finish with the paper.

I take the book he hands me but I hate crosswords; if I can't get a clue at once then I'm just not interested. I inspect my camera on the seat next to me. Glen has told me to be ready. Never roll up unprepared, he says, get your camera ready, make sure it's got fresh batteries, the card's in, you've got a fast shutter speed and your lens cap's not on. I laughed when he said that because who would be stupid enough not to take a lens cap off? 'Believe me,' said Glen, 'it happens.'

'Why will we be here a while?' I ask.

'If the *Express* and the *Mirror* stay then so do we, darling.' Glen sighs like this is obvious. 'It's Saturday, we all need something for edition tomorrow, so we can't go if those boys are here. But if you ask me, Macca's not even in the area.'

'Are we allowed to just sit outside like this?' I ask.

'Course we are, darling. You can't stop someone taking a photo from a public place and we're not doing anything wrong per se. If you were to try and get in, though, into Macca's house or just through the gate, that would be trespass. Although trespass is still not a criminal offence, at least not in England and Wales,' he nods at me, 'not unless you're a silly bugger and trying to get in to a military base!'

I watch as one of the *Mirror* men gets out of the Hillman and comes over.

'Alright, Glen,' says the man as Glen winds down the window. He's a tall man with a good few days' growth on his chin and a nose that looks like it's been broken more than once.

'Alright, Fred,' says Glen. 'Been here long, mate?'

'Just arrived,' says Fred. 'You doing OK?'

'Yeah, bro, fine.'

I smile at Glen saying 'bro'; he sounds like he's twenty years younger than he is.

'Thanks for that frame the other day,' says Fred looking bashful.

I start fiddling with my camera; Fred hasn't even acknowledged me and I don't know what they're talking about.

'What was he saying?' I ask when Fred goes back to his car.

'We were both on a watch at Jude Law's,' says Glen. 'Law was putting this big fucking fence up. He's an *actor*, you see, Jude Law, not a celebrity, and actors need their privacy.' Glen laughs. 'So our friend Fred wasn't even there, see, he'd nipped off to watch the match in the pub. So when he came back I gave him one of my frames.'

'But aren't you rivals?'

Glen gives his high girl's laugh. 'We look out for each other, darling, we're just the shutter monkeys down at the bottom of the pecking order. We've all got the desk on our back, we're all just trying to make a living, we get paid whether we get a snap or not. At the end of the day that's how it is. One day, who knows, I'll need Fred to do a favour for me. Now, I'm just going to have a bit of a snap, darling; wake me if Macca comes out or if there's a traffic warden about. Traffic wardens,' Glen sighs. 'The bane of my life.'

I turn to put my camera down, but Glen stops me. 'Never put your camera on the back seat, darling, because you won't have time to turn round to get it. By the time you do the shot's gone.'

So I sit there, concentrating, watching Macca's door, my

camera on my lap. I think about my pictures of the bus in Tavistock Square. They're still on my old little digital. I haven't printed them or put them on my Mac, and I haven't deleted them either. I don't know what I'm saving them for, but it's like I can't get rid of them. Glen starts to breathe heavily and then to snore. The double wooden gates to Macca's house open electronically and a man who looks like security or perhaps a bodyguard comes out, waves to the man from the *Express* sitting in his car, and goes back inside. Fred from the *Mirror* gets out of the Hillman and comes back with a paper bag from Starbucks. A group of people who look like tourists congregate outside Macca's house, film it with their camcorders, and eventually move on. I drink some water. Then I'm startled by an urgent tapping on the van window. I wind it down and find a young woman, in her twenties, with jet-black hair and a strikingly beautiful face.

'Excuse me,' she says.

'Yes?' I whisper back. I don't want to wake Glen.

'I would like to know if Paul McCartney lives here?' The woman nods towards Macca's house. I think her accent is Italian. 'I come to London only to see Paul,' she says pleadingly. 'Please, is this his house? It is very important!'

'Yes,' I say, 'this is the one.'

The woman's face floods with excitement. She gives me a quick thumbs-up and hurries over to the house. I watch while she stops a man walking by on the pavement and asks him to take a picture of her standing there alone in front of the big double doors of Macca's house. How sad is that, I think, as I watch the woman leave. I flick through Glen's crossword book. Drink some more water. It's late afternoon and nothing has happened. Then Glen's phone rings and he wakes up.

'Hello? Alright, mate, yeah yeah, good one.' Glen laughs. 'Oh, OK.' He puts the phone down.

'What is it?'

'That was the desk, Macca's in the States. Silly buggers, they've only just found out. "Stand down, Glen." That's what this plank Ray on the desk says. "Stand down", like we're on military manoeuvres! "Stand down!" I haven't even stood up yet, mate.' Glen takes a pouch of tobacco from the glove compartment and separates a rizla from the packet. 'The desk wants a GV of the house before we leave.'

'A what?' I watch him roll his cigarette. He does it gently, licking with the very tip of his tongue, smoothing down the cigarette with real appreciation. Then he lights it.

'A GV, a general view. They're only asking for it to make sure we're here. You take it, Bel, just do it from the car because you can't see anything of the house from outside anyway, not without steps. And you wouldn't put steps up outside Macca's house in case security decides to *accidentally* walk into them.'

'Why would they do that?'

'To knock you off, darling! Because you'd be a cheeky fucker putting steps up outside Macca's house, wouldn't you? Take a GV, Bel, then they want us on Ant and Dec.'

'Who?' I feel a bit of a thrill that Glen has said 'us', like I'm his partner in crime.

'Those planks on TV, Ant and Dec, the Geordie double act. They must be on the piss or something. So it's a schlep

180

down the Thames for us, darling. Be dark by the time we get there and with any luck they'll call us off,' Glen laughs. We watch the *Express* man drive off and the car belonging to the *Mirror* men follow. 'Guess they got a call from their desks too,' says Glen.

I look out the window at Macca's house. I feel like I know it really well after sitting outside it all day, it almost feels like it's mine. I pick up my camera, ready to take the GV, when the electronic gates open and a blonde woman comes out. 'Who's that?' I ask as the woman stands on the pavement and looks around, like she's looking for something or someone. She's wearing white trousers that are so long the ends drag on the ground and she's holding a smart handbag like it's a shield.

'It's the Mrs!' says Glen. 'Fuck, Heather Mills, snap her. Through the window, quick.'

The window is the only clean part of Glen's van; he keeps glass spray in the glove compartment and I've seen him cleaning the window several times a day. I hold up my camera and snap quickly. Shit, this camera is good. The focus comes instantly and silently and the moment I press the shutter it fires away, five frames a second. I can see Heather Mills in the viewfinder as clear as anything; with a camera like this I can capture every expression, every slight change on her face.

'Jesus Christ,' says Glen, tapping on the steering wheel with both hands. 'That fucking nutcase is here. Him, see the fella with the beanie hat on running up the road there? What's he doing? Is he crazy?'

I turn and watch a giant-sized man with hunched shoulders come lumbering down the road. Something about him makes me think of a train spotter. The lens hanging round his neck is so long it's like he's running with a dildo.

'He's having a laugh,' says Glen. 'What's he going to do, jump on her back? He's on a long lens, he won't get her with that anyway.' The moment Glen says this a car drives out through Macca's gates and Heather Mills jumps in and the car speeds off.

'Is he a pap?' I ask, watching the lumbering man left stranded on the pavement.

'Thinks he is,' says Glen. 'Don't know anyone who will hire him, though. He's worked for the agencies and got fired. I've heard of him going into schools, for Christ's sake, and taking snaps of kids! He's two frames short of a roll if you ask me.'

'She was looking a bit glum,' I say. 'Even before that bloke went after her.'

'Yeah, you're right. Wonder what's up, why's she here when Macca isn't? If Macca's in the States, how come she's here?'

I chew my cheek, thinking about this. Then I laugh, I can't believe I'm wondering why Heather Mills is not in the States with Paul McCartney. Like I care. Like I even know them.

'We'll wait here a while,' says Glen, 'make sure none of the others come back. If the plot is clear and they don't come back and the Mrs doesn't come back either then we've got an exclusive.' Glen smiles, starts rolling another cigarette. 'She usually loves attention, Heather Mills,' he muses. 'Yeah, she's usually only too happy to be papped. That's what some people crave, you know, darling. Oh they want it on the way up, can't wait for some snapper to notice

182

them. Then something goes wrong, they get caught playing away or with some drug up their nose, and then it's all, "Where's my *privacy*? This is an invasion of privacy!" But on the way up, well, the paps are their best friends, see, because that's all some people want, darling, fame.' Glen starts laughing.

'What?' I ask.

'You remember that muppet of a singer Jay B?' asks Glen, still laughing.

'Yeah,' I say with a stab of something odd, like something is where it shouldn't be, like something feels out of place. First Jodie in the office was listening to Jay B on the radio. Now Glen's talking about him. I thought he went out of style years ago.

'I was at this nightclub,' says Glen, 'this was years ago, he'd just broken up with his girlfriend, can't remember her name . . .'

I nod. I'm not going to say her name because maybe it's not Ashley; maybe he's talking about someone else.

'So he comes out the nightclub,' says Glen, 'nicely wasted, and stands on the steps having a chat. Four in the morning, me, the *Mirror*, couple of agency monkeys. He's posing away, drunk as a fucker. Then he suddenly goes barmy, starts throwing punches, man from the *Express* gets it right in the eye, so we all wade in to pap him before the police turn up. Then he's standing there, this Jay B, blood pouring down his face, yelling at us, "You're all living in poverty!" and the *Mirror* man turns to him and he goes, "Not after these pics, you ugly fucker!"' Glen chuckles.

I smile too because Jay B was an ugly fucker. I don't know

what Ashley ever saw in him. 'I know someone who went out with Jay B,' I tell Glen.

'Wooah!' He puts his hands up. 'Don't tell me, I don't want to know.'

'Oh.' I'm a bit put out. I think it's funny Ashley went out with Jay B and I want to tell Glen about it.

'If the desk even *thinks* I know someone who knows . . . well, they'll be on my case. So you know anyone famous, I'd rather not know.'

'OK,' I say. Ashley isn't famous anyway. But I wonder if she's going out with anyone now. If she'd turned up at the bar that night of the bombs I might have found out because Loreen would have asked her, but then of course she couldn't be bothered.

'You did a good job just then with Heather Mills,' says Glen. 'You're a fast mover. You'll be better than me!'

I don't know whether to take this as a compliment or not because he's laughing again. 'Good job she didn't have the little one with her, though.'

'Why?'

'Don't snap kids, darling, not if the celeb hasn't given the go ahead. Sometimes they do, sometimes they love trotting the kiddies out and having family snaps taken or selling an exclusive to *Hello!*. But otherwise, if they have a kid, leave well alone. That's my morals, darling. Some paps will do it, there's money in it, but not me. The parent might want fame but the children haven't asked for it, have they? They can't help it if their mum or dad is a celeb. Some papers will publish kiddies, others will pixelate them out.'

'Why's that?'

'Well if it's Beckham's kids, say, then they won't show the faces because they could be targeted, for kidnapping or what have you. Right,' says Glen, 'the plot is clear.' He starts the van and pulls away from Macca's house, then he stops in a side street, gets out his laptop and uploads my pictures. 'You'll have to learn how to send snaps, Bel, if you want to get into this game, because it's a job in itself. The FTP software's still working on that laptop I lent you, so you can use that. Have a play with the Photoshop as well. In the old days getting a snap to the desk was easier in a way, a courier would pull up, collect the can and that would be my job done. Now I've got to download these snaps, edit them, send them in and make sure they're all captioned. You know what some paps used to do? Develop their snaps in the boot of their car, then run the film through a drum scanner.' We wait until my pictures appear on Glen's laptop and then he goes through them, singling out a handful, cropping them, adjusting the contrast. 'This is a good one.' He points at one of my close-ups of Heather Mills. Her face is twisted a little, her neck is going one way and her face the other and she has an odd expression on her lips. It could be a smile, it could be a snarl, it's hard to tell.

'I don't think it's that good,' I say.

'Oh it's not *good*,' Glen laughs, 'but it's got that snatched feeling and you could go with all sorts of headlines with a snap like this. Is she happy? Angry? Sad? Dejected? Is she beautiful? Is she a nutcase? Why's she looking like this?' Glen picks up his phone, starts searching for a number. 'Right, as far as the desk is concerned we're not on Macca, darling, we're on Ant and Dec. So these snaps, Bel, were not taken by

185

you, or me, because we weren't there, are you with me? We were pulled off that job; we're on Ant and Dec now, so I'm not letting the desk have these. What I'm going to do is . . .' Glen finds the number he wants and I hear the phone ringing, '. . . see if an agency wants these. If Macca's marriage is on the rocks, like the journos have been saying, then they might be interested.'

Chapter Twenty-One

I'm sitting on the sofa eating Cheerios dry from a bowl because I've run out of milk. My housemates aren't here, I've got the front room to myself, and I'm watching our new TV as part of research and development. I bought it with the money Glen gave me for my snap of Heather Mills. Four hundred quid! That's what the agency paid. Not bad for holding a camera for less than a minute. It's Tuesday morning and the last thing I want to do is go to the office. I've rung in sick so many times recently they're getting used to it now. The window is wide open, it's going to be another warm September day and I want to be out there, doing something. Then my phone rings.

'Alright, Bel?' says Glen. 'I've got a court job at the Old Bailey this morning, you interested?'

'Definitely!' I say, putting down the Cheerios. 'What's the job?'

'The Jones gang,' says Glen. 'Remember them? The gang that beat that little ten-year-old boy to death last New Year's Eve. They said he'd disrespected them, so they set on him with a bicycle chain. There were twelve of them, the poor boy was only going to the shops for his mum when . . .'

'OK,' I say quickly, because I don't want to hear any more. I remember this, I remember Loreen talking about it because the boy was about the same age as her son Anthony.

'It's been a three-month trial,' says Glen. 'With any luck they'll be convicted today. And two of them aren't underage any more, so we can snap them now. My van's at the garage this morning, darling, and I've got to go and pick it up, but if you want you can catch the tube to St Paul's and meet me there.'

'Will do,' I say, standing up. Maybe today's the day I can take and sell another snap, maybe one day I could make edition, have my name in the paper, maybe even do this for a living. But first I have to prove myself to Glen.

I sit down again. It's still early, I don't need to leave for an hour or so. I pick up yesterday's *Evening Standard* and the *Metro*, flick through them, keeping an eye on the TV. I'm beginning to look at things differently now. I pay attention when there's a celeb in the paper, I follow what they're up to. I look at all the snaps to see which ones are used, I note every byline. When I'm out I've even begun looking for famous faces too, just in case. I can't believe people pay good money for a snap of someone like Heather Mills doing nothing. But if they pay me, I won't complain.

The phone rings.

'Hi hon! It's Loreen!'

'Hi Loreen.' I pick up my bowl again, pop a couple of Cheerios into my mouth. 'What's up?'

'Nothing, nothing, just fancied a chat.'

I look at the TV, see what time it is. 'Aren't you at school?'

'Oh the boys have just gone back but I've got an inset.'

'A what?'

'An inset, you know, a training day, the school's closed to the kids but we still have to come in, but I've got a bit of a cold so I'm just lying here in front of the telly.' Loreen sniffs. 'Oh it's that idiot,' she says.

'What idiot?'

'The one on the telly right now. Oh, I forgot you don't have a telly.'

'I do now,' I tell Loreen.

'Really?' She sounds shocked. 'Why?'

'What channel is he on?' I ask. I don't want to answer the question about why I have a TV because I can't tell her about Glen and the *Sunday Post* yet. It might not work out, it's not like I have a new job, all I've done is sell one snap. If I tell Loreen now it might all fall apart.

'I'm watching BBC1,' says Loreen.

I switch to BBC1 and see a newsman on a red settee. He's got his head turned to one side, talking to a man whose face is up on a screen with Big Ben in the background. The man on the screen has the face of a hamster. When he opens his mouth his chin sinks down into his shirt collar, which is so white and so sharp it looks like he's being strangled. I wonder what's got Loreen so upset about hamster face. I keep staring at him; his lips remind me of someone's, they remind me of Dad.

'Who is he?' I ask.

'Oh, every time I see him he's going on about single parents, he's some home affairs minister, and he's always going on about how we're eroding away the moral backbone of society.'

'Ha!' I say, popping more Cheerios into my mouth. I don't really have any opinions about single parents but Loreen does, obviously, because she is one. 'What a plank,' I say.

'What a what?' Loreen giggles.

189

'A plank, you know, a tosser.'

Loreen giggles again. 'I didn't tell you, I've joined a dating site!'

'Really?' Shit, I think, here we go again. You would have thought Loreen had learnt her lesson. She's always been doing these things. It started with the pen-pal section in the girly magazines she used to read, then the lonely-heart columns in newspapers, which is how she met the boys' father. You would have thought that would have put her off, but at one stage she even joined a dating agency. Now she's obviously gone online.

'You should do it too, Bel.'

'No thanks.' The Cheerios feel like wet sand in my mouth. 'So,' I sigh, because I know she wants me to ask, 'have you met anyone?'

'Not yet, no,' she says, and I can tell she's smiling, 'but there's this one man, Mark, who's been emailing me for a few weeks. He's called Mark, did I just tell you? He seems really lovely.'

I grunt. Loreen thinks every man seems really lovely.

'I could do it for you too.'

'No thanks.'

'Oh come on, Bel. I could do a profile for you and put on a photo and weed out the replies and . . .'

'Anyway,' I interrupt, 'how are you feeling? You must be bad if you're not at work.'

'And why aren't you at work?' Loreen sniffs.

'I am,' I say brightly, like I'm heading off to the office. 'I'm just on my way.'

*

190

I get the tube to St Paul's and it's a couple of minutes' walk to the Old Bailey. I've heard about the Old Bailey, I know its name, but I've never been here before. I stop, impressed by the Gothic way the building rises up before me. I'd like to take some snaps; I'd like to get it really monumentalised against a thunderstorm sky. I look up at a golden statue of a woman balanced impossibly on top of the dome of the building. I can just make out she has a sword in one hand and a pair of scales in another. What's that supposed to mean? It must be something to do with fighting for justice. I'll ask Glen. He knows everything; he seems to know about every building in London.

But I can't see Glen. I can just see a whole scrum of paps standing behind a metal barrier set about five yards from the court's front doors. They're all men, all beefy-looking. It's hot now but half of them have anoraks on. They see me heading their way, one even puts his camera up, but then he puts it down again. I still can't see Glen. I walk nearer, they're watching me, they can see I'm heading towards the barrier and I can see there's no other woman back there.

'Morning,' I say, my camera bag swinging from my shoulder. I've got a holster bag today, Glen lent it to me so I can get the camera out faster than if it's on my back in a rucksack.

Two of the men nod, look at me with a mixture of suspicion and derision. I know what they're thinking: who's this silly little girl?

'I'm with Glen,' I say. 'From the *Sunday Post*.'

One of the men laughs. 'Oh, the *Sunday Poke*,' he says.

'And you?' I ask.

'*News of the World*,' says the man, and the others start

laughing at him now. 'Where's Glen then?' he asks, smiling in defeat.

'He's on his way,' I say, walking around the barrier to join the paps.

'Yeah, having a snap in his van more likely,' says the man. 'Room in there for both of you, is there, love?'

I want to tell him to fuck off but I suppress it. 'Yeah,' I smile, 'but the gear stick can get in the way.'

All the men laugh. 'Nick,' says one of the men, shaking my hand. 'I'm with the *Mirror*.'

'Ben,' says another man. 'From Getty.' He has a round bald head and, when I look down, the shiniest shoes I've seen in my life.

'Bit hot, isn't it?' I ask. I look around, there must be a café somewhere. 'I'll get the tea then, shall I?'

The men get animated.

'Tea, one sugar, love,' says Nick from the *Mirror*.

'Coffee, black,' says Ben from Getty.

'Nice and milky for me, love, with lots of sugar,' says the man from *News of the World*. 'And a bacon buttie wouldn't go amiss.'

I head off to find a café. If Glen's not here then I must be early and nothing must be happening yet and I won't miss a thing. Dealing with pap men is like dealing with my brothers, I think, as I spot a café nearby. Make a joke, don't take any shit, don't take any offence because they'll know they've got to you, and offer them something to put down their throat or in their belly.

I come back and join the paps behind the barrier outside the court. They're talking about a new SLR that does ten frames a second and can send snaps wirelessly straight to your laptop. Then I see the crazy man with the beanie hat we saw outside Macca's house the other week, the one who ran after Heather Mills. He's trying to barge his way to the front of the barrier but no one's allowing him to make any headway.

'He wants to watch himself,' says one of the paps. 'He gives this game a bad name, people like him.'

'Otherwise we'd all have an excellent reputation,' says a tall man just to my right. 'Paparazzi, the men the public love to love, right?' The man has only just joined us and now he tips an imaginary hat and says, 'Morning, gentlemen.'

The paps laugh. They seem to be looking at the tall man with some admiration, even making room for him a little. 'All right, Jimmy,' says one. 'Things a bit quiet at the *quality* papers today? Forced to join the plebeians for the morning?'

I turn and study Jimmy with interest. He must be from a broadsheet and I haven't seen a snapper from a broadsheet yet. I don't think there were any broadsheet snappers when we were at Madonna's gym or at Macca's house. He's wearing a white shirt, unbuttoned to show a tanned neck, and his camera bag looks brand new. Then I look at his face and see how good-looking he is, late thirties, bright blue eyes, full bottom lip, an artful spread of hair around the chin.

But I can't study him any more because, to my left, the court doors are suddenly flung open. I catch a split-second glimpse of a young man coming out in a blue shirt, walking cockily, looking very pleased with himself. He must have been let off, I think; if he's been convicted then would he walk out the court door like this? But he's not prepared for the paps out here and as he catches sight of all the cameras his bravado disappears. He holds his hand up next to his cheek, shielding his face from the cameras. The pack of paps closes in, hard against the barrier, and the young man is obscured from view. I can't see a thing. A moment ago the paps were talking to me, now they've closed ranks and there's no way I can get in there.

'Excuse me,' I say to the men in front but there's no response. I try squeezing myself between them, but it's impossible, they won't let me in. I look around, feeling desperate. If I can't take a snap from here then where can I take one from? In a panic I run away from the barrier and out into the road; maybe I can get a shot from the other side where no one else is. I'm halfway across the road when something makes me glance to my left. A police van with blacked-out windows comes tearing out of the side doors next to the court. I don't even have time to think, the moment the van gets caught up in traffic, I just hurl myself towards it, put the flash on double power, flick to manual focusing. Then I hold my camera up as high as I can and start snapping. A minute or two later the van has passed me and is disappearing down the road and I'm left standing here, fingers trembling.

'Did you get anything?' asks the broadsheet man. He's crossed the road along with four or five other paps and he's standing right next to me. 'I'm Jimmy, by the way,' he says, holding out his hand.

'Bel,' I say, offering mine. I want to talk to him but even more than that I want to see what I've got, and as I look at the snaps I've just taken I can't help it, I'm beaming from ear to ear. I've got them. I've managed to snap two young men sitting in the back of the van and they must be the Jones gang men, the ones that have just been sent down. The window was blacked out so I couldn't see what I was doing, if anyone was even in there, but my flash was on double power and I've got a snap. The men are sitting close to each other and their heads are held back because they're laughing. They're sitting in a police van on the way to prison and they're having a laugh, these young men who murdered a ten-year-old boy.

'Wow,' says Jimmy, looking over my shoulder. 'You were lucky. Are you with an agency? I don't think we've met before . . .'

'I'm with Glen,' I say, 'from the *Sunday Post*.' I look up from my camera; Jimmy is staring at me and I get a flash of blue eyes that seem to go right through me. It unnerves me, the feeling I get from his eyes, so I busy myself putting my camera over my shoulder, looking away.

Broadsheet Jimmy laughs. 'Oh, the *Sunday Post*! I know Glen quite well actually. He's helped me out more than once, especially in the early days. You were lucky there,' Jimmy repeats and looks back at the court building, 'they could have had you for that.'

I shrug like it's nothing to me, but I don't know what I just did and why I was lucky.

'I spent six months doing criminals at the Old Bailey once,' says Jimmy. 'It's not the easiest place to work.'

'I'm new,' I say. 'I'm not even a pap. I just hang around with Glen.'

'Oh, right,' says Jimmy.

'So,' I say, because he seems disinterested now and I want his attention, I want his blue eyes focusing on me. 'So, you used to take snaps in court?'

'Not *in* court,' says Jimmy slowly, like he might be thinking of smiling at me, 'because that would be illegal.'

'OK,' I say, nodding like I know this. 'So, what, you took them outside court?'

'Not quite, because that could be illegal too.' Jimmy smiles now and gestures to the court building again. 'That's why we're all herded behind that barrier, which is where you should have been. Not only can't you take a photograph in court or *outside* court, you're not supposed to take any in the court precincts either, but as to where the precincts of the court actually are, that's open to debate.' Jimmy ruffles his hand through his hair. 'They'll often turn a blind eye anyway, because it's less hassle for them that way. Anyway, that's me done for the day, I was only covering for someone else. If you fancy a cup of tea, I only live in Holborn.'

Jimmy takes an expensive-looking soft blue wallet out of his pocket and flips through a wad of cards, then he hands me one with his name and address.

I'm about to say yes. He's good-looking, he's available, he's asking me for tea, and how many months have I been without sex? Maybe Loreen has a point, maybe I should let her find me a date, and I'm about to say yes to Jimmy, yes I would fancy a cup of tea, when I get a slap on my shoulder.

'Bel,' says Glen. He's just arrived and he's just slapped me on the shoulder like I'm one of the boys, and now he's here I am one of the boys.

'I got them,' I say. 'I got two of the gang in the van.'

196

'You did?' Glen looks surprised. 'Anyone else get a shot in the van?'

I shake my head.

'Nice work. If the desk knew I'd got here late they wouldn't be happy. They don't want to know about a broken-down old van, they don't want excuses, they just want someone on the job. Nice work, Bel. Let's go and have a proper look at the snaps.'

I wave to Broadsheet Jimmy and, just as I turn my head away, I see him giving me a wink.

Chapter Twenty-Two

KAREN

I wonder, if I saw Ashley's picture in the newspaper and I didn't know her, what would I think of her? Because that's what I appear to be looking at now, a goddam picture of Ashley in the paper! I'm standing in a store on Green Lanes with a whole bunch of people; waiting at the little one-man checkout, holding the *Guardian* because that's the paper I used to read as a student, when I see the guy in front of me reading the *Sun*. He has the paper held right open in his face so that I'm looking straight at a photograph of a woman with a white Alice band in her hair. And I'm thinking how funny that is because that was what Ashley used to wear, when we were at primary school she used to wear a white Alice band in her hair, and it's funny because all the way to this store I've been thinking about her. I've been in London two months now; I've spoken to Bel and to Loreen a whole bunch of times, but not to Ashley, and even Loreen doesn't seem to know what she's up to these days.

The photograph isn't clear, it looks like it's been taken from a long way off, and all I can make out is a man and a woman sitting on a park bench. He appears to be saying something into her ear and she appears to be laughing and the headline says, 'Donny Green's new squeeze?' I don't want the guy in the checkout line in front of me to think I'm a freak, but I move even closer and peer at the photograph. The paper wants to know if any readers know who the woman is and I could swear it's Ashley. Could it be her?

I duck out of the checkout line, get myself a copy of the *Sun* and queue up again, and all the time I'm thinking, who the hell is Donny Green and why does the paper want to know who he's with? I'm still standing here, waiting to pay, looking at a rack of magazines up against the wall, when I realise this guy is all over the place. This Donny Green in the paper I'm holding is the same guy on the cover of all those magazines up there. I go over to one, open it, and see page after page of Donny Green. Then the checkout guy coughs and I look up; he's got his eyebrows raised like he wants to know whether I'm going to pay for this magazine or not. I close it, a little embarrassed, and come up to the counter and I'm about to pay for my papers when I see a row of biscuits on a shelf behind the counter and, in the middle, a packet of digestives and I'd forgotten how much I loved digestives. 'Can I get a packet of digestives?' I ask the checkout guy, and the moment I say this I can hear it's all wrong. I should have said, 'Can I have . . .? Do you have . . .?' 'Can I get . . .?' sounds out of place. In California it sounds polite, here it sounds like I'm ordering someone around. And I can hear the way my voice goes up at the end of a sentence and I know people think I'm American. I have to relearn everything, relearn London and relearn how to speak. The first time someone said to me, 'Alright?', the first day I took a bus to the British Library, I was thrown for a moment. Did I not look alright; did I look as if something was wrong with me?

'And a bottle of squash,' I say to the checkout guy, because I've just seen some bottles at the end of the shelf. I've always hated squash, I used to have to force myself to drink it at Loreen's house, but I buy a bottle because if Stella saw such a thing she would laugh. Stella would say, what sort of name for something is *squash*?

'Thanks,' I say to the checkout guy, and I have to bite my tongue not to say, 'Have a nice day.' I can't remember the way I used to talk, but maybe when I see Bel and the others next weekend I will. I turn off Green Lanes and onto my street; this area is all new to me, but a contact at UC Davis got me the apartment for the next twelve months so I've been trying to get to know it. The atmosphere in London is quieter than I remembered or expected, and less crowded with tourists because of the bombs the day I arrived. I've hardly seen any Americans at all, but yesterday I saw a young woman selling roses by the overground station and I thought of Willa Cather and her *roses of London town, red till the summer is done.*

I've read that Green Lanes is the longest street in London. It used to be a route to drive cattle to Smithfield Market; now it's a road of jewellery and food stores, and some of the food I don't even know because there's not much Turkish food in my part of California. In the window of one diner I've seen a woman making what looks like paper-thin pancakes, crouched down in front of the glass. I don't know if seeing a woman crouched in the window working away like this is supposed to bring people in, and I sure hope not because she looked hot and exhausted and like she needed a break. I pass the fish shop near my road and I smell disinfectant through the open door, and then I pass one of the guys from the fish shop out on the street in heated discussion with another guy who is selling DVDs from under his jacket. The fish shop man in his white apron smiles leerily as a young woman passes by.

London feels very bricked up compared with California and no one says 'hi!' on the street. In the British Library, where I go most days, it's real quiet because people take their reading seriously over here. You can't even get into their reading room until you've proved who you are. I can't stay away from the place, I can't stay away from a place that describes itself as the world's knowledge, that has 150 million items, that adds three million new ones a year. When I'm at the British Library I feel like I'm at an all-you-can-eat buffet.

My street is long and curved and it seems to take an age getting to number 70. There are three apartments in the house I'm staying in and two of them are empty, or at least I haven't seen or heard any signs of life. I'm beginning to feel isolated here, a semi-Yank in London.

Just as I get to my house I see a removal van stopping outside and a woman in a white boiler suit and red hennaed hair jumps out from the back, followed by a huge strong-armed man in green overalls and then two kids. I watch as the woman unlocks the front door of number 70 and wedges the door open with a box and then everyone troops in with their things. So it's a family moving in, it will be nice having a family upstairs. I like having kids around; I like talking with them and then handing them back to their parents. I would never have wanted to be a parent myself. Loreen is a mother now, she's sent me plenty of pictures of her boys Anthony and Dwaine over the years, but I can't get my head around Ashley being a mother as well. There is a whole section of her life I know nothing about because I've been away and out of touch for so long. When I left England Ashley was a single woman going to university to study design; now I come back and she's a divorced mom of two. The woman in the photograph in the *Sun* laughing with the man in the park doesn't look like she has two kids at home, but then I guess it's not Ashley in the paper anyway because what would she be doing with this Donny Green guy, and I feel crazy for even buying it now.

I hear the woman in the boiler suit shouting at the driver. She's making a joke and the big guy with her laughs, then she gets busy removing more boxes and crates from the van. She looks arty, maybe she's a sculptor or a painter and that's why she's wearing a boiler suit. 'I'll take that,' says the guy with her. 'You need to mind your back.' The woman hesitates, I can see she doesn't want help, she wants to take the box in herself, but then she nods and puts it down. One of the kids, a short black-haired boy, says something to her and she laughs and ruffles his head.

'Hi!' I say, getting to my front door just as the woman is coming out again.

'Oops! Sorry!' she says, and she flattens herself against the hallway wall so I can get by, but then the big guy comes in behind me with a picture frame and he doesn't seem to realise I'm here and I stand for a moment totally wedged between them. The guy's face is close to mine and although he's smiling a little there is something about his face my body

202

doesn't like because I can feel my chest flutter as if I'm in a plane that has just hit turbulence. He's got a long, thin nose and there's sweat on his forehead.

'That's OK,' I say. 'I'm Karen, I live downstairs.'

The couple look appalled that I have said my name and I think, hell, I've done it again, because people in England don't go around introducing themselves like this. I wait for a response but then I realise they're not going to give me their names, because they think that giving their names to a stranger is a too goddam intimate thing to do! I squeeze past them to get to my front door and they seem relieved. I watch as the big guy walks up the stairs with the picture frame and when he gets to the landing he's so tall he has to hunch down his shoulders and duck his head so that for a moment it looks like he's using his body as a battering ram.

I get into my apartment just as the phone rings and I think, what time is it in California? Please let it be Stella, please. It's too empty in this flat and the phone echoes and I feel empty and echoey too. Only my books are here, the ones I had to ship over, the poems of my poets who came to England, my Sylvia Plath, my Elizabeth Bishop, my Willa Cather, my HD. Nothing really is in its place yet, only my books. I rush for the phone but it's an automated voice saying I've won a prize and I listen for a while and then hang up. From the apartment upstairs I can hear the bang of a door, water in a pipe as someone turns on a tap, a young voice calling out in laughter.

The phone rings again and again I rush for it. 'Hello?'

'Karen.' It's my mom. She's supposed to be on her way to see me, I got brunch all prepared before I went out, I was going to make an omelette with home fries on the side, but I know immediately what she's going to say, she's going to say she isn't coming round after all. 'I'm dying to see your place,' she says.

'Good,' I say, because although I've been to see her a bunch of times she hasn't managed to visit me once since I've come over from California.

'It's just that your sister . . .'

'What?'

'Don't be like that,' says Mom.

'Like what?'

'Your sister has a bit of a crisis.'

'Freaky,' I say. 'That doesn't sound like Romana.'

'So I can't come,' she says.

'That's just fine. I'm really busy anyway,' I say, and I hang up the phone and as I do I wonder, does my mom know what she's doing when she does this to me? She just keeps on doing this to me because, as far back as I can remember, Romana has always come first, and I wonder, if my sister hadn't been born premature, if she had waited, like me, until she was fully grown before bursting into the world, then would our mother have been so overprotective of her? But Romana came early, early and by caesarean, and she was tugged from our mother's stomach with her arms raised high in protest and she's still protesting now.

Romana was the weak one, that is what our mom always said. Only she wasn't; she was weak at birth and for a few weeks that followed and she didn't feed properly and she lost weight and our mother fussed and worried, and even our father must have worried too, but that was in the beginning. After that, my little sister was fitter than me.

Yet I was the strong one, that's what our mother always said, the one who could withstand anything. That was why I always had to take second place. There couldn't be two girls in the family who screamed like Romana, who demanded like Romana, who threw tantrums that rattled the plaster off the wall; one of us had to back down and that one was me.

My sister's premature birth and the fact that in my mom's eyes she always came first explains why, of all my friends, I was the one who had to get away, because if I'd stayed at home I would have continued, for ever more, being in second place. I look at the phone and I will it to ring again, and this time for it to be Stella. I'll wait a while and if she doesn't call I'll go swim. What is she doing now back home? I picture her in her Davis kitchen standing at the window looking out across her yard, and I picture myself coming up behind her and my hands cupping themselves around her body. I hear the sound of a radio from upstairs and it's a song that Stella loves, a song about walking away from a lover and pretending not to care.

That day of the end-of-quarter potluck at Professor Greer's house I knew I'd fallen for Stella; what I didn't know was if she'd fallen for me. And I wondered what she saw in Nick Givenchy, what purpose he could serve in her life. Perhaps, I thought, they had married young, perhaps she knew what a terrible mistake she had made and now, for some reason, she couldn't leave him. Perhaps she was indebted to him in some way. Perhaps, I thought a little guiltily, he was rich and she needed his money.

I didn't see Stella again until classes convened the next

quarter, but then I walked into the faculty meeting and found her sitting in the chair that was usually mine. I hesitated for a moment, and then when she waved and patted the chair next to her I headed straight over. The room looked as it always did, thin white drapes at the window, fresh coffee on the table in the corner, a basket of donuts Macey Bloom had brought along to share. Professor Greer opened the meeting, he apologised that Annie, the principal department secretary, had had to rush home because her kid was sick so she wouldn't be able to take the minutes.

'Well I vote Karen takes the minutes then,' said Bill Turnbill, an East Coast man who got away with doing as little as possible and who forever had an unlit pipe in his mouth, unlit because no faculty member at Davis would have been crazy enough to smoke on campus.

'I don't think so,' I said, feeling bold because Stella was there and because Bill Turnbill knew as well as I did that Professor Greer would never get an assistant professor like me to take the minutes, because what if I went and put down something a tenured prof said and got in trouble?

'And I don't think so either,' said Professor Greer with a smile, and Bill sucked on his pipe and stared at me in distaste.

'Bozo,' said Stella next to me, and for a wild moment I wanted to laugh. I didn't think Bill Turnbill had heard her, and I didn't think he would even think she was referring to him if he had, and this made it even funnier. I coughed, to hide the laugh that I thought was coming, and my colleagues looked at me, as if seeing me for the first time, as if they weren't looking at Karen, the one who always came on time, who always dressed and behaved appropriately, who always took on the thankless menial jobs like representing the department at the Academic Senate or being put in charge of the Placement Committee. Instead they looked at me as if I was someone else entirely. The only person not looking surprised in that room was Macey Bloom. She was smiling at me from where she sat in the corner eating a chocolate-covered donut, because Macey Bloom had said I would love our new staff member Stella Givenchy and she was right.

That afternoon I helped Stella move into her office and I carried up her things, making several trips down to the SUV she had parked outside, and on the last trip I came into her office to find she had opened a tin of paint and was dipping a roller in a tray of orange.

'What do you think?' she said, taking the roller still dripping with paint and slapping it straight on the middle of the faded white wall.

'I like it,' I said, but my voice trembled slightly because my head was saying, but that's against the rules! How could Stella Givenchy turn up here on the first day in her new office and paint the walls? And paint them goddam orange! But I stopped myself from saying that the administration wouldn't like it, that the janitor would be sure to notice it this evening, that it wouldn't be long before a maintenance worker was sent round to paint it back to white again, because I didn't want Stella to know how anxious I was. Instead I stood back and watched her and she did it so boldly, she hadn't tested a small corner first, she hadn't thought about whether or not an office painted all in bright orange would work, she'd just gone ahead and tried it out. And the smell of the paint in that small office room made me dizzy, and so did Stella when she came and stood next to me, so close our elbows were touching, when she stopped at last to survey her work.

'Jesus Christ, Prof,' said a man's voice, and I didn't have to turn to know that Nick Givenchy was there. 'Your students are going to need shades when they come see you.'

Stella smiled at her husband but it was a tight smile, a smile that said, 'I am aware you are here and I will be tolerating you, but not for too long.' Then I made myself busy helping Stella unpack her books and I thought that I could not wait until we knew each other better so that this day, the day she painted her office orange, would be a day we could say, 'Remember when . . .?', the way that lovers do.

What is it with swimming pools in London, what the hell have they done with them? When I was a teenager we swam a lot, Bel and me and the others. We used to go to Park Road and save our bus fare for the way home and buy chips. This is the first time I've been swimming since I got to London and I don't know the routine any more. I go up to the front desk and wait while three people before me pay to go to the gym, then they walk through double glass doors, through a waiting area with tables, chairs and vending machines, and I see them trotting up metal steps to where the gym must be.

I pay for my swim and go through the doors, down a ramp, past three old hairdryers fixed to the wall, and into the changing room which smells of chlorine and apple shower gel and unflushed toilets. This is how I remembered swimming pools in London: rusty old lockers, some with taped-on handwritten signs saying 'Out of order', slippery wet floors, forgotten hair bands left on cracked wooden benches.

Quickly I change, fix the locker key on the rubber band around my wrist, and head to the pool. But this has changed. I was expecting to get in and swim how I liked; now I see it's all been organised for us. The pool is roped off into three lanes, and at the end of two of them are signs showing which is the fast lane and which is the slow, and a series of arrows to show the direction we should be swimming. I look at the people in the pool in dismay; it's too crowded, the smell of chlorine is overpowering. I thought going to swim would be a way to ease my irritation with Mom and my sister, and a way to clear my head of Stella, and now I'm not so sure.

At the end of one lane, on the side of the pool, I see a young guy limbering up. A pair of blue goggles envelops his eyes and he's wearing tight black Speedo trunks that glisten as he does his stretching exercises. A woman comes up from behind me and I watch as she lowers herself into the lane for slow swimmers and I see her push off. Why has she got into the slow lane when she can move as fast as that, I think, why do so many women pretend to not be as good at something as they actually are? Then I see an elderly man getting into the fast lane and he begins to churn at the water, getting nowhere at all. Then the guy in the Speedo trunks finishes his warm-up and he dives in, into the fast lane too, and he begins to swim and he's doing front crawl like it's his own goddam private lane. This is what Nick Givenchy would do, I think, get his dumb ass body into the fast lane and then churn up the water like it was something that needed a beating, like it didn't matter that anyone else was there. I picture Nick Givenchy drowning.

When I get out of the pool and shower and take off the

tight rubber band that holds my locker key I see that the skin on my wrists is changing. When I bend my wrist towards me and then relax it the skin stays there, gathered in little wavery lines. I wonder when this happened, when my skin started to change like this. I turn my hand over and look at the inside of my fingers and my thumb and I think suddenly of our holiday in Portugal when Loreen got us all to cut our thumbs with the razor and swap blood. It was so like Loreen to want us to promise to all stay together, and I couldn't see the point in it myself but I liked the romance of it and the pact of friendship. I can see us now, the four of us sitting outside Ashley's parents' place in Portugal, so young, so unafraid, so full of anticipation of what might come, and I can see Ashley slicing herself quickly, efficiently, with the razor blade, and I can see the look on Ashley's face as she bent forward to Bel. What was it about the two of them on that holiday?

Chapter Twenty-Three

DUDU

I am sitting in my kitchen on this gentle autumn day, waiting for my kitty cat to seek me out, and as I sit here I am remembering the girls the morning they set off for their holiday in Portugal. I remember it well for they met at our place and I was up and ready long before my little Loreen. I had bought her a new suitcase for her trip which was cleverly compartmentalised inside so that her underwear and her other things would all be separated, and I had even offered to do her packing for her. I was anxious about my little Loreen going abroad, that I wouldn't be there to protect her should she need me, but anxious too that I didn't hold her back from this great English love of independence. It was independent of her to go on holiday on her own, but then again she was going with three friends, one of whom at least was sensible. I trusted Karen; if my little Loreen was with Karen then I didn't worry so much. Bel took risks, but she was daring rather than reckless, whereas Ashley was an unknown quantity, I never quite knew where I stood with Ashley. I knew that other people found her clever, and I knew that other people found her pretty, but as the years had gone by I had begun to find her neither. What she lacked most, I thought, was a sense of loyalty.

Loreen was buried under her duvet that morning and her room had a sunny, musty smell about it. She had painted her walls a bubblegum pink some years before, but now they were covered with posters and I wondered that Loreen was not bothered, as I was, with all these people on her walls staring down at her. There was only one thing on her wall that I approved of and that was a map of the world I had given her one Christmas, for as a child my little Loreen always loved being told where it was in the world her parents came from.

Bel arrived before Loreen was even dressed that morning, which was unusual because Bel was a girl who was usually late. I opened the front door to find her on the step wearing an oversized denim jacket covered in all manner of buttons and safety pins and badges, along with trousers that had seen better days. The girls were on their way to becoming women by then, and they weren't too sure about how to keep up with the changes their bodies were undergoing. Ashley favoured fashions that accentuated the changes, Karen and Bel favoured ones that hid them, and my little Loreen veered from one extreme to the other.

'Hello Bel,' I said, seeing the rucksack on her back, the same rucksack she took to school every day, so it was hard to believe she was setting off to another country for two weeks. 'Come in, Loreen is just getting ready.'

Bel came bounding into the flat, she was very excitable that day; she had dyed her hair, as she was always doing, and it was a strange green colour that morning. I knew this holiday meant a lot to her, for at first her mother had refused to

212

allow her to go. Then, when everyone else had said their daughter could go, Bel's mother had agreed, but only if Bel earned the money for the trip herself. How Bel had managed to do that, I didn't know. I had saved for six months to allow Loreen to go, and she had worked at her Saturday job to earn her spending money, and it had been hard to save for my salary was pitiful and whenever there was a promotion at the hospital I was never the one to get it. But pain is relieved by pain, and to get out of hardship a person has to toil hard. Then Karen arrived, with a smart suitcase on wheels, and a bag over her shoulder that was, of course, to carry her books. She wore a long white shirt that made her look somewhat like a very large ghost, and her straight black hair had been crimped into crinkly strands.

'Hello Karen,' I said. Karen waved to her mother who was standing out on the pavement with her younger daughter, but her mother barely noticed the wave for Karen's sister Romana was fussing. She was a big grown-up girl now, and still she was fussing.

'Why can't I go?' she asked, though it was more of a demand than a question.

'Because it's my holiday,' said Karen. 'Mum, tell her . . .'

'The girls are in Loreen's room,' I said quickly, before Romana had the opportunity to come into the flat as well, and Karen went off to join the girls and at once I heard the sounds of their chattering.

There had been, for months, such quarrelling over who would go to Ashley's parents' house in Portugal. At first Ashley was inviting six girls from their class, then her father had limited it to three, and each week it seemed Ashley had

213

changed her mind over who was going and who was not. There had been at least one night when my little Loreen could barely sleep for worrying about it all; would she be invited, and if she was then would Bel be invited too? I didn't know why Ashley had to change her mind, why she could not have made her choice and then stuck with it, instead of using her parents' holiday home as a prize that she wanted the others to fight for. This is what I mean when I say the girl lacked loyalty.

I thought all along that Ashley would have to invite my little Loreen because they had been friends ever since that first day of primary school, but then again the girls were so changeable that year they turned sixteen. It was a time when my little Loreen seemed to change from day to day; one day she would lie awake worrying about her friends or her exams and want my advice and comfort, and the next day she was a sulky bad-tempered girl who saw me as an adversary. That was how she had been just two days earlier, the day Victor Kudumane, my late husband's eldest brother, arrived out of the blue. I had only met Victor Kudumane a few times, after I first met my husband and before I left for the UK. He was one of six brothers and, aside from my late husband, he was the most successful in what was then a poor family. Coal gives birth to ash, it is said, for a gifted family may produce a misfit, but in the case of my late husband and his brother Victor, ash had given birth to coal, for Loreen's father had excelled in his studies at Fort Hare and his brother Victor had already set up his own small business.

Victor Kudumane called me from the airport, giving me very little warning about his visit, simply saying he was on a business trip to the UK and would arrive shortly. I should have known, I thought then, to expect something because my horoscope for that day had been very clear: *a visitor you haven't seen for a long time will be seeking you out today*. I had such a panic, in those few hours while Victor Kudumane made his way from the airport to our house. I had to clean the flat from top to toe, make myself presentable, and get everything how it should be. There was no one in my family, neither on my side nor on my late husband's side, who had moved to the UK, and I felt I would be taken as a representative, whether I wanted to or not, and so it was important to me that Victor Kudumane saw us at our best.

'Why are you doing that?' Loreen asked, coming back from school to find me on my knees cleaning out the cupboard under the sink. 'Mum, I need a new towel to take on holiday, Ashley says we have to bring our own towels.'

'OK,' I said. 'Your uncle is on his way.'

'So?'

'So?' I sat back on my behind and looked at her.

'You don't want him to think we live in a shit hole.'

'Loreen!' I said, shocked. Where had she learnt to speak like this? In the last few years at secondary school she had been growing sharp and rude and impatient, and I read in my newspapers and magazines that it was because she was a teenager now. Back home in Africa I didn't remember any such thing as a teenager, you were a child or you were an adult, but in England that was how it was, they had a whole social group for the years they called teenage. They had clothes for teenagers, music for teenagers, food and drink for teenagers, and a behaviour that was excused on the grounds that it was teenage behaviour.

'It shows respect,' I told my little Loreen, 'to keep a place clean. Prepare the meat. It's in the bowl on the counter there. Cut it up and get it into the pan, the big one with the lid. Don't you understand, your father's brother is coming!'

'Yuk,' said Loreen, looking on the counter for the meat and finding it, for she had begun to take a dislike to meat and to object to the idea of animals being killed. 'What is it?' she asked.

'Goat,' I said, standing up, my work in the cupboard done. Of course I knew Victor Kudumane would not be looking in my cupboards, and especially not the cupboard under the sink, but it made me feel better to know my place was clean, that I was prepared.

'Goat!' said Loreen. 'Double yuk.'

'I want you to behave yourself today, Loreen,' I said. 'As I have said, this is your father's brother.'

'And so?'

'And so! He is your father's brother.' But I knew my little Loreen was an English girl now, an English *teenager*, and she had no idea how an elder should be treated according to our beliefs back home. I was fearful for a moment, that she would disgrace me, and even more fearful that Victor Kudumane would be disapproving of the way I had brought up my child over here in the UK.

'So, we're running around cleaning and everything because he's a man?' asked Loreen. She was at that age then, when she was very righteous about things and especially about things between men and women, because she was growing very aware of how the world was. She could see that men were in charge and sometimes she seemed to blame me for this. 'I

216

thought you always said never run around after a man?' said my little Loreen, and she went to the fridge and opened the door and then she just stood there, with the door open, because she knew it annoyed me when she did that.

'This is not "a man",' I said, exasperated. 'Will you close that door? This is your *malome*, your uncle.' And I thought, she has no idea how it is to be brought up to run after a man, no idea of the way in which as a girl in my home village of Manyana I had been trained to serve the men in my family. No sooner could I walk and hold a cup without spilling the contents, than I was to serve the men water to wash their hands, hand them the food, take the food away again, provide them with more water to wash their hands, and all the time I was to curtsy a little and keep my eyes on the ground. And now that my late husband's brother was coming I could not stop myself from acting the way I had been bred to and the way he would expect, and after all, I thought, soon he would be gone. 'Show respect,' I said again, and my little Loreen looked at me as if I had asked her to stand on her head.

Two hours later my late husband's brother arrived. I saw him get out of the mini cab and tip the driver and then there was Victor Kudumane in his fine blue suit. It seemed like a long time since I'd seen a man dressed so smartly, and while he did not resemble my late husband in his physical appearance, there was a grace about him that made me remember the love that I had lost.

'*Dumela, Mma*,' said Victor Kudumane when I opened the front door, and there he stood on my outside step, a hat held carefully in one hand. It was clear he was an African, for an English man would not wear such clothes on such a warm summer's day, in fact an English man may well have taken off his clothes altogether.

Behind me I could feel Loreen hovering in the hallway. '*O tsogile jang?*' asked Victor Kudumane, and I answered him and for a moment, standing on the step of my London flat, the road and the houses and the chimney pots and the planes overhead melted away and I was in my mother's compound in Manyana with the sand under my bare feet welcoming a visitor.

'*Dumela, mosetsana,*' said Victor Kudumane, spying my little Loreen behind me.

'*Dumedisanang ka matsogo,*' I said to Loreen sharply. 'Shake his hand.' It was so rarely that I spoke Setswana to her by that time that she didn't look as if she knew what I was saying, but she came forward and shook her uncle's hand and he chuckled and put his hat back on his head and came inside.

'*O apaya eng?*' he asked, stopping for a second to sniff the air.

'*Podi,*' I told him.

'Good, good,' said Victor Kudumane, slapping his lips together.

We sat then in our front room, which I had just finished vacuuming, and I wished we had at least a yard so that we could have sat outside and felt more comfortable. Back home in Africa a person didn't sit inside their house unless they were sleeping in it, or if it were raining too harshly outside, and there is something about sitting inside a person's house that is very intimate and, at times, uncomfortable. I served Victor Kudumane his tea and I kept my eyes away from my little Loreen because she was staring at me like she couldn't believe what she was seeing. It was true, I had always taught her not to believe that a man deserved her servitude, but then this was her uncle and I had to do things right.

'So, *mosetsana*,' said Victor Kudumane after he had drunk his tea. 'Are you doing well at school?'

Loreen sat on the sofa next to me but I answered for her. 'She is doing very well.'

Victor Kudumane nodded. 'You are growing big, you'll be married soon. I can find you a nice man from home, with plenty of cattle!'

Loreen snorted.

'So how are things back home?' I asked quickly. 'How is everyone, how is the village?' I smiled and sat back on the sofa and waited to hear the news. I thought of my family and how everyone must have grown since I'd seen them last, during a visit I had made a few years after my little Loreen was born and her father had passed away.

'Oh, Gaborone is changing so fast these days,' said Victor Kudumane.

'Gaborone?' I asked, surprised. 'Is that where you live now?'

'But of course,' said Victor Kudumane, and he listed the other members of the family who had moved to the capital as well, a cousin who was at the university there, an aunty who worked for Air Botswana, an uncle who ran a car hire company. But the things Victor Kudumane mentioned so casually were things I didn't know existed in my country now, and I looked at him, trying to hide my amazement: a university, an airline, a company renting cars? I thought it couldn't really be true, that he was showing off about these things.

'And who has stayed in the village?' I asked.

219

'Oh there are some, here and there. Ma Mafoko still has her shop . . .'

I nodded, relieved. 'And does the village look the same? How is the Kolobeng River this year?'

Victor Kudumane laughed. 'The village looks the same, my dear. In Gaborone we anticipate a construction boom, but the village is only growing smaller. I haven't been there since, let me see, last Christmas.' Then he gave a yawn and stretched back on his chair and gave his belly a rub.

I looked at Loreen, waiting for her to see it was time to serve the food, but she wasn't paying me any attention at all. 'Get the food,' I hissed at her, and then I turned and gave Victor Kudumane a big smile to show that everything was well.

My little Loreen came back, walking reluctantly, dragging her heels, holding the plate of food I had prepared. Then she plopped the plates on the table and sat down on the sofa again. She hadn't even offered him water; she hadn't even set out his cutlery! I could imagine Victor Kudumane telling everyone back home that my little Loreen was a very ill-man-nered child and that that was how it was if a person brought a child up far away from her family and culture.

'No meat for the girl?' Victor Kudumane inquired, seeing what was on Loreen's plate, stopping with his own fork halfway to his mouth. I could tell he was a very rich man now, rich enough to question if a child had no meat, whereas in my youth if there was meat then it was the adults who received it.

'No,' I shrugged, like it wasn't of any importance. 'No meat.'

'I'm going to be a vegetarian,' said Loreen, and I could see she wanted to start an argument about this, 'because meat is murder.'

Victor Kudumane burst out laughing and put down his fork. 'You don't eat meat? My dear, without meat I wouldn't have a job!'

I looked at him inquiringly, because he hadn't yet mentioned his work.

'*Ee*,' he nodded, 'I'm on the board of the Botswana Meat Commission.' Then Victor Kudumane took the napkin I offered him and tucked into the food.

'I'm going to Portugal in two days,' said Loreen suddenly. She hadn't touched her food, she was just staring at her uncle and I wanted to tell her to leave him to eat in peace; it wasn't according to our culture to be talking at the same time as eating.

'Is that so?' Victor Kudumane asked politely, dabbing at some oil on his chin.

'Yeah, it should be fun.'

'Fun,' echoed Victor Kudumane as if this was a term that was foreign to him.

That night Victor Kudumane went to bed early and I sat alone in the kitchen listening to the radio until it was late. And my little Loreen who had been sulky all evening, came down around midnight and sat with me a while and put her long young arms around my neck.

'He's weird,' she said, holding on tight.

'He's your uncle,' I replied.

'I don't like it when someone else is here,' said my little Loreen. 'I like it when it's just us two.'

221

And I smiled and held her hands around my neck because that was how it had always been, just us two.

I open the back door and I put my head out and smell the air and I can sense that indeed autumn is here. I wait until my little kitty cat comes strolling in and then I sit at the table with my toast and listen to the radio. I don't have much to do today, not until this afternoon when I pick up my little grandson Dwaine from school. First they are talking about the bombers on the radio, then they begin to speak about Piano Man again, the man found wandering the streets in a soaking wet suit who wouldn't or couldn't say who he was or where he was from. Only now it has been established who the man is, he is a German man from Bavaria and now he has gone back to where he came from. The radio says that some believe that the whole incident was a hoax, that Piano Man couldn't play the piano at all, he only played one key over and over again. But, I think, at least he is back home. Then the radio says he has told his family he had no idea what happened and how he came to be in an English seaside town and that one day he just suddenly woke up and realised who he was. It has been suggested by the man's lawyers that it was a psychotic episode. But what I can't understand is this, his family had reported him missing when he had left Germany and they did not hear from him for a while, but although there were photographs of their son in newspapers all across Europe, they did not recognise him, and what I am wondering is this: how could a family not recognise their own child?

I take a crust from my toast that is still warm and buttery and I drop it in my kitty cat's bowl and I think again about that day my Loreen went on her first holiday without her mother. Ashley was the last to arrive that morning and I opened the door to find her dressed as if for a fancy dress party. She wore a shiny yellow top that was cut so that her left shoulder was bare, on her arms she had long lacy gloves without fingers at the end, and down below she wore a very short skirt.

'Is Loreen ready?' she asked. 'Only Dad says we've got to hurry.'

I looked over her naked shoulder to where her father sat in the car, for he was driving the girls to the airport. He took one hand from the steering wheel and waved and I waved back.

'They're not quite ready,' I told Ashley. 'Why don't you both come in?'

'Dad!' shouted Ashley.

I led the way into the kitchen where on the table the newspaper was open to the horoscopes I had been reading that morning, and this is what it had said for my little Loreen: *You are about to set off on a journey that could change your life.*

'Checking the weather in the Algarve?' asked Ashley's father, seeing the paper open on the table.

'Yes,' I said, hurriedly closing the paper. 'Is it hot there?'

'The Algarve in August?' said Ashley's father incredulously. 'It's boiling! But at least the beach won't be swarming with Brits. Our house is in a very quiet area, the girls will love it.'

'Hiya!' Bel shouted, coming into the kitchen with Loreen and Karen behind her.

Ashley turned and I could see that she looked put out to see the three girls together and I could sense the way her body tightened up as she looked at them. They were always quarrelling, these four girls, forever falling out with each other and then making up again, always suspecting that things were being said behind their backs, always forming alliances and then breaking them up again.

'What cossies are you taking?' asked Ashley.

My little Loreen looked worried; she always liked to have the other girls' approval about what she wore. 'I've got two bikinis, will that be enough?'

'Bel?' asked Ashley.

'I've got a bikini as well,' said Bel, 'and a new camera! A proper one.' She took off her rucksack and began rummaging around in it and out fell two t-shirts rolled up like sandwiches and a pair of shorts as crumpled as a used handkerchief. Finally she found what she was looking for and she took her camera out and held it up to her face, squinting and turning it around, fiddling with that camera in a very particular way, adjusting one button, swivelling the front part one way and then another, making a loud clicking sound.

'Really?' asked Ashley, and she raised her eyebrows as if the image of Bel in a bikini wasn't a nice one. 'What colour is it?'

'Blue,' said Bel, still with the camera in front of her face.

'*Blue?*' said Ashley like she couldn't believe it, and she giggled and my little Loreen and Karen started to giggle as well, though I didn't know why and I didn't think they knew why either.

'Let's go, girls!' said Ashley's dad. 'We haven't got all day.'

'Is your mum in the car?' asked Bel, taking a photograph of Ashley's father.

'No,' said Ashley. 'She's not coming. Do you have to keep doing that?' she snapped at Bel. 'She's not feeling well.'

'Oh dear,' I said sympathetically, and I was about to ask what the matter with her mother was when Ashley pulled harshly on her fingerless gloves and turned her back on her father and led the way out. Then I remembered what I'd heard: Ashley's father was having a love affair with one of his patients. I couldn't remember who had first told me this, but they had, and in the manner of someone who pretends not to want to talk badly about someone else but who can't in the end prevent themselves. Then I had seen Karen's mother at a parents' evening at school and she had told me as well. So as I watched Ashley stride out of my place in her fingerless gloves, and as the others followed her, eager for their holiday abroad to begin, and as my little Loreen stopped for one final kiss, I felt, perhaps for the first time, that Ashley was not the lucky spoilt girl she had always appeared to be. I stood on the steps and I waved after the girls as they climbed into Ashley's father's car and I asked myself whether Ashley's parents would get a divorce and, as divorce was still a big thing in those days, then what that would do to Ashley? For I had never seen a girl as close to a father as she was.

Chapter Twenty-Four

LOREEN

Hi Simon, hi Gene, ha! So here we are again. I may as well sleep in this wardrobe the amount of time I spend in front of it. Why don't I just get everything out of here, sort out the boxes, and chuck out what I don't need? I've just found a pile of old annuals but I shouldn't stop to look at them, I should be cleaning up instead. My bedroom looks like an over-crowded office, with piles of post I haven't dealt with, bills I can't afford to pay, another briefing paper from our head which I haven't even taken out of the envelope, the card from social services still on my bedside table. I'm supposed to be getting ready, but I'm dithering because I haven't been out since that night with Bel when the bombs went off. It's been ages since then but Dwaine still cries out at night some-times and there is still that feeling on the streets and in the buses that people are wary. I feel trivial getting ready to go out for a date really, but other people are probably getting ready for dates too, all over London people are getting ready to go out on a date. I pick up *Jackie,* this will tell me what to do. *Jackie, the best thing for girls – next to boys*. Ha!

I hold the annual in my hands, lift it to my face and sniff the glossy cover that smells of faded nail varnish. God, how

I loved *Jackie*. Even when the others outgrew it I still bought it. I loved it because it had photo stories and quizzes and features about teenage things and in the centre there was always a big pull-out poster. There used to be free gifts inside too; once I got a twin heart ring.

I open the annual and here on the inside page is what used to be one of my favourites: *A very special love chart*. I can't help it, I look up Pisces on the downward column and then I look up Mark69's star sign on the top column so I can see how compatible we'll be. I know he's Scorpio because I know his birthday's this month because I asked him. And the result is: *He'll two-time and lie so plausibly you'll feel YOU should apologise.*

This isn't what I was looking for, so I have a look at the next sign instead, Sagittarius. When I match Sagittarius with Pisces it says: *Your Saturdays will be the happiest you've known.* That sounds better; maybe I'll pretend Mark69 is a Sagittarius. I turn the pages of *Jackie* and see a big picture of Wham! Oh my God, George Michael and Andrew Ridgeley! Oh how I loved you, George. And just look at your hair, that's a real bouffant you've got there, and such brooding eyebrows and what about that gold earring? Very nice. Oh my God, remember that song 'Wake me up before you go go'? I can see you now all in white, hip wiggling across the stage while Andrew pranced around with a guitar. And then you changed outfits, didn't you, and put on tiny little shorts and all the audience were waving their arms and I wanted to be there waving my arms too. Was that when you had a shuttlecock stuffed down your pants, George?

Now, here's the sort of thing I really used to love, a two-page spread on how to read hands. Mum would love this too, she probably tried it herself. OK, my heart line is which one? It's the one going across the top. I compare my left hand to the fifteen left hands drawn on the first page. None of them really look like the heart line I see on my hand, which is very long and slopes all the way down from left to right. So I pick which heart line I'd like to be, the one that means *Happy marriage*. How about my life line?

Oh God, it's ten to seven, Mum will be here in half an hour and Dwaine hasn't even had his bath. I've told her I've got a date and that's why I asked her to baby-sit, but she didn't ask me for any details.

I turn the pages until I get to a feature on how to work out what it means if a boy does something in a certain way. I remember doing this, I remember doing this exact thing with Bel, saying look at so and so with his feet crossed, because feet crossed meant the boy was definitely intrigued with you. I'd like someone to be intrigued with me. I'm so excited about tonight I've got butterflies in my stomach. We've been emailing back and forth for weeks, me and Mark69, ever since that first email the night of the bombs, and I can't help it, I think maybe he's the one. How do you know when someone's the one? Mum always said she knew with Dad, that she saw him in that church in South Africa and she knew at once.

'Hi Loreen,' said the first email from Mark69, 'you sound so nice from your profile that I just wanted to drop you a note to say hi. No worries if you don't think we'd get on.' You see, he sounds so nice and easy, doesn't he, George? There I was feeling scared and lonely in my flat, even though Mum was there, even though the boys were there, and I could imagine Mark69 sitting somewhere in south London, which is where he lives, in a darkened room writing to me, searching for his soul mate. Now I come home from work and make the boys a snack and rush to my computer to check if I have any mail. 'Loreen,' I read with excitement, 'you've got another message from Mark69!' And I think that I should be doing the washing or checking what the boys are watching on TV or catching up with marking, and instead I sit down to write back to Mark69. It's like I have someone out there, someone just for me.

God, what's this? I put down the *Jackie* annual and pick up a book from the top of yet another box. It's a diary, I don't ever remember keeping a diary, but that's what this is, 'Diary 1989'. So I was sixteen. I open it with a bit of trepidation. I'll just flick through, have a quick look. It says 'University Diary 1989' on the inside. Why did I have a university diary?

It's empty. I open it and nothing is written on the thin blue lined pages at all. That's a relief; I don't really want to know what I wrote about at sixteen. It was probably about you, George, because you were on your own by then, weren't you? You'd dropped the clean-faced look and gone all macho and moody with leather jackets and stubble on your chin and that crucifix earring. Then I see that there is something written here. The writing is really small so I must have been writing something private, secretive.

Ashley says she's not asking Bel to come to Portugal and that I've got to tell her and I said are you asking me or telling me and she said telling. Oh thanks so much your majesty. Cunt. Why do we obey Ashley's opinion so bloody much?

I sit down on my bed, stunned. I can't remember ever feeling that way about Ashley, I can't believe I ever used that word, I still never use that word, and I always adored Ashley, she had everything. She was blonde and pretty, she had a mum and a dad, she had that house in Hampstead, she was clever at school. And she was nice and she was kind and she was generous and she took us all to her parents' place in Portugal. I never could have hated Ashley. I feel guilty even having written that. What if Ashley saw this now? God, I hope I haven't written anything else like that, then I won't be able to tell the girls I found a diary from when I was sixteen. I was just thinking I'd tell them at the weekend, but if I do they'll want to know all about it.

Feb 2. Karen came over and we made our speciality: pizza with extra cheese and loads of butter with coleslaw and 1 hard boiled egg each smothered with mayonnaise. I wanted to go to Camden and buy a ra ra skirt but Mum said she didn't think it was a good idea due to revision. Bel says she hasn't revised at all. Christ, we've got our mocks in a month. My God!

That sounds more like me, making food with Karen, worrying about exams. I remember Karen always used to come round on a Saturday and we'd go shopping or swimming and then back to mine if Mum was on a weekend shift. And we'd paint our nails and eat Nutella from the jar and listen to records and I would read my *Jackie* annuals and Karen would laugh at me. I must ask her at the weekend if she remembers that; people are probably writing dissertations on *Jackie* by now.

I wonder if Karen has gone all academic. She sounded really Californian on the phone last week. She went on about how strange London feels to her and then she insisted she'd seen Ashley in the paper with Donny Green! As if! But I don't know what's going on with Ashley, she's only rung once in the past few months and when I asked her if she was OK and why she hadn't come to the bar that night of the bombs she sounded really hurried. So I wonder what's going on with her.

It's quarter past seven, I've got to stop going through all this junk, Mum will be here any minute. But, oh my God, here's another one. This one's big, a big brown book of a diary and the pages are bumpy so I can see there are things inside. A bus ticket falls out and I remember how we used to add up the numbers on the ticket; there was some way we added them up and it said if a boy fancied you or not. And here's a piece of card where I've written a list of subjects and percentages and ticks and crosses; I must have been trying to work out what I would get in my GCSEs. And here're some photos; there's something odd about them, they're all square and a bit cracked. Here's Mrs Greenrod when she was still our teacher, and here's Karen standing in front of a school bus. But why would I have kept this one, it isn't square like the other photos and it isn't even anyone I know, just a couple up against a rock or something. Jesus, are they having sex standing up? Then I do know them, I do know who they are because I know that red and white spotty bikini, and if that's Ashley then who is the boy?

'Mum!' Dwaine shouts. 'Nan's here!'

'Coming!' I shout back, stuffing the photos back in the diary, the diary back in the box and the box back in the wardrobe. I'm doing it all in a rush because I don't know why I have that photo, or who put it here, or how Mum got hold of it. But most of all I'm doing it in a rush because I'm in a complete fury; that picture is from Portugal and Ashley said that was the boy who fancied me. She said that, she said, 'he fancies Loreen', and we were on the beach and I was so excited and I wanted to go and find the boys because no one ever fancied me, they only ever fancied Ashley.

'Anthony!' I shout. 'Have you run Dwaine his bath?' Then I take a last look at myself in the mirror. I can't decide what I look like. Do I look like a thirty-something woman going on a date, or do I look like a harassed single-parent teacher who hasn't had a good night's sleep in years?

'You look lovely, my dear,' Mum says as I let her in and she starts taking off her coat and hat.

'How's your leg?' I ask, because the way she's standing looks like she's trying not to put any weight on it.

'Fine,' says Mum. 'Dwaine,' she says, looking down at my smiling boy, 'I've brought some crumpets for you.'

'You look s-e-x, Mum,' says Dwaine, and he goes on tip toe and puckers up his lips for a kiss. Mum's watching and she looks shocked. I wait for her to say, 'In Africa a child would never say . . .', but then Anthony comes out of the kitchen and he looks at me and raises one eyebrow and walks without speaking into the living room. Anthony's getting really good at this; now he's in his last year of primary school he's started to spend a lot of time walking slowly from room to room with a put-upon air. Tonight it's because he thinks he's too big to have Mum look after him, but someone's got to look after Dwaine.

Mum laughs. 'Off you go now, Loreen,' she says. She's urging me to go, just like she used to urge me as a kid, to get into line at school in the morning or to go and ask for something in a shop or to join in at a friend's birthday party when I was feeling shy.

I leave quickly before I can change my mind or have any second thoughts about meeting Mark69. I feel like I'm seven years old and I've been sent on an errand and I'm really self-important. I leave the mansion block, walk down to the road and put my hand in my coat pocket. I find an old mint imperial and put it in my mouth and begin to suck. It's dusk, people have come home from work and now some of us are going out again. Like me, I'm actually going out for the night. I'm going to be one of those people who has had a bath and washed their hair and put on nice-smelling creams and is now about to wait at a bus stop in the soon-to-be dark and head into the city. Well, not the city, only a bar in Camden.

Mark69 wrote, 'Where would you like to meet? Somewhere near you then you can get back easily?'

That was thoughtful of him.

I feel the butterflies in my stomach again as I get on the bus. I don't mind that there's an empty chip packet on the floor and an old newspaper on the seat, I don't even mind that the man next to me smells of cider and pee. I get off the bus in Camden and see myself in the window of Sainsbury's and quickly I button up my coat; this dress looks like an old cocktail dress, like something someone who doesn't go out much would wear, and I want to cover myself up. I start thinking about Ofsted, there's only a week to go before the inspectors come, and then I think about whether the boys will behave themselves with Mum, and then I try to stop thinking about these things and just have a night out.

I open the door to the bar and walk in. I hate coming into places on my own but at least Mark69 will be easy to spot: six foot two, mixed race, muscular build. Immediately I see a man like that sitting on a stool at the bar and he's got a coat on the stool next to him so he's keeping it for someone and that someone must be me. Hurrah! Hurrah! I'm so excited I can't bear it. Then a blonde girl comes rushing up and kisses the man on the lips and he takes his coat off the stool for her.

'Loreen, I presume,' says a man's voice.

I turn and look at the man behind me. His face has an odd familiarity about it, like it's the face of someone I knew once at primary school. He's wearing a FCUK t-shirt under a denim jacket and he smells like someone who has put on five years' worth of Christmas aftershave presents all at once.

'I was worried I'd be late,' says the man.

Oh please, God, don't let this be him.

'It's a lovely evening,' says the man, and I know it's him, it's Mark69, it's the man looking for his soul mate. He looks familiar because I've been gazing at the photo on his profile page for months; his face is ingrained on my mind. But something is wrong, and then I see everything is wrong, because he's shorter than me, he's no more than five foot six. He does look mixed race, but there is no way in the world he's six foot two, and his build is about as muscular as Dwaine's. How could the photo on his profile page have lied so much, how could I have not realised that the person in that photo wasn't a muscular six foot two? And there is no way he's thirty-seven, he's far older than me, he could be

234

forty-seven, he could even be fifty. For the first time I wonder why he calls himself Mark69, why did he choose '69'? Oh God, I don't want to know.

Mark69 looks around the bar – we both do – at the fake deer antlers on the wall and an old black and white photograph of Camden Town with the streets full of trams. I want Mark69 to look embarrassed, to say, 'I'm not how I described myself, am I? Sorry about that.' But instead he touches me on the arm and says, 'We could even sit outside? What are you having, vodka and tonic?'

He knows I like vodka and tonic; we've emailed back and forth so much we know all these things about each other, and I nod pathetically. He knows my favourite colour, where I went on holiday last year, what I like to eat.

And Mark69 says, 'Are your boys OK? Is your mum looking after them tonight?'

I nod again, he knows about my boys, he knows their names, their ages, their favourite sports, their favourite pop stars and TV shows, he knows all about my mum too.

Mark69 gets the drinks and I follow him outside, to a patio at the back of the bar. There is a raised area with wooden tables like picnic benches, with thick white candles on the tables and ivy on the walls, and it's very nice out here. It feels warm for some reason; I could take my coat off but I don't want to because what am I doing wearing a black cocktail dress here? Mark69 sits down, puts the glasses on the table. 'Do you come here often?' he smiles. He doesn't seem self-conscious at all; perhaps he really thinks he's thirty-seven, six foot two with a muscular build. Maybe he's completely deluded; maybe he doesn't think he's been lying at all. Or maybe he just described himself as he'd like to be and hoped no one would notice the difference. 'So, how's the teaching going?' he asks, but I can't answer because I'm thinking, did he really ask me that, did he really say, *Do you come here often?* We sit on the patio outside the bar and I watch him drink four pints, one after another, and I realise that was why he used to write me emails in the middle of the night, he was drunk. I'm so crushed I could sink through this wooden picnic bench and be gone, and the only thing keeping me here is thinking about the look on Bel's face and how she's going to wet herself laughing when I tell her about this at the weekend.

Chapter Twenty-Five

BEL

Shit, I'm going to be late. All the girls will be there and I'm not. Loreen's going to kill me. She's been trying to set this evening up for months, ever since Karen came back from California, and I can't disappoint Loreen. But it's day seventeen of my new life as a press photographer and it's been like a non-stop car crash. I've been going on shifts with Glen every day since the snap I took at court, when the paps squeezed me out and I got the gang men through the van. Now Glen's gone on holiday and he's lent me his van so it's just me, on my own, hoping for work. Glen said to expect a call from the desk – they know he's on holiday, they know I'm covering for him. I know the routine; ten am is the magic hour after the morning conference. That's when the desk rings and gives out shifts. But I didn't get a call this morning, or this afternoon. So I've been mooching around at home, reading old papers. I've just had a look through last week's *Sunday Post*, which didn't take long. There was a four-word headline on the front page: *Sex; John and me*, and a photo of a woman in full colour, only I couldn't think who she was. This is it, I've been waiting like this all day, looking at crap, and in the meantime I completely forgot about tonight. Shit. It's eight o'clock already. Loreen's going to kill me. I'll drive there, park the van by the tube and pick it up again tomorrow. That way I'll get there quicker and can drink.

I see the girls the minute I walk into the Canary Wharf bar, through a revolving glass door that goes so slowly I want to butt my head against it. Inside it's all mirrors so I'm almost forced to look at myself. I haven't had a bath in three days. It's so hot in here it's impossible to believe it's winter outside.

'Bel!' Loreen shouts from the table by the window, waving as if she is drowning. 'Bel!' she cries again as I push my way through the Friday night crowds, women in heels, men in suits, office workers drinking doubles at the bar like it's the day before prohibition. I don't like places like this, I don't like all these mirrors, is there some design statement going on here? Is this why Ashley chose it? I push my way over to where the girls sit, scanning people's faces just in case there are any celebs in here.

Loreen's sitting with her back to the window, Ashley and Karen are opposite her. I almost reach for the little compact camera in my pocket because I could frame them now, the three of them, each sitting in their own particular way. I wish they hadn't seen me so I could photograph them like this. Ashley has her chair pulled back a little from the table and her legs are crossed over on one side like a chat show host. It's an uncomfortable way to sit but somehow she manages to look comfortable. Her face is very bright, like she's just been dancing. Karen is next to her and she has both elbows on the table, her hands framing her face the way people do when they're sad. But she's sitting like this because she's listening to Loreen telling a story. I watch the way Loreen's hands move as she speaks, her mouth is open, laughing, and I'd like to frame them like this because I think, somewhere, I have a picture of the three of them in just these same poses.

'We thought you weren't coming,' says Loreen. She gets up and gives me a kiss and a hug as if we haven't seen each other for ages. Then the others stand up too. Ashley's skin feels creamy and cold and she smells of vanilla; our lips are nowhere near each other's, only our cheeks. Karen kisses me on the forehead like a mother might do, and then we all look at each other and laugh. Loreen scoots along the bench so I can sit down. She has some shiny-looking black dress on, like the ones you see in magazines that suggest every woman should have one in their wardrobe. These are the sort of magazines I read these days, part of my research and development. Then I see we're all wearing black: Loreen in her shiny black dress, Ashley in a sparkly black skintight top, Karen in a well-ironed black shirt opened at the neck, and me in the old black t-shirt I didn't have time to change.

'Sorry I'm late,' I tell Loreen. I put my mobile on the table, even though the desk won't call now.

'Some things don't change,' says Ashley, the bracelets on her arm jangling as she sits down.

'And where were you last time?' I ask. I'm still pissed off that Ashley left me and Loreen sitting for hours in that bar in Soho. 'Loreen was really worried about you.'

'Was she?' asks Ashley.

I can feel Loreen next to me, she's going to protest and say it doesn't matter when it does. 'Yes,' I say, 'she was. She thought you were caught up in the bombs.'

'Well,' says Ashley lightly, 'you two were there, right?'

'Yes, so where were you?'

Karen laughs because she wants to diffuse the situation and I turn to her, because I haven't seen her for years and none of this has anything to do with her. 'So, Bel, where have you been?' Karen asks.

'You mean where have I been all your life? Or why am I late?'

Karen laughs again, rests her arms on the table. 'Bel, you always were goddam late. I mean where have you been this evening?'

'Waiting for work,' I say. I've taken my jacket off and I realise I'm sitting with my arms folded like I'm hiding something and I make a conscious effort to unfold them. I'm not going to tell them about my new job because I still don't know if it will work out, if it will last, and they'd only take the piss at the idea I'm working for the *Sunday Post*. 'Why are we all wearing black?' I ask, looking round at the three of them.

'Because,' says Ashley smoothly, 'black is flattering for women of our age.' She takes out a mobile with a shiny blue cover that looks brand new and puts it on the table next to a pair of specs in a yellow see-through case.

'Oh my God,' says Loreen happily, nudging up against me. 'Isn't this amazing? How long has it been? When was the last time we were all together like this?'

'Nearly fifteen years,' says Karen seriously. She starts drawing circles with her finger on the tabletop and I look at her, see a shadow of her teenage self, the way she was always the sensible one, the one who always had an answer to everything.

'It can't be!' says Loreen.

'It is,' says Karen. 'I worked it out on the way here. The last time all of us were together was fifteen years ago before we went to uni and I'm kind of jealous you guys still see each other all the time.'

We three *guys* smile, but Karen is wrong, we don't see each other all the time. Why is that? Maybe it's because we don't want to, only Loreen wants us to. I never suggest meeting up with Ashley and I don't think Ashley ever suggests meeting up with me. It's Loreen who holds us together just as she always has. 'Your hair is still so black,' I tell Karen. 'You would have thought it would have got bleached in all that Californian sun.'

'Yeah, she hasn't changed at all,' says Ashley.

I'm surprised to see Karen's expression is angry and I wonder what I've missed and what they were talking about when I came in. Loreen gives my arm a squeeze and smiles at me like she's going to tell me something later on.

'So do you dye your hair?' asks Ashley. She's talking to Karen, but before Karen's even answered she's started looking around, checking who is coming in the bar through the revolving doors.

'No,' says Karen, and she blushes like she always used to. 'It's just black, I guess that's just the way it is.'

'Last night,' says Ashley, 'I found my first grey hair.'

'*You* don't have any grey hairs,' objects Loreen. 'You don't even have any wrinkles!'

I look at Ashley and see it's true, her face is as smooth as it was as a teenager. I only know she's older because of the expert way she wears her makeup.

'On my fanny, babe,' says Ashley. 'Not on my head.'

'Gross,' says Karen.

Ashley flashes a look at her.

'I mean gross in general, not gross in particular.'

'Shall we talk about something else?' I ask, wishing I'd never mentioned Karen's hair. We're together again after fifteen years and we're talking about hair dye.

'How are the kids?' Loreen asks Ashley and she smiles; Loreen is good at finding out how people are.

Ashley looks blank for a second. 'They're with Afina.'

'Who?' asks Loreen, still smiling.

'The au pair,' says Ashley. 'Afina. Romanian. Very good.'

Loreen smiles some more. She could be envious that Ashley can afford an au pair, but Loreen doesn't do envy.

'This is really weird,' says Karen, leaning across the table. 'I mean, I never even saw you two,' she looks at Ashley and then Loreen, 'pregnant. Now you're mothers! With kids!'

Loreen smiles, takes it as a compliment.

But Ashley is impatient. 'What are we drinking?' she asks. She looks around again, checking who is coming into the bar. I'm beginning to think she's positioned herself deliberately in order to be able to do this.

'Not another one of those,' laughs Loreen, pointing at the cocktail glasses on the table. 'I'm tipsy already!'

Ashley goes off to the bar. I see the way she manages to get people to part, she doesn't have to barge through them the way I did when I came in, she sails through. I see her blonde hair at the bar, see two men make way for her and the way she gets served at once. In a few minutes she's back with another jug. She hands me a glass, pours me a drink.

'Cheers!' says Loreen giggling and we all clink glasses. I feel the drink sink into me and I feel my body relax, but at the same time I get the sudden urge to move on. I still can't stand all these mirrors. Then, out of nowhere, there are two men at our table, holding pints. They're wearing suits, if I had to guess I would say lawyers, maybe bankers.

'Evening ladies,' says the taller man, his eyes hooked on Ashley. Ashley begins to stroke the side of her cheek and then slowly, carefully, runs her fingers through her hair. 'Mind if we join you?' asks the man. He's not looking at the rest of us, he's only looking at Ashley. I stare at him, so does Karen, so does Loreen. He's interrupting us. I want to tell him to fuck off. He can see we're talking, he can see there isn't any room for him and his friend. But the two men beam, wait, seem certain we will say yes because they are so sure that four women sitting together at a table must just be waiting, longing, for some men to come along. They are transfixed by Ashley running her fingers through her hair. We all stare at Ashley but when she doesn't say anything eventually the men shrug and slope off.

'The shorter one was quite nice,' says Loreen, watching the men as they approach another table of women. 'Really funny eyebrows though, never trust a man whose eyebrows join in the middle. Oh my God! Do you remember *Jackie*, that magazine? I've been going through all my stuff that Mum's kept and I've got all these old annuals. Remember *Jackie*, "the best thing for girls – next to boys?"'

'Shit,' I say. 'You and Karen used to read that crap all the time.'

'No I didn't,' says Karen.

'Yes you did.' I laugh, to show I'm not trying to start an argument.

'And how about Simon Le Bon?' Loreen giggles.

I groan. I had to put up with Loreen's crush on Simon Le Bon for years.

'Remember "Girls on Film"?' Loreen asks.

'Yeah,' I tell her, 'I do actually. That was the video that started with the close-up of the camera, someone opens a camera and loads in the film and then they start firing off shots. Fuck, that seems so old-fashioned now!'

'I don't remember that,' frowns Loreen. 'But Simon was wearing a white scarf in his hair and . . .'

I lean forward because I've just seen that one of the men has left his wallet on the table. I pick it up, feel the soft brown leather.

'Oh, that guy dropped his wallet,' says Karen. 'Hey!' she shouts, but the men have gone. 'You should take it and hand it in at the bar, Bel. What are you doing?'

'Nothing,' I say. I've opened the wallet. I want to look inside, I want to take a peek into someone else's life. If someone's stupid enough to leave their wallet on the table then why shouldn't I take a look? I see credit cards and business cards and a little photo. I take the photo out, think who it might be.

'Bel!' says Karen again and she holds out her hand. I sigh and close the wallet and give it to her, then she pushes her chair back from the table and heads off to the bar. Maybe this is what Ashley meant when she said Karen hasn't changed at all, maybe she didn't mean what Karen looks like, maybe she means what she is like.

'Wow,' says Loreen when Karen comes back. 'I still can't

believe we're all together again!' She takes her drink, shifts up close to me. 'Now we're *all* thirty-three!'

'Oh hell,' says Karen, looking at me. 'She means it was your birthday. Hell, I totally forgot your birthday was October, Bel. I'm sorry. I'm a real bozo at the moment.'

'Bozo?' asks Loreen, giggling.

'Doesn't matter,' I say, and I try to remember the last time I cared about my birthday.

Ashley doesn't say a thing. Then she takes her handbag from the side of her chair and brings out a small box wrapped in silver paper. 'Sorry it's a bit late,' she says, pushing the box across the table.

I don't know what to say. I thought we gave up giving each other birthday presents years ago. I should be happy Ashley is giving me a present but instead I feel disadvantaged. I remember this feeling. I start searching through my mind to think where I remember this feeling from and then I know, it was in Portugal. It was just before we went to Portugal and Ashley gave me the money, a wad of ten-pound notes in an envelope, and I took it because otherwise I wouldn't have been able to go. But Ashley didn't seem that happy about giving me the money, just as she doesn't seem to get any pleasure from giving me a present now.

'Oh my God!' says Loreen, leaning forward, looking at the box. 'That's from that shop in Covent Garden.'

Now I feel even more disadvantaged because Ashley's giving me something expensive. I open the box carefully, feeling them all looking. I'm worried it's going to be jewellery and I don't wear jewellery. 'It's beautiful!' I say, because that's what you're supposed to say when you lift a lid off the box and see

245

a patch of blue velvet and a tiny silver chain. I look up at Ashley but she's looking away, checking a group of people coming into the bar.

'Put it on,' says Loreen.

So I fix it round my neck and feel the metal cool against my skin until it warms up and I can't feel it at all.

'Very nice,' Loreen says, and she twirls me left and right by the shoulders so the others can admire me. 'Hey! Let's do something all together before you go, Karen, let's go away together or something.' She puts her hand on my arm, gives me a squeeze again and I feel like I'm back at school and Loreen wants me to join a club or be in her group or be on her team.

'Good idea,' says Ashley. She turns her attention back to us, picks up her drink. 'Let's go to Portugal.'

'Brilliant!' says Loreen. 'Do your . . . parents still have that house in Portugal?' She looks a bit embarrassed that she's asked about Ashley's parents, as if she'd forgotten they split up.

'My father does,' says Ashley, and she says 'father' like it's something nasty.

'Do you remember that holiday when we were sixteen?' Loreen leans across the table, she's not giggling any more, she looks different now, like it's vitally important that Ashley remember it. 'I used to think that was one of the best holidays I'd ever had.'

'Yeah, I remember it,' I say, and I look at Ashley. She glances at me, cool as anything. Then I wonder why Loreen said she used to think it was her best holiday ever, like she doesn't think this now.

'You were going out with, what's his name?' says Loreen. She hasn't sat back in her seat, she's still leaning forward. 'You remember, that really skinny boy who used to wait outside the school gates?'

Ashley doesn't say anything, she just turns and glances at the revolving doors.

'Remember?' urges Loreen. 'The one who was in that band.'

'Steve,' says Karen. 'Ashley was going out with Steve Donut and the band was called Steve and the Vibrators.'

We all look at Karen for a second, then we piss ourselves laughing.

'Are you seeing anyone at the moment?' Loreen asks Ashley. 'I thought maybe you'd met someone because you haven't rung for ages.' Loreen sits back finally, she sounds quite plaintive now, but Ashley doesn't seem to notice, she just turns the empty cocktail glass around with her fingers, fingers that have nails so perfectly formed, so perfectly painted, they could have been stuck on. Maybe they have been stuck on, but I'm not going to start a conversation about that.

'No one,' says Ashley, and she does that thing where her cheeks tighten and her eyes go narrow.

I look at her and I know she's lying. Why is she lying? We all stare at Ashley, wanting more, but she's looking around at the door again. This is really irritating me. Who's she expecting? Who is she waiting for? It's almost like she's waiting for someone to come in and recognise her.

'Hey!' says Karen. 'I forgot! I thought I saw you in the paper.'

Ashley's head whips round.

'I was going to bring it with me tonight. I forgot. Bozo!'
Karen mimes slapping herself on her forehead.

'What paper?' asks Loreen. She blinks, looks confused. I
think she's had too much to drink.

'It was really *weird*,' says Karen. 'I was in this store near
where I'm staying and this guy was reading a paper in front of
me, the *Sun*, and there was this picture of a woman with an
Alice band in her hair. And I thought, no way! Because she
looked just like you.' Karen turns to Ashley. 'She was sitting
on a park bench . . . with this guy, some famous somebody,
and I thought it looked just like you!'

We all look at Ashley, but Ashley doesn't answer.

'Who was the guy?' I ask.

Karen frowns. 'Donny somebody, Donny Green.'

Loreen starts giggling. 'Yeah, like Ashley is going to be
going out with Donny Green!'

We all look at Ashley, waiting for her to say something, to
make a joke. But she just abruptly stands up and walks off.

'What happened there?' asks Loreen.

But I don't answer because my mobile rings and I just
know who it's going to be.

Chapter Twenty-Six

Shit. I've had a drink and it's the desk. I can't work if I've had a drink. But I have to, I can't afford to say no, because this is the first time I've been put on my own shift alone. If I say no, they might never ask me again. And I've only had one drink, I can still drive. 'Hi,' I say, standing outside the bar, holding the phone to my ear, freezing. All around me people are yelling at each other as if they're still inside the bar.

'Alright, Bel, how's our girl snapper?' It's Ray. Ray is the man on the desk who thinks we're on military manoeuvres. I've spoken to him a few times, answering the phone for Glen or leaving a message from Glen, and he always calls me his girl snapper. Glen thinks Ray is a plank, but I like the way he gives directions quick fire, like we're on a cop show.

'Glen says you're available?'

'Yeah,' I say. 'I'm available.' My heart speeds up. 'Where do you want me?' I ask, then I wish I hadn't because I'm giving him a chance to be a wise arse. 'What's the job?' I add quickly.

'Café 200,' says Ray. 'Brick Lane.' He lowers his voice, brings his mouth right up to the phone. 'Operation Pete.'

'Right,' I say, equally seriously.

'Pete Doherty,' says Ray.

'Yup,' I say, like I knew this all along. I try to think what I know about Pete Doherty, which isn't much. I don't know his music, but I've seen pictures of him in his pork pie hat and his guitar, and I've read he's going out with Kate Moss. I'm getting up to date with celebs now; I'm really trying hard.

'He's gone AWOL from Kate,' says Ray, like we're best mates having a gossip. 'Talk about a walking car crash. The tip-off is, he's turning up at Café 200 with some fan. An art student. Get us a picture of whoever he's with and we'll ID it. But don't flash them up unless there's a pack there, OK?'

'OK,' I say. 'Will do.'

'This might be an all-nighter, Bel,' Ray laughs. 'How's your night vision?'

'Yeah, fine,' I say. I haven't done a night shift before, even with Glen. The desk has always sent a night man to relieve us. But I can't see that'll be a problem. I'm saving up for a car and a few day shifts plus a few night shifts and I'll be able to get one. If it's an old banger.

I rush back into the bar, fight my way over to Loreen and the others. 'I've got to go,' I say, grabbing my jacket. 'Sorry.'

'Why?' wails Loreen.

'You just goddam got here!' laughs Karen.

'Sorry,' I say again, and as I put on my jacket and leave I see Ashley staring at me, totally unperturbed.

I pick up Glen's van where I left it near the tube, find his A to Z and plan my route to Brick Lane, even though I know where Café 200 is. The East End is where I went to art school so I know it well. I feel like a kid driving Glen's van, like it's a grown-up thing to do and I'm not a grown up. It's hard making room for my gear in the nest he's created, but I've got my own Thermos now, and my own bucket in case I need a wee. Glen's showed me where he keeps the clingfilm, in case I need a shit. He says he's never used it, but you don't want to get caught short, Bel, he said with his high girl's laugh. As if I'm ever going to shit in a piece of clingfilm.

Getting to Aldgate takes forever; it's Friday night, the roads are jammed. I pull over twice for an ambulance, then again for the cops. I pass drivers on their mobiles, drivers eating food, drivers getting stoned. Everyone is out in their cars tonight. Eventually I get to Whitechapel. Once I'm settled I'll ring Loreen and Karen and apologise again. I feel bad leaving them. I never had a proper chat with Karen, and I want to know what's up with Ashley. But still, it's good being on the move.

I see the turning for Jewry Street and my old art school. I want to shout, look at me, I'm a snapper! I'm so glad I'm not at art school watching a grown man cry because his loom has broken. And I'm so glad I'm not at Tavistock Square any more, in an office listening to what Jodie is going to do at the weekend, having Clive breathing down my neck. I'm so glad I'm not where the bomb went off.

I'm not far from Café 200 now. It's a café by day, a club by night. I had coffee and cake here at lunchtime once. There was a sign in the toilet saying the shelf below the mirror had been coated with oil to prevent the use of illegal substances. So if they put up a sign like that, then you know the sort of people who go here.

The problem is, Café 200 is on a private road, so where am I going to park? I need to find somewhere handy where I can sit in my car and wait half the night. It's all a matter of logistics. I check a couple of nearby roads and recognise two cars: Fred from the *Mirror* is here, so is Sam from the *Express*. So we're all on Doherty tonight. I drive past Fred in his battered Hillman and he sees me and gives a nod.

Nothing's going to be happening for a long time, so I park and settle myself down. I put on a jumper and a scarf and a pair of gloves, fingerless so I can still take snaps.

An hour later my phone rings. Ray's still on the desk.

'Alright, Bel? How's our girl snapper?'

'Fine,' I say, shivering.

'Any sight of our target?' asks Ray.

'Not a thing. But there are a couple of other paps here.'

'Uhu,' says Ray.

'The *Mirror* man's here,' I say. I'm only offering this information so Ray will know I'm here on the job and not lying somewhere warm in bed making things up. Glen taught me that but it annoys him, the way the desk is always trying to catch us out.

'Lima, Yankee, Foxtrot?' asks Ray, reeling off the last three digits of Fred's number plate. I tell him he's got that right and he rings off. I get Glen's mini TV from the back of the van and plug it in, putting it on the passenger seat. I'll watch the ten o'clock news. Pete Doherty won't turn up for a while yet – who goes clubbing at this time? The news has already started and some politician is in the middle of being interviewed.

'So, Minister, a return to family values?' asks the interviewer.

The minister is up on a screen with the Houses of Parliament in the background. He's wearing an odd green-coloured suit jacket, and his neck looks like it's being strangled by his collar. Shit. I know who this is. It's the minister that pissed

Loreen off a few weeks ago. It's hamster face. He's wearing glasses tonight, which he wasn't last time; they're tipped forward a little on the nose. I bet he's wearing them because he thinks they give him a scientific air and make him look less like a hamster.

'What we're talking about is the breakdown of the family,' says the minister. 'The moral backbone of our nation. Marriage is no longer regarded as sacrosanct. One in four children are now growing up in single-parent homes . . .'

'And what's wrong with that?' I ask the TV. It can be better than having some drunkard of a father around. Like mine. And Loreen does all right, she loves her boys and her boys love her. They couldn't wish for a better mum than Loreen.

'Fatherless children,' says the minister, 'from broken homes are far more likely to have social, behavioural and academic issues, and be far less likely to succeed.'

'What do you mean, succeed?' I shout at the TV. 'What do you mean, *broken* homes? Fuck off.' I switch the TV off, chuck it in the back of the van, dig out my mobile and text Loreen to apologise again for running out of the bar.

It's one am and I'm keeping my eyes on the door to Café 200. People come in and out, shouting, wasted. But there's been no sign of Pete Doherty. I'm feeling edgy; I've been here for hours. I'm going to take a drive around. No one expects a snapper to be on a watch without a break. And I've just seen both Fred and Sam drive off.

I cruise around, noting the streets. It's raining now. I pass a posh French restaurant, and when my mobile beeps I pull over for a moment. It's a message from Loreen. She says she got my message from earlier and she's sending me lots of love. I count seven kisses at the end of her text, only one of the 'x's is a 'z' so she must be a bit drunk. I look up as a group of people come out of the French restaurant and I watch for no particular reason. It's not fun now, being cold and on a watch. One of the men coming out of the restaurant hangs back from the others and he seems to be deliberately keeping his head down. That makes me want to see him; I want to know why he's keeping his head down like that. It's not like there are that many people around to see him. Then the man puts his head up for a second, fiddles with opening an umbrella, and I see him: it's the fucking minister off the TV! It's hamster face! Same green-tinged suit, but no glasses on now. He looks younger without them, but I'm sure it's him. He puts up the umbrella, takes out a mobile and studies it. Then he looks around, what's he looking for? Is he waiting for a cab, is that why he's been checking his mobile? I think he's looking at me so I put my head down. Should I snap him? The camera's all ready on the passenger seat. No, I'm supposed to be on Pete Doherty at Café 200 with the other paps. And this minister isn't that famous, he's not doing anything anyway. But I could snap him to show Loreen. If he's drunk and falls over I'll snap him for Loreen. Maybe the desk would want that too.

Where's he going now? He's walking down the street towards me and he's not walking that steady. Fall down drunk, I think, fall down drunk, hamster face.

The minister stops at the entrance to an alleyway just on his right and I see him nod at someone standing there. I'm craning forward in the van to see. Then a figure comes out, it's a girl, and she's young, maybe not even eighteen, wearing a mini skirt and high boots. You have to be joking. Mr Minister is meeting a young girl in an alleyway at night? My hand twitches for the camera. Mr Minister who preaches family values and the breakdown of the family is meeting a young girl in an alleyway at night? I have the camera in my hand, but I resist. If I take a snap now they'll know. I'll have to flash them up and they'll know and he's not doing anything anyway. This girl could be his daughter. This could all be totally innocent. And if it's not, and I flash them up now, then this will stop them from doing whatever it is they are going to do.

Then the minister steps away from the alleyway, holds out his hand and a car comes down the road and pulls up just under a streetlight. The minister waits until the car parks and then he opens the car door and the girl gets in. This isn't any good; I can see the driver but I can't see into the back of the car at all. I need to move, I need another spot. Quickly I pull Glen's van onto the road, and then pull in again. No one's noticed me. Now I can just sit here and look through my rear-view mirror at the minister's car and see everything. They're not driving away yet and it's perfect; I can see them both. I can see the minister sitting on the back seat, he loosens his tie and leans towards the girl. I can see them both in profile as he puts something down the front of her dress and then his head covers her face and I know they're kissing.

I rise up in the seat, clip the quantum Glen's lent me onto my belt, because with the quantum in place the battery will recharge in no time, and check the cable leads into the flash. I reach for the car door, gently release the catch. The rain's stopped now. I step onto the road, run as quickly as I can to the minister's car. I get to the back window, hold up my camera and set off an instant series of flashes: the first flash fires and the minister and the girl are oblivious to what's going on, they haven't even realised I'm out here snapping away because they're too busy. The girl has one leg wrapped over the minister's thigh and I'm so close I can see his tongue pushing into her mouth. The second flash startles him, though; he throws his head back, his eyes are confused, and then he sees me by the window. With the third flash, the driver's realised what's going on too and he's leapt out of the car. But my job's done; all I need is to get out of here. I run back to Glen's van, sling my camera in and pull off. Mr family values indeed. Bingo, as Glen would say.

Chapter Twenty-Seven

KAREN

So now I know what we'd make of each other if we all met for the first time, if we hadn't known each other for most of our lives, if we were just four women meeting in a London bar on a Friday night. It's two-thirty in the morning and I've just got home and I'm in my kitchen fixing a snack and I feel so wired that I want to go over the whole evening like it's a story I'm reading and when I've finished it I can go to sleep. I guess it's better than lying in bed and wondering why Stella hasn't given me a call in goddam five days. She called me from her mom's when she went there for Thanksgiving, told me her pumpkin pie didn't taste so good when I wasn't around, but she hasn't called since then and it makes me anxious because I don't know if Nick Givenchy went with her to her mom's or not. Thanksgiving means family and Nick Givenchy is part of Stella's family while I am not.

I'm surprised at how many people are up at this time; when I got in just now I could see lights on in the apartment upstairs, and when I looked up I saw the figure of the big guy. He was just standing at the window, looking down, and I don't know if he could see me or not but something about him standing there didn't feel good to me. There is something sinister about this guy.

Early this evening, before I went out, I heard the boy upstairs shouting to his mom for something and the mom shouting back and the boy laughing. I heard the sound of someone walking on the floor, their kitchen floor must be wood because every sound carries, and I could hear plates being clattered into the sink, water in the pipes as someone ran a bath. The domesticity soothed me then as I sat on my living-room floor and wrote up my notes for the day. I already know that a year is not going to be enough; my book is going well but I need more time and I'm going to have to extend my stay and apply for a grant.

Then just before I left I saw from my window the woman and the little girl going out the front door and they were carrying suitcases and I wondered, idly, where they were going and when they would be back and why the boy wasn't going with them. Perhaps that was why the big guy upstairs was standing at his window just now, perhaps it was nothing sinister, perhaps he was just thinking about this too.

I take my snack, my cheese on rye, to my bedroom so I can lie down and eat while I think about this evening and how strange Ashley and Bel were. I got to the bar first tonight, the tube was much quicker than I'd expected and so was the Docklands Light Railway. I got onto the first carriage where the driver sat, a small guy in a dark grey uniform, and from the windows, in a mauve blue sky, I saw shiny futuristic office blocks with hundreds upon hundreds of windows, some with lights on, most without. The view outside was so gleaming; it wasn't London as I remembered it at all. Then the driver got off and I thought, there's no one driving the goddam train! But it wasn't the driver at all, it was just a passenger in a grey suit I had taken to be the driver, because I'm a semi-Yank in London and I haven't been on the Docklands Light Railway before and I didn't know it doesn't have a driver.

I spent a while wandering around Canary Wharf, enjoying the busyness of a Friday night in London, seeing a bunch of guys coming out of an office, a bunch of girlfriends on a night out. Still I felt a foreigner and I liked it tonight because it gave me a sense of anonymity so that I could look and look but no one, it seemed, looked at me. Then Loreen texted to ask if we could meet outside the bar, as she didn't want to go in on her own. It was the third time she'd texted me today; everyone seems to text everyone about everything over here, it's non-stop goddam bulletins.

I didn't much like the look of the bar Ashley had chosen. I would have preferred something small and cosy, a traditional English pub with a swirly carpet and a roaring fire and upside-down horseshoes on the wall, but the bar Ashley had chosen was very modern. I saw Loreen at once. I was standing outside the bar and I could see even from the other end of the road that she was smiling. She was walking a bit unevenly, she had heels on and I don't think she normally wears heels, and that was cool in a way because it meant she'd dressed up for the evening. 'Karen!' she cried. 'Oh it's so good to see you!' And she gave me a big hug and a kiss and then she linked arms with me the way she did as a kid. Then just as we were going through the revolving doors, just as Loreen was asking me something, a black cab pulled up outside the bar and we

259

both turned at the same time and saw a glamorous woman in white pants and a little black top get out as if she was going to a summer pool party.

'Ashley!' whispered Loreen next to me, and I laughed because Loreen always said Ashley looked like the girl from the Tampax advert and I looked at her and thought, she still does.

'Come on,' I told Loreen, 'we're going to get caught in these doors.'

We were already sitting opposite each other at a table by the window, by the time Ashley came over, bringing with her a smell of perfume that was sweet and intense, a smell that made me feel dowdy and unbelonging in a bar like this, full of people ten years younger than us.

'Karen,' said Ashley, in that flat way she has of speaking. 'You haven't changed a bit.' She put down a handbag on the table, a handbag I could guess was expensive because of the way Loreen was looking at it, and scraped her hair behind one ear so I could see a glint of gold hooped earrings. I looked at her, irritated. What did she mean I hadn't changed at all? How could I have lived abroad for over ten years and not have changed at all? I wanted to have changed, I wanted to be different. I didn't want her to think I was the same old Karen because I wasn't.

'It's a compliment,' said Ashley. 'What are we drinking?' She looked over her shoulder as if to call a waiter.

I picked up a menu from the table, hoping for food, but seeing it was just a long list of drinks.

'What are you looking for?' asked Loreen as I started fumbling round in my bag.

'My glasses,' I said.

'Oh, do you wear glasses?' Loreen giggled. 'I think I'm going to have to get some too.'

I put my glasses on and all of a sudden I felt like a little kid playing dress up.

'Sex on the beach?' asked Loreen, holding her finger on the cocktail menu, looking up.

'Yes please,' said Ashley, without smiling.

'Or slippery nipple?' Loreen giggled.

'What the hell is that?' I asked.

'I would have thought you knew what a slippery nipple was, Karen,' said Ashley.

'Or how about,' said Loreen, oblivious to the tension that was now building in the air between Ashley and me, 'slow, fuzzy screw up against the wall?'

'I'll get a jug of margaritas,' said Ashley, and again she looked around as if for a waiter.

'I think you have to go up to the bar,' said Loreen. 'I'll go.'

'No, no,' said Ashley, and she took out a credit card from her handbag and I could see it was gold and she said, 'I'll set up a tab with this.'

Then Loreen and I sat there by the window and Loreen leant over and gave my arm a little squeeze. 'So how *are* you?' she asked.

I smiled and squeezed her back because it's been a while since anyone asked how I am, because the only person who asks me this and means it is Stella.

'How long are you going to be in London?'

'A year,' I said, thinking of Stella, wishing she were here. 'Longer if everything works out.'

261

'And what are you working on?' asked Loreen.

'It's a book,' I told her, 'about American poets in London.' And all at once I could imagine what Bel's reaction would be if I told her this – 'sounds boring' she would say – but Loreen was still beaming at me, wanting to hear more.

'How's your girlfriend . . .?'

'Stella,' I said, and it was like a light came on in the bar, like I'd just pulled a switch and there was her name before me all written in lights.

'You've been with her for a while, haven't you?'

'Yeah, I have.' I took a deep breath and I was about to tell Loreen all about Stella, far more than I'd been able to tell her in a letter, but then I felt real exhausted at the thought of telling Loreen how complicated things were between Stella and me. 'And how are *you*?' I asked instead.

Loreen laughed. 'Actually, things are really good right now. The boys are doing well, I can't wait for you to meet the boys, I've got a bigger flat, you'll have to come over, Mum's OK, the job is OK, and yeah, things are good right now, *really* good actually.'

'Who is he?' I asked.

Loreen bent her head, looked coy. 'Well, he seems really nice . . . he's forty, he works in the City. He's got his own house. And he's nice-looking, from the photo.'

'You mean you haven't met him?' I asked, and wished I hadn't because I sounded so disapproving.

'Not yet, no. He contacted me on this dating site. I've talked to him but we haven't met yet because he's been really busy.'

'Oh.' I smiled at Loreen but I didn't think it sounded good, that somebody would contact someone and then say they were too busy to meet.

'But we're going to meet soon,' said Loreen happily. 'I did meet this one bloke, off the same site, he was called Mark but that was a complete disaster! I'll tell you about it in a minute. But this one, well he's got a lovely sense of humour. We talked on the phone last night for the first time, and God, Karen, I mean we talked for hours! I know it sounds mad but I think he's the one.'

'Who's the one?' asked Ashley, coming back from the bar. She had managed to get a waiter after all; a man in black pants and a white shirt was following her holding a tray on which were three large cocktail glasses and a large glass jug.

'Thanks,' I said, taking the drink. 'Loreen's telling me about this guy she's going to meet.'

'Go on,' said Ashley, not acknowledging my thanks, just looking at Loreen.

Loreen took a sip. 'Mmm yummy, is this a margarita or is this sex on the beach? Well, I met him on a dating site. Have you ever tried any of these dating sites, Ashley?'

Ashley gave a blank smile.

'Oh, well I guess you don't have to!' said Loreen, and she laughed. And then Bel arrived, looking like she'd just got out of bed, like she'd just remembered she was supposed to be somewhere, and she wore what she has always worn, jeans and sneakers and a t-shirt.

'Shit,' Bel said, coming over, whacking the back of somebody's chair with a bag she had over her shoulder. 'Don't have a go at me for being late, OK?' She put her cell phone down on the table, picked it back up and squinted at it, and I wondered who she was expecting to call.

What the hell was that? Something real heavy has just fallen in the apartment upstairs. I've finished my cheese on rye and I'm just lying here in bed, thinking. I wait to guess what it might be, to see if there are any clues. What time is it, three am? It must be something real bulky that fell down to make a noise like that, a box perhaps or a case, something big but not something that has done any damage or I'd hear the sound of people too. I wonder when the mom and the girl are going to come back; if they went with suitcases they might be gone a while. I put my bedside lamp on but the light is so cool and harsh that I turn it off again just as I hear another noise, a muffled noise like someone is trying to speak and someone else is trying to stop them. I sit up and my back feels rigid against the bed. I could swear I just heard a kid cry out. I look up at my bedroom ceiling; I can hear footsteps now and I stare up, track the direction in which the steps are going. It must be the big guy; the steps are heavy and he's walking slowly across the floor, almost as if he is dragging something from one side of his room to the other. He takes a few steps, stops, and then takes a few more, and as he does flecks of white plaster float down from my ceiling and fall on my bed like snow.

Then I hear the big guy reach the window. He stops and I hear the frames of the window shake a little as he opens it, and then there is a thud, a single quick thud as if something has just been pushed hard, up against the glass. A tingle goes through my body, it works its way down, leaves my toes stinging. What is the big guy upstairs *doing*? Why is he opening the

264

window in the middle of a freezing night like this, and was that the boy I heard crying out? The thud could be the boy, the big guy could just have thrown the boy against the window, or maybe he's even going to throw him *out* of the window. Quickly I get out of bed and grab my dressing gown, walk over to my window and pull aside the drape and look out at a layer of shiny ice on the cars below. Then I hear the window above me rattle shut, so he's closing it again. There's silence now.

The Stillness in the Air /
Between the Heaves of Storm.

I stand very still, listening intently, wondering what the big guy is going to do now.

Chapter Twenty-Eight

DUDU

I am sitting in my kitchen on this frosty winter's morning listening to Christmas carols on the radio and thinking of what to buy my little grandsons this year. And as I spoon some sugar into my tea and as I stir my cup and think about this, I remember that first Christmas I spent without my little Loreen. That was the year she turned eighteen and she was at university and she chose to go away with her new friends rather than spend it at home with her mother. And then I think of my Loreen the day her A-level results came out and she found out where it was she would be going, for I recall the post came late that morning and I took the letter into her bedroom to show her. 'Loreen!' I called from the doorway, as she didn't like me just walking into her room any more. Loreen gave a mumble from the bed and I came in and went over to the window and opened the curtains because I didn't like to see her waste the day. I had been brought up to wake with the sun and sleep with the moon, but my little Loreen lived a different lifestyle. Since she'd finished her A-levels she was up at midday and out until midnight and there didn't seem to be much I could do about that.

266

'Mum!' Loreen complained as the sun squeezed its way into the room, and she rolled over, annoyed, in the bed.

I looked around the room, at the dust I could clearly see on the top of her chest of drawers, at the mess of clothes on the floor and at the empty single mattress set out next to her bed. 'I thought Ashley was staying?' I asked.

My little Loreen didn't answer.

'I thought Ashley was staying the night?' I said again. 'Where is she?'

Loreen fidgeted on the bed and eventually sat up. 'If her dad asks, say she stayed with us.'

'But where is she?'

'She's not here.'

'I can see that!' I had come into her room in a cheerful mood and already the conflict was starting, a conflict that could make me more weary even than the day-to-day weariness of disputes at the hospital.

'She's at Steve's,' Loreen mumbled.

'Oh,' I said. I didn't like Ashley's boyfriend. I'd seen glimpses of this boy, I'd seen him outside the school gates once when I'd met Loreen from school, I'd seen him another time with his friends in the park, and I'd seen the way he thought he was something, walking like a cockerel among chickens.

'Just say she stayed here,' Loreen said again.

'But I can't do that, Loreen.' I sat down on her bed and thought back to when Ashley was younger and when she couldn't say a thing without bringing her daddy into it. But now that Ashley's parents had divorced it seemed Ashley did everything she could that would make her daddy mad, like running around with an unsuitable boy and lying about where she had spent the night. She had told him she was staying with us and she hadn't, and that put me in a very difficult position. 'Loreen,' I said, 'I can't lie to her father.'

'Why not?' Loreen asked, and she yawned and stretched out her arms as if the question of telling a lie was such a simple one. I looked at her lying there on the bed and I thought of that day when I had come into her room to find her playing mummies and daddies with Ashley and how Ashley had said it was my little Loreen's idea and I knew it was not. And now, all these years later, her friend still expected my little Loreen to lie for her. When I didn't move, Loreen sat up again and I held up the letter to show her what had arrived.

'Oh my God!' she cried. 'It's come! I can't bear to open it. Mum! What if I've failed?' She looked at me, no longer the eighteen-year-old who had stayed out doing who knew what half of the night, but my worried little girl wanting to know if she'd passed or failed her A-levels.

'You will have done fine,' I told her, patting her leg under the sheet. 'Open it.'

I saw her fingers trembling as she tore at the envelope and brought out a slip of paper. 'Two As and a B. *Two* As and a B! Mum! I passed, I got it. An A in English! Wow, I thought I'd totally fucked up that last essay.'

'Loreen!'

'Sorry, sorry, Mum. Yippee!' And she jumped out of the bed and took my hands and began to dance me round the room and I knew that was it, my little Loreen was leaving. This was the beginning of the end, she was going to university and I had to be happy about that. The English call it flying the nest, and when a young bird leaves the nest it doesn't come back.

'Shall we go to Brighton?' I asked. 'For a special day?'

Brighton had always been special to me, I had gone there with Loreen's father a year or so after we'd arrived in the UK and it had been my first sight of the sea and my first taste of what the English do on holiday, the way they set deckchairs on stones and put handkerchiefs on their head and drink tea from flasks, all the while looking out at a silver sea that separates their island from the next. I liked the deckchairs in particular, the way they folded up simply like the chairs the men in Manyana took to the Kgotla on the days the Chief called a meeting, and I was amused at the way people stripped off their clothes and lay like pink chipolatas on towels made endlessly uncomfortable by the stones underneath. There was a holiday spirit in Brighton, a feeling that everyone had rushed down from the capital for a day at the seaside, and I had taken my little Loreen there several times as a child and she had loved it too.

'Yeah, OK,' she said without much enthusiasm. 'Can Bel come too?' she asked, brightening up, and I nodded, a little saddened that my daughter no longer saw a day out with her mother in Brighton as anything special to do. Then we heard the doorbell ring three times, and I knew it was Bel because that was the way she rang it. I opened the front door and there she was, her finger out, about to ring the bell again. She looked quite extraordinary that morning, with big, thick boots on her feet and thick black eyeliner around her eyes so that she looked like a young warrior.

'I passed!' Loreen shouted from inside the flat. She came running down the stairs and she threw herself at Bel. 'What did you get?'

I bit my lip and disappeared into the kitchen. Loreen shouldn't have done that, I thought, she should have waited to see how her friend had done in her A-level exams. I heard the girls confer in the hallway and then they came into the kitchen.

'Mum! Bel passed too!' Loreen said.

'Congratulations,' I said, but I could see Bel's eyes all dancing in her face like they couldn't keep still.

That weekend we went to Brighton, all four of us on the train, for at the last moment Ashley joined us. I hadn't known my little Loreen had asked Ashley to come, and I was a little confused that she had, for I knew Bel and Ashley were not as close as they had been and that all during their exams they had argued. I wanted a peaceful day out, I didn't want quarrelling between the three of them, and it was a shame, I thought, that Karen had to remain behind to keep an eye on her younger sister, for Karen had a way of deflecting arguments between the girls.

Ashley met us at Victoria station and her eyes were dancing almost as much as Bel's had been when the exam results came out. The three girls sat together on the train, chatting in loud voices, not caring if they were disturbing other people, leaving me to read my paper which I did with great concentration. And then we arrived and we stood outside the station and I could smell the sea that lay down at the bottom of the hill and I could hear the squawk of a lone seagull in the air above. I looked up, the wings of the seagull were outstretched and the white bird was hovering like something held up by God on an invisible string. The sky was a palest blue, an African sky diluted a thousand times so that it looked in danger of losing any colour it had and becoming white like the shop fronts on the street before us.

We walked down Queens Road until we reached the clock tower standing on its own on a little island amid the roads and all the traffic. I stopped for a second to look, remembering how my late husband and I had walked this way many years before and how he had told me about the clock. There was a golden ball at the top, he had explained, which in the past had risen up the pole on which it was perched and had then come crashing down at the stroke of every hour. But then, he had explained, over time the vibrations that this caused were found to be destroying the entire structure of the clock and so the authorities had put a stop to it and the ball stayed where it was. It had seemed so odd to me back then, that the English were a people to whom time was so important that they wanted it marked hour by hour, so that even when they were walking down the street they wanted to hear the sounds of a ball crashing down a pole in order that they should know the time.

And it was then, at the clock tower, that the girls left me. Although I had thought we would spend the day together, instead they linked arms and said they would wander the shops on Western Road and from there they would go to the pier and then they would meet me later. And so then I knew what I would do. Each time I had come to Brighton, I had walked along the seafront near the pier and I had read the signs under the arches of the road and I had thought which

271

palm reader I would go to if I had the opportunity. And today I was alone.

First I went down to the sea, down the steps lined with turquoise-painted rails that were rusty in parts where they had been sprayed and battered with salt water over the years. I looked to my left, to the Palace Pier, hazy in the morning like a factory producing smoke, and I wondered as I had done before how the pier stood there, far into the water, on its metal legs as if hundreds of giant spiders had been joined together.

I knew there was a tarot consultant on the pier, who sat inside a little wooden wagon and read a person's cards, but I also knew that anything on the pier was more expensive than that on the seafront. So I came down onto the beach, stepping awkwardly on the pebbles, crunching my feet, looking down as I had done when my Loreen was very little to hunt for shells or special stones, stones that had holes big enough to fit a pen, or stones with swirls and dashes of colour that looked so pretty on the beach and would look so dull once taken home. And soon my eyes began to glaze; all the stones and the pebbles began to form into one dancing pattern that only stopped at the sea. And then I reached the shore and the sun forced its way out from behind a cloud and with a blaze of furious light the beach was transformed into something magical and I felt excited about what I was going to do.

I went back up to the promenade and I walked slowly along, past the little shops selling flip-flops and beach balls and Brighton rock that crunched in the mouth and stuck in a person's teeth, until I got to the palm readers. I liked the look of one in particular; his name was written in lovely white letters upon a green awning: *Prof Shiraz*. And below this it said: *Consult the great mystic of the east*. There were signs in front, one of a large white hand with red lines, another a board leaning against the wall: *Any problem you have. Marriage, Love, Money, Litigation*. And then there was a red arrow pointing in towards a door.

I pushed my way gently through a multi-coloured bead curtain and it rattled nicely like jewellery in a box as I felt my way in. 'Hello?' I called.

'Come in,' said a man's voice.

So I came into the room and it was very small, as would be expected under an archway under a road. The radio was on, I could hear but not see it, and there was a smell of dust and fried fish. Behind a table was Professor Shiraz, and all around him on the walls were postcards, turned so that a visitor could read what the sender had written: *Dear Prof Shiraz, thanks for your help. My opinion of psychics has totally changed. Everything you said came true!*

'How much is it?' I asked, sitting down on the chair that Professor Shiraz had indicated and clasping my handbag on my lap.

Professor Shiraz smiled and he laid his hands flat out on the table, very relaxed. He had a kind face with a little black moustache and long brown eyelashes. 'Well if you want to know everything then it is five pounds, but . . .'

I waited.

'. . . Some people require another offer . . . which is slightly less.' He looked at me in a disappointed fashion and when I didn't comment he said, 'There is no pressure. But if you want to know it all, then . . .'

273

'Alright,' I said quickly, before I could change my mind, 'five pounds.' And I heard in my head Loreen's father saying I was being foolish and wasting my money and I shook my head a little and told him to hush.

Professor Shiraz held out his hand then, indicating that I should give him mine, and he took both of them and turned them palm up.

'What is your date of birth?' he asked. So I told him the date of my birth and he wrote it down and then he came back to my hands and I sat there thinking how my old German landlady Adelaide would enjoy hearing about this and how I wished we had not lost touch so that I could tell her.

'You will live to ninety,' Professor Shiraz said, quietly, as if thinking about this. 'You have a very long life line.'

I relaxed a little then as well, for if I was to live to ninety then I still had more than half of my life to go.

'The luck line underpins this life line,' said Professor Shiraz, tracing a finger along my right palm so softly it almost tickled. 'But there is a major split here. A major split at the age of . . .'

I sat up a little straighter; there was only once my life had split and that was when Loreen's father had died.

'A major split at the age of twenty-two,' and he gave out such a deep sigh that I sighed too in agreement and felt a shiver along my back, because that was when it had happened, when I was twenty-two.

'I can see great grief at the time of this split,' said Professor Shiraz. 'I can see a loved one going on a journey from which he never returned. But whatever grief has

274

happened is in the past; everything will be all right from now on, work, love . . .'

I nodded, letting his words soak through me, letting them give me comfort like a hot drink on a winter's night.

'This is my advice: don't do things you don't want to do . . .' Professor Shiraz looked up at me then, at my face, and I nodded because it was true that sometimes I did things I didn't want to do, doing them only because people asked me.

'You will marry twice more,' said the professor, leaning back away from my hands. 'You will have a flat abroad. And you will be rich.'

And just as he said that my little Loreen came looking for me, bursting into Professor Shiraz's place with Bel and Ashley, giggling and being silly, bringing in with them a shaft of sunlight, a smell of smoke and chips, voices from the outside world.

'Your daughter,' said Professor Shiraz, looking at Loreen as she stood with Bel and Ashley on either side.

'Well duh!' said my little Loreen.

I looked, embarrassed, at Professor Shiraz, but he gave a kind, slow smile as if the situation was entirely unavoidable and I shouldn't worry myself about it.

'Mum!' said Loreen. 'I knew I'd find you in one of these places, it's so *embarrassing*.' She and her friends looked around and their youth and their energy and their conviction of their own rightness made the place feel shabby all of a sudden, secretive and shabby, and Professor Shiraz looked like a man who had not seen daylight for some time.

Embarrassing was Loreen's favourite word at that time. Everything was embarrassing – in particular everything about

275

me. She was embarrassed if I sucked my teeth in disgust over something a newsreader said on TV or when discussing her school report with her teacher; she didn't like the wrap I wore in the mornings, and even more she didn't like it if I opened the front door still wearing it; she didn't even like the way I ate, she said she could hear the food in my mouth and that that was embarrassing. But I ignored Loreen and I paid the money to Professor Shiraz and I left my kindly palm reader and I didn't wait for my little Loreen and her friends to catch me up, and this of course made them want to all the more.

'Mum! Slow down!' called Loreen. But they had disturbed me and they had mocked me and I wasn't waiting for them. I went up the steps to the seafront road, passing children eating chips, carrying beach balls, enjoying themselves, until I was forced to stop by the crossing outside the Grand Hotel, for it was too busy and there were too many cars.

'You shouldn't waste your money, Mum,' said Loreen.

'I know you're not a believer,' I retorted, not looking at her, still looking at the traffic, still waiting for a chance to cross.

'A believer!' Loreen rolled her eyes and nudged her friends. 'Mum! These people will tell you anything they think you want to hear.'

I was about to tell her that Professor Shiraz had told me exactly when my life line had broken, that he knew far more about me than she thought, such as when and how her father had died, but now Bel joined in as well. 'They can tell all sorts of things about you just by the way you walk in.'

'Yeah,' said Ashley, 'they can just look at you and guess what your problem is!'

276

'Is that so?' I scanned the road, still looking for a break in the traffic. 'And what could they tell about me and my *problem*?' I turned to Ashley, this eighteen-year-old who lied to her father about where she spent the night and expected my little Loreen to do the same, and who came to Brighton for the day when I, at least, had neither wanted nor invited her.

'Well,' said Ashley with a toss of her golden hair, 'he'd see you were a short little African lady who is obviously a bit . . .'

But I didn't listen to the rest of her words because just then I stepped out into the road and car horns blared all around me.

Chapter Twenty-Nine

LOREEN

Hi Tony! Ha! Long time no see. I've just found you here in this *Oh Boy!* annual. God, how old is this? I just opened it and here you are. Tony Hadley, Mr Spandau Ballet himself. Very nice. Oh how I used to love *Oh Boy!*, even more than *Jackie*. I don't think it lasted as long as *Jackie*, but it looked pretty similar except there was usually a boy on the front not a girl. But it had the same pin-ups and true-life photo stories, the same hairstyles for white girls, the same horoscopes and problem pages, like 'Can you pass the BO test?'

Here's the picture of you, Tony, in a two-page spread in glorious colour, with the other four band members. Someone has written a number in thick blue pen on each of your noses and then circled it. That must have been me. So Tony, I can see you're number one. But poor old Gary Kemp, you're down at number 5. Oh my God, what an odd-looking bunch. Tony, your skin looks like a waxwork dummy, you all look like waxwork dummies, squishy white faces with wispy little fringes. And why on earth are you all wearing suits and ties?

Oh my God, remember that song 'True'? The one where you wore that suit, Tony, with a little white handkerchief peeking out of the pocket, and you held the microphone so delicately, with both hands like you were praying, and you were singing that song to me, weren't you, Tony?

What is Tony's favourite sport and hobby? This is the question under the picture in the *Oh Boy!* annual. I know the answer, horse riding. I look under John Keeble's photo. *What is the name of his pet slow-worm?* And it's out of my mouth at once, Slimline. I turn the *Oh Boy!* annual upside down to read the answer and check I'm right, which I am. I laugh at myself, then I stop. Because why would I ever have wanted to know the name of John Keeble's pet slow-worm and how could I ever have fancied Tony Hadley and marked a number 1 on his nose? I'm a bit disgusted with myself.

It's the start of the New Year blues; I always feel like this at the beginning of a new year. Christmas is gone, there is nothing left that I can use to entice the boys with any more. They're punishing me now, as they always do when their father's been to drop off all the presents they've been asking for and I've been saying no to all year. Then he leaves again and I'm left to pick up the pieces. Bel's dad used to do this, I remember, he would turn up every now and again and give her something and it was always something she really wanted, like a camera, and she hated not being able to say no. She used to show off whatever he'd given her, just like my boys do now, but I knew she hated him for it.

It's depressing me, the whole situation with the boys' dad; and work is depressing me too. Even though I dreaded the Ofsted inspection, now it's over there's a feeling of anticlimax. The school year should start in January; I'd like the structure of that. Instead January and then February seem aimless, like leftover months no one really likes. Why does the social worker have to come today?

He said, 'Ms Kudumane? Chris Raymond here, from social services.'

And I said, 'Who?', because I'd answered the phone expecting someone else, Bel perhaps, or Mum. And then I remembered the card they'd sent, the card I'd never replied to.

'Chris Raymond, Ms Kudumane, from social services?'

'Yes?' I said, still not sure what was happening.

'We had an appointment, Ms Kudumane? Your son Dwaine's school had made a referral?'

'You mean last summer?' I said.

'That's right, yes, I'm sorry there's been quite a backlog.' The man paused, he didn't sound very sorry. 'So if we could make another appointment, Ms Kudumane?'

'Another appointment about what?'

'Just to have a chat, Ms Kudumane,' said the social services man smoothly, 'about your son Dwaine? The school has been expressing some ongoing concerns.'

So here I am, with the afternoon off work. It's two o'clock, social services are coming at four, and Jayden's mum is picking Dwaine up from school and dropping him here. So I have two hours left to myself on a miserable January day. I should make the most of the time I have alone. A new year, a new me. I rummage through the boxes in the wardrobe and take out the *Jackie* and *Oh Boy!* annuals and put them in a small pile so that looks a bit better. Then I make another pile of my old teaching folders and the diaries I found before. I'm still worried that I wrote Ashley was a cunt; I still don't quite get that. It kept on running in the back of my mind when we all met up. I almost wanted to lean forward at that fancy bar in Canary Wharf a couple of months ago and say, *I found an old diary of mine! From when we were sixteen! And I wrote that you were a cunt!* I could have said it to Bel, she would have laughed and called me a cunt too. I could just about have said it to Karen, but not to Ashley.

And what about that photograph, the photograph of Ashley in her red and white bikini up against the cliff with the boy I fancied in Portugal? I didn't mention that because I just didn't know how; I haven't even told Bel about that because I don't want to feel so angry about it and bring it up again, but it's niggling at me like a nasty secret. I pick up the diary, the one with the photograph in, and open it, and this time a sprinkling of tiny shell pieces falls onto my bedroom floor. They must be from Brighton, because that's what Mum and me used to do, go down to Brighton for the day and bring back shells. Only we didn't bring back any that day, that day Mum got run over. We'd been under the Palace Pier getting stoned, me and Ashley and Bel, and then Bel had said, 'Let's go and find your mum,' and we'd wandered along the beachfront looking at the signs for fortune-tellers until just by chance I'd guessed the one she'd gone into. And we'd found her and interrupted her and made her so furious.

We called the ambulance; I don't remember which one of us did that but it can't have been me because I was frozen with fear. Then I sat in the back of the ambulance and Mum was still unconscious and I held her hand and squeezed it so

281

tight and I kept on squeezing it and saying, 'Mum!', because I wanted her to wake up.

Oh God, it's the buzzer. Is it four o'clock already? Is this Dwaine or is this social services? I hurry out of my room, close the door behind me. I press the intercom, hear Dwaine's voice shouting something muffled from down below, and I press it again. I wait a few minutes, enough time for Dwaine to get up to the flat, and then I open the door. And here is my son and right next to him is a man I don't know. How did he get in? That's the only thing I don't like about these flats, the fact that anyone can let anyone in.

'Mum!' says Dwaine. 'I came up the stairs all by my own! Jayden's mum didn't even come up with me!'

'Hi babe.' I bend down and give him a kiss but for once he pushes me away and I stand there feeling silly because the man's watching me and I know he's got to be from social services.

'Ms Kudumane,' he says, holding out his right hand. 'Chris Raymond.' He's young, far younger than me, with a long, thin face and the tip of his nose is flat, like someone poked it in with a finger.

'Do come in,' I say, and this sounds so silly I almost want to giggle. Dwaine runs into the flat, he doesn't seem to have taken any notice of the fact there's a strange man at our door, and he heads into the kitchen. The man from social services stands back so I can lead the way, like he's asking permission as to whether it is OK for him to come in even though he knows I don't have any choice. He's wearing a suit and, oh God, he's even got a briefcase and a clipboard. He feels like an intruder, I don't want him here, what right does he have to come into my home and inspect my son and me? But if the school really has made a referral then there's nothing I can do but let him in.

'Tea?' I say as the social services man follows me into my kitchen. 'Would you like some tea?'

The man shakes his head. 'No thank you very much, Ms Kudumane.'

'Oh.' I wish he'd stop saying my name, and if he doesn't want tea then I don't know what to do with myself, and I wish he wasn't being so polite because it's making me really nervous. 'Shall we sit in here?' I ask. 'Or we could go in there . . .?' I nod towards the front room.

The man from social services gives Dwaine a big smile. 'Here is fine, but I'd like to speak with the little fella alone later if that's OK.'

Alone? Why does he want to talk to Dwaine alone?

'I'm starting juniors soon,' Dwaine tells the social worker man while I open the fridge, take out some butter and a cucumber and make him a sandwich. 'After the summer, then I'm going to be in the juniors.'

'That's nice,' says the social services man. He looks a bit embarrassed and I don't think he knows what juniors is, and that means he doesn't have kids of his own and that makes me even angrier because if he doesn't have children then what does he know about anything? I see him look round the kitchen. Yes, OK, the dishes are piled up in the sink because I haven't had time to wash them, and the breakfast things are all over the table, and someone hasn't put the lid back on the bin. From the corner of my eye I see the social services man

283

take a pen out of his suit pocket. Is he going to make a note about the state of my kitchen? Why didn't I clean it up before he came?

Dwaine takes his sandwich and he goes, unasked, into the front room, and the man from social services sits down at last at my table.

'So,' I say. 'I don't really know what all this is about.'

The man puts his clipboard down and I can see there's a fresh stain of Marmite on the table and he's put the clipboard right on top.

'This is just a routine visit,' says the man.

I nod, that is what I've been telling myself. I know the procedure, I've referred students to social services myself, only Dwaine's a good boy at school, he's never got in trouble the way Anthony used to.

'If I can just check the information I have here,' says the man from social services, and he lays some forms on the table. 'You are Ms Kudumane?'

I nod.

'Ms Loreen Kudumane? And this is a council flat?'

I nod again; he must know this is a council flat because this is a council block.

'And you are a single parent?'

I nod for the third time and I feel like all these nods are going to be held against me in some way.

'So,' says the man from social services, 'as I think I said on the phone, the school was concerned about some of the things your son Dwaine has been saying.' He starts leafing through the forms. 'And the pictures he's been painting.'

'Oh!' I say, and suddenly everything falls into place. 'You

284

don't mean the drawing of the willy? His teacher told me about that. That was ages ago!'

The social services man looks at me seriously. He's got very odd eyes, I can't decide if they're blue or green.

'I didn't think that was anything to worry about . . .' I tail off because I'm expecting him to agree with me and he isn't.

'Well,' says the social services man, 'any sexually explicit or inappropriate behaviour needs to be followed up.' He gets some pictures out of his briefcase and lays them on the table too. My table is beginning to look like a crime scene, a table-top of evidence.

'I haven't seen these,' I say. I pull a picture towards me and see two figures, possibly a man and a woman, and something small in the corner, probably a child, or possibly a dog because Dwaine really wants a dog.

'Your son has been . . .' the social services man hesitates. '. . . Talking about sex quite a lot. And the pictures he draws are quite . . . explicit.'

I turn the picture around. I can't even tell if the figures are dressed or naked because Dwaine has scribbled all over them. For a second I get a lurching feeling in my stomach. What if something has happened to Dwaine, something sexual that he hasn't told me about? But he hasn't shown any signs of being disturbed, he hasn't asked me about S-E-X for a long time; his only anxiety is about starting juniors in September.

'So, the school gave you these pictures?' I ask, and I wish my voice sounded stronger, more assured. 'Without telling me first?' I'm thinking of what the procedure is, can a teacher refer an incident with a child to social services without telling

285

the parents? They can only do that, I think, if they suspect the parent of doing something to the child. I'm beginning to feel sick. 'And so they're really worried about these?'

'And the incident with his classmate,' says the man from social services.

'Sorry?'

'When your son and his classmate, a girl, were found without their clothes on?'

'They were? They didn't tell me about that.'

'No, well, it was referred to us.' The social services man stops, looks at me. He sighs a little. 'I'm sure it's all perfectly normal but we have to check up on these things.'

'Of course,' I say, and I pick up a leftover piece of toast from breakfast and start to chew on it. Then I hear the door open; Anthony is back from football practice. He gets to the kitchen door and grunts.

'Hi babe.' I smile at him but he scowls and I quickly finish chewing the toast and swallow because Anthony says I chew too loudly and it's embarrassing. I don't look at the social services man; maybe he's going to make a note about this as well, maybe he thinks my older son is a budding delinquent seeing as he's black, the son of a single parent and lives in a council flat.

Anthony goes out again and the man from social services turns back to me. 'I wonder . . . does your son Dwaine watch a lot of TV?'

'No,' I say and I stare at the man. We can both hear the sound of the TV in the front room. 'Not usually,' I say.

The man nods. 'Perhaps he's seen something on TV? Something, ah, sexual, that he replicates in his drawings?'

'He only watches kids stuff on TV.'

'Perhaps he's seen something else . . . perhaps you've had a male friend round?' The man from social services leans forward, lays his hands on the pictures my son has drawn and I think, this is why he's come. He thinks my child is drawing sexually explicit pictures because his mum is a single parent and she lives in a council flat and she brings men round and has sex with them on the kitchen table. 'A boyfriend perhaps?'

'I don't have a boyfriend,' I say, and I look away from the flushed young man sitting at my kitchen table and my voice sounds like a wail.

Chapter Thirty

BEL

Shit. I just left my watch for ten minutes and the bottles have gone. I got here before six this morning, a nice warm spring morning, still dark, and there were four milk bottles on the step. So I sat here, outside this house in Islington, waiting. I'm supposed to be snapping some bloke off last year's *Big Brother*. But as I didn't watch last year's *Big Brother*, as I didn't have a TV then, I'm a bit hazy about who I'm after. I just know he's supposed to be running around with some footballer's girlfriend. Another day in the world of important news.

I got here just before six am, parked up close by, and waited. This bloke likes his milk, I thought. Four bottles is a lot of milk for one person. But no one came out to take the bottles in. Either he knew someone was out here waiting to snap him, so he wasn't coming out to collect his milk, or he's gone away and forgotten to cancel the milk, or he did cancel the milk and the milkman's made a mistake. I waited all of four hours.

Ten minutes ago I got fed up, nipped off to the bookies to have a wee, came back and now the bottles have gone. Shit. Someone has come out and taken them in. So I've missed a snap. It's a good job no other paps are here; if there was a pack here then I'd really be in trouble with the desk.

I see the blind on the front window move, so someone's still in there. This is beginning to piss me off. He can't have it both ways; he goes on *Big Brother* to become a celeb and now he is a celeb he's playing cat and mouse. I'm exhausted. I've worked ten days in a row. It's been one undercover watch after another and I've barely even taken a snap. I'm beginning to wonder what's the point of the job if I don't even get to take pictures. But this is the point, my new car, my new laptop.

And that's all thanks to my snap of the philandering minister, Mr 'lone parents are destroying the moral backbone of our society'. I've been in this job for seven months and the minister snap is still my best because it had that illicit quality. You could see him clearly enough, him and the young girl, and you could see they were in the back of a car and you could see they were kissing and it was close up like you were sneaking up on them. But although you could see them clearly it still had that grainy quality so it didn't look like a set-up, it looked like a snatched photo and that's what made it so good. And the desk didn't care I'd left Café 200, that I'd been supposed to be waiting for Pete Doherty. They may have forgotten they even put me on him. They flagged the minister story up on the front page, and all the broadsheets followed suit, the way they do. It was on the radio, that story, and the TV too. There were phone-ins about cheating husbands, features about privacy laws, retrospectives on great political sexual scandals, and when Glen came back from his holiday I couldn't wait to show him, that was my pic on the front page! I did that! I got a lot of work after that; ever since then I've been on one shift after another. Now I'm stuck outside the *Big Brother* man's house cursing the missing milk bottles.

My mobile goes and it's Glen. 'Alright, Bel?' he asks.

I yawn loudly down the phone, kick at some of the rubbish that's been collecting in my car, a modest little second-hand Nissan Primera. It's not in as much of a state as Glen's van, but it's getting close. This old Nissan is my home now, my mobile office and my home. I look on the back seat; I can see the frame I got from a charity shop yesterday. I'm pleased with that, a frame like that, real slate, costs a fortune new.

'You working, Bel?' Glen asks. I can hear him light a cigarette.

'Yeah, I'm working.'

'What are you on?'

'I'm in Islington playing cat and mouse with some bloke from last year's *Big Brother*,' I say. 'You?'

'Chantelle,' Glen sighs.

So we're both on *Big Brother* planks.

'Desk sent me down to Brighton last night. I've been sat outside the plot all morning,' says Glen. 'How's your mum?'

'Fine,' I say, although he knows how she is better than me. Mum and Glen are getting serious. Whenever he's not at work, he's at hers.

'You wouldn't believe the number of press down here,' says Glen.

'Yeah?' I ask, but I'm not really listening. I'm thinking, he's in there; the *Big Brother* plank is in that house there because someone just took the milk in. So I need to get him to come

290

out again. It's got to be something he – or the girlfriend, if she's there – will want to come out for.

I get off the phone with Glen and open my new laptop and Google Interflora. Then I ring them and get the cheapest bunch of flowers they have. I have to choose between a single rose gift set and the perfect spring gift. Either way it's twenty quid, ten more to get it delivered within the next three hours. I go for the single rose. Now I need to wait.

The hardest thing in this game is keeping focus. When I'm on a watch hours go by and nothing happens, yet I have to be alert. I've learnt to do things with one eye only. I can read the paper, send a text, even do a fucking crossword with one eye. I start sorting through the crap on the passenger seat, looking for something to eat. I find an empty packet of Jaffa Cakes. I ate those while waiting for George Clooney last week. Then a family pack of salt and vinegar crisps, that was two weeks ago outside Kate Moss's place.

I've got nothing left to eat today so I pull over last week's *Sunday Post*. The front page is nasty. The *Post* has been shadowing a convicted paedophile, he's living in a hostel and they've snapped him in a park with some children. They say it's a moral outrage. I turn the page, stop at a picture of a girl who looks about fourteen. She's posing in a schoolgirl's uniform and twirling her tie, licking the tip in what is supposed to be a provocative fashion. Do the people who put this paper together realise how hypocritical they are? I chuck the *Post* onto the back seat and pull over one of the freebie London papers from yesterday evening. I haven't looked through it yet. I cast an eye over the snaps, recognising some of the bylines. Then I see my snap, my snap of the minister.

What are they using that old snap for? I start reading and see the story's not about him, it's about her. *Disgraced minister's wife in suicide shock*. That's what it says. There are two snaps, mine of the minister and the girl kissing in the car, and a family snap. A street cleaner walks by my car window and I jump. Oh please, I think, don't let that be true. But it is. The minister's wife has been admitted to a London hospital after a suspected overdose.

My mobile goes and it's Glen again. 'Alright, Bel?'

'Yeah,' I say, and my voice sounds weak.

'I forgot to say, check the London papers, they used your minister snap yesterday.'

'Yeah, I know. I've got it here in front of me. What am I going to do?'

'What do you mean? They've used your snap, that's all, good on you, mate. Did the *Post* ask you for it?'

'No.'

'Well they should have, the copyright's yours once they've used your snap. You should get paid for that, Bel.'

'Yeah but, Glen,' I say, 'it's my fault.'

Glen doesn't say anything; for a moment I think we've been cut off.

'It's my fault, isn't it?' I say. I'm beginning to feel woozy. 'It says here she took an overdose. She's tried to kill herself because of the picture I took, didn't she?'

'Hang on a minute, darling,' says Glen, and his voice is strong again, reassuring. 'Think of the whole scenario, Bel. She knew about her husband, she knew he was playing away, right? Or if she didn't, then she would have found out anyway. With or without your snap. To tell you the truth, if you hadn't got it, eventually someone else would. It's him that's to blame, not you, mate. You're not in this game to make friends.'

'I'll call you back,' I say. The Interflora van has just pulled up. I throw down my phone, happy for the distraction, and pick up my camera. The Interflora man parks, gets out, has a look at the house numbers and then opens the gate to the *Big Brother* man's house. I watch as the Interflora man rings the doorbell and stands back, holding the flowers. I see the slats on the blind on the front window moving again. Then the door opens and that must be him, the man I'm after, the plank from last year's *Big Brother*. He's in his late twenties, squarish body, squarish face. He's nearly naked. He's got nothing on but a pale blue towel wrapped round his waist, like he's just stepped out of the shower. What sort of plank opens the door like that? His chest is smooth with a burst of hair right in the middle. I snap him at once through the window, the moment he opens the door to the Interflora man. I hose off ten frames. Then the girlfriend, only of course she's not supposed to be his girlfriend, comes out too. She's got a flimsy little nightie on and she's come out to see who the flowers are from. I snap them together, another ten frames. Bingo, as Glen would say.

Then the *Big Brother* plank looks across the road and sees me. 'Hey!' he yells and comes tearing across the road. I haven't locked the passenger door and before I've even had time to think about this he grabs the handle and swings it open. Shit. He's halfway in my car.

'Give me the camera!' he screams, grabbing at my lap. He's got an ugly little face, flushed in the cheeks, a snarling mouth. The towel has fallen off and I'm looking at a scummy pair of grey Y-fronts. I'm trying to get the memory card out but he's got his paws on my camera and we're both tugging on it. I feel a slice of pain in my left hand. There is no way he's getting my camera. I can't do my job without my camera.

'Give me the fucking film, you stupid bitch!'

'Hold it, hold it,' I say, still holding onto my camera. Film? What planet is he on? 'It's not a film,' I tell him, 'it's a memory card. There you go.' I hold out a memory card and that stops him. He lets go of the camera and takes the tiny little card and I shove him out of the car and lock the door. What a nutter. If he doesn't want to be snapped, then he shouldn't go on a fucking reality TV show.

I start the car. In the rear-view mirror I see him brandishing the memory card in the direction of his girlfriend. It's a blank, I tell him, as I drive off. It's a fucking blank, mate!

I pull into a side street and put the real memory card back in the camera. My left hand feels funny. I hold it up and see there is something embedded in the side of my thumb. It's hard and a little yellow, like a piece of shell. I poke at it, hoping to flip it out of my hand, but it's stuck fast. Then I realise, the plank off *Big Brother* has left a piece of his fucking fingernail in my hand!

I take a pair of tweezers from the glove compartment and pull out the nail. My thumb's gone all red. What if it gets infected? I blow on it, as if that will help, then I get my laptop out and quickly download the snaps and send them to the desk. Then I sit back in my car, nursing my sore hand.

My mobile rings.

'Alright, Bel, how's our girl snapper?'

It's Ray from the desk. 'Alright, Ray.'

'Where are you, Bel?'

Where am I? I just sent him the pics of the *Big Brother* plank, how can he not know where I am? 'North London,' I say. 'Islington.'

'Good, good, we need you on a follow.'

'OK,' I say. I like follows. After six hours sat in the car on a watch, I need to move.

Chapter Thirty-One

'Who am I on?' I ask Ray, grabbing a pen and a scrap of paper from the glove compartment.

'Operation Katy,' he says.

Who? I think, but don't say. I still can't keep up with some of these celebs, the ones who once had a part in a soap or who once dated some celeb and now they've become a celeb themselves. Or the ones who go on reality shows, and then call you a bitch and leave a fingernail in your thumb.

'Katy?' I ask, casually, as if I'm just checking, as if I'm making sure it's Katy and not Kate.

'Katy Koogan,' says Ray.

Who's she? I think.

'Bravo, six, four, nine . . .' says Ray, reeling off a number plate.

I scribble down the number plate and address Ray's giving me. Then I put down the phone and open up my laptop. I Google Katy Koogan and find a site with a biog. It describes her profession as 'socialite'. She was once crowned Miss Beach Queen in Scarborough. She's a former model. Oh, OK, she used to be married to that pop star. I find some pics, so now I know what she looks like, now I know who I'm supposed to be following.

It's late afternoon by the time I get to the address Ray's given me. I park just down the road but before I've even turned the engine off I see her. Perfect timing. Katy Koogan is at the front door of number 28, wearing a short little flowery dress. She's got something under one arm; it looks like a picnic hamper. She waves at someone up at one of the windows and then she walks down the front steps and gets into a car. I don't need to snap her; the desk just wants to know where she's going.

I feel a little odd as I wait for her to pull off and I can't think why. Then I realise I haven't done a woman alone before. I've been out with women journos, I've taken snaps of women who have sold their stories to the *Sunday Post*, I've done women on red carpets at film premières, I've done plenty of couples, but I haven't followed a woman alone before. Not that it will make any difference.

Off we go. I follow Katy Koogan through London for a good half an hour. I think of what Glen's always told me: if you're on a follow on your own then it has to be covert. You know you've been spotted if the person you're following does something stupid, like slowing down at a green light and then zooming through just as it goes red. Then you know they know you're there, so you just pull off. What option do you have? If you put your foot down as well when the light goes red, Bodie and Doyle style, then they'll know. And celebs have more powerful cars than paps. How fast am I going to do in my second-hand Nissan? But at least I've got a full tank; I can follow Katy Koogan for hours. I fix on my hands-free just as my mobile rings.

'Alright, Bel?'

'Yeah, Ray,' I say. 'I'm on it, I'm after her now.' I make my voice low and urgent, like the paps do when they're speaking to their desk and they want to pretend something's going down. That's how the desk likes it; they have no idea what we're doing half the time, but they like the drama.

We get onto the M1 and I relax. There's nowhere you can go on a motorway, all I need to do is follow. We get to Watford Junction and I can see Katy Koogan about five cars ahead. I stay in position until we pass the turnoff for Whipsnade and then she moves into the slow lane. I get bored and pull ahead; she'll never think I'm following her if she's the one behind me. Glen taught me that. We drive on, past the Milton Keynes junction, and suddenly Katy Koogan decides to overtake. I look to my right as she passes me and I can see straight into her car and I see there's someone else there. Shit, she's got a kid in there. I didn't see there was a kid in there when we started this.

I'm looking at Katy Koogan's car in front of me now and I can clearly see the top of a child's blond head in a bucket seat on the back seat. I watch as Katy Koogan leans one arm over the back; she's giving the kid something. A drink per-haps, or a book. I think of Glen. Don't snap kids, he says, it's not right to snap kids, it's not their fault if their parent is a celeb. Katy Koogan's face is turned towards the road but her arm is still stretched out towards the kid. I think of Mum, she used to do this. On car journeys, when I was little, I always sat in the back inbetween my brothers and Dad drove and Mum sat in the passenger seat. Joe and Rich would be bashing me on the head and Mum would lean one arm into the back to separate us.

Katy Koogan looks in her rear-view mirror. Then she speeds up. We're going fast now. I have my foot down; I'm well over the speed limit. I don't think she knows she's being followed. But what if she does, what if she's speeding up because she knows I'm following her? She's driving like a crazy woman now, swinging from one lane to the next. And there's a kid in the car. If something happens now, if she crashes on the M1, it's going to be my fault. And for what? I don't even know why I'm following Katy Koogan. I don't know what the story is, if there even is a story. Who cares where she's going? Who cares who she's meeting? She's in a car with a kid and she's speeding.

I ease my foot off the gas, slow down, change lanes. I see Katy Koogan disappearing into the distance. She overtakes a blue Mercedes and she's gone.

I drive on; I don't even know where I'm driving. There's something about a motorway that makes it hard to get off. One more junction, I think, and I'll stop and turn round and head back to London. But I don't. I just keep on going. Everything is grey, except for the white broken lines of the lanes. I'm part of one crazy conveyor belt of cars and lorries and vans and trucks hurtling along, unable to stop. I put the radio on and sing, loudly, like I haven't a care in the world. But thoughts are popping up like headlines. I took a snap of the minister. The minister's wife tried to kill herself. I followed Katy Koogan. I lost my nerve.

The desk doesn't call. When they do I'll say I lost my target. It happens all the time. I'll just say I lost her. I won't say, this felt wrong all of a sudden, she's got a kid in the car with her. As if the desk would care about that. Should I ring Glen? I don't want to, I don't want to have to explain myself.

It starts to get dusky, the sky is a thick cloudy blue and it's darkening, the sun's going down. I've been driving too long, I need to get off the motorway and get back to where I started. Otherwise I'll end up in Leeds. But it's like I can't, I'm being overtaken and I'm overtaking and it feels like a video game that I can't switch off. On every side of me I see car lights and they become one long stream of light like a firework. The motorway narrows suddenly into a single lane lined with cones and I feel hemmed in. I can't bear single lanes; the cones on either side make me want to crash my way out of it. When's it going to end?

And then it does end and the motorway opens up again. A lorry overtakes and I'm up its arse and I peer at the back of the lorry where someone has written, *this is dirtier than my girlfriend*, and the words are white against the black dust that coats the van. I'm still looking at this when the back of the lorry flaps open and something falls out. I swerve, not enough to take me out of the lane but enough to miss whatever it was, something long and bulky, something like a wrapped-up body.

I drive on and my heart is hammering. What the fuck just happened? I look in my rear-view mirror, I can't see anything on the road behind, I can only see other cars. How come none of them have stopped? Who has hit the body if I didn't? There's going to be a pile up, any minute now there's going to be a pile up. But there isn't, everyone just keeps on driving normally, because nothing has happened, no body fell from the van. I'm just losing my mind, that's all.

Two hours later I get back into London, negotiate the North Circular. I still don't know where I'm going but I head into town. I need someone to talk to. It's night now and I've got to stop driving and talk to someone. I could go to Mum's. But then maybe Glen will be there. Or my brothers. And I'm a failure. I was supposed to follow Katy Koogan and I didn't. Why am I in this game if I couldn't even do that? I need the work; I need to pay for my car, my laptop, all my camera gear. I can't get precious about this job now.

I pull into a petrol station and have a think. I'm not far from Holborn and Holborn is where broadsheet Jimmy lives. That's what he said, last summer outside the court, that he lives around here. I rummage through the glove compartment, looking for the card he gave me.

It was six months ago that he offered me tea, but maybe it's an open invitation. Maybe he'll remember me. I should have gone with him then, when he asked. I find his number on the card and dial. It rings a long time but there's no voice mail. I'm about to hang up when he answers.

'Hello?' he says quickly, like he's in the middle of something. Maybe he's on a job. Maybe he thinks it's his desk.

'Jimmy,' I say, 'this is Bel. From the *Sunday Post*.'

'Hello, Bel!' he laughs. 'How are you?'

'That invitation for tea,' I say. 'Is that still on offer?'

He laughs again. 'You sound rather stressed,' he says. 'I'll put the kettle on.'

I smile, put the radio on again and sing along. I think about the chat I had with Jimmy outside the Old Bailey that day. I picture him in his white shirt unbuttoned to show a tanned neck. I think about when he watched me leave with Glen and I looked back and he gave me a wink. I start whistling, I feel lucky. I'm not going to think about anything else. It's a game, it's all just a game. Katy Koogan will have

301

had her picnic. The minister's wife will recover, and then she'll leave her husband.

I pull up outside Jimmy's address, see a row of four-storey houses with attics on top. It looks very 'young professionals' around here. These buildings are probably listed. It's a nice road, plenty of trees, and it's surprisingly quiet, like I'm not in London any more. I lock my gear in the boot, except for my SLR which I put in my holster bag. The cherry blossom on the tree under the street light looks beautiful. I stop for a moment to frame it; the tree is laden with sharp little tight petals, pink and white against the night. I feel my body relax as I take some pictures, as stray petals float to the ground. The petals float so slowly, this way and that, that standing by the cherry blossom tree under a street light in the dark I'm in a moment of suspended time.

I ring his bell. Then I hear a window open above.

'Hey Bel, it's open, come in!' says Jimmy, leaning out of the window, looking down. I push at the front door and it opens easily so in I go. 'Up here!' Jimmy shouts. He's standing at the top of a landing, so I walk up the soft-carpeted stairs towards him. When I get to the top he's standing there with one arm held flat against the door, keeping it open. He stays there while I edge past him and I feel a crackle of friction between us, the friction you get when you fancy someone and you think they might fancy you back. It's been so long since I did something like this I don't know what to do next.

I get into the flat and it feels like a converted warehouse, a long room with white walls and a shiny wooden floor. There's lots of stuff from IKEA in here, a three-seater white

302

sofa, a white coffee table with hard, sharp corners, two beige bookcases set in alcoves in the wall. It feels like I've walked into a catalogue. It's all wood and white and beige, and very clean. I look around, see two cups on the coffee table. It smells nice in here, like someone made a good meaty stew. I'm hungry, I haven't eaten all day. My stomach feels empty and weak.

'Hey Bel! Nice to see you!' says Jimmy, following me into the flat. 'I'm glad you called.' He looks just as I remembered him, only something is a little different. He looks like he hasn't shaved in a while and it suits him, gives him an edginess he didn't have before. I see now that he's wearing shorts. Maybe he wasn't working today, or maybe he's just knocked off.

'What can I get you to drink? Tea? Or I was just going to have a beer.'

'Beer,' I say.

Jimmy goes off and comes back with two bottles of beer; I don't recognise the brand, it's something expensive and imported. I sit down on the IKEA sofa and feel my limbs go soft. Jimmy sits next to me, his leg against mine. I'm glad I came.

'What have you been up to?' he asks, shifting himself so he's sideways on the sofa, so he's even closer to me.

I sigh. I want to talk to someone in the same game as me. But I don't want to go into it all now; I don't want to talk about the follow and how I lost my nerve. 'It's been a long day,' I say.

'I'm sure it has, working for the *Sunday Poke*!' Jimmy laughs. 'What were you on today then? Who's poking who? Come on, you can tell me!'

303

'What were you on?' I ask, because I'm too tired to be teased.

Jimmy scratches his chin. 'It's a political story, a big one.' He frowns and lowers his voice. 'I can't say more than that, but I've been out of town for three days and I'm only coming up for air now. It's difficult, isn't it, Bel, having a social life with a job like ours? You have an eyelash there . . .' Jimmy leans towards me, his hand is aiming for somewhere around my eye. 'You smell great,' he says, and I feel his finger on the skin of my cheek and I have to stop myself, stop my entire body from turning towards him.

'Your girlfriend out then?' I ask.

Jimmy's hand jolts back. He's going to say something, then he changes his mind and laughs. 'Yeah, she's out. How did you know?'

I look around the room; there are plenty of signs, not just the two cups. There's a bottle of nail varnish on the mantelpiece over a closed-up fireplace. There's a noticeboard at the far end of the room and I can see photos of a man and woman in different places and different poses. I stand up, drink some beer, put the bottle down. Jimmy puts out his hand, touches me on the arm.

'Hey Bel . . .' He says it softly, like we know each other.

'I'm not into that,' I say. 'You didn't say you had a girl-friend.'

'Well, hey, it's just a bit of fun,' says Jimmy. 'You were the one who called me!'

'Yes,' I say. 'But I'm not into that.'

Jimmy shrugs. 'We could go for some food? There's this Italian place, my treat because you've had a rough day?'

I nod, although I don't know why. But I'm thinking of pasta, lasagne perhaps in a brown earthenware dish, the mince packed with herbs, a thick white sauce, a little burnt on the top. It's been so long since I ate real food or had a real conversation. Shit. Why did I have to pick a bloke that's already taken? Shit, I fancy him though.

'Make yourself comfortable,' Jimmy says as he leaves the room.

I pick up my beer, drink some more. I don't have the energy to move. I want food. Then I look up because I can feel Jimmy's back in the room. He's standing there smiling at me. And then I take in what he's wearing: a bright red one-piece vinyl costume. A sound comes out of my mouth like a gasp. This can't be happening. But Jimmy's still in front of me and I can't not look. The costume is wrapped tight around his neck like clingfilm, but then there's a big hole where I can see his naked chest. I look down, there's another hole around his crotch; I can see the hair on his naked thighs and his cock in a big red pouch as shiny as a tomato. Jimmy's heard my gasp and he seems to take this as approval, and so he turns, shows me how the costume is cut away at the back so I can see his dimpled buttocks. Then my mobile goes, it's the desk.

Chapter Thirty-Two

KAREN

I don't need to wonder any more what it would be like if Stella were here because now she is, she's asleep in the bed next to me and I'm lying here reading a book and it's one of those everything moments when I feel both that I have everything and that I want everything. It's a feeling that comes with being with Stella again. I can hear the sounds of summer outside, someone mowing the lawn in a back garden with a rackety old machine that keeps stopping and starting, birds gathering in the rowan tree just outside my bedroom window, two women chatting on the street in cheerful voices. It's been six hours since Stella arrived, landing on my doorstep in the middle of the night like she just dropped down from goddam outer space and I just can't believe she's here.

She murmurs in her sleep and I rest my book on the bed for a moment and reach out my arm and curl it round her and feel her stomach as soft as flour. But she doesn't wake, she's sound asleep, and for a moment I want to push her and wake her up and make her look at me.

'I've left him.' That was what she said when I opened the door last night and I just put my arms out and pulled her in.

I never thought it would happen, it's what I have wanted to happen more than anything in the world, but I never thought she would do it. I never thought she would leave Nick Givenchy. He must be mad, I thought, he must be real mad, and I followed Stella into my apartment, watching the careful way she put down her bag, just a small carry-on bag so that for a moment I wondered if she really had left him and if she really was here to stay. I saw that the usual glow of her face was dulled by a night spent in a plane, and when I took her hand she began to stroke up and down my palm with her thumb, slowly as if unaware that she was doing it. I wanted to ask her so much, I wanted to ask how she'd made her mind up to leave him and what she'd said and had he begged her to stay and was this all for real and why now, after all this time?

'This is cool,' she said, looking around my apartment. 'I'm sorry I didn't tell you I was coming, honey. I missed you so much, Karen.'

I smiled at the way she said 'Karen' because she said it in a way I'd totally forgotten. 'How did you get to the airport?' I asked, and then wished I hadn't because it didn't matter how she'd got to the airport; it only mattered that she was here.

'Macey took me, with her bozo of a rabbit,' Stella laughed.

'And you've left him?' I asked as Stella began stroking my palm again.

Then there was a bang from upstairs and we both looked up at the high ceiling of my living room. 'Hell,' I said, 'it's starting again.'

'What's starting again?' asked Stella, and she sat down on my sofa and she took off her shoes and stretched out her feet. It was dark in the room; I had only put a small lamp on and it was still the middle of the night.

'There's a family in the apartment up there,' I told her, 'and I think the guy's a little crazy. Last year, around Thanksgiving, there were some really weird noises coming from up there.'

'I missed you so much at Thanksgiving,' Stella said, and she kissed me on my forehead, my nose, my lips. And then the bang came again and she stopped. 'What do you mean,' she asked, 'weird noises?'

'The guy shouts a lot,' I said, looking up at the ceiling. 'Things fall down. One night, I thought I heard him drag his kid across the floor and open the window and I thought he was going to throw him out.'

Stella looked at me, her face worried, and I was glad because now someone was here with me to hear these things and to decide what to do. 'There were two of them,' I told her. 'To begin with there were two adults up there, a guy and a woman, they moved in last summer, just after I'd arrived. There were two kids too, a boy and a girl, but it looks like the woman left with the girl, so I guess it's just the boy now. I never see either of them, though, the man or the boy.' Then I looked at Stella. I didn't know why I was talking about this when what I wanted to talk about was what had brought her here and was she really staying and why now? Then we heard the voice of a boy calling out upstairs, 'Dad!', but it was a happy voice and I thought perhaps the boy was calling out for reassurance in the night and Stella closed her eyes and smiled and said, 'I always wanted a little boy.'

'You want to sleep?' I asked. 'You want coffee? I could do you a decaf?' I felt like a hostess who wasn't doing her job properly because I wasn't used to thinking about another person's needs after a whole year alone in London.

'Sleep,' said Stella, and I took her upstairs and she got into bed and went to sleep and I thought of all the time we had known each other, the evening we met at Professor Greer's potluck party, the day she painted her office orange, the first time I knew she was mine, the day of the annual Davis Picnic.

I hadn't been looking forward to Picnic Day that year, because Saturdays had become days I tried to keep for myself, so I could sit on my balcony after an early morning swim and drink my coffee and plan a trip to the farmers' market, or further afield into Sacramento. Officially there was no pressure on faculty members to attend Picnic Day, or to be present for the Chancellor's opening words, but the hype surrounding the event meant I felt I had to go and so I went. I remember what I was wearing, a pair of white pants with a drawstring waist that were cool and comfortable and easy to untie.

I sat with the rest of the American Studies faculty; Macey Bloom was just at the end of the row with her bunny Wilamena under her chair. I had looked around for Stella when I'd arrived and she was nowhere to be seen and I'd felt disheartened about this, wondering why I'd felt I had to come, why I couldn't treat official things with the amusement that Stella Givenchy seemed to do. And then she arrived, just as the Chancellor was beginning to speak, and she walked quite deliberately towards me, apologising as she made her way to the chair next to mine, only apologising in such a way that the people she was disturbing began to apologise to her as well.

'Hey!' she said, a little out of breath as she sat down, and the moment she did I could smell something sweet that hadn't been there before. Perhaps I even sniffed the air without realising it for Stella smiled at me and then she opened up a white paper napkin to show four freshly made brownies. 'I thought I might get real hungry,' she said, 'if we had to sit here for too long.' And then, the brownies still on her lap, she took a book out of her bag and opened it to where I could see a bookmark and she began to read. She just sat there at the Chancellor's address eating her brownie and reading her book and not being afraid to show anyone she was doing either. And I sat beside her and I ate a brownie she gave me and it was perfect, a thin crispy layer on top and then a sunken mound of still warm, still sticky chocolate beneath.

'Delicious,' I said to her, my voice a whisper.

'There's nothing like a hashish brownie, is there?' Stella smiled sweetly at me.

I almost choked. I was sitting there watching the Aggie marching band all in blue, beneath the beady eye of the Chancellor, and my colleague had given me a brownie goddam laced with drugs!

'I'm kidding, honey,' she said, and she laughed and so did I because Stella always made me feel like this, that we were in on something no one else was. 'Okey dokey,' she said when the address was over and the marching band gone. 'What shall we do now?'

And then I knew she was free, that her husband Nick Givenchy must not be about, that she was suggesting we spend the day together.

'Now we go to mine,' I said. And that was when it happened, when we got into my apartment and I followed her in and I thought I do this now or I do this never and I came up behind her and I kissed the back of her neck. Stella remained there for a moment, her entire body still, soft, waiting, and then she turned quickly to me and her lips were as sweet as the chocolate brownie.

And here she is, my Stella, sleeping next to me in London and I'm going to have to get up otherwise I won't be able to hold back and I'll wake her and she needs to sleep. I come down the stairs and busy myself around the apartment, fixing things, wondering how long she will stay. My grant came through, I have another year in London, but will Stella stay that long? Has she come for a visit or has she come to stay? I clean up the kitchen, putting away the washed-up dishes from last night, grinding some fresh coffee beans for when Stella wakes, checking I have what I need for scrambled eggs on rye. I open my kitchen cupboard and take a bottle of squash down from the shelf; I've been keeping it all this time, I haven't even opened it.

I go back into the living room and pick up Stella's bag and put it on the coffee table. It's heavy, there are all sorts of in-flight magazines she must have picked up on the plane. I take out one of the magazines and lay it on the table. It's all bent out of shape so I smooth it down and then I open it to see what Stella was reading about on the plane. There's a photograph of a young guy standing on a sidewalk squinting into the sun, and as I scan the text beneath a name jumps out at me, Donny Green, and I can't think why this name is of any significance until I realise, this is the guy I thought I saw

311

Ashley with in the paper that morning at the newsagent's on Green Lanes. I wonder why, when I asked her about this at the bar that night, she stood up and walked out. I wonder what the big secret is.

When I can't keep myself busy any more I go back to the bedroom and as quietly as I can I make space in my wardrobe for Stella to hang her things, and as I do I think, she's here, she's goddam here and I've woken up and gone to heaven! Stella stirs again, I think she's waking up at last, but then she makes a little satisfied mumbling noise and goes back to sleep.

I close the bedroom door and go downstairs again and just as I get into the kitchen there is a crash from upstairs. I stop by the sink and look up at the ceiling as a man's voice shouts out, 'Christ, you fuck me off!' Then I hear a whimpering noise. I look at my clock on the kitchen wall, it's nine-thirty in the morning, why isn't the little boy at school, is it summer recess now? 'No, Dad!' I hear the boy scream, suddenly and in fear, 'No!' I look round my kitchen, take hold of a pan lid and slam it on the counter, slamming it real loud so that the big guy upstairs will know I'm down here, that I can hear him yelling at his boy. I slam the lid a couple of times and then I wait. For a moment or two there is silence, but then the big guy starts again. 'I said,' he yells, and it's a warning, it's a threat, 'I said, you are beginning to FUCK ME OFF!' I slam the lid again. I think I hear a whimper but I'm not sure. Then I wonder have I made things better for the little boy upstairs by letting his father know I'm listening to what he's doing in private, or have I made things worse?

I get dressed, leave a note for Stella, and grab my swim things. Outside the street feels friendly in the sunlight;

312

everyone seems to have their windows open today. Opposite, a woman is washing her front steps, while a man wearing just a pair of shorts is up a ladder chipping away at a window sill. I open the gate and step onto the sidewalk just as a woman comes out of the house next door.

'Hiya!' she says when she sees me. I haven't spoken to any of my neighbours before; I've been in this apartment for a year and I still don't know any of my goddam neighbours. It seems like she's heading off to work. She's wearing a black skirt belted tightly at the waist and a white shirt with a thin red tie around her neck. I wonder what job she does, she looks a little like a flight attendant, but she would probably take offence if I ask her where she works, so I just look at her and smile. She adjusts a handbag on her shoulder, and I see how her curly yellow hair bounces around her face like she's just had it cut. I wonder if she's saying hi to me only because the sun is out?

'Morning,' I say. 'Isn't it lovely?' I smile some more, pleased with myself because my neighbour is nodding and smiling too and I'm sounding more like a Brit now.

'Everything OK in there?' my neighbour asks, because we are still smiling at each other, and she looks up at the apartment upstairs. 'It gets a bit noisy in there, doesn't it?'

'Yes,' I say eagerly. 'Do you hear it?'

'Every word,' the woman nods. 'Especially that carry on this morning. He's notorious. The council should do something.'

'The council should do something,' I echo. I want to ask my neighbour what this means but she's said it like I should know what it means.

'Oops!' says my neighbour. 'Got to go, I'm going to be late, as usual. Bye!' And she opens the gate and hurries off down the sidewalk, her curly blonde hair bouncing, just as I was about to ask what she can hear and why the big guy is notorious and whether there is anything we should or could be doing, and I think she knows this, I think that's what made her hurry away.

I get to the pool and the fast lane is so crowded I choose the slow lane, and I put my new goggles on and I'm off, in the water, up and down, feeling the strokes stretching my body, clearing my mind. The water is churning, I'm doing backstroke right by the ropes, and a guy in the next lane is doing front crawl and the water is rolling like we're on a massive waterbed. I speed up, increase my strokes, kick harder because I want to reach the end first, I want to win against the front-crawl guy. But I have a troubled feeling just below the heady, rhythmic feeling of swimming, because I'm thinking of what Stella said before she fell asleep last night, when she said, 'I always wanted a little boy,' and I wonder why, after all this time, she's never said anything like that to me before.

Chapter Thirty-Three

DUDU

'You always say you remember when we girls were little, but you never talk about now.' This is my Loreen speaking as we stand here in her bedroom, and I have never seen a bedroom in such a state. Her dressing table looks like a market stall and the doors of her wardrobe are wide open because they can't close; there are too many things inside because even now, after all this time in her new flat, she hasn't sorted out her boxes. I can see childhood things all over the place, the things I have kept for her, her special things like school reports and prizes, Brownie badges and sports certificates, diaries and posters and the annuals she used to read.

'Mum,' says Loreen, 'I'm not being horrible, I'm really not, but have you noticed? Have you noticed the way you're always going on about . . . you're always talking about when we were little, me and Bel and Karen and . . .'

'Ashley,' I say, picking up a pile of loose jewellery from the dressing table and dropping it piece by piece into a box I gave Loreen for her birthday when she turned twenty-one. That was a good year, the year she turned twenty-one and she was finishing university and she stopped seeing me as her adversary.

'And Ashley,' says Loreen, watching me. She takes a long silver chain from my hands and puts it round her neck. 'So, if I say anything to do with Bel or anyone then you immediately say, "I remember when you girls were little . . ." It's like a button gets pressed.'

I go to her bedroom window and it's a little open so I close it; it's cold enough in here already and I don't want to share a private conversation with other people in these flats that are built so close together that if a neighbour coughs another neighbour can hear it. I think maybe she is right, for a seer does not see something on her own head, and that is the way with shortcomings, you don't see your own. 'A button gets pressed,' I say.

'Yeah.' Loreen carelessly pulls the duvet across her bed and my fingers itch with wanting to do it properly for her. 'So, for example, if I say, "I'm trying to get Bel and everyone together before Christmas," you'll say, "Ah, I remember you girls that one Christmas when . . ." Or if I say, "I've got to get the boys to school," then you'll say, "Ah, I remember when you girls were little and the day you started school," and blah blah blah.'

'Blah blah blah,' I say, echoing my Loreen. I wonder why she's doing this, causing a quarrel like this, only it's not a quarrel as such because a quarrel is a two-way thing and this is not. But I do know why she is doing this now; she is doing it because I am going away, because I am going home and this is making her anxious and keen to pick a quarrel. Rise above it, I hear my late husband say, rise above it.

'Where's that t-shirt?' asks Loreen, riffling through a pile of bags on the floor. 'Where's that t-shirt I got for Bel for her birthday?'

She sounds just like a sixteen-year-old, wanting her mother to find things for her and to stop myself from doing this I sit down on the one chair in her bedroom, whose covers need a good clean. 'How's your leg?' Loreen asks when she sees that I have sat down. My back, and my leg, have become part of our day-to-day routine: How are you? Isn't it cold today? How are the boys? Isn't it getting darker earlier now? How's your leg? I shrug to show my leg is as it always is.

'What time is your flight?' she asks.

'Six.'

'This evening?' she asks.

'This evening.'

'So what time will you check in, what time do you need to get to the airport? You have to check in three hours early now, Mum, and don't forget you're not allowed to take on any liquids.'

I smile, I don't need my daughter to get me to a plane on time, I am more than capable of doing my own travel arrangements. 'I just came by to say goodbye to the boys, Loreen, and to ask if you have anything you want me to take with me.'

'Anything to take with you?'

I nod.

'Like what?' asks Loreen.

'Anything for your family back home.'

Loreen looks annoyed. 'I haven't thought about it really. Um, I just didn't think about that, that I should be getting things for you to take back.' She looks at me a little guiltily now. 'The thing is, Mum, it doesn't really feel like *my* family. You know?'

I don't say anything because no, I do not know. Those people back home are her family because that is the way it is.

'I mean, Mum, when was the last time I saw anyone from Africa? When I was a baby, right? After Dad died? And I can't really remember that.'

I flinch because she says it so easily; she says this like she has no trouble saying it at all.

'Oh, I suppose there was that time when weirdo Victor came over . . .'

'He's your uncle,' I say.

Loreen ignores me. 'And it's not like I actually come from Botswana . . .'

'Loreen!' I am shocked. The fact that she wasn't born in Africa doesn't mean that her mother and father weren't born in Africa and that our culture back home isn't a part of her. She knows I'm going home, she should have thought of giving me things to take to the family, to the people who are worse off than she is. I stop myself from saying this, for I do not want to continue the quarrel or provoke her, and instead I look across at her wardrobe. I can't keep my eyes away from it. My daughter is thirty-four years old and still I want to clean up her wardrobe and her clothes and her room. But I stop myself and instead I think of the day she left for university and how I went with her to the tube station and watched her get on a tube just like her father had done all those years ago, when he had never come back. And then I returned home alone and sat in her room, just as I am doing now, and I examined all the posters she had left on the wall and on the back of her door and on her wardrobe, and I wondered who the people in the posters would have to talk to now their owner, my little Loreen, had gone.

'How do you mean I don't talk about now?' I ask, standing up, feeling my leg pulse with a pain that is so familiar I am almost alarmed when it's not there.

Loreen looks at me, puzzled, like she's forgotten what she has been saying. 'I mean, it's not a criticism or anything, Mum, but it's like, when something is going on with us now, me or Bel or Karen or . . .' She opens a drawer and pulls out a cardigan which is rumpled because she should have hung it on a hanger and put it in her wardrobe if it wasn't so full of boxes. 'Or Ashley, you don't want to talk about it, or you're not as interested in it.'

'Like what?' I ask. Today is the day my daughter has chosen to tell me about all my shortcomings.

'Like,' my Loreen sighs. 'Like anytime I go on a date.'

I hold onto the knob of her open bedroom door. What does she want me to say about her dates?

'I mean, Mum, I told you about Mark last year . . .'

I nod that she certainly did.

'But you never said anything, like whether he sounded nice or not, what you thought of him.'

'Loreen,' I object, tightening my hold on the doorknob, 'I never even met that man!' And would she have listened to what I had to say about him anyway? He sounded like a very dubious individual, as would any man looking for a woman on this Internet thing everyone loves so much, but Loreen couldn't see this and I wouldn't have been able to make her see this, so what was the point? And the reason I don't comment on all these men she meets is because I don't want my child to get hurt. I see how excited she gets, how sure she is that one man or another will be the man she's looking for and I just don't want to see her get hurt, for it is not possible for a parent to ever stop protecting their child.

'I know you didn't *meet* him, Mum, I know,' says Loreen, exasperated, 'but that's not the point, the point is ... Oh I don't know what the point is. Have a good trip, OK, Mum?' And she comes and puts her arm into mine so we are standing together hooked onto the knob of her open bedroom door.

'Mum!' yells Dwaine from the front room.

'What?' yells my Loreen.

Why is there always so much yelling going on in this home? Dwaine shouldn't be yelling like this, demanding his mother's attention, an African child would never behave like this, shouting for their mother through the house.

'What does your horoscope say?' asks Loreen, squeezing my arm playfully. 'You are going on a journey . . .'

I take my hand off the knob. 'You know I don't believe in those things anymore.'

'Well, you used to!'

'I used to,' I say. Indeed I used to, ever since my kindly German landlady Adelaide told me about horoscopes and I thought I could use them to see the future and protect my child. I had believed them when they said, that first day of primary school, that the friends my little Loreen would make that day would be her friends for life. And the day of the Hampstead Heath fair and the fortune-teller who told me my little Loreen would be famous, that I would meet an older man, that I would have another child, I believed that too. But

320

she knows what happened, she knows I lost my faith that day we went to Brighton to celebrate her A-level results. That was when I lost my faith in horoscopes and everything else because how could that fortune-teller, how could that kindly Professor Shiraz, not see that when I left his place then I would be knocked over by a car and admitted to hospital for three months, and so many years later still have this stiffness in my back and this pain in my leg? How could he not have seen that? How could he not have had even an inkling that that was going to happen and how could he not have given me some sort of warning, to be careful on the road perhaps, to stay away from my daughter's silly friend in case she made me so mad that I would . . .

'Mum?' Loreen looks worried, she's tugging on my sleeve. 'You OK?'

I smile, I take her chin with my hand and I smile, but I am thinking of Ashley and I am thinking that a louse bites after hiding inside your blanket. I never liked that girl or the way she behaved with my little Loreen, the way when she came over for tea that first time she asked, 'Don't you have a whole house? A garden? A car?' The way she laughed when I spoke my language, the way everyone seemed to think Ashley was cleverer than my little Loreen when she was obviously not. And I know it was Ashley who led the way when they burst into the palm-reader's room in Brighton, I know it was Ashley who encouraged my little Loreen to mock me.

'When are you back?' asks Loreen. 'Two weeks, right?'

'Right,' I say, but I don't tell her I have an open ticket. I just make my way into the front room with my poorly leg and say goodbye to my little grandsons.

Chapter Thirty-Four

I am sitting waiting to be called for my plane and I am thinking, I don't remember this, I don't remember this at all. I don't remember escalators going up and down, I don't remember so many shops and bars and restaurants and cafés, I don't remember Johannesburg airport like this at all. I want to get back to what I know. I have been waiting for some two hours now, but the nice man at the check-in desk said if I was to sit here, to one side, then he would call me when my plane is ready. I have slept all the way from London and now I am wide awake.

And then at last I am called and I am jostled along in the crowd of people and put onto a little bus and driven to the plane. I look out and see there is a lady in a uniform standing at the open door to the plane that is painted in the Botswana colours, and as we come nearer she puts out one hand and gives a thumbs-down sign and the people around me complain as the bus starts up again and it drives slowly round the plane that will take me home. We drive three times around that plane until the lady at the open door finally gives the thumbs-up sign and we stop and we board. My neighbour is a man in green, everything about him is green: his shirt, his cap, his shorts and his socks. He is a tourist.

When the plane lands at Sir Seretse Khama airport I am one of the first to stand up and I take my bag and walk to the door. The flight attendant does not even nod at me as I get off, but even her indifference cannot spoil my mood. I am home, and I stand on the top of the steps and smell the flat sandy dryness of a hot land. There are people waiting behind me, I can hear them beginning to complain, but I want to enjoy the moment, the moment before I step off this plane and my feet stand again on the land of my birth.

I come down the aeroplane steps, feel them shake a little as I clutch the railings to steady myself, and then I am on the tarmac which is steaming in the sun as if it is water. I look around, see people hurrying off another plane that is parked right behind us, see passengers with trolleys and suitcases, cameras and handbags. I watch as a little white truck trundles to the side of my plane and as two men begin to load off our luggage. And I know for me this is a special day, but for everyone else it is just normal, a day in which a person arrives somewhere or leaves, a day in which the person who unloads baggage does as he always does; it is only for me that everything about today is different.

I get through immigration without trouble because this is my country and I don't have to give any explanation as to why I am here, and as the glass doors slide open I see my late husband's brother Victor Kudumane waiting for me. He is looking immaculate in a blue jacket over a white shirt. He is a chief executive now; I know this because he has written to tell me. There is a woman next to him, a young woman with a shiny face and hair piled high up on her head, but I'm not sure if they are together or not for when Victor Kudumane sees me then the woman walks away as if she shouldn't be there.

'Good journey?' he asks, taking me by the arm, but watching the back of the shiny-faced woman as she walks away. 'My driver is outside,' says Victor Kudumane, and I wonder why he is speaking to me in English; either it is for the benefit of those around us, to show what a successful man he is, or it is for my benefit, as if I have been away for so long I have forgotten my own language!

We get outside and something odd has happened outside the airport. There are wild animals everywhere. Amid the sand-coloured stones and the tall grand aloes and the spiky bulbs of cacti, are animals: an elephant standing majestically with its trunk raised off the ground; two zebra, their bright black-and-white-striped bodies facing in opposite directions about to run. Then as we walk past them towards the car park, I see that, of course, they are not real. They are fake animals. I see a group of children rush towards the elephant, then they stop and begin to walk cautiously around it, and then they dart forward and touch its skin, although now I can see there are signs saying this should not be done. And I think, you stupid old woman, of course they are fake; there would not be real animals outside an airport, in the midst of a car park, in the midst of all this traffic. The journey has been long, it is playing tricks with my mind and I am not sure any more about what I am seeing. But I wish my little grandsons were here, I wish they could see this place that their grandmother was born.

Victor Kudumane stops by a large shiny white vehicle and I see a man waiting in the driver's seat. 'This is all very new, *Rra*,' I say, getting into Victor Kudumane's car, and it is so high off the ground that I feel I am getting on a bus.

324

Inside the car the seats are soft and I sink onto them and the skin of the seats is cool because the car has air conditioning that I can hear humming away. Victor Kudumane gives a smile and I know he thinks I am talking about his car. 'This airport terminal and these animals,' I say, 'they are all very new.'

'Oh everything in Gaborone is new,' says Victor Kudumane, nodding at the driver that he should start the car. 'You go away for a few weeks, come back and there's a new shopping centre! We live off Independence Avenue.' He looks round at me as if I should know this, as if I should be impressed. 'The shopping centre near us is very good, it has an excellent Italian restaurant, we may go there tonight if you're not too tired.'

And I think, Italian restaurant? I haven't travelled across the world back to my home in Africa to go to an Italian restaurant! But of course I don't say this, I just slip the seat belt across my chest as we drive along a motorway, and as we reach the city I look out of the window and I look and look because this is not how things used to be at all. There are new blue buildings of glass and steel, there are traffic lights and road signs and modern expensive cars. A person would not think this is a place built in a valley, between Kgale and Oodi Hills, or that this is a place that lies on the Notwane River. And I remember how, when Victor Kudumane came to stay that one night with me and my little Loreen in London, how he tried to tell me things were different back home and how I didn't believe him.

'How is your wife?' I ask. 'And the children?'

But Victor Kudumane doesn't answer me, for he is busy

now, chatting away on his mobile phone. I hear him say he requires rice for his lunch.

'Are the family well?' I ask when he finishes his conversation.

'Yes, yes.' He looks over at me where I sit in my comfort on the back seat. 'My wife will be back later this afternoon, she's at the gym. That woman is always at the gym.'

At the gym! What would Mrs Kudumane be doing there, I ask myself as I look out of the window again, at the billboards I see advertising mobile phones and televisions and condoms. 'What's happening, *Rra*?' I ask as we slow down and I see cars stretching out on all sides.

'Traffic jam,' says Victor Kudumane. 'We shouldn't have come onto Nelson Mandela Drive,' he looks at his driver in irritation, 'it's always like this.'

We sit in the traffic jam and it gives me time to look around again, and I see that the houses by the road have walls around them and the walls have rigid strings of brown barbed wire and thick pieces of broken glass on top and I wonder why the people of Gaborone feel the need to turn their houses into fortresses.

'OK?' asks Victor Kudumane.

'Fine, *Rra*,' I say, 'just fine.' But I feel the pain in my leg pulsing so hard that I grasp my thigh with both hands as if to hold it in. Then suddenly the driver swerves the car left and onto the sand on the side of the road, and now we are travelling parallel with all the other cars, in a place where cars should not be at all. And just as I am worrying about this, Victor Kudumane's driver sees a space between the cars in front and he swerves the car off the sand and back onto the tar road and there are a lot of people blaring their horns at us as we turn left and onto a road that I see is Independence Avenue.

We pull up at the gates to a private complex and a watchman comes out from a little wooden house and he waves and Victor Kudumane's driver drives us in. I see six houses in a row, they are very new, and when we stop at the last house I see the garage is the most prominent part of the building. Above the garage is a large curved white satellite dish fixed to the wall, and down below a porch of sorts, half-covered in panes of frosted glass and with a large fridge freezer waiting to be taken in perhaps, or waiting to be collected and taken away.

There is a single tree, a sturdy twisted shepherd's tree, in front of the house on a square patch of reddened sand, but other than that the sand on which the private complex stands has all been concreted over into beige and orange paving stones.

This is not what I was expecting. I don't know what I was expecting but this is not it and I wish with a longing that is painful that my late husband was here, that I was taking this journey with him and not by myself alone. I had forgotten that most of the family were in Gaborone now. Then I do know what I was expecting: I was expecting to go to my home village of Manyana. I was expecting a long drive along bumpy tracks and then to reach the outskirts of the village and to see the low-walled compounds and thatched houses, the raked yards the colour of a peach, the rock-strewn pathways along which the cattle trek.

Victor Kudumane helps me out of the car and I stand a

little dazed by the twisted shepherd's tree outside his brick and glass Gaborone house. 'Dorcus!' he shouts. The door to the house is thick brown wood and it is open. 'Dorcus!' he shouts again. '*Modimo*,' he mutters. '*O kae Dorcus?*'

'What?' a girl's voice shouts back, harsh and annoyed. Then a young girl of perhaps fourteen comes to the doorway. She wears skintight jeans that end just above the knee and an orange t-shirt. 'What?' she says again.

I expect Victor Kudumane to give her a thorough telling off, I expect him to tell her what she should be doing and to greet her guest, not to be shouting out like this and asking, 'What?', but he just walks past her with a sigh and into the house. I look at the young girl's face and wonder which of my family I can see in her features, what relative she will be to me, but she stands there in the doorway with a rude stare on her face.

'*Dumela mosetsana*,' I say as I reach the door and as I hold out one hand to steady myself. 'My bags are there,' I tell her when she doesn't reply.

'Oh pick them up yourself,' she says, and she moves back into the house. 'I'm busy.'

I stand there, utterly speechless. Has a child really just spoken to me like this, has an African child just spoken to an elder like this? Does she not know respect, has she not been brought up to show respect? But I don't have time to ask her this because Dorcus has gone, and so I come into Victor Kudumane's house and I see at once that this is a house whose insides are more important than its outsides. There is no room out on the porch with the fridge freezer there, but in here there is plenty of room. There is a square of blue carpet on the polished tiled floor and in the exact middle of the carpet is a table with a glass top and it is covered with newspapers and magazines and cords and leads that fit I don't know what, and three cans of St Louis beer and an empty bottle of guava juice. I come further into the room and see that along one wall are two very new armchairs still with the imprint of whoever has recently been sitting on them, and the colour of the armchairs is alarming, it is the colour of algae. I sit down on one of the armchairs, unsure where Victor Kudumane has gone, and I lean forward and take one of the magazines off the glass-topped table and peer down at the words. I see I am looking at a horoscope: *Give your feelings new life, be creative and sexy. Enjoy top-notch professional entertainment.* That is what it says for Pisces, my Loreen's star sign, and I wonder if Dorcus has been reading this magazine and if she is a Pisces as well, for someone has circled this horoscope and then drawn little pictures of hearts all round it. Perhaps it is not Dorcus who has been reading this, perhaps it is Mrs Kudumane, perhaps this is what she does before she goes to the gym. *Be creative and sexy?* What sort of horoscope is that and when did newspapers here in Botswana start printing horoscopes?

I put the magazine down and I see that I am facing a very large television screen on a wooden cabinet and that there is a music video showing. I see some young people grinding up against each other and I cannot believe at first that these are Batswana. I listen to the music, try to hear the words they are singing; I cannot be sure of the language but then I know it is English and that this is what the young men are calling each other: nigger. They are singing a song, these Batswana, a song with the word nigger and they are smiling in their tiny little clothes and I am so shocked that, once again, it is as if all my breath has been taken away. And as I sit here on this chair the colour of algae I see that this room extends into another area which has a curved wooden bar and four bar stools with blue on the top. What sort of room is this, I think, is this a bar or is this a family home?

'It is very . . .' I say as Victor Kudumane comes back into the room.

'*Ee*,' he nods, and he looks pleased, he looks certain I was about to admire his home.

'Where has the girl gone?' I ask.

'Who? Oh, you mean Dorcus.' Victor Kudumane gives another sigh. 'She's my last born, you've not seen her before, I suppose. She's the family dropout.'

And then I hear a baby crying, far off in another part of the house, and then the young girl Dorcus comes to the doorway and eyes me as if I am the one who is making the baby cry.

Victor Kudumane ignores Dorcus and he ignores the baby crying and he holds his hand out, inviting me to wander further into the house, and so I do and I put my head into a galley of a kitchen, where everything is fitted tightly together, the units on the walls, the tiles beneath the units, the black marble of the counter tops. I see then that the back door is closed, the glass of the door is covered in white burglar bars, and outside in the yard is nothing, nothing but sand and an empty white metal clothes dryer. It is utterly and completely colourless and I think with a feeling of panic that is almost like drowning, what am I doing here?

330

Chapter Thirty-Five

LOREEN

Hi Fonzie, how you doing? Ha! Here you are in my old *Look-in* annual in your trademark leather jacket and white t-shirt. Very nice. You look hot, Fonz, with both your hands giving that thumbs-up sign you used to do. But then again, you're looking rather middle-aged. I remember you as young. What's the date of this annual? 1983. So I was ten. What was a ten-year-old doing having a crush on a thirty-year-old, Fonz? Oh my God, I'd forgotten your real name was Henry Winkler. We used to giggle at that, me and Bel, because Winkler sounded a bit like willy, didn't it?

Oh how I used to love *Happy Days*, because it was so happy, in a 1950s drive-in, cheerleader sort of way. You were supposed to be a bit tough, though, weren't you, Fonz? You used to snap your fingers when you wanted to stop the juke-box, you had an endless supply of girlfriends, and of course you wore a leather jacket. But even that family, the straight-laced Cunninghams, ended up loving you, didn't they?

Oh God, I'm wasting time when I should be thinking about what to wear tonight. It's been over a year since we all met up and this time we're meeting at Ashley's house, and I haven't been there for years.

Who else was it that used to wear leather jackets all the time? Bodie and Doyle on *The Professionals*. Now you really were hard, weren't you, boys? In fact you were pretty violent, always running through empty building sites, dangling crooks off balconies, waving your little guns. I liked Bodie the best, I really fancied Bodie, he was the one with the pout, the ex-mercenary, the real hardman. Bel used to laugh at me and call you Bogey, but she liked that programme too, she liked the cars and the chases and the way you always leapt over a car bonnet rather than walking round it. I don't remember any women in *The Professionals*; were there ever any women?

I flick through *Look-in*, wondering if you're in here too, Bodie, but you're not. I can't find much to read in this, it's all crosswords and comic strips. There aren't any girly quizzes or questionnaires. There's a joke page, though. *Q. What did the policeman say to his stomach? A. You're under a vest.* Ha! I'm going to tell that to Dwaine. It might make him laugh. He's feeling down because Mum's still gone. She was supposed to be back three weeks ago and now I'm beginning to wonder if she'll be back for Christmas. She hasn't even rung, only weirdo Uncle Victor has rung to say Mum is fine. Well of course she's fine, she's back home where she wants to be in her beloved Africa. She's back where everything is how it should be, where mums and daughters live together and where children don't shout or talk back to their elders.

I pick up another *Look-in* from the pile. This one looks more recent. Oh my God, it's Bros. You were massive, weren't you, boys? God, remember that song, 'When will I be famous?' Matt Goss, I can see you now with your white

332

quiff and your baby-blue eyes, dancing like a seven-year-old, floppy arms all over the place.

Oh this is ridiculous. I chuck the *Look-in*s back in the wardrobe, kick at some clothes on the floor. I've got a baby-sitter tonight, I don't want her to think I live in a pigsty. Then I hear Dwaine yelling from the front room.

'Hey Dwaine!' I shout. 'I've got a joke for you. What did the policeman . . .'

But he's still yelling, he's not listening. He's a bit hyper at the moment, now he's seven and in the juniors.

'Mum, you know what we were talking about before?' he says, coming to find me, standing at the doorway to my bedroom.

'Yes?'

'Well can we talk some more about it?'

'OK,' I say very reasonably, although I realise now I have no idea what he's talking about. I sit down on my bed and wait.

'Mum, can a child have S-E-X with an adult?'

'No,' I say at once. It's been a long while since Dwaine talked about s-e-x and I wasn't expecting this. 'Well they can, but they shouldn't because an adult shouldn't do that.' Why did I say that? I should have just said no, it will only confuse him.

'Have I had S-E-X with you, Mum?' Dwaine asks, sitting next to me on the bed.

'No!' I nearly put my head in my hands. What would the social services man make of this? But the young man with the clipboard hasn't been in touch again; he said he didn't think he needed to take things further, unless something else happened. Like what, what did he think would happen? It still seems crazy to me. Dwaine's just a kid who drew a willy on a piece of paper, a kid with a natural interest in his body and everybody else's. Why didn't the school talk to me first? What did they think they were doing referring it to social services when there are kids out there who really need help? I need to go and meet with Dwaine's teacher, I need to ask about this, but I'm so angry I can't face it.

Dwaine shifts away from me, looking rejected because I've said he hasn't had S-E-X with me. I put my arm around him. 'No,' I laugh, 'of course you haven't.'

Dwaine nods. It's an I-thought-so sort of nod.

'Why?' I ask in alarm. 'What has someone been saying?' I start thinking all sorts of things, why would he ask if he has had sex with me, where would an idea like that come from? What do the boys say to each other in the juniors' playground? Has he heard someone say motherfucker, has someone called my little Dwaine a motherfucker? 'Dwaine, what has someone been saying, about S-E-X and everything, have the big boys been saying anything?'

'Nothing,' he says, squirming away from me. 'Mum?'

'Yes, right here,' I say.

'Have you ever had S-E-X?'

'Yes.'

'Yuk! Have you really?' Dwaine looks amazed, like this was the last answer in the world he was expecting. 'Oh!' he says, looking suddenly relieved. 'With my dad, right?'

'Right,' I say, and as always when either of the boys mentions their dad I get a sickly feeling because I can't say what I want to, I can't be honest. It's not like I'm talking to Mum or to Bel; it's their father and I have to let the boys grow up and find out for themselves what sort of person he is.

'And,' says Dwaine, 'that was to make me and Anthony?'

What? I've lost track for a moment. 'Yes,' I smile, 'that was to make you and Anthony.'

Dwaine nods, he approves of this. 'But Mum, why can't Dad live with us, if you made us together?'

'Because . . .' I stand up. Dwaine's never asked me this before. He has always seemed to take it for granted that his father comes once a year at Christmas and then leaves again. What can I say? 'We don't live together because your dad doesn't want to' – can I say that? 'We don't live together because actually your father never wanted to, he ran away when I was pregnant with your brother, he didn't even come to the hospital to see his son being born, he just came round a few years later, and stayed long enough to make you, and then left again. We don't live together because your dad does-n't love me, he never loved me, even though I loved him, and anyway he has no idea what it is to be a father.'

'Sometimes, Dwaine,' I say, 'people just don't get on any more.'

Dwaine nods. I study his eyes, try to work out what he's taking in, what he thinks of this. 'So, Mum . . .' he says.

'Yes?'

'How will Santa get down the chimney if we don't have a chimney in this flat?'

This is exactly the worry he had last Christmas. I look at my son's serious little face. His mind jumps so quickly; one minute he's trying to get his head round the fact his mother has sex and why his father doesn't live with him, and the next

335

it's back to being a little kid and believing in Father Christmas.

'Mum!' says Dwaine, and he falls over backwards on the bed and makes himself comfortable in my duvet. 'I've made a Christmas list!'

'You have?'

'Yes. I want a Nintendo DS.'

I laugh; I can't afford one of those.

'And Mum,' he sits up, 'I want a Donny Green CD.'

'Oh come on, Dwaine!'

'But Mum! Donny Green is really cool,' and Dwaine gets up from the bed and begins dancing in front of my wardrobe. 'Mum?' he calls as I make to leave the room.

'Yes?'

'You really should clear up all this mess, you know.'

Me and Dwaine set off to Mum's place to feed her cat. Her neighbour has been doing it, but now she wants me to take over. Anthony's at football practice and he wouldn't want to come anyway.

'Is Nan ever going to come back?' Dwaine asks as I let us in with Mum's key. 'It's spooky in here, isn't it?' he says as we walk down Mum's tiny hallway and into her front room.

'Don't be silly,' I say. 'Of course she's coming back.' But he's right, it is a bit spooky in here. Mum has left the curtains closed even though I told her not to, because with the curtains closed it's obvious she's away. It's freezing in here. I open the curtains and look around the room, everything is as it should be, only even more so. Mum must have washed the sofa and the cushion covers before she left because they look very clean and starched, and all the surfaces have been dusted. 'Careful!' I warn as Dwaine starts picking up Mum's bits and pieces from the side table. She has a row of things from Botswana: a small wooden candle holder that's become cracked over the years; two place mats decorated in a zebra design; a Botswana stamp encased in a hard square of plastic. They are lined up so carefully, with equal spaces between them and a gap at the end of the row where perhaps she's thinking of adding something new. I have a sudden feeling of doom. What if she doesn't come back? What if that gap is never filled and would what I do with all these things then?

I start calling for the cat, noisily, to distract myself. 'Cat!' I shout, because I can't remember its name.

'Its name is Kitty Cat,' says Dwaine reproachfully. He gets down on one knee and calls quietly, 'Where are you, my clever little Kitty Cat?'

I smile at the way he is imitating Mum so exactly, then we both shout in alarm as the cat leaps out from wherever it's been hiding and lands on the carpet in front of us.

'Don't go out tonight, Mum,' Dwaine says. He picks up the cat and cuddles it and the cat dabs gently at Dwaine's face with one black paw. 'I'll be so lonely without you, Mum.'

'Don't be silly,' I say. Don't do this to me, I think. When I don't want to go out, like the night of the bombs when I met up with Bel, then he wants me to go, but when I do want to go out, then he doesn't. But we're meeting at Ashley's tonight and I can't remember the last time the four of us were there and there are so many things I want to know about. I want to meet Karen's girlfriend, I want to know what Ashley's been up to that she can't keep in touch, and I want to know why

Bel has been so hard to get hold of and why, having hated every moment of her job for years, she suddenly seems to be working all the hours there are.

'Ah, Mum . . .' Dwaine pleads, and he looks at me and cuddles Mum's cat.

I shake my head because no, I want to go out tonight, I want to see my friends.

Chapter Thirty-Six

I'm walking down the road with my mobile in one hand and a bottle of Pomagne and a bunch of flowers in the other. We always used to drink Pomagne, me and Bel and Karen and Ashley. We thought it was champagne, because it was fizzy and in a big, heavy bottle with sparkly wrapping on the top, but when I bought it at the off licence just now I had a look at the label and saw it's just cider. Ha! All those times we thought we were being sophisticated drinking champagne and it was cider.

I'm holding my mobile in my hand in case it rings, and because somehow it makes me feel safer like this. I don't much like walking out at night, and with my mobile in my hand I feel connected to my boys. I texted Karen to see what time she was coming to Ashley's but she hasn't texted me back. I texted Bel too, but for some reason the text wouldn't send. Oh my God, I feel a bit lopsided, clutching my mobile and the Pomagne and the flowers. I've got my winter boots on and I haven't worn them for ages and the heels are a bit high, like if I wanted to run quickly I couldn't.

I never really liked Ashley's parents' road. It's big and wide, the spacious four-storey houses rise up impressively on either side, but there's something about the street I don't like. There aren't many street lights, there's two at one end and two at the other, so inbetween it's quite dark. The houses have lights on but they are so far back from the road that they don't help much. There is an alleyway halfway down the road that's dark and overgrown, with wet graffitied walls, where Ashley used to sneak out to smoke or where we'd take a short cut to the shops. It's the sort of short cut that these days I would only use in daylight. Maybe I was braver when I was younger, but no, I know I wasn't, I never took risks even as a kid; it was Bel who did that.

I walk quickly past the alleyway and as I do I see the figure of a man sitting in a bashed-up white van parked right at the entrance. I wonder what someone's doing sitting in a dark, parked van at night; perhaps he's waiting for someone or perhaps he's broken down. I speed up even more, with some silly idea that the man might suddenly jump out. Then a light comes on inside the van, a dim light like that of a child's torch, and I see now it's an elderly man with white hair and he's using a pen torch to fill in a crossword. It's such a cold night that he must be freezing, why doesn't he go somewhere warm and light to do his crossword? As I pass the man in the van, I see him put down his crossword, pick up a paper cup and drain the contents, and then he starts the engine and drives off.

I slow down now and I look down into the basement rooms on the right-hand side of the road. They are much of the same these houses: the basement rooms have all been knocked through so the kitchen and dining areas join, and in each house are thick wooden slatted floors and bright ceiling lights, shelves lined with books, wine racks and abstract paintings on the walls, large dinner-party-sized tables, bowls stuffed full of fresh fruit. It's a wealthy road. We're only in mid-December but several houses have Christmas lights up already, one has sparkling little red globes strung up in the big tree outside.

I'm trying to remember what number Ashley lives at, and I think it's this one, 24, because I remember a black door and a gold knocker. There's a wreath on the door for Christmas. I don't know whether to go up the steps to the front door or go down and use the basement door because I remember Ashley used to use both. I can see lights on downstairs, but the blinds are drawn so I can't see inside. This is silly, Ashley's my friend, I could just shout out her name.

I knock on the front door and wait. Nothing happens so I lift the letterbox and look through and I get a blast of warmth and a smell of mulled wine. I haven't been here for years; I'm not sure how long Ashley has been living here, although I think it's only about six months, or even where her parents are now. I think her mother kept this house after the split, not that Ashley will ever talk about that. When Ashley's dad moved out she acted like her father was dead, just like mine.

Even walking up the steps brings back all sorts of memories, like Ashley's dad standing here and saying, 'Hello girls!'; like coming here after school; like coming to one of Ashley's birthday parties, the first one I ever went to, and Mum nudging me in and being overwhelmed by everything, the food, the presents, the party games. I thought they had everything then, Ashley and her family. She lived in a big house, she had every item of clothing I ever wanted, she had all the dolls, she even had a kitten when she asked for one. Maybe that was why I called her a cunt in my diary. Maybe one day it all just got to me.

I take the big brass knocker and bang on the door again.

The Christmas wreath is woven from holly and ivy and though the berries are bright and red and alive, it makes me think of a funeral.

'Hello,' says Ashley, opening the door. 'You're early.'

'Sorry,' I say. For a second I think she's going to tell me to come back later and close the door, but she opens it and waves me in. I give her a kiss and her cheeks are hot and soft. She's wearing a plastic apron with big pink tits painted on the front and she sees me looking at it and laughs and unties it from behind with one hand.

'That's your mum's,' I say.

'I know, hideous isn't it, babe?' She drops the apron on the floor and I step around it and follow her downstairs. I'm holding my bunch of flowers and the bottle of Pomagne and when we get into the room I wish I hadn't brought either because there are flowers all over the place, big new bunches of flowers in tall glass vases, and a fully stacked rack of wine and real champagne bottles near the cooker. I put down my offerings on the dark marble counter, next to a big pile of newspapers, and they look pathetic. Why did I bring Pomagne? It looks so cheap.

There's a Christmas tree by the window, bushy and thick and green, with gold decorations: baubles and tinsel and icicles. It's a very coordinated Christmas tree and I can't believe kids would decorate a tree like this.

'Where are the girls?' I ask Ashley. I can't wait to see her girls. I can't even remember when I last saw them. I always thought our kids would be friends and I don't really know why they're not, except that her girls go to boarding school. 'Are they back for the holidays yet?'

'They're upstairs,' says Ashley. 'They only board during the week now.'

I wait, listening out for the sound of children.

'They're with Afina.'

'Who?'

'Afina. The au pair. Romanian, very good. We've turned the upstairs into a self-contained flat.'

I don't know what Ashley means by 'we'. She can't mean her ex because she'd never do anything with him, she won't even talk about him, just like she won't talk about her father. And that's what is so odd, that we've been friends for so long, for most of our lives, and yet still there are things we don't talk about. None of us ever got to know Ashley's husband; the first time I ever spoke to him properly was at the wedding, and so when they divorced none of us really knew what to say. And if Ashley can't talk about these things with us, then who does she talk about them with? I'm lucky I have Bel, I can talk about anything with Bel, there's nothing we wouldn't tell each other.

'I hope we see the girls later,' I say.

'Mmm,' says Ashley. Now that she's taken off her mum's old apron and we're standing in the light of the kitchen, I see she's not really dressed. I'm not sure if she's wearing a nightie or a little party dress but her feet are bare and I have the sudden feeling she just got out of bed. Then I see a man's black jacket thrown over the back of a chair. Oh my God, is there a man in here?

There's a knock at the front door and Ashley says, 'Will you get it, babe? I've got to get dressed,' and she says it like I often pop round and open the door for her. I hope the boys are behaving themselves with the baby-sitter, I think, as I go back up the stairs and open the door, and Karen is standing there with a woman who must be her girlfriend. I giggle as I open the door because it's like it's my house, and I give Karen a hug.

'This is Stella,' she says. 'And this is Loreen.' Stella puts out her hand to shake mine but I've already gone forward to kiss her, and so we meet, laughing, in the middle. She has beautiful hair, with highlights that are almost orange, and she's wearing a green velvet dress that gives her an incredible cleavage. In comparison Karen is looking very sensible in black trousers and a black top like she's about to address a conference.

'You look lovely,' I say to both of them. I remind myself to tell Karen about the *Look-in* annual I found so we can reminisce about *Happy Days* and the Fonz.

'Hey, cool place,' says Stella as she follows me down the stairs and into Ashley's dining room. 'I haven't seen a Christmas tree like that for years, is it one of those ones that lasts for months? Mom used to have a tree like that and me and my sister decorated it and argued all the way. We were like, Mom, *please*, can I get to put the angel on top this year?'

'Where is she?' asks Karen, all impatient, like she needs to get something over with.

'Ashley?' I say, and I shrug to show I don't know.

'And just look at these decorations,' says Stella, still transfixed by the Christmas tree. 'This one is really sort of gross, isn't it?' Then she laughs, like she realises she might have just been rude. I like Stella; I wish I'd met her before. I wonder why Karen has been hiding her away. I'm going to ask her this but Karen has started marching through the dining room, shouting, 'Ashley!'

'Coming!' Ashley calls from somewhere at the back of the house. I think she must be in her parents' old bedroom, a massive room at the back with glass doors onto the garden and a built-in wardrobe which used to be full of Ashley's mum's things which we'd try on days when we bunked off school. 'Get yourselves a drink!' Ashley shouts.

I see a jug on the table, a big jug with rose-coloured liquid inside and I sniff it. I think it's Pimms, which seems odd for a winter's evening, especially when I thought I'd smelt mulled wine. I open a cupboard in the kitchen area and, oh my God, it's full of sparkling wine glasses turned upside down on the shelf, huge ones that could fit half a bottle of wine each. I take down three glasses, carefully in case I break them, and put them on the table, then I go back and take another two.

'No thanks,' says Karen when I offer her a glass, 'I'm driving. Where's Bel?'

'Probably on her way,' I say. 'I love your dress,' I tell Stella, and when she turns away from the Christmas tree to take her glass of wine I see there's a mark on her left hand. She has a light tan everywhere except for a thin white piece of skin where a wedding ring must have been. So she was married? Karen never mentioned that. I wonder if Bel knows.

Then Ashley floats into the room. Her dress must be made from silk, and it's probably designer because she moves like a butterfly, but for some reason her feet are still bare. 'Hi all,' she says, sweeping into the kitchen area and pulling open the door of the fridge and taking out plate upon plate of food. It's lots of expensive nibbly things: chunks of chicken,

345

little mini scotch eggs, fat jumbo prawns on wooden skewers, a plate of hams and salamis.

'I didn't know we were doing food,' says Karen. I notice now that she has a small white box in her hand and I hope it's something sweet, it looks like the sort of box that holds luxury chocolates. 'Ashley, this is Stella, my partner.'

I'm surprised at the way Karen says this, there's a sort of challenge in her voice. This wasn't how she introduced Stella to me. She introduced Stella to me like she was introducing two friends, now her voice sounds harsh. Ashley turns from the fridge, she doesn't seem to have noticed Stella until now, and I can see she's a little taken aback. 'Hi,' she says, holding out one hand then taking it back and wiping it on a beautiful blue tea towel, and then holding it out again.

'Hi,' says Stella, and she says it in a very slow, appraising sort of way. 'So you guys have all known each other since you were kids, hey?' She stops to sip her Pimms. 'And you've still kept in touch.' She looks at the three of us, smiling. 'That is cool. Sometimes I think I should join one of those reunion sites and find my old friends, you know? But then I'm like, there must be a reason we all lost touch! Are these your kids?' she asks Ashley, moving over to the fridge and pointing to a photo. It's very small; I've just noticed it myself.

'Yes,' says Ashley.

'They're beautiful,' says Stella, and she stares at the picture of Ashley's girls for so long it's like she wants them to come alive. I wonder if she has kids herself? If she does then she's really missing them, and if she doesn't then she really wants them. I wonder how old she is.

346

'I brought this,' says Karen, holding out the small white box she still has in her hands.

'Truffles,' says Ashley, taking the box, turning it around on her hand. 'Lovely.' She puts the box on the counter next to my Pomagne and the pile of newspapers and continues bringing things out of the fridge: sausages and a little ceramic pot of mustard, a plate of stuffed vine leaves, a large bowl of hummus, a tray of sushi, neat and tiny like doll's house food.

Karen looks offended; Ashley hasn't even said thanks for the box; but I see Stella wink at Karen and that makes her smile. Then Stella strokes the front of her green velvet dress and she and Karen exchange a glance so intimate that I turn away. Why haven't I got someone to love?

'Can I help?' I ask Ashley.

'No, babe, you're fine.'

So I sit down on one of the bar stools at the table in the middle of the room and Karen and Stella join me. I nudge Karen and make her see there's a man's leather jacket hanging over the chair and she raises her eyebrows as if to ask me whether I've asked Ashley about this and I shake my head that I haven't.

'How's your mum?' Ashley asks, once she's laid down all the food on the table and sat down herself. She puts one hand on her cheek and tips her face to one side and looks at me, and it's like she's asking about someone who's ill, someone for whom there's no hope.

'Fine,' I say. 'Yes, she's fine.' I smile, but I don't really feel like smiling because there's something about the way Ashley has just asked about Mum, and I realise it's the way she has

347

always asked about Mum, and it's patronising. It's like my mother is to be pitied in some way. I feel a jolt of fury, I feel as furious as I did when I found the picture of Ashley and the boy I fancied up against the rock in Portugal.

'What the hell was that?' asks Karen, as there's a loud bang on the basement window. Ashley goes over and picks up a corner of the blind and looks out. 'Bel,' she says as if she's not at all surprised. Ashley goes into a little passageway that leads off the kitchen and I hear her unbolting a door and opening it.

At once Bel comes hurtling in. 'Shit, I'm late, aren't I?'

'Yes,' says Karen.

'Oh fuck off,' says Bel. 'It wasn't my fault. What it is, is . . .'

'Bel, this is Stella,' says Ashley.

'Oh, *hi*,' says Bel, but she still wants to finish her story, 'I thought I'd walk so I went across the heath . . .'

'In the dark?' asks Karen.

'It wasn't dark when I started,' says Bel dismissively, 'but then when you come down over Parly Hill, I took that path on the left? The one that . . .'

'Why didn't you drive?' asks Karen.

'I'm not into driving at the moment,' says Bel, taking off a denim jacket.

'Why?' Karen and me both say at the same time, because Bel loves driving.

'No reason,' says Bel, and she comes over to the table, has a look at it, and puts a whole mini scotch egg in her mouth. She wipes the crumbs off her hands and down her jeans, quickly, several times with one hand and then several times with the other. She seems stressed tonight; I haven't seen her

348

doing this for a long time. 'Any lemon?' asks Bel, taking a skewer and biting at a jumbo prawn.

Ashley hands her half a lemon without saying anything, then Bel starts walking around, inspecting the drawings and photographs on the fridge, working her way around the kitchen area. 'Pomagne!' She lifts the bottle up and laughs. 'Let me guess who brought this . . .' She turns and beams at me and I feel better about having brought it now. 'You don't read this, do you?' Bel asks, sounding amused, lifting up one of the newspapers on the counter. 'Ashley,' she says mockingly, 'I didn't know you read the *Poke*.'

'The what?' I ask. Bel holds it up for me to see. 'Oh, the *Sunday Post*.'

'So, do you read it *every* Sunday, Ashley?' Bel says. She opens up the paper and pretends she's reading something shocking and amazing, widening her eyes and letting her jaw hang open. She's taunting Ashley and I wish she wouldn't because Ashley's face has gone all tight, and however angry I felt with Ashley just now I don't want another evening like the one we had at Canary Wharf.

'It's quite funny actually,' says Ashley lightly, taking ice from the freezer. 'I have to read it really.'

'What do you mean, you have to read it?' Bel won't leave this alone, she still has the paper in her hands and I don't know why this matters so much.

Ashley laughs like she was only joking. 'Well, Bel, I just *have* to know who's bonking who. Plus I really *have* to keep up with the celebs.' She empties the ice tray into a big jug and puts it on the table. 'Come on!' she says to Bel, tapping the ice tray briskly on the table corner, trying to get out the last

349

cubes. 'What would I read it for? It's not even a proper paper.'

'What do you mean, a proper paper?' asks Bel.

'Oh, you know,' says Ashley lightly, 'one that carries actual news. Everything in the *Poke* is made up, everyone knows that.'

Bel looks like she wants to keep this argument going but then a mobile beeps and we all, except for Stella, look around to see if it's ours. Ashley picks hers up from the kitchen counter, Karen pats her trouser pockets, but Bel already has hers out in her hand. She looks at it and frowns.

'Everything OK?' asks Karen.

'No,' says Bel.

I go over and Bel holds out her phone for me to see the text: *When am I going to see you again?*

'Ah, that's nice,' I say. 'Who's that from?'

Bel rolls her eyes. 'It's this bloke I met on a job, a snapper. I went back to his place, this was months ago, and it was a fucking disaster, I can't even tell you what a disaster it was, and now he's been sending texts.'

'What's a snapper?' I ask.

'A photographer,' says Bel, and she puts another prawn in her mouth and bites off the head. 'From a broadsheet. A *proper* paper,' she says, looking at Ashley.

'How did you meet a photographer from a broadsheet?' I ask.

'What do you mean?' Bel says. She is doing that thing where she deflects everything I ask her; whatever I ask she asks what do I mean and then avoids answering the question.

'I mean, what TV job were you doing to meet him?'

Bel looks stumped, then she waves her hand off to the side like she can't be bothered. 'He seemed OK at first,' she says, 'but he was a real "I'm a broadsheet snapper and I'm up my own arse". He did actually have a nice arse, the problem was that he showed it to me when I hadn't asked him to.'

I start to giggle. 'You didn't tell me about him.'

'Didn't I?' asks Bel.

'Anyway,' says Karen, 'go on.'

'Oh I thought he was nice, you know, I went back to his and it was obvious from the minute I walked in he had a girl-friend.'

'You didn't?' asks Karen, frowning.

'Of course I fucking didn't.' Bel sounds annoyed. 'I do have some morals, you know.' She glances at Ashley quickly and then looks away again. 'And when I said no, he went off and then he came back in and he was all dressed up in red vinyl bondage gear.'

'Oh come on!' says Ashley, and she's giggling now as well.

'I'm telling you,' nods Bel. 'It was completely bizarre. One minute he was Mr Serious I work for a broadsheet, and the next he looked like a tomato.'

'The *Guardian* is what you guys call a broadsheet, right?' asks Stella. 'That's the paper you read, honey?' She looks at Karen. 'I read an interesting interview in there about a woman who'd been married to one of your ministers, some bozo of a politician who the papers caught cheating on her with a prostitute.'

'Oh, I remember that!' I tell Stella. 'I can't stand that man.'

'Hamster face,' says Bel. 'That was the *Post* that broke that story.'

'So they can do some good after all,' says Ashley sarcastically. She looks at Bel, but Bel just starts stuffing sushi in her mouth.

'So this interview,' Stella continues, 'I was reading it and I thought, come on, honey, leave the bozo, but then she explained why she'd stayed when she'd first found out, then how she couldn't take the press intrusion and the lies any more, and then how she tried to take an overdose. Then she explained why she went back to him.'

Karen leans forward suddenly at the table and pours herself a drink. I thought she said she was driving?

'She's gone back to him?' asks Bel incredulously. 'When did that happen?' She picks up her mobile and looks at it even though it hasn't rung. 'So I suppose she's OK then,' she says quietly, like she's talking to herself. She puts another prawn in her mouth and she nods as she eats; she looks happier now than when she first came in.

'So Bel,' says Karen, 'where's your camera tonight?' She turns to Stella, 'Bel always has a camera, she never goes anywhere without one.'

'It's at home,' says Bel, and she rubs her hands down one leg and then the other.

'Eat!' says Ashley, bringing a final dish to the table.

'So, Pimms . . . all this food . . . what's the occasion?' asks Karen, and the moment she says this the door opens and we all go absolutely silent. I want to say, I know you from somewhere, haven't we met before, are we related in some way, as a man in a dark blue shirt and jeans comes into the room.

'Hello, girls!' he says, and I see he's smaller, slighter than he looks in his pictures or on the TV. But he still looks like a boy from one of my old annuals. He looks incredibly energetic, there's no spare flesh on him, and he looks like he has a gym membership and uses it. His jeans look deceptively old, when I'm sure they're brand new; they're exactly the right length and fit. His shirt is a deep, rich blue and it looks new as well, like it's just come out of a shop, because the collars are sharp and so are the cuffs where they are rolled up on his sleeves. The creases I see in his shirt as he walks into the kitchen are not old, unironed creases, they are being made right now by the stretch of the shirt against his chest. As he gets nearer I see his hair almost comes over his eyes and it's thick and golden and a little wet like he just washed it. Maybe he just had a shower – oh my God, maybe he just had sex. He moves about us, shaking hands, and as he does it's as if he's on stage or as if he's expecting someone else to be watching him, Donny Green. Then he stands by the counter in the middle of the kitchen, one hand in his jeans pocket, the thumb of the other hand looped into his belt, and he says, 'So, girls . . .'

Ashley has put on her Christmas lights, little gold sparkly lights that hang from the walls and the windows, and we're sitting round the table in the middle of the kitchen, except for Donny Green. He doesn't seem to want to sit down. He pours me a drink, gives me a smile and I can't help it, I'm as hypnotised as I was when he first walked in. I can't wait to tell Dwaine. His face is so clean, like George Michael when he was still in Wham!, and I don't know what he uses on his skin but it's blemish free, and under his eyes I think he's got some concealer because there's a silver shimmeryness that doesn't look natural. He's put a tie on now, a thin silver tie, and a waistcoat that's silver too. I think him and Ashley must be going out later.

'Can I fix any of you girls some coffee?' he asks. He's been doing this all evening, asking if we need or want anything, and all the time Ashley has been in the background, cleaning up, putting things away, doing it silently, not contributing to anything we're saying. I thought she'd brought us here to show off, to show us she's going out with Donny Green, but if that's the case I don't know why she isn't even smiling.

'No thanks,' says Karen. She and Stella are sitting close together, their fingers intertwined; they are only really interested in each other now, they're not that interested in Donny Green because neither of them really knows who he is. They say they've seen him in magazines but they don't really know him, they have no idea how famous he is, because of course they don't live here.

'So, Ashley,' says Karen suddenly, looking around, searching for Ashley in the shadows of the kitchen, 'I just thought, so it *was* you I saw in the paper.'

'Babe?' Ashley looks up, she's stacking the dishwasher and she's doing it very slowly like she hasn't done it before.

'That time we met up,' says Karen, 'and I said I thought I'd seen you in the paper with . . .'

'With me?' asks Donny.

'With you,' says Karen. 'There was a picture of you, on a park bench, and they were asking if anyone knew who Ashley was.'

'Well, girls,' Donny Green laughs, 'that's what you get if you go out with a celeb.'

Chapter Thirty-Seven

BEL

Shit, that Donny Green is a prick. I've just heard him on the radio and I had to turn it off. I can't stand his voice; there is something totally insincere about it. He doesn't sound real, he doesn't even look real. Donny Green! Where the hell did Ashley meet Donny Green? We never asked her that, we were all too surprised when he walked into the kitchen at her parents' old house. I just thought shit, don't tell me Ashley's going out with a celeb! That's why she had a copy of the *Sunday Post*. And he just kept on staring at me. At first I thought he knew me, that he knew I was a snapper, but if he did he didn't say so. He never asked what I did; he just kept on looking at me. Every time I looked up, there he was looking at me.

I'm on an early shift in Esher today. It feels like no one is up in the world but me, sitting in my car, turning off the radio because it's Donny Green. Not even the milkman is up. I head through central London, but something feels wrong, it's not just that the streets are quiet and deserted, but something feels out of place. It's the boot. Did I lock the boot just now before I set off? If I didn't, and my cameras fall out, it would all be over for me.

I pull over. It's still black and silent outside. I walk to the back of the car, try the boot. Yes, it's locked. But my hand goes out, independently, and tries the boot again. Yes, it's locked. I do it one more time for luck, then twice more, then I make myself get back in the car. Shit, why is this happening, why did I just pull over like that? I haven't had the urge to check like this for a while. I take some gum from the glove compartment, start chewing, force myself to drive on; I'm going to drive all the way to my watch in Esher and not stop.

An hour later I get on the M25, see the commuters streaming into London. I'm glad I'm going in the other direction. A few miles go by and it gets easier. I know the boot is locked. My cameras won't fall out. It's just a case of mind over matter. A few more miles go by. I'm driving calmly now. I'm almost not thinking about the boot. It's still dark outside but I can feel the beginning of a nice spring morning. I look to my right. Door locked. To my left. Door locked. In my mirror, back doors locked. And the boot, I know that's locked. I can't stop on a motorway anyway. I can't pull over and check on a motorway.

Then suddenly I know why I've got this urge to check, why something's been feeling wrong and out of place; it was this time last year, a spring day like this on the motorway, when I lost my nerve following Kate Koogan and then I went mad and thought a body had fallen out of a lorry. The checking flared up for a while after that, it lasted all through Christmas, then it died down again.

I hope I'm going to be taking snaps today. When I take snaps then things focus down to what I want them to be. When I have a camera in my hands and I'm looking through the viewfinder then there's only one thing I'm thinking about and that's what's inside the frame. I pass junction 10. I can't help it, I'm thinking about the boot again.

When did all this checking start? It's been going on so long I can't remember. As a kid I had the urge to line things up: my books, my crayons, my toys. I couldn't leave my bedroom for school until everything was lined up. So I must have been about five. If I did leave the room without everything lined up, then it was like I had unfinished business. And the more Mum tried to get me out the house before I'd finished, the more insistent I became. I can feel that agony now. Knowing I had to, I just *had* to, line everything up. And she was trying to stop me. But sometimes I wanted her to stop me, because I couldn't stop myself.

Then when we got to school I'd have these things I had to do. Like stand at a certain place in the line. Because there was a faint black spot on the playground floor and from my very first day of school I knew that was my spot. I *had* to stand on it, something was telling me that if I stood on that spot everything would be OK. If I stood on that spot then Dad would come back. *Stop it*, Mum would hiss, *why does it matter where you stand? People are looking.*

I had other things too. My hair, that really bothered me. Mum used to make it into plaits but she never got it right. One plait was always tighter or longer than the other. I wanted the plaits to be equal and Mum just didn't get it. And I had rituals, like when I went to the toilet at night I had to get back to my room before the toilet finished flushing. My brothers knew about that one; Joe used to hold my door closed so I couldn't get back in time.

357

And under my bed I had all the dolls that relatives were always giving me at Christmas and on birthdays even though I never played with dolls. They were set out in a particular order and every day when I came home from school I checked they were still like that. Back then I didn't think I was crazy, with the hair and the crayons, the dolls all lined up and the spot on the playground floor, it just felt like magic spells, like things I could do that would make things OK. Otherwise, if I didn't do them, something would go wrong. I don't know how I knew this, I just did, and I couldn't ignore the impulse, the thing that was telling me what I had to do to make things right. It played in the background of my mind, like an irritating song.

At secondary school I had to get things so right that I was always rubbing out my work. I'd start off really carefully, then I'd make a mistake. Something wouldn't look right: a letter, sometimes a whole word. So I'd rub it out and I'd start again and I'd rub it out again. I failed my French exam like that. I failed my A-levels like that. I rubbed so hard I made holes in the paper. And then what? Then things calmed down again. Until art school. That was why I dropped out, because if your life is dominated by checking then it's hard to get anything else done.

My mobile beeps and I grab it, banging my hand against the edge of the passenger seat. My thumb starts to throb; I've still got a scar from where that *Big Brother* plank assaulted me with his fingernail. I look at my mobile, hoping it's not broadsheet Jimmy again. Ever since that evening at his flat he's been texting me. A first it was jokey. *Sorry bout the other eve, my mistake! Fancy a drink sometime?* I deleted it at once. As if I'd go meet with him in his red vinyl bondage gear. Then it was *When am I going to see you again?* That was at Ashley's around Christmas, that night when she got us all together and then out came Donny I-think-I'm-hot-shit Green. Things were quiet over New Year, but then I got another text. *Hey Bel, how come you don't reply? Xx* What was he doing sending me a text with kisses at the end? I thought about texting back: *Fuck off Jimmy.* But it's better to ignore him. Not let him know he's getting to me. Then, last night, about 2am, he texts again. *Lying here thinking of you.* That wasn't funny, that was creepy; he wanted that to be creepy.

I flick open my phone and read the message even though I'm driving, even though I'm on the M25. It's from Loreen. She says she's found me someone on her dating site. I laugh out loud. What's she doing up at this time? It's not even dawn. I fix my earpiece on just as my mobile rings.

'Alright, Bel, how's our girl snapper?'

It's Ray on the desk. I'm not that happy with Ray. He's been sending me on real goose chases recently.

'Fine,' I say, a bit sharpish.

'You available, Bel?'

'Yes.' Of course I'm fucking available, you rang me last night and said to go to Esher. That's why I'm in the car on the M25 at five am.

'Right, here's the plan. Chelsy's arriving at Heathrow.'

'Chelsea?' I think for a moment I'm on a football story.

'Chelsy, Prince Harry's girlfriend? Are you with me?'

'Yeah, yeah, go on.' I slow down, concentrate.

'Where are you now?'

'On the way to Esher.'

'Oh right,' says Ray. 'Well you're nice and near then. She's on a flight from Cape Town, arrives 0700 hours. Harry will be there to meet her. He's been at that strip club right, so she's not going to be best pleased, is she? And this is a quiet one, Bel. We're the only ones on this. Terminal Four, OK?'

'OK.'

'And Bel?'

'Yeah?'

'Hook up with Glen, he's on his way there.'

I speed up, pleased I'm on an airport job and not another watch. I'm already at junction 14. It's just ten minutes to Terminal Four. And I'm pleased that Glen's on the case because I haven't seen him for a while. We lead different lives now, we're on different shifts, different celebs.

It might be first thing in the morning but it's chaos inside Heathrow. I can't even get to the barrier where people are coming out from behind the sliding doors because of a crowd of taxi men with signs. I see arriving passengers can go either way, right or left, so I need a good spot to stand. I feel a tap on my shoulder and it's Glen.

'Alright, Bel!' he smiles, gives my shoulder a squeeze.

'Hi,' I say, 'haven't seen you for ages, what have you been on?'

Glen looks sleepy. His hair is whiter than ever and his shirt is crumpled. He touches his nose with his right forefinger and gives a smile.

'Top secret?' I say.

'That's right, mate, top secret!' And he gives his high girl's laugh. I wait; now I really want to know what he's been on. 'It's a pop-star story,' he sighs. 'They've had me on

360

and off it for months. I've told them I don't think it's worth it; but they've bought up the girl's story, now they want him.'

'What's her story?' I ask.

'Who?'

'The girl.'

'Oh, well, her mother says this pop-star plank contacted her daughter on a website, sent her pictures of him playing with himself.'

'He what?' I laugh.

Glen shakes his head like he can't believe the state of the world. 'The mother found the pictures on her daughter's computer, she's only sixteen, and she recognised the pop star and contacted the *Post*.'

'As you do,' I say.

'As you do,' laughs Glen. 'So of course the *Post* were dead keen the mother didn't go to the police because then they couldn't have a story. And they've had me all over the place, trying to find what else he might be up to. I've been on his mother's place, his brother's, any ex they can dig up. He's got a girlfriend now, so they're keen on her too.'

'Which pop star is this?'

But Glen is distracted by a young man in baggy grey trousers and a short, tight black suit jacket who has just crept up behind us. 'The *Sunday Post*?' the man whispers. I turn round and study him. He looks about eighteen, he looks like a boy. Maybe he's some deranged reader. Maybe he should get a suit that actually fits. 'Glen and Bel?' he asks, still whispering. We nod and he opens his jacket to show us an ID hanging round his neck. I've never seen any *Sunday*

Post ID before, but it looks like this is what he's wearing. 'Brian,' he says. Then he looks around, quickly to his right and then to his left, as if expecting, hoping, that someone might be trying to overhear. 'They said to meet you here,' says Brian, closing up his jacket. 'Action stations, hey?' He pats his trouser pocket; I can see he's got a big fat notebook in there.

Glen pulls his sunglasses down over his eyes. If he wasn't so polite he'd groan. Glen hates being sent out on jobs with overeager boy journos. 'Right,' he says to me, 'long-haul planes can be early, darling. Check the monitor, see what's going on.'

I don't like being told what to do, especially not in front of a boy journo, but with Glen it's different. I owe him; I owe him everything. I go off and check the monitor and come back. 'Nothing on it about any flight from Cape Town.' Brian the boy journo gets his notebook out and starts scribbling, although nothing has happened.

'It should take forty minutes to an hour for them to come through after landing,' says Glen, getting out a pouch of tobacco. 'Earlier because she'll probably have security with her. If Harry's coming then there'll be royal protection too. When you see the message that the baggage is in the hall, then she's on her way. Where did you park, Bel?'

'Short stay parking,' I tell him.

Glen rolls his eyes. 'You won't be able to get out of there in a hurry, will you?'

'Where are you parked?' I ask.

'I'm with another snapper, he's in my van now, at the pick-up point. If he gets moved on he'll just do the airport loop

362

and come in again. Anyway, we've got a while, so you have a stroll around.'

I feel for my camera bag because I'm so used to having it over my shoulder, but I've left it in the boot of the car and just brought a little point and shoot. I don't want to be too obvious.

'Right!' says Brian the boy journo, and he takes out a baseball cap and puts it on his head and pulls it low down over his eyes. I think he thinks he's incognito. I get away from Brian as quick as I can and wander around arrivals, but there's not much to see or do. The arriving passengers have gone, so have most of the taxi men. I have a look in the toilets and come out again. Then I see the back of a familiar figure at the cash machine. It's Fred from the *Mirror*. He's pretending to get money out. Then I see another familiar figure leaning up near the bureau de change, a newspaper held open over his face. I recognise the shoes and the bald head. It's Ben from Getty. Shit, now I can see two planks from the *Star* inside WH Smith, flicking through photography magazines. At the entrance to the shop is a man from *News of the World* picking his nose, and just behind him is a snapper from the *Mail*. So much for a hush-hush job.

I approach WH Smith and inspect a rack of newspapers. Then I see airport security, two big men in blue, and they're heading this way. I open a paper, stick my nose in it, and wait. From the corner of my eye I see security approach the planks from the *Star*.

'Morning, gentlemen, you photographers?'

Both the *Star* men have fucking massive camera bags, what are they going to say, no?

'Yeah,' says one of the men, a bit sheepish.

'No photographs in the airport without permission,' says the security man.

'Oh come on, mate,' says the man from the *Star*.

'No permission?' says the security man. 'We'll do you for trespassing, this is a private building.'

Come off it, I think, what's private about an airport? But then if it's BAA men and BAA own and run the airport building and all the shops, maybe they have a point. In that case, that would make this private property. I know the score now, where I can take snaps and where I can't. I'm not the innocent snapper I was when I started, when I didn't even know you couldn't take snaps outside the Old Bailey. The *Star* men have to decide. They shrug that they'll leave and I watch the security men head for Ben from Getty. I'll be next. On the whole I get less agro as a woman, apart from the *Big Brother* plank and his fucking fingernail. Men are more territorial. The security men think this is their territory, the *Star* men think it's theirs. Personally I don't give a shit. The security men walk past me, I'm not holding a massive camera bag, they don't know my face. Then I see two men in grey suits and I see the way they're strolling, checking out the place, and I wonder if they're undercover, if they're with Prince Harry.

I put down the paper and dash back to Glen. 'She's on her way,' he says quietly, indicating the baggage sign on the monitor. Brian the boy journo rushes over, starts bouncing up and down on the spot.

Then all hell breaks loose. The sliding doors open and out comes a blonde girl with a sleeveless white top and tight jeans, torn carefully on one knee. She's got a minder with her, a big bloke sucking in his bottom lip. I snap a few frames, as does everyone else. It's got to the point when, at the second I take a snap, I can already see it in the paper. There's no creativity in this, but it's still a buzz. Chelsy hears the first clicks of the cameras and she looks away. That's what famous people do, look away when they hear the click of a camera. The non-famous people look towards a camera when they hear it click because they don't think it's going to be pointed at them. Jesus, she's getting the royal treatment now, there's two armed cops meeting her at the barrier and escorting her through. We rush after them, still snapping away, out to a waiting Range Rover.

'What did you say to Harry?' yells a man I don't recognise; he must be a journo from a daily. 'You give him a ticking-off about the lap dancing, love?'

'Hey, hey, Chelsy!' Brian the boy journo shouts out frantically, waving his hands. 'Yeah, what did you say to Harry?'

Chelsy has her head down. She gets bundled into the black Range Rover and inside I can see the top of Harry's head. He's got his face down, studying something on his mobile phone. There's another Range Rover behind, it must be for protection, and there are five cops on motorbikes. Passengers coming out of the airport stop to stare, they can't believe what they're seeing.

I rush up to parking, pay and get my car and I'm lucky, something must have delayed Prince Harry and his entourage leaving Heathrow because the moment I get on the M4, I see them. Glen's already in front of the Range Rovers and the paps who were thrown out of the airport building are close behind. It's getting even warmer now and I open the car windows, feel a breeze coming in, happy to be moving. I drive on, anticipating a call from Glen. I've never been on a royal job before, I don't know the protocol. But still, I'm driving along after Prince Harry and no one's stopping me.

What the fuck is this nutter on my right doing? I look out my window as a little blue Mini overtakes. It swerves in front of me and takes up position right behind the second Range Rover. Then it swerves out again and takes up position behind the first Range Rover, the one with Harry in. I've seen the driver as he passed me; it's beanie man, the man I first saw lumbering after Heather Mills outside Macca's house, the man who none of the other paps would let anywhere near that day of the Jones gang at court. People like each other in this game, but no one likes beanie man.

Is he mad? I see him trailing right behind Harry's Range Rover. I don't even know how he managed to squeeze himself in there. You can't stop cars moving on a motorway, that's obstruction, that's a criminal offence. And you can't stop the police carrying out their duties either, that's obstruction too. If I know this and I've only been in the game so long, how come beanie man doesn't? And if he does know then why is he behaving like this? Two cops on motorbikes come roaring up beside me, move ahead, get parallel with beanie man and wave him down. If he refuses they'll arrest him. And then it hits me, I'm a snapper. I'm a snapper and I'm following Prince Harry and his mother died when snappers were following her. How did I get into this, how am I part of this frame?

Chapter Thirty-Eight

It's early evening when I pull up at Mum's. After Heathrow the desk sent me back on the Esher job; it's been a fourteen-hour shift and I'm exhausted. But I haven't checked at all, I haven't checked the boot once since this morning; today I'm winning in the battle against myself.

'Look at the state of you!' says Mum when she opens the door.

'Hi Mum.' I see she's got a new doormat. It's divided in two: the part I'm standing on says GOODBYE in black letters on a brown background; the part she's standing on says WELCOME in brown letters on a white background. Mum must think it's funny to have it turned the wrong way round.

'Have you been wearing those clothes all week?'

'Are you going to let me in?' I snap. 'Or are you going to cross-examine me?'

Mum moves off down the hallway and I follow. 'Smells nice in here,' I say, to make up for snapping.

'Roast chicken,' says Mum. 'You staying to eat? It should be another half an hour because I want it all crispy on the top; you like it crispy on the top, don't you? You haven't been answering your phone, I've left you two messages today. Your brothers are here.'

I stop in the hall. I haven't seen Joe or Rich for months. I can't remember the last time I saw them, Christmas perhaps.

I don't feel ready for them. I'm too tired to spend the evening with my big brothers teasing me. It doesn't matter that I'm thirty-four years old, I don't think they even realise I'm thirty-four years old, I'm just a kid sister to them. I think about making some excuse and leaving, but Mum's yelling at me to come into the kitchen and here they are. Joe has his elbows on the table and he's flicking through a paper, not reading, just flicking because he's always been too impatient to stop and actually read through something. He has a pint glass on the table next to him, and a row of bowls: peanuts, crisps and twiglets. Mum knows Joe likes salty things; she will have got them especially for him. Rich is sitting opposite. He's got his jacket on like he's just come in, and his head is bent, writing in a Sudoku book. He's sitting right under one of Mum's spider plants and he doesn't seem to be bothered by the fact the plant is tickling the top of his head. Rich doesn't get bothered by much.

'Well look what the cat's dragged in,' says Joe, looking up. He's eager to start the wind-up at once. It's like he's been sitting here, at a loose end, just waiting for me to walk in. I see he's got a tan; he must have just been away. Joe can afford to go away.

'Very funny,' I say. I sit down between my brothers, kick off my shoes and Joe holds his nose, pretends there's a bad smell.

'Joe's just come back from Spain,' says Mum.

'That's nice,' I say.

'Don't be jealous,' says Mum. She opens the oven, pulls out the roasting pan. She's wearing an oven glove decorated with dancing monkeys. 'Shall I do some rice with this then?'

368

She looks at Joe and then at Rich. 'I don't know if I've got enough potatoes with you all here. I'm going to do broccoli and peas, but I don't know if these potatoes are enough. I'll do some rice and then if it's not all eaten I can always reheat it tomorrow, although they say not to reheat rice.'

'Lovely, Mum,' says Joe, closing the paper in a satisfied way and stretching his legs out under the table. His eyes look droopy; they've always looked droopy, like one of those dogs with saggy faces. In the corner of the kitchen I can hear the washing machine droning. It's an old machine and on the final rinse it rattles and shakes up and down on the floor. Joe must have brought his washing for Mum to do. He's thirty-seven years old, he works in a bank, he has a pension and a house and a girlfriend, but he still can't do anything domestic.

'So how's the new job?' Rich asks me. He puts down the Sudoku book and smiles. His hair is still thick and black. Rich was always the good-looking one in our family. 'Mum says you've been working with her, uh, friend.' Rich looks a bit embarrassed by this; he doesn't know how to deal with Mum having a boyfriend because my brothers want Mum to be Mum, to cook and wash and grill them about their lives. They don't feel comfortable with her having her own life too.

'It's not new,' I say, softening a little because Rich has never teased me as badly as Joe. I look at Mum, trying to work out what she's told them. She must have only told them recently or they would have brought this up at Christmas, always an ideal time for a family row. Why did she have to tell them anything anyway? I wonder who else she's told. 'I've been doing it for over a year now,' I tell Rich. I slide over the paper Joe's been reading, take a look at the front page.

369

'Hell of a job,' says Joe. 'Being a paparazzi. Stalking famous people. Hidden in any dustbins recently?'

'It's not stalking,' I say, and wish I hadn't. 'And I'm not a pap.'

'Well what are you then?' asks Joe.

'I'm a press photographer.'

Joe smirks and I have to hold back from kicking him under the table. This is just like old times.

'Is Glen about?' I ask Mum. 'I was with him earlier, I thought he'd be coming here.'

'No, love, he's gone to Portugal.'

'What?'

Mum nods. 'He left about an hour ago; he'd only just got here when he got a call. A little English girl's gone missing, terrible,' Mum shakes her head. 'He's on his way there now.'

'Well,' says Joe, because he wants to continue our argument, 'if it's not stalking, you being a *press photographer* and all, what is it then? Hiding outside people's houses, running around taking pictures of people when they don't want it?'

I pull over a bowl of peanuts and start eating them one by one. 'It's all a game,' I say. 'Most of them pretend they don't like it, when they do.'

'Public property, are they?' asks Joe a little aggressively, and he glances at Mum as if wanting her agreement on this.

'In a way, yes,' I say. I'm not going to let Joe wind me up.

'So what was Lady Di then?' asks Joe, like he's thought of something really original and clever. 'Was she public property? I don't know how you square it with your conscience. You people chase a woman through a tunnel at night, she's trying to get away, and she ends up dead.'

370

I look at him, raise my eyebrows. If I show any weakness with Joe then he will go for me. I'm not going to be apologetic, why should I? I wasn't there chasing after Lady Di. I'm nothing to do with that. I stare at him, not saying anything. Shit, I hope he doesn't know what story I was on this morning. I hope Glen didn't tell Mum about that. 'Her driver was drunk,' I say. 'That's why they crashed. And who was it that wanted all the pictures of her anyway?' I eat some more peanuts, take my time. 'If people didn't want snaps of Lady Di,' I tell Joe, 'then there wouldn't have been any photographers there in the first place, would there?' Joe snorts. 'And they were there because the pictures sell, and they sell because people wanted to buy them.' I look at Rich to see if he's getting what I'm saying, but he's opting out of this argument and writing in his Sudoku book again.

'People blamed the paps . . .' I start to tell Joe.

'I thought you said you're not a pap!' He laughs and holds up his hands like it's impossible to have a decent argument with me.

'But,' I say, 'the people who blamed the paps were the ones who bought all the mags and all the newspapers with Di's pictures slapped all over the place! And it was the paps who were there, at the scene of the crash, who gave first aid.'

'Did they?' Rich sounds surprised.

'I haven't snapped anyone who didn't want to be snapped,' I tell Joe. This sounds nice and certain but I don't know if it's entirely true. I start listing the jobs I've done in my head, those who wanted to be snapped and those who didn't, like the Jones gang and the *Big Brother* plank and Hamster Face the cheating minister. They all deserved what they got.

371

'Bel did Kate Moss the other week, didn't you, love?' says Mum, putting the kettle on to boil, measuring out some rice. How does she know this, does Glen tell her everything?

'Kate Moss?' asks Joe, sitting up. He picks up his pint, opens his mouth.

I laugh, he's interested now.

'Well, she's gorgeous,' he says. 'Who else have you done?'

'She did Beckham,' says Mum, 'didn't you, love?'

'Beckham?' asks Joe. He puts his pint down, leans forward. He might mock Beckham but he can't resist wanting to hear about him.

'Yeah,' I say casually, like me and Becks are best friends.

'I just saw an interview with him on the TV,' says Rich. His head is down, he's still writing in his Sudoku book. 'He's got OCD, hasn't he?'

'He's got what now?' asks Joe.

'Obsessive compulsive disorder,' says Rich, putting a pen in his book to mark the page. 'When you obsess about doing certain things, you know, like washing your hands or checking things, and you have to do them over and over.'

I look at Rich, feeling little pricks of nervousness all over my body. What are we talking about here, what is this conversation that has just got started?

'Beckham puts all his socks in order,' Rich tells Joe, 'stuff like that.'

'Oh!' says Joe. 'Yeah, I saw that in *Hello!*. He counts his Coke cans in the fridge. He has to have things symmetrical, so that if he's got three cans, he'll throw one away because three is uneven!' Joe laughs. 'Nutter!'

'So,' I say nicely, 'when did you start reading *Hello!* magazine, Joe?'

He looks pissed off. 'It wasn't *mine*, it was Irene's.'

'What, and your girlfriend just *made* you read it?'

Mum opens the oven door again, but she's forgotten to put her gloves back on and she swears as she burns her finger.

'You OK?' asks Rich.

'Anyway,' says Joe. He doesn't want to be distracted from an argument even if Mum has burnt herself. 'Yeah, I remember that, Beckham admitted he had OCD.'

Rich looks at me over the top of his Sudoku book, his expression sympathetic. 'It's quite common,' he says. 'A lot of people have OCD in one form or another, it's not something you have to admit to.'

'Not if you don't want people to think you're a completely irrational crazy nutter it isn't!' Joe laughs.

'It usually starts in childhood,' says Rich, using his pen to open up his book again. 'You used to avoid the cracks in the pavement.'

'So?' says Joe.

'Well, why did you used to avoid the cracks in the pavement?'

'I don't know! It was just what we did, wasn't it? It was bad luck or something, if you stepped on a crack. Everyone did it.'

'Was it rational?'

'What do you mean, rational?' Joe laughs, but he's annoyed because his big brother is interfering.

'What I'm saying is, we all have little rituals and compulsions,' says Rich patiently. 'Avoiding the cracks in the

373

pavement is perfectly normal in that plenty of kids do it, but what if it gets really extreme? What if you can't walk down the road without avoiding the cracks? What if you can't get out of the house in the morning because of all the cracks on the pavement?'

Joe yawns like he's just not interested.

'Some kids can really get into checking things,' continues Rich, 'like locks and things, or toys, but the checking doesn't stop them from checking them again, it only makes it worse. So someone can know that a door is locked, for example, but that doesn't stop them from checking it again. Once it interferes in everyday life, then that's OCD.'

I'm so nervous now that I don't know what to do with myself. Is Rich talking about me?

'How do you know all this?' asks Joe.

'Ah,' says Rich, looking down at his Sudoku book. 'I've been seeing someone.'

'Oooh!' says Mum. 'Who?'

'I just met her, you don't know her. She's training to be a psychologist.'

'That's nice,' says Mum. 'How old is she?'

'Anyway,' says Rich, 'I'm just saying it usually starts in childhood, and it can run in families.'

Mum gets busy all of a sudden, putting the rice and water in a pan, opening a drawer, taking out knives and forks. The washing machine gets to the final rinse and starts shaking up and down like the whole thing is going to explode. It's so loud there's no point in talking until it's done. I clench my left hand under the table, stroke the scar on my thumb, three times with one finger, then three with the next. I work my

374

way through the fingers on my left hand but then when I get to the little finger Mum puts the plates on the table and that distracts me and I have to start again.

'Remember all that crazy stuff you used to do?' asks Joe, and he finishes his pint and looks at me slyly. I've been waiting for this; I knew this was where this conversation was heading. I press a fingernail into the scar on my thumb, hard. I look at Rich with his head back down in his book. He brought this up, he needs to help me with this. 'Remember, Mum?' asks Joe.

'What's that, love?' asks Mum.

I know she heard him; the washing machine has finished jumping up and down, it's quiet in the kitchen now.

'Remember all that crazy stuff Bel used to do?' asks Joe with a smirk. 'All that checking with her dolls and stuff? Lining things up all the time, going mental if anyone touched anything! And her hair,' Joe takes a handful of twiglets, starts munching on them. 'She used to go mental about her hair. And remember when she used to shrug her shoulders all the time?'

I feel my face going red; they're talking about me like I'm not here. I'd forgotten about the shrugging, the way I had to shrug my shoulders every time I swallowed. There wasn't any reason, I just had to do it. This is private, I think, this is my private doubting disease, it's nothing to do with any of you.

'Oh it was just a stage,' says Mum. She turns to me and smiles and her face is flushed. She takes out the roasting tin, scrapes some of the juices into a glass jug for the gravy and puts the chicken back in the oven. 'I always said you'd grow out of it. I blamed myself really.'

'You what now?' asks Joe, mystified.

'Well,' Mum sighs, still with her back to us, 'we didn't know about things like that back then.'

'Things like what?' asks Joe.

Rich frowns at him over his Sudoku book.

'This OCD business, I didn't know how to handle it,' says Mum.

I'm pushing a fingernail into the scar on my thumb so hard now that it hurts. Is this what she's saying, that I have OCD? Is that the name for it? And if I had it then, as a kid, is that what I have now?

'If I tried to get you to stop,' says Mum, 'you went mad, and if I let you do whatever you were doing you went mad too. I just didn't know what to do. So I blame myself really. It started when I threw your dad out. You,' she turns and nods at Rich, 'got all withdrawn, couldn't get a word out of you some days, and you,' she waves a tea towel at Joe, 'wouldn't stop whining and crying. And you . . .' she smiles at me, 'started all this fussing.'

So I was right, what I was thinking about earlier, it did all start when Dad left. But Mum's wrong, it was more than fussing, it was a whole way of life, it was how I saw the world. Everything had to be right because obviously everything wasn't right. I had to get to the playground spot. I had to get home and check the dolls. It was up to me to put things right. I feel sorry for my five-year-old self. I feel so sorry that I could cry, and I can't remember the last time I cried. I was just a little kid, nothing I did was going to change anything or make things right. I could put things in order and line things up and stand in the spot in the playground as much as I liked, but I couldn't bring Dad back.

My mobile rings and I grab it and stand up, happy to have an excuse to leave the kitchen, to get away from this conversation. 'Hello, Bel.' It's the desk, but it's not Ray because he's knocked off now; it's Pete. He's new on the desk and he has a posh voice. 'We heard about the *drama* at the airport this morning,' he says.

I go into Mum's front room, see the monkeys are taking over, the sheep have been moved out. There are monkey pictures on the wall, a monkey light switch, a ceramic monkey just under Mum's green lady picture.

'Apparently two snappers were arrested,' says Pete.

'They were?' I sit down on Mum's old blue sofa, then stand up again because I'm going to get covered in dog hairs. I face the three-monkey statue on top of the TV. I remember how Glen said sometimes there's a fourth monkey too: see no evil, hear no evil, speak no evil, do no evil.

'Yes, indeed they were,' says Pete.

I smile; I hope one of them is beanie man. He should be locked up.

'Many thanks for the snaps of Chelsy coming out,' says Pete. 'We may possibly use one of those, if nothing better comes in.'

'Good,' I say, pacing around Mum's living room, rubbing my shoe up and down on a new hairy rug shaped like a big fat monkey.

'Would you be available tomorrow, Friday?' asks Pete.

'Yup.'

'Do you have a pen and paper?'

Of course I have pen and paper. I write down the address he's given me. 'Who's this?' I ask, although I know I'm not supposed to, I'm just supposed to do what I'm told.

'It's a follow-up from last week's story,' says Pete. 'That mention on the gossip page?'

'Uhu,' I say, because I don't know what he's on about.

'Bel, you do *read* the paper, don't you?'

'Not usually, I just look at the snaps.' I laugh, but Pete doesn't laugh; some people just take themselves too seriously. I don't read the *Sunday Post* because it's just not that funny and because every time I look at it I see a story I don't want to read. I just want to take the snaps.

'Well if you did bother to read the paper,' says Pete sarcastically, 'you would realise who you're on.'

'Who's that then?'

Pete laughs. 'Donny Green.'

Chapter Thirty-Nine

KAREN

Stella's asleep next to me in the bed, sleeping so solidly that I wonder if she's not a creature in hibernation storing up its energy for the spring when it wakes and comes to life again. Only it *is* a spring morning and there's no reason for Stella to be bundled under the sheet like this, and I wonder if all this sleeping is a way for her to recover from something or whether it is to save herself up for something that I'm yet to find out. *Sleep is supposed to be . . . The shutting of the eye.*

For months Stella has been travelling on her own from country to country because she said she always wanted to travel Europe alone and Nick Givenchy never allowed her, so how could I raise any objections? And now she's back, just when I'm getting ready to return to California, and if I don't go now there won't be a job for me any more; I've had my sabbatical, I've had my leave, I have to go back or stay here and totally start again.

When I had a bath earlier, before coming back to bed, I found Stella's clothes on the bathroom floor and I picked them up, her orange pants soft from where they had been stretched against her body in the train from Calais, and I thought, what's in her pocket? I closed the bathroom door to have a look, emptying out the pocket of her orange pants to find a ticket, a credit card receipt, a notebook with a soft silvery cover like a small travel journal. I opened the note-book, thinking, this is wrong, I shouldn't be doing this, this is totally wrong and not like me at all, and then I was disap-pointed to discover that inside every page was blank. What had I been expecting? I'd been expecting to read something about me and about what Stella plans to do, because I'm expecting that Stella will leave me, like Jen left me, and I want to find out now, before it happens.

I bend my knees up and balance my book against my thighs. There are crumbs in the spine of the book from my breakfast, which I had alone because Stella was sleeping. We need to have a talk, I need to sit her down and talk and ask about what will goddam happen when we get home. Will she move out of her house with Nick Givenchy, will she rent alone, will she move in with me? I don't even know if she'll stay at UC Davis. 'I don't want to go there,' is all she will say when I ask. 'Let's just leave it, honey.' I know Stella; I know she loves to talk and that words are as spontaneous as thoughts to her, so I don't know why she isn't talking to me now. And I want to know if Nick Givenchy has con-tacted her since she's been here, since she left him last summer, and I feel the jealousy that I've always felt, only now it's eating me up from the inside. I wonder if he's rung her on her cell phone when I'm not around, when I'm in the library or at the pool or at the store; maybe he's written to her, maybe he got my address off of someone at UC Davis, like Macey Bloom. Perhaps Stella even gave him my address herself.

When she was travelling, did she stay in touch with him; did she send him postcards from Vienna or Budapest, did she write to him on hotel paper from Barcelona or Rome, and if she did then what did she say?

I can't read this morning. I'm turning the pages, my eyes are looking at the words, but I'm not actually reading. I put my legs down, the book falls onto the sheet. I can see on the bedroom shelf where Stella has put her wallet. I can see it half open, and I can see something, a card poking out, and I want to go and search through it and see what's there, but I can't because it's wrong. This is what I told Bel that night she picked up the guy's wallet in the bar. I told her it was wrong to go through someone's private purse, and I told her she had to hand it back, and yet look at me, this is what I want to do now.

I get up and change, not even trying to be quiet, annoyed that Stella can sleep while I'm so fraught, putting my bathing suit on under my dress, all the quicker to be able to get into the pool. It's later than I would usually go, it will be full already, and hurriedly I put my keys and some money in a purse around my waist and close the door to my apartment, stopping only in the hallway to go through a pile of leaflets from local restaurants, from pizza places and Indian takeouts, in case there is any actual goddam mail hidden in here. Then the door to the upstairs apartment opens and I look up and see a boy on the landing and he sees me and his shoulder twitches as if he's going to run back inside.

'Hey!' I say, giving a little wave, still with the takeout flyers in my hand.

The boy closes the door, puts his back against it and leans

against the frame, tightly, as if there is someone on the other side trying to push it open.

'I'm Karen,' I call up. 'From downstairs?' I know a boy of his age isn't going to want to chat to me; he's ten perhaps, and on his way out of childhood, and his hair is shaggy and hanging down over his forehead so that his eyes are partly, but very deliberately, covered. But I don't want to lose this opportunity because this is the first time I've seen the boy up close since the day he moved in. All this time I've heard him, when he runs in or out of the apartment, when he watches TV, when he shouts out to his dad. I think of that strange night when I thought I heard his father drag him across the floor to the open window, and that night Stella arrived and his dad was cursing him, and yet I've never seen him up close until now, when I'm only two months away from packing up and leaving. 'What's your name?' I ask.

'Dylan,' he says.

'Dylan? What, like Bob Dylan?' I smile like we're best of pals but he just stares at me so I pretend it's no big deal and finish going through the mail. Then I glance up and he's gone.

I step outside and the moment I come onto the sidewalk and into the sharp spring air of a London morning I realise I've left my towel inside, so I come back in and from the apartment upstairs I hear a rattling noise. I look up, up to the landing, and there is Dylan, his body hunched. 'Dad,' he's saying, rattling the letter box, his mouth right up against the door, 'Dad Dad Dad.' He starts rattling furiously; his father must be able to hear him so why isn't he letting him in? 'Dad Dad Dad, it's me, Dylan, Dad Dad Dad. Let me in, Dad Dad Dad.'

I tip toe into my apartment to get my towel, feeling awful for this little boy who is trying to get his dad to let him in, and I wonder once again what happened to the mom and the little girl and then I think, perhaps I got it wrong and they were never together, they never were a family at all. All this time I thought they were a family, I thought the mom and the girl had gone on holiday and I'd wondered why they hadn't come back. But what if they never were together, the mom and the dad, what if she wasn't the boy's mom, what if the man isn't the boy's dad? But he must be, I've just heard him shout out, 'Dad!'

When I come back into the hallway with my towel, Dylan is just ahead of me at the front door. I see the back of him as he goes down the steps, as he grabs a scooter that he has left lying by the railings, and he hops onto it and scoots off. His father hasn't let him in, Dylan must have given up. I stand and watch him, and then I hear a front door close; my neighbour has come out of her house as well.

'Hiya!' she smiles at me. This is as far as I've got with my neighbour. We have not gotten further than this in all the time I've been here, except for the morning last fall when she said the council should do something about the big guy upstairs. Her hair is not as blonde and bouncy as it was that day, it looks a little limp. She's got a newspaper under one arm and I can see a picture of the little girl that vanished in Portugal; Stella was talking about her last night.

'He's a lovely little boy,' says my neighbour, shaking her head as we watch Dylan scooting off, right in the middle of the road, his right leg hammering away like a frantic cartoon character. My neighbour must be on her way to work; apart from the newspaper under one arm she also has a thin case and a bunch of letters. 'It is a shame about the father,' she says.

I come a step closer, I want to know what she knows, but I have a feeling that if I ask she'll run out on me again. 'He was trying to get in just now,' I say. 'Dylan.'

My neighbour shakes her head again. 'His father's from around here, like me. We were at the same school together but I wouldn't mess with him now.' She switches her case from one hand to the other, then she laughs. 'Listen to me standing here gossiping!'

I smile at her politely but I wonder if this is gossiping or is this just looking out for a young child who is our neighbour? 'I can't work out what's going on up there,' I tell her. 'It can be real quiet for months and then it starts again. Sometimes I think he's . . .' I lower my voice, '. . . hitting him.'

My neighbour nods and starts going through the mail in her hands.

'So what do you think we can do?' I ask.

'Oh I don't think it's a good idea to get involved,' says my neighbour, and she puts her mail away in her case. 'You can't go around messing around in other people's private lives, can you?' She looks at the watch on her wrist, says, 'Late again!' and flashes me a smile and she's off. That's it, the conversation is over just like last time, and I wonder what it is she's so afraid of when the only one getting hurt around here is the little boy. I look around and see a figure at the window opposite. A woman is standing at the side of the window, she's drawn back the net curtain enough to allow her a view of the road and her face is looking in the direction where Dylan scooted off. I wonder what she's heard as well. Then the woman sees me and the curtain falls back into place. We are all voyeurs, I think. We listen in on Dylan's life, we hear him, we see him scooting away down the road like this, and yet we do nothing but watch.

When I get to the pool there are five people waiting in the area where the counter is, waiting in that English way that no matter how casually someone is standing by the counter or waiting a good few paces apart from the next person, everyone knows who got here first. I have to guess where to place myself, make real sure that it doesn't look like I'm pushing in. 'Hi,' I say to the woman behind the counter. 'One swim, please.'

'The lanes are closed,' says the woman. She's wearing a t-shirt with a bunny rabbit on and her hair is tied up playfully in two bunches with pink ribbons around the ends, but her face is hot and annoyed and she doesn't look like she wants to be at work today.

'When will they open?'

The woman shrugs. 'We're waiting to be told.'

I head for the glass doors and the seating area by the vending machine. I bought a paper on the way, I'll sit and read it.

'Sorry!' says the woman. 'You can't go in there any more.'

I look at her; I've sat there before many times.

'We had an email about it this morning,' says the woman. 'We can't let anyone wait in there any more.' A phone on the counter starts to ring but she doesn't make any move to answer it.

'Oh?' I wonder what the danger is in letting people sit on a bench while waiting to swim.

'Especially because there are children around,' says the woman significantly. We both look through the glass doors at a straggle of kids with wet hair and rolled-up towels and a harassed-looking teacher trying to quieten them down. 'We have had a couple of . . . incidents,' says the counter woman.

I stare at her, wondering what sort of incidents she means, but she turns away from me now, starts looking at her computer screen, finally answers the ringing phone. Then a woman comes in on crutches and we all watch and yet try not to watch as she painfully hauls herself to the counter. 'One swim,' she says. She looks exhausted, like it's taken all her effort to get to the pool today, so much so that she's ignored the people waiting and come straight to the front.

'Sorry,' says the counter woman, putting down the phone. 'The lanes aren't open yet.'

'Oh God,' the woman on the crutches groans. 'I'll wait in there then.'

But the moment she moves one crutch in the direction of the glass doors the counter woman stops her. 'Sorry,' she says, 'but you can't. Health and safety.' And she goes back to her computer, starts to print something out, and we all stand there, all of us waiting for a swim, and I wonder at these new rules that we are not allowed to wait anywhere where children are in case we do them harm somehow, and I wonder what the rules are when it comes to the little boy Dylan upstairs. I think my neighbour feels I am being a busybody, that I am interfering in something which doesn't have anything to do with me, but it does have something to do with me because if I do nothing then I will be as complicit as my neighbours.

At last we are allowed in and I hurry down the ramp

towards the dressing rooms, passing the three hairdryers bolted to the wall, a new sign about veruccas. At once the air changes, it becomes the air of a changing room: bathing suits soaked in chlorine, someone's apple-scented shower gel. I take off my dress as fast as I can, throw my things in a locker, put the rubber band with the key attached round my wrist and head for the pool. I try to pretend I'm back in California and it's a sunny day and the water in the pool will be clean and fresh and not like this London swimming pool water, murky and full of chlorine and other people's urine. I need to swim, to think about things and clear my mind; I need to swim until I'm not so worried about Stella and all the things she hasn't said, until I'm not so worried about what I can do about the boy upstairs.

There's only one person already in the fast lane, he must have just got in: a guy in goggles chomping up and down doing front crawl, the guy I often see here in the pool. I look at the slow lane, there are already five people in it, and as I'll be going as fast as goggle guy I get into the fast lane and push off into the lukewarm water, timing it so that he is just kicking off from the other end of the pool as I start my lap. I pass him in the middle of the lane, we're going in opposite directions at the same speed, and that means I can do some proper laps today. I can think until I'm not thinking any more, until I'm just swimming.

I lose count of how many laps I've done; goggle guy is tiring now but he's still fast enough not to stop my sprint. I'm about to touch the edge of the pool with my hands and to turn and push off again just as an elderly woman sits down on the lip of the pool. She must be seventy, eighty even, and

387

she won't get in here because me and goggle guy are going too fast for anyone else to get in. But just as I touch the bar at the edge of the pool the elderly woman starts lowering herself in slowly and I take in a bathing suit of pink and yellow swirls and a bathing cap with large white petals on the top.

I'm about to turn, to push off again, but she's getting in the pool right in front of me. I turn to face the way I've come and see her setting off down the lane, her head held out of the water like a turtle, and if it wasn't for the fact I can see her legs kicking from behind I would think she wasn't moving at all she's going so slowly. I wonder why she has chosen the fast lane to do this in, perhaps she's not aware that there are lanes designated for fast and slow swimmers and she just liked the look of this one. I feel bad for her, a comical figure going so slowly in the fast lane.

But I can't swim with her in front of me. I'm forced to stop and wait and press myself against the tiles of the pool, feel their smoothness against my naked back. My heart is hammering from my laps and I need to keep going but I'm forced to wait until the elderly woman has progressed a little way down the lane because the only other option is to push off and overtake her. And I can't do that because goggle guy is pushing off from the opposite end of the lane and he starts to churn the water next to the elderly woman in the bathing cap and the waves splash her and she looks a bit confused. But she keeps on going, her legs kicking further and further under the water like a top-heavy drowning turtle.

I wait until she finally reaches the other end of the lane and I push off at last, feel the muscles in my calves tighten, my stomach stretch out, and then suddenly my hand connects with something and it startles me. It's turtle woman, she's swimming in the wrong direction.

'Hey, sorry,' I say.

Turtle woman looks at me, she blinks, her eyes look wavery and bloodshot from the pool and I'm about to ask if she's OK. Her face is wet and wrinkled and her bathing hat has been pushed crookedly over one side of her head so some grey hair is escaping and two of the white flowers are flopping over her forehead.

'Maybe,' I say kindly, patiently, 'you could swim in that lane?' and I nod to the slow lane, which is nearly empty now. There are only two women in it, elderly like her, one sunk in the hole of an inflatable ring. I nod at the slow lane some more, showing her that she could happily swim up and down in that lane and not be disturbed by the likes of goggle man.

'Why don't *you* swim in that lane?' she snaps. 'Fuck off!' Then she punches me hard on my arm. I want to hit back but I can't, I can't hit a little old turtle woman swimming in the fast lane. I move back, but it's real difficult moving back in a pool, and she lifts up her hand and it's balled into a fist. I'm trapped. I can't hit her back and I can't swim on because she won't get out of the fast lane, and that's my morning, my swim, gone.

I look around, see a lifeguard at the end of the lane. 'Hey!' I shout. He doesn't hear or see me because he's chatting to a girl in a bikini who just got out of the Jacuzzi. 'Hey!' I shout and wave. He frowns, starts walking along the edge of the pool. 'She's hitting me!' I shout as turtle woman's fist collides wetly with my shoulder.

I come home, shaken, feeling like I misjudged something and not knowing what made the woman go crazy like that. All along I thought I was behaving the way someone should behave, I wasn't like goggle man, I was waiting while the woman swam, and then she hit me.

'Stella!' I call out, opening the door to our apartment. I want her to be up, if she's not up I'm going to wake her up because I want to tell her about what happened in the goddam pool.

'Hey honey!' she shouts back. She's in the kitchen.

'You wouldn't believe what just happened,' I say, putting down my towel, walking across the living room, untying the purse from around my waist.

'What happened?' Stella says, looking up from where she's sitting at the kitchen table, her face smiling, waiting for me, looking delighted like she's just made something, some new cookie recipe perhaps, and it's turned out real well and she can't wait for me to taste them. Then I see him, sitting at my table eating from a bowl of cereal, the boy Dylan from the apartment upstairs. He looks startled to see me and his shoulders flinch like he's going to get up from the table and run away.

'Hi!' I say brightly, but with my eyes I'm asking Stella, what is going on in here? I gesture with my head that she come out into the living room, and as she does I close the door behind her. Stella sighs and leans her back against the wall.

'I had to ask him in,' she says, her voice low. 'After you'd gone, I went to the store to get some juice? And when I came back he was sitting there on the steps outside and he looked real forlorn, so I told him to come on in.'

I look at her worriedly. 'Does his father know he's here?'

Stella frowns. 'He had a bruise on his arm, honey.'

Dylan has gone, Stella is in the kitchen, cooking and swaying along to music on the radio, and I sit down by the phone in the living room. If Dylan has a bruise, if his father has been hitting him, then I have to do something, I have to call inquiries and get the number for the council.

'Hi,' I tell the woman on the council switchboard, 'I need to talk with someone about my neighbour. I'm not sure who but . . .'

The switchboard woman doesn't reply. I think she's transferring me. The phone rings a long time and then at last a man answers.

'Hi,' I say, 'I wondered if I could talk with someone about my neighbour? I'm concerned because there are strange noises and . . .'

'Name?' asks the man with a sigh, like I'm interrupting him and he wishes he'd never picked up the phone.

'I don't know his name,' I say.

'I meant your name.'

'Oh!' I laugh. 'Karen.'

'Karen what?' says the man.

I find myself hesitating for a moment; it must be the English part of me that is reluctant to give my full name to a stranger, like I'm not sure what he will do with this information once he has it, like it makes me vulnerable somehow. But I take a breath; tell him my name. 'Karen Macintyre.'

'And your address?'

Again I hesitate because suddenly my name and address

391

are pieces of information I want to keep to myself, because what if the big guy upstairs knew what I was doing now, and if he did then would he come after me? But I tell the man from the council and I wait to see what comes next.

'And what is the problem, Mrs Macintyre?'

I stand up with the phone. I don't like this guy, I don't like the way he's called me 'Mrs' and I don't like the way he's not making this easy for me. 'The problem,' I tell him, 'is that I have some upstairs neighbours and there's a lot of noise, shouting and swearing coming from up there, and I'm concerned because there is a little boy and I'm concerned about his safety.'

'And have you confronted your neighbour about this?'

'No.' I want to tell him my neighbour is a big guy, but this sounds foolish. 'But the council knows about him.'

'And how do you know that?'

I start pacing with the phone in my hand. What is wrong with this guy? I want to tell him about the little boy who doesn't go to school, who knocks and pleads for his dad to let him in, who is dragged across the floor in the middle of the night, who is cursed at, who has a bruise on his arm, but he's making things real difficult for me. 'Because a neighbour told me.'

'Because a neighbour told you?' The man's voice has risen a little, as though he is ridiculing me. 'What you need to do, Mrs Macintyre, is you need to put this in writing.'

'Why?'

The man doesn't answer and I hear a sound, like a spoon against a cup, like he's taking a break to stir a cup of tea. 'Because,' he says at last, 'that's how we do things here.'

And I think, does he mean that's how we do things here at the council or that's how we do things here in England, because he's heard my voice, he thinks I'm a Yank and he thinks that I'm not handling things the way I should be. 'So,' I say, 'I need to write this all down?'

'That is correct,' he says stiffly. 'And it would help if we have complaints from other neighbours as well, or is it just you that's being bothered?'

'No,' I say angrily, 'it's not just me. So if I write it all down, can you tell me what you will do then?'

'I will write to your neighbour,' says the man, 'and request that he takes steps to either stop or reduce the nuisance that is causing annoyance.'

'The nuisance?' I ask. I haven't been talking about a nuisance, I've been talking about a little boy and his father and I can't understand why this jerk doesn't get this.

'If the problem continues,' he says, and I sense he is trying to wrap this conversation up, 'then more formal action may be considered, in which case I would ask you to be aware that the council may need to call you as a principal witness in any hearing.'

A witness? Does he mean a witness at court? I hang up and as I look through the open door into the kitchen and see Stella still swaying to the music, I realise my fingers are trembling.

Chapter Forty

DUDU

I am climbing up Dimawe Hill and everything is dry, the air around me and the sand below me, even my fingers where they clasp the stick Victor Kudumane has given me. Creatures scurry away as I walk up through the brown bush land, rough-skinned lizards the colour of chalk slip under the rocks and disappear. The rains have come and gone; they were not like the rains I remember as a child, when the world was wet day after day. I hear cicadas singing in the air and I smell the scent of the tea bushes all around me as I continue to climb. My leg has not pained me at all today, I do not even need this stick, but I decide to stop a while and lean on it and as I do I think of my father. I can almost hear his penny whistle, see him as he sits in our yard on an old upturned pail and tells the children about the battles that took place here on Dimawe Hill and the people who fought the Boers.

I walk a little further up, towards the skyline ridge of orange stones above me, the stones positioned so carefully it is as if there are still people up here on the hill who have arranged them each to be in a certain place. Some of the stones are as big as boulders, just as I remembered them to be, they are not smaller because I am an elder, they are just the same. They are square at the corners and stained with deep brown veins, and on the top of one boulder is a small round stone the colour of a summer's evening.

Still I climb up Dimawe Hill, and I am glad I am alone, that Victor Kudumane has left me alone this morning, and I am even gladder that I am no longer in Gaborone. The time I have spent in Gaborone reminds me of the time I spent in hospital after my car accident all those years ago; people were friendly, they were kind to me, but all I could think of was when I was allowed to leave. Victor and his wife took me to the shopping malls and to the Riverside complex and we went to the President Hotel to sit on the terrace and drink tea, but the hotel was being renovated and it was noisy and dusty and the walls were coming down. Everywhere in Gaborone, everywhere we went, people were talking on mobile phones, just as they do in London, and when they were not on their mobile phones then they were watching television or reading magazines, even newspapers with horoscopes and the naked women they call Page Three. I thought perhaps the things of life that I didn't like about England had somehow followed me to Botswana. And there was a difference not only in what people did, but also in how they related to each other, for Victor Kudumane's family is as fragmented as families in England are, and he and his wife and his last-born child Dorcus and the unwanted grandchild lived together like strangers.

I pause again and look up at a group of stones that look as if the hand of God has come down from the heavens and split them open in a fit of annoyance and left them there, forever split. I walk on, towards a particularly large rock, as round and as smooth as the clay pots my mother used to make, and the patterns on this rock, made perhaps from minerals, or perhaps from the wind and the sun and the rain, make dancing faces. Then I come upon a little wall, a jumble of stones laid on top of each other, cleverly, like a jigsaw puzzle, and I step over this ancient wall behind which people used to hide and look out for the Boers, and continue to wind my way upwards.

Finally I stand high up amid the trees and the bushes and I survey the compounds and the houses and the scrubland below. I think of the day I arrived here in my home village of Manyana, my tiny village tucked so neatly among the hills. Victor Kudumane drove me from Gaborone and everything was the same: the gentle slope that leads to my family's compound, the sand inside the compound neatly raked in zigzag lines, two mosetlha trees like look-out posts. We drove in and everything was still, the mosetlha trees, the sand and the air, and I saw a wooden pestle, the sort I was taught to pound mealie in as a child, and I saw a metal bath set in a patch of grass like the bath I washed in as a child. And then I saw a little girl in pink shorts halfway up a mogotlho tree, balanced between its two main branches watching the visitors arrive, just as I used to do. Still I stand on Dimawe Hill and look below and I have the strangest feeling that I am seeing this land both for the first time and for the last. I think to myself, perhaps I should remember this sight because perhaps I am not going to see it again, and so I look around and I notice everything: the sad brown leaves on the trees in front of me, the soft flat valley below, a roadway made in the reddish sand, the glint of metal-roofed houses in the sun. It is so vast this land that if I were a bird, an eagle perhaps, then I would swoop down from the hill and float in the air that is still. And then I know what I have known since I arrived in Botswana, that even though now I have found the place I was looking for and it has not changed, it is just as I remembered it, I cannot stay here because my family, my Loreen and my two grandsons, are on the other side of the world, and if a person doesn't know how much time they have left, if they feel the thread is running out and the reel is almost empty, then it is best to be with the ones you love more than yourself and who need you the most.

I come down from Dimawe Hill and Victor Kudumane drives me to the banks of the Kolobeng River and I am pleased when his big new car has a puncture and we are forced to sit on the stones by the river bank and drink our tea from a thermos flask and watch the cattle pass, slowly, quietly, their flanks of silver and beige and brown and black rippling in the sun. And I am even more pleased when Victor Kudumane suggests we visit the rock paintings, although I am surprised to see a fence around the rocks, because the National Museum is in charge of the rock paintings now, and this is good I suppose because the moment we arrive I can see people have been drawing graffiti on them, just as London children would do, even though they are our history and our heritage.

The rock paintings are nearly as tall as I remember, giant-like men with bulging stomachs, and I walk along them searching for the three giraffe that were my favourites as a child. I find them and they are faint, as faint as they were when I was small, but they are like old friends, these outlines of the animals drawn so many hundreds of years ago. I find a place to sit, a place I remember sitting as a child, tucked into the wall of one of the rocks where the surface is so patterned it is as if a waterfall of colours has been this way and frozen. Victor Kudumane takes my picture and I know what it will look like once he has developed it at a photo shop in Gaborone, for I feel how small I am, just a small old woman against a sea of rock, fragile like an insect that has been blown off course by the wind.

Chapter Forty-One

LOREEN

Oh my God, it's so hot for May. We've chosen the perfect Saturday to have our picnic and the minute I've got dressed I'm going to call Bel and check what time we're meeting. But first I'm going to box up these annuals so I can take them to Oxfam on the way. I haven't seen this *My Guy* before. I pick it up and it's heavy and the cover feels a little rough and the orange background is faded like something left out in the sun. I remember *My Guy* always had a couple on the cover; sometimes they were celebs, sometimes just ordinary-looking people. The couple here have their arms wrapped around each other; in fact the boy has his hand right up the girl's yellow t-shirt. They both have their mouths open a little, like they've been kissing and they've just been disturbed and have turned round to see who it is.

I open the annual and here are all the things I used to love, the photo stories and the girly quizzes. I stop at *Your supernatural guide to getting a guy!* It's a special pull-out which will tell me all the hidden secrets I need to know to bewitch a boy and get him under my spell for ever and always. I'm a bit disappointed when I look at the pull-out and it just tells me what it means when a boy takes his clothes off. This is pathetic really. But I remember this: I remember that if a boy takes his socks off first then he's the sensitive type, because this was the sort of information I would memorise, in the slim chance I would ever be around when a boy took his clothes off. Here's a test, *Why can't you be in love like this?* I can't help it; I start reading. *Are you ever afraid of falling in love? Yes/No. Are you pleased with the way you look? Yes/No. Would you rather kiss a real boy than a pin-up? Yes/No.*

No! I'm not going to read any more of this, I'm not going to get drawn into these stupid tests, and as for you, *Jackie*, one last flick through and it's Oxfam for you. I turn the pages and find a knitting pattern. It's to make a yellow beret with a fried egg, a big rasher of bacon and a portion of peas on top. They must have been kidding. They must have been sitting in that *Jackie* office just making things up. But no, it's a real knitting pattern and here's a girl modelling it and you can make a bag to go with it, also with a fried egg but this time with a big brown sausage and five chips as well. That is completely ridiculous. How could they expect young girls to make this? Did they want us to look stupid? Did they sit there thinking, what idiot advice shall we give our readers this month? I turn the pages, find a piece on *21 Ways to Make Him Notice You*. Number 1 is *Get wise to his favourite haunts, and just be there, ever so casually*. Number 6 is *Wear an all-white trouser suit*. Number 20 is *'Faint' in front of him*. I remember that tip; I remember the boy I was going to pretend to faint in front of, it was a friend of Ashley's boyfriend Steve. I really was going to faint in front of him. I really thought that was a good idea. I would faint in front of him and he would scoop me up, and then we'd get married and have babies and live in a rose-covered cottage.

How could these *Jackie* people do this to us, tell us to pretend to faint in front of boys and knit a fried-egg hat?

That's it, I'm giving up dating. I'm giving up spending sleepless nights wondering if the profile I've written on the dating site is good enough, or trying to find just the right photo. I'm fed up with waiting to see if anyone will choose me. I've spent most of my life waiting to see if someone will choose me. That's what these annuals taught me, and I'm still doing it now. I begin taping the annuals into a box so I can get rid of them.

I pick up my handbag from my chest of drawers where the head's latest briefing paper is, drowning under a pile of bills. I haven't even opened the last three. I don't know how come my phone bill is so much. The moment I get paid it all gets taken out of my account again. Anthony wants to go to a football camp this summer and how can I afford that? I pick up my Key Stage 3 scheme of work; on Monday I need to teach the final unit, *The role of the individual for good or ill?* It's all about why certain people are famous, and usually the kids find it much more interesting than the other units, the ones on how medieval monarchs kept control or the French revolution. But every time I teach it they confuse fame with being a celebrity, they're supposed to discuss historical figures like Karl Marx or Nelson Mandela, but instead they want to talk about Robbie Williams or, God help us, Donny Green.

Right, I'm dressed. I'm going to ring Bel to see what time we're having our picnic. I'll take whatever food I've got in the fridge; I'm too broke to buy anything. Maybe when Dwaine's not looking I'll raid what's left of the money he got for

401

Christmas, then I can take him on a boat on the lake. It's just as well no one's mentioned going to Portugal again because I couldn't afford it and, anyway, what would I have done with the boys?

'Mum!' shouts Dwaine from the front room.

'What?' I yell back.

'Donny Green's on telly!'

I come into the front room because Dwaine's yelling like something really exciting is going on. 'You know him, don't you, Mum?' Dwaine asks, and he sounds so proud that I know someone on the TV.

'Well I don't know him, Dwaine, but I told you I met him at Ashley's house.'

Still Dwaine looks impressed. 'And I've got his CD, haven't I, Mum, because Dad bought it for me at Christmas, didn't he?' Dwaine shifts over on the sofa so I can get down next to him. I stare at the TV. Donny Green is in the centre of a small round stage and he's miming a song and two women are dancing behind him. He's standing quite still and he's frowning a little like he wants to look tough. The bristles on his chin look like they've been airbrushed on.

'Do you think he's pretty?' Dwaine asks as we watch Donny Green finish his song.

'Pretty? I guess so.'

'You fancy him!' says Dwaine, and he nudges me in the stomach. 'My mum fancies Donny Green!' He gets up and starts chanting, 'Mum and Donny Green sitting in a tree, k-i-s-s-i-n-g!'

'Come on,' I say, laughing, and I think it's Ashley that Donny Green is kissing. No one kisses me, Dwaine, except

402

for you. 'You need to get dressed,' I tell him, 'And don't forget Nan's coming back tomorrow.'

Dwaine looks astonished, although I told him this last night after Mum rang and said, 'Loreen, I'm on my way home.' And I said, 'OK, Mum,' like this was perfectly normal, but it's not normal at all because Mum never, ever calls England home. I don't know what's going on with her; she said she was going to Botswana for two weeks, she disappeared for months, and then last night she calls.

'Yippee, Nan's coming back!' Dwaine jumps up and down on the sofa. 'Kitty cat has really really missed her, hasn't she, Mum?'

'Yes,' I say, because I can't believe Mum left her precious cat for so long. I stand up, fetch my phone and call Bel.

'Hi,' she answers the phone on the second ring, which isn't like her. Usually she lets the phone ring until I'm just about to hang up.

'Hi hon, it's Loreen.'

'Oh.' She sounds sort of confused.

'What's up?'

'Nothing, nothing, I thought it was . . .'

'You thought it was who?'

'Nothing,' she sighs.

'Well we've got the perfect day, haven't we?' I ask. 'For our picnic? What time d'you—'

'Shit, I'm sorry, Loreen, but I can't do today.'

'Oh. Why?' I'm standing at the door to my little balcony now and the sky is blue outside and I want to go for a picnic.

'It's work, I'm working today.'

'On a Saturday? You never work on a Saturday.' I open the balcony door, let some fresh air into the room.

'It's a new job,' says Bel.

'Oh! You got a new job, you didn't tell me!'

'It's not really that new. Loreen, it's complicated, I'll tell you when I see you, OK?'

'OK,' I say, only I don't feel it's OK, I feel like I'm a kid and everyone has somewhere to go and something to do on a lovely sunny day, except for me. That's what friends are supposed to be for, people you can do things with.

'How's Dwaine?' Bel asks.

'Fine,' I say, a little coldly because I still want to go on our picnic. 'Oh! Did you see Donny Green on TV just now?'

'No,' Bel sounds surprised. 'What was he on?'

'Kids TV.'

'Was it live?'

'I don't know. Why do you want to know if it's live?' I laugh.

'If it's live then that's where he is, isn't it?'

I laugh again. 'Why would you want to know that?'

'What?' says Bel, because she's playing the game she always plays and not answering the question.

'Have you heard from Ashley at all?' I ask.

'Who?' asks Bel, although I'm sure she heard me.

'Ashley. Have you heard from her at all? I haven't heard from her since the last time we were at her place and I've left her loads of messages since then.'

'She's busy, isn't she?' says Bel, and her voice sounds muffled like she's put the phone down and is doing something else. 'With her toy boy.'

404

'Where are you?'

'In my car.'

'Well she can't be that busy,' I say. 'Is she still with him, do you know? Is Ashley still with Donny Green?'

'Mum!' shouts Dwaine excitedly, trying to get in on the conversation.

'How would I know?' asks Bel. 'Sorry, I've got a call coming through, catch you later.' And she hangs up. I didn't even get the chance tell her more about the man I found for her on my dating site. I think she's going to love him. Bel says she's not interested in meeting anyone but I know she is. He's about our age, but he looks younger in his photo and he works in the media. He says he used to be a photographer. I didn't use her real name and I didn't put a picture, but I must have written her a great profile because she got more replies than I ever did.

Dwaine is dressed in his favourite little black t-shirt which has no sleeves. He looks too small to be in this; you need to be big with adult muscles in your arms to wear a t-shirt like this. He's got a tennis ball and he's bouncing it in the hallway, urging me to come. 'Let's go, Mum, you said we were having a picnic with Bel.'

'Yes, well we're not,' I say, following him into the hall.

'Why?' he wails. His ball hits the wall, flies off down the hall and he runs after it.

'Because,' I say. I feel annoyed now. Dwaine picks up his tennis ball and struggles to open the front door; he can't quite get the latch off so I lean over him and pull it myself. Oh my God! There's a man in the corridor and he's so close to my front door he almost falls into my flat. I let out a shriek.

'Sorry,' he says. 'Didn't mean to frighten you.' He's wearing an ill-fitting suit, the trousers are black and too loose, and the jacket is grey and too tight. He can't be waiting for me because my buzzer never went, someone else must have let him into the block and he's ended up at the wrong flat. I take Dwaine by the hand, waiting for the man to move so we can get down the corridor and to the stairs, but he doesn't. Instead he holds out his hand. 'Loreen?' he asks.

'Yes,' I say. Maybe he's here to deliver something.

'Ashley's friend? Ashley Brown?'

'Yes,' says Dwaine, and I squeeze his hand to show him he should stay quiet, because how does this man know my name and why is he asking about Ashley?

'Brian Barker,' says the man, and he takes back his hand because I haven't shaken it and he wipes it on his trousers. 'From the *Sunday Post.*'

'What?' I say.

Brian Barker leans against the corridor wall and puts one foot up against it so it looks like he's standing there with one and a half legs. 'Ashley Brown,' he says, nodding his head. 'You and Ashley go back quite a while, don't you?' He's trying to sound casual and chatty, but it's not working and I'm even more suspicious than I was when I opened the door. How does he know we're friends and why would he care anyway?

'My mum knows Donny Green,' says Dwaine.

I give his hand another squeeze, hard.

406

'Does she, hey?' Brian Barker takes his leg down from the wall and moves forward, gives Dwaine a little chuck on the chin. 'Can we have a quick word?' he asks, looking over his shoulder and up and down the corridor as if people might be listening. 'Inside?'

Chapter Forty-Two

BEL

Shit, Loreen's not going to be happy I hung up on her, but work is work and I need everything I can get. I had three days the week before last when the desk didn't call at all. It's all so uncertain, this game. I'll work twelve days on the trot, until the money feels like it's rolling in, and then suddenly it all goes quiet and I panic. I've got a car to pay for, a laptop and all my other gear; I can't afford not to work. So then I'll ring the desk, trying to sound casual. 'Hi Ray,' I'll say, 'Bel here.' 'How's our girl snapper?' Ray will say. 'Fine,' I'll say. 'Just to let you know I'm available, if you need me this morning.' What I mean is: give me work! Why aren't you giving me any work? Did I do something wrong? That was what it was like the week before last, but now it's Saturday and I've been working non-stop since Tuesday.

I wasn't thinking straight when I told Loreen I'd go for a picnic with her and Dwaine today. Saturday is the day before edition and I always work on a Saturday. I'm going to have to tell her what's going on. I don't like keeping things from Loreen, I never meant to. When I was put on Donny Green on Thursday, I was going to tell Loreen then. I was going to tell her and ask her what I should do, and whether I should tell Ashley. I was going to tell her that I'm a snapper; even before that I was going to tell her, when I took the snap of the single-parent-hating minister, I was going to tell her then. The longer I go without telling anyone the harder it gets. But the desk pulled me off Donny Green before I'd even got to his house in Notting Hill, and they put me on Macca instead, and I thought, why should I? Why should I tell Ashley, she never shows any interest in what any of us are doing. Sometimes I could shake Loreen. Just now she was upset that she hasn't heard from Ashley. I just think, Ashley has got what she wanted. Ashley has always got what she wanted. Ashley has always been looked after, she's never lacked a thing. Now she's got a pop-star boyfriend and that's why we are nothing to her any more, that's why she doesn't even answer Loreen.

Ray has just put me on Operation Amy. There'll be a whole scrum of paps outside Amy Winehouse's place in Camden today; she's the new big thing. Plus she just got married, Ray says. I drive towards Camden, my car windows open. It smells stale in my car because I just don't throw anything out any more. There's enough Polo wrappers to wallpaper my room, and so many newspapers and supplements still wrapped in cellophane I could insulate a house. I can barely see my back seat, but I can see the frame I got yesterday at a junk shop in Muswell Hill. It's an old frame and the mount is an unusual shape, curved at the corners rather than the usual square or oblong, and the wood around it is as shiny as a freshly opened conker. It's unlike any of my other frames, the ones I have piling up at home, under my bed, under the sofa, behind the door to my bedroom, leaning up against the wall. And I know which photograph I want to put in this frame; I took it yesterday at a churchyard in St John's Wood while I was supposed to be at Macca's. It smelt of early summer in there. The grey tombstones were scattered with grasses and wildflowers and I could smell sweet, dusty nectar in the air. I liked the contrast in the churchyard, the cool darkness under the trees by a wall wrapped in ivy, the sort of green you see only deep beneath a lake or the sea, and then the open sunniness of the graves themselves and the shiny little petals of the buttercups. By the gate was a plane tree with thick, low branches that made me think of being a kid, of climbing a tree as high as I could until, best of all, there was a feeling that perhaps I wouldn't be able to get down, that I might fall. The bark of the plane tree was like a dried-up riverbed. That's the photograph I'll put in that frame, if I ever get the time.

I turn onto Camden High Street, it's early still. Two men are sweeping the pavement, while a punk stands on the side of the road consulting his A to Z. On the right, by the underground, are stalls selling multi-coloured socks and union jack flags and a row of leather jackets hanging up like shiny carcasses. There's a splatter of clouds in the sky now and while the brightly painted houses are just lit by the sun, the street is in shadow and the people who are out this early are silhouettes on the pavement. I look the other way, at a record shop and a small stall set out with drugs paraphernalia: bongs and rizlas and magic mushrooms. A woman opens the awning over her shop front, begins putting out boots: high-heeled and low, some with zips, some with straps, black and white and brown. She is doing it so carefully and with so much planning I almost want to stop and take a snap. I should have charged my battery up last night, I think, as I pass over the bridge and look down onto the canal and at a weeping willow like a big green puffball just exploded. And then I think, as I stop at the lights, did I blow out that candle in the bathroom?

When I was having a bath this morning, the bulb had blown so I'd lit a candle. But I don't know if I blew the candle out. Yes I did blow it out, I bent over it. And I blew it out. I looked at it. There wasn't a flame. But what if I saw it wrong and it never went out? What if right now, while I'm waiting at the lights on Camden High Street on the way to Amy Winehouse's, it flares up? What if it flares up and keeps on burning and burns right down to the end of the candle and then starts to burn the top of the cabinet it's on because that's wood, that could burn. What if right now the cabinet is on fire and then the bathroom is on fire and then the landing and then the whole house. And I lose everything and so do my housemates and it's all my fault? And there's an investigation and it's clear the fire happened because the occupant, me, left a candle on. How stupid is that, to go out and leave a candle burning? I could call them now, find out if everything is OK, but then they'd know, they'd know they were living with a crazy woman.

Shit, it's happening again. Ever since my brothers started talking about OCD it's been getting worse; it's like that conversation made my brain flare up into craziness. It's like them talking about it has given my mind licence to come up with new, scary thoughts, far scarier ones than whether or not my car boot is locked. And once I get the thought, that's it, it takes me over. I can't not address it, I can't not think about it;

411

even if I'm not thinking about it, I'm thinking about it. I grip the steering wheel, I'm still stuck at the lights. Why won't they change? I want to turn the car round and head back home and check the candle. My teeth are pressing down on each other. I have to get to Amy's place. I can't go back. I hear a fire engine a street or so away. Shit shit shit. The lights change, I'll have to go on. Someone would call, wouldn't they, if the house was on fire?

I'm here and so are ten other paps. I've been here once before and it's not easy in terms of access. The road is tiny and cobbled and you can't get to any of the flats because they're in a courtyard and to get into that you have to get through a metal black gate. I can see the paps now, in a semi-circle in front of the gate, shoulders squared, cameras raised. In the thick of it I can see the familiar figure of beanie man; I thought he'd been arrested after the Prince Harry fiasco. I slow down as I see the gate open and the paps go mad. But even from here I can see it's not Amy. It's a man. The paps start hosing off shots as the man walks tight-faced into a car. Perhaps it's her dad, if the paps are snapping away like that. So I missed it.

I park up, annoyed I missed the dad coming out, grab my gear and get out. Then I realise, I've forgotten about the candle. When I'm working there's no time for anything else. That's why I need to keep on working. Of course the candle was out.

I walk up to the scrum of paps. A handful have gone after Amy's dad, mainly the agency monkeys, but the others, the press men, are hanging around having a chat. I see Sam from the *Express*, he gives me a wave. I stopped being the new girl on the block a long time ago. I can see beanie man from the corner of my eye and I remember the day of my first court job, when one of the paps said beanie man gives the game a bad name; that's how I feel now too.

I walk nearer, my jeans are sticking to me it's so hot. I see Fred from the *Mirror* and I head in his direction, but then, too late, I see who he's with. Fred has his hands scooped, lighting someone's cigarette, and I see the someone is Broadsheet Jimmy. You'd think a press photographer for a broadsheet would be too high and mighty to be on Amy Winehouse. But perhaps not. Shit shit shit. I can't leave and I can't go anywhere but past them and Fred's already seen me and I have to walk on.

'Morning!' I say, all cheery.

Fred smiles. Jimmy whips around. There is a leer on his face when he sees me. Jimmy's still sending me texts. The last one was two days ago. It wasn't nice. He doesn't ask when he'll see me any more, he's calling me a prick tease now.

'You're a bit overdressed today,' says Jimmy, looking me up and down.

I see what he's wearing – a beige t-shirt and tight corduroy trousers – then I look away, ignore him. 'Been here long?' I ask Fred.

'Hours, mate,' he says. 'I thought I'd see you here yesterday, it was quite a circus.'

'No,' I say, 'I was at Macca's.'

'What d'you think about Macca's divorce then?' asks Fred. He looks expectant but also sympathetic, like we're talking about mutual friends we've both known for years. 'The *Post* has been having a field day with that, haven't they? Joint custody of the little one, though, so they say, that's good. It's the kids who get hurt most in a divorce. Think she will get the house? Fuck, I'm hungry.' Fred rubs on his belly. 'Anyone cover for me while I nip to Sainsbury's? I fancy a bit of sushi.'

'No problem,' I say. I can sense Jimmy right beside me now. He's annoyed that I'm so deliberately ignoring him.

'You want anything?' asks Fred, getting ready to leave.

'No thanks,' I say. 'Not hungry.'

'You seem a little stressed, Bel,' says Jimmy, like he can't hold back any longer, and he steps back so he's standing just behind me and puts both hands out and begins to knead me on the shoulders. 'How's your love life?' he asks, and his breath is hot and smells of stale garlic.

'Fine,' I say, shaking him off. 'How's your girlfriend?'

Fred from the *Mirror* puts his SLR over his shoulder and looks at me; he can sense something's going on and even though his belly is leading him to Sainsbury's he's hanging back.

'Amazing, isn't it?' I ask him.

'What is?' asks Fred.

'Well,' I say, 'it's amazing that in a job like this, where we're usually rushing from one plot to another, some people still have time to sit down, day after day, any time, day or night, and send texts . . .'

Fred looks confused.

I hold up my phone, press my message inbox, start scrolling down. 'That's fifteen you've sent me in the last two weeks, Jimmy.' I turn the phone, showing it to Jimmy.

Fred laughs, but he still doesn't quite follow. I turn my phone back towards him.

'Look at this, here's the latest one,' I say, opening the message. 'This is the one when he calls me a prick tease.'

Fred looks at my phone, reads the message and frowns. 'Oh, that's not on,' he says. 'Do you know who it's from?'

'Yes I know who it's from, like I said, it's from Jimmy.'

Fred looks confused, glances at Jimmy.

'She's making it up,' Jimmy laughs.

'Well, let's see . . .' I say. I've unsettled him now, like he wanted to unsettle me, because he's been relying on his texts to stay private. He doesn't want this in the open; he wants this just to be between the two of us. 'If I was to reply to this text,' I say to Fred, 'this one here that says, "Bel you little prick tease . . ."' I hold up the phone so Fred can see what I'm doing, press the 'reply' button and then the 'call' button. Jimmy's phone starts to ring. We can see it vibrating in his trouser pocket.

'That's harassment, bro,' says Fred. He turns to Jimmy, sets his feet wide apart on the pavement like he's marking a line that he won't allow Jimmy to cross. 'My sister-in-law had something like that, she kept on getting rude texts from someone she'd only met once! She reported it to the police. Why would you want to do that, mate? That's harassment, that is.'

Jimmy's about to say something when there's a disturbance at the gate. It looks like someone is coming out of Amy Winehouse's place; paps are running in from every direction and I just see the back of Fred's head as he dives into the scrum.

Chapter Forty-Three

It's lunchtime. Nothing's happening at Amy Winehouse's. It wasn't her after all, coming out of the gate. Fred's come back from Sainsbury's, Sam's still here. Jimmy has sloped off because I've humiliated him in front of another man and he didn't like that. I take a few GVs of the house, get back in my car and send them to the desk. That will show them I'm here. Then Fred says he'll cover for me so I set off to Mum's. I'm hoping she might have something I can eat. I never cook at home any more, not that I did much anyway, but I'm a fast-food junkie now, always eating on the go, in the car, walking down a street, on a watch. Camden High Street is rammed with people, pedestrians milling across the road, carrying bags, talking on mobile phones, wearing backpacks, dragging trolleys, just looking to get run over. A hot Saturday morning is always like this and I wish I could go for a picnic with Loreen and Dwaine. I could be in a park now, under a tree, in the peace and quiet.

I get to Mum's and see she's still got her doormat turned the wrong way round. I stand on GOODBYE and wait for her to answer the door. When she does, a small, white, hairy fur ball leaps at me.

'Shit!' I say, thrown backwards.

'This is Titch,' says Mum. She picks up the dog and holds it against her chest, like it's a big baby. The dog licks Mum's neck and Mum laughs. Dogs lick their balls and their bums and other dogs' balls and bums. Then Mum lets it lick her neck.

'Where did you get it?' I ask, keeping as far away from the dog as I can.

'It's a she,' says Mum. 'She's six months old. At least we think she's six months old. I just got her yesterday from Battersea. Poor little thing, someone found her tied to a plank in the street and brought her in. Hasn't she got an intelligent face?' Mum puts her hand around the dog's face and turns it towards me. I can't see any sign of intelligence.

'Smells good in here,' I say, trying to get past Mum and the dog. 'Are you just having lunch?'

'You working, Bel?' Mum says, following after me. 'What are you on today?'

We get into the kitchen and I take a package out of my jacket pocket. 'I got you this,' I tell her. It's a little monkey statue I found in a junk shop yesterday, when I found the frame. Mum opens it, has a good look, puts it down again. 'Thanks very much,' she says.

She doesn't seem that excited by it. I wonder why she's not more enthusiastic, then I poke my head through the hatch to the front room and I see why. The monkeys have gone, all except the three on top of the TV. Now there are squirrels taking over. I can see a grey felt squirrel with a tail as big as Basil Brush's sitting in the middle of the coffee table. There's a black squirrel on the window sill, sitting up on its hind legs holding a shiny green wooden acorn. On the wall above the TV is a flying squirrel, its arms and legs stretched out like a taxidermist's specimen showing a soft white belly. I look down; even the draught excluder on the floor by the door has the face of a squirrel – the body of a snake and the face of a squirrel.

'Do you see my squirrels, Bel?'

'Yes, Mum. Why squirrels?'

'Why not?' shrugs Mum. 'Titch loves squirrels, don't you?' She nuzzles the dog in her arms.

I'm still peering through the hatch, looking round the room, when I see Glen is on the chair in the corner fast asleep.

'He just got back,' says Mum.

'From where?' I ask, my voice low, not wanting to wake him.

'Well as you know he's been in Portugal,' says Mum. Her voice is still loud and I remember that nothing wakes Glen unless he wants to be woken. Then his phone starts ringing. I expect this to wake him but he stays in the chair, eyes closed, snoring. The phone stops. A minute later it starts again. But still he doesn't wake up.

'What's up?' I ask Mum.

She shrugs. 'I think he's just had enough.' For a crazy second I think she means he's had enough of her and I feel shivery because Glen is something solid in my life and I don't want him to have had enough of her. I want him to stay.

'He's had enough of what?'

'Being a pap,' sighs Mum. I sit at the kitchen table while she finishes off lunch. The entire kitchen window is now blocked with plants, twisted and knotted into each other, leaves flattened against the glass. The fur ball of a dog is in the garden, I can see it through the open door. Why does

418

Mum let the plants go crazy in here when she could just move them outside? 'I've got four lamb chops,' says Mum, 'which is just as well because I didn't know Glen was going to be here and I didn't know you were going to show up either. All we need now is your brothers to turn up and I'm buggered. Shall I do potatoes with these? Or macaroni? Bel?'

'Yeah, lovely,' I say. I open my phone, I've just got a text.

'Anyone nice?' asks Mum, seeing me checking my phone.

'It's from Loreen.'

'Oh,' says Mum. 'How's she?'

'She's fine.' I close my phone. I'm not going to tell Mum what Loreen is texting about. She just won't give up on this idea of finding me a date. She has actually done what she said she was going to do and advertised my personal life on the Internet. I don't know whether to be pissed off or not. She says I've got to ring her, to say when I can meet this man she's found for me. I'm going to tell her to forget it, but then I think what have I got to lose? I text back that I'm free tomorrow night. It's Sunday. And Monday is my day off.

'You awake then?' asks Mum as Glen comes to the kitchen door.

'Just having a little snap, darling,' says Glen. He looks a mess. He looks like he hasn't slept, eaten or washed for days. His hair is sticking up. 'Hello, Bel,' he says. He slaps me gently on the shoulder and then smiles and sits down at the table, picks up a saltshaker in the shape of a squirrel. 'Interesting animals, squirrels,' he muses, turning the saltshaker around in his hands.

'Really?' I ask.

'Yes. How high do you think a squirrel can jump, Bel?'

'Ten feet?'

'Twenty.' He keeps turning the saltshaker around. 'Double-jointed back legs, see. Five toes on the back feet, four on the front. And a squirrel,' he puts the saltshaker down, 'can see some things that are behind them. Quite clever really.'

'Mmm,' I say.

'So, Bel, I haven't seen you since the Heathrow job. When was that, Thursday? What are you on today?'

'Amy Winehouse,' I say, 'along with everyone else.'

'Ooh!' says Mum. 'The one with the beehive hairdo.'

'I'll have to get back there in a bit.' I take the plates from Mum and put them out on the table. I skive off much more than I used to do. I used to arrive early for every shift, stay religiously where I was supposed to be – except for that one time at Café 200 – wait without complaint for a night man to take over. Now I take short cuts. Now the game is how little I can do while still appearing to do my job.

Mum takes the chops out of the oven, swears as she almost loses grip of the pan. From the front room we can hear Glen's phone ringing again. At the kitchen table Glen puts his head back and closes his eyes. It looks like he's going to have another snap. After a few minutes he opens his eyes again, looks round the room like he's forgotten where he is. The fur ball that is Mum's dog runs in from the garden. 'Hello, girl.' Glen smiles and pats at the dog as it tries to jump up his leg. 'Good girl,' he says as the dog sits.

'Don't say that!' Mum shouts.

We both look at her, startled, and then the dog lets out a steaming yellow torrent of wee on the kitchen floor. 'Don't say what you just said,' says Mum. 'If you say "good you know what" then she wees. Someone must have tried to train her, they must have said, "good you know what" every time she had a wee. Now she thinks it's a command.'

'Righto,' laughs Glen.

Mum gets the mop, starts cleaning up the dog's wee. Again we hear Glen's phone ringing in the front room. 'Why aren't you answering it?' I ask.

Glen slumps a little at the table. 'Do you know what it's like out there, Bel?' he asks, and his eyes look tired and swollen. 'Have you any idea what it's like in the Algarve? On the missing girl? I was only there, what, two days, and I've never seen anything like it in my life. I mean, never. It's a fucking freak show over there. Journos, paps, TV crews, on every street in the town, every bar, every pub, the beach, the lot, the entire place is crawling with them. The parents of that girl, they're shadowed wherever they go. They come out of the house, the press are there, they go to church, the paps are there. They get in their car. They get out. They . . .' Glen grabs the saltshaker in frustration and he tips it up and begins to pour a little mountain of white onto the table. 'And there's nothing happening and the police won't talk to them, so they make it up, that's what all these muppets are doing, making it up. It's a fucking feeding frenzy over there. One journo makes something up, it's headline news here, the papers need something for the next day, the TV needs something for the next hour. Because that's how it is now, reporters can't wait for anything to develop, they can't take their time with a story, they need something now. And they need a new story, a different one from the other journos. Right now they're

421

saying a mad man took the little girl. The next thing you know they'll be pointing fingers at the parents.'

'Oh they can't!' objects Mum.

'They will,' says Glen. 'So you know what, darling? To be honest with you, I've had enough.'

I think of the first time I met Glen, nearly two years ago, here in Mum's place, and this was what he said. Perhaps this is what he's been saying for years, perhaps this is what he always says. And maybe in five years, ten years, fifteen years time, that will be me as well. Just like Glen, trying to get out of the game. Again his phone rings from the front room. Glen puts out one arm and pats me on my right hand. One single, sad pat.

The doorbell rings and Mum goes to answer it and I hear the voices of my brothers as they enter in tandem. Joe's got a big supermarket bag in his hands. He must have brought his washing. He puts a case of beer on the table. 'For the match,' he says. 'You staying to watch it?' he asks Glen. Rich comes in behind him, he's got a battered Sudoku book wedged in his armpit like he's keeping it warm. The room feels too much now, it feels claustrophobic. The dog starts whining. There are two many men, too many plants. It's all too hot. I start tapping under the top of the table, where the wood is pale and a little soft. I tap three times with one finger and then another and then another, then Mum asks me something and I have to start again. When my phone rings I'm thrown for a second. Then I leap up, shit, I'm meant to be at Amy Winehouse's in Camden. I run through Mum's flat and rush outside. 'Hi,' I say, one finger in my ear, running to my car.

'Alright, Bel.' It's Ray on the desk. 'How's our girl snapper?'

'Fine, fine,' I say, lunging for my car door, opening it as quickly as I can and clambering in. Ray will be able to hear if I'm in my car or not, if I'm where I'm supposed to be.

'Anything happening, Bel?' he asks.

'No,' I say, feigning boredom. 'Nothing.' What if there is, though? What if something has happened at Amy Winehouse's place and Ray knows this and he's testing me? What if she's come out of her house and is standing there right now giving an impromptu press conference?

'Alright then,' says Ray. 'Stand down from Amy. You're back on Donny Green.'

Chapter Forty-Four

KAREN

It's Saturday lunchtime and I'm standing in my back yard looking around at the plants and the herbs that have shrunk in the dryness overnight. I almost wonder if it's worth watering the rosemary and the chives and the thyme considering I'm going back to California soon and can't take them with me, but I want to keep them healthy and growing for the person who will be living here after me. I picture my garden back in Davis, the lushness of the place, reddening tomatoes, clusters of grapes on the vine. I don't want to be here any more, I don't want to be in London, a city of long, grey days, a city where neighbours don't talk to each other, even when a child is being abused. Today the sun is out and it makes me long even more to leave. I can taste California on a day like this.

Stella is asleep; we were out late last night and when we came home at one am we found Dylan sitting in the hallway, his back against our door, his feet stretched out on the carpet, his sleeping head soft against his chest. Stella woke him gently, and as he stirred and looked up I saw again the bruise that Stella noticed yesterday on his arm, as dark as a thundercloud. He seemed wary of me at first, but he allowed

Stella to let him in and call him 'honey' and make up a bed for him downstairs. And then for hours we whispered to each other about what to do, about whether we should call the council again, about whether we should call the police, and several times during the night I woke, thinking I heard Dylan get up and leave or that I could hear his father coming for him. But the big guy never came and there doesn't seem to be anyone in the apartment upstairs right now. I told Stella we needed to ask the boy about this, about where his father was, about why he was sleeping outside our door, about whether he'd been beaten, but she told me to let him be. Stella cannot see a boy asleep in a hallway and not want to let him in.

I wrote a letter to the council this morning, like the jerk on the phone told me to, and now I need to mail it. The two of them are sleeping still, so I go inside quietly, grab my swim things, leave a note for Stella and head out the door.

I've timed it well because my neighbour is just leaving too. 'Gorgeous morning!' she says.

'Lovely!' I agree, but today I'm not going to stand here and try to get her to talk; I'm going to walk with her and goddam force her to talk, because I'm going soon and I want to know that someone will do something about the boy. I want to know when we are all going to stop watching and listening and pretending we are not involved when we are. I wait until my neighbour opens her gate and leaves her driveway then I fall in with her and we walk along the road together.

'I rang the council about the boy,' I say.

My neighbour stops in her tracks. 'Really?'

'They weren't very helpful.'

'No,' she says, walking on again. 'Well they wouldn't be.

425

But they're the ones responsible, aren't they? They know all about *him* in there, they're the ones who should do something.'

'I've written to them,' I tell her, and I hold up my letter so she can see, but my neighbour doesn't say anything, she just keeps on walking, she doesn't even look at the letter in my hand. Then she waves to a woman on the other side of the street and the woman waves back and then we part to let a young woman with two children in a double-storey buggy pass between us. One child is in the bottom compartment, the other is in the top, and they look like passengers on an Amtrak train.

'Hiya!' my neighbour says to the young woman with the buggy, and the woman says, 'Alright!' and passes with a wave. How come everyone seems to know each other today? Am I the only neighbour who doesn't know anyone, and is that because I just haven't been here long enough, and if I stayed, if I lived here for years and years, then would I know people too?

'I've just written down what's been happening upstairs,' I tell my neighbour. 'I thought, if you could too then perhaps the council would intervene. I don't think he's safe. He spent the night at our apartment last night.'

My neighbour looks shocked. 'At your place?' she asks, like my place is somewhere very far from here.

'He's still sleeping there now,' I tell her. 'So will you write to them too?' I slow my steps, bend down and retie a lace on my sneakers, and when I look up my neighbour is watching me suspiciously. 'If there are two or three of us, that would help, and then if it did come to court then we could testify together.'

'*Testify?*' asks my neighbour, her voice shrill. 'You mean in court? Oh I don't think I could do that.' She laughs nervously and I know what she's going to do now, she's going to look at her watch and say, 'Oops! Running late, time to go.'

'But if we don't do something,' I tell her, 'it's just going to continue, isn't it?' I look at my neighbour, search her eyes, but she won't look at mine.

'Well, you know,' she looks flustered, 'my husband said, after our last conversation, not to get involved.' She tails off; perhaps she can hear how weak this sounds, that she knows what she should do but her husband is preventing her and she is unable to go against his wishes. Then she does look at her watch and she does say, 'Oops! I'm late!' and off she goes as fast as anyone in high-heeled shoes can go and I'm left watching the back of her. I'm feeling utterly defeated when I see the woman who lives opposite me coming down the road, the woman who I have seen at her window, watching Dylan on those times he scoots off down the middle of the street on his frantic cartoon feet when his father won't let him in. We have never spoken before, but today it will be different.

'Hi,' I say as the woman reaches me. I can see she wants to nod and walk on, that she has a bag of shopping in one hand, that she doesn't want to be delayed. 'I'm Karen,' I say, 'I live opposite?' The woman has a soft-skinned face and I see it sag a little as she lowers her chin and passes a shopping bag from one hand to the other. 'I was wondering,' I say, 'about what you can hear from your house?'

The woman looks blank.

'Do you hear, you know, noises, from in there?' I nod back

427

in the direction of my house. 'I know you've seen the boy locked out . . .'

The woman nods but she's watching me warily.

'I've written to the council,' I say, and I hold up my letter. 'I thought if we could get together and perhaps do something, for the sake of the boy?'

The woman's face closes up and the softness has gone. 'I do feel for you,' she says, swapping the bag from hand to hand again, 'living underneath all that. But it's domestic, isn't it, love?'

I get to the pool and I'm angry now, and when I undress and get to the water and see goggle man smashing his way up and down the fast lane I jump straight in. I'm not going to be polite and careful today, I'm going to act like this is my own private lane, my own private pool and if turtle woman turns up today I'm not stopping for her either. And as I swim I wonder why no one will get involved with the boy Dylan and whether he will still be there when I get back, and then I think, is Stella safe at home if the big guy comes looking for his son?

Chapter Forty-Five

I get home from the pool and my body is buzzing, my hair is still wet and I feel alive again. I have my gym bag over my shoulder and I swing it through the open door into my apartment. 'Stella!' I shout, and then I wonder why the door is open and for a second I'm afraid. But then I realise it is women's voices I can hear, and then a child's as well. 'Mum,' says the child, 'are we going on a picnic or not?' I don't know the child's voice but I know the woman's when she says, 'Will Karen be back soon?' because it's Loreen. Loreen! I haven't seen her in months. I've been so caught up with finishing my book and then Stella coming back from her trip that I haven't even called her.

I hurry into the kitchen and Loreen is sitting at the table with her arm around her little boy Dwaine who has a tennis ball against his chest. Stella is pouring out two cups of peppermint tea. 'Here you are, honey,' she says, looking up.

For a moment I feel I'm interrupting, that I haven't come into my apartment but into someone else's, but then Loreen gets up and gives me a hug and a kiss. 'I'm sorry for just turning up,' she says. 'Me and Dwaine were going for a picnic with Bel in Regent's Park. But then she said she couldn't and he was so keen to get out I thought we'd pop in on you . . .'

'That's great,' I say, 'I love it that you came by,' and Loreen smiles and sits down again.

'Where is he?' I ask Stella.

'Dylan?' she says. 'He's gone upstairs.'

Loreen looks at the two of us and smiles, even though she doesn't know who or what we're talking about, and I'm about to tell her all about Dylan when I sense she has something she wants to tell me and that this is why she's come. 'I've had this really weird morning, Karen,' she says, and then she looks down at her son as if she's trying to decide whether to speak in front of him or not.

Stella must be thinking this too because she gets up from the table and says, 'You want to come out and put a hoop up with me?'

Loreen's son moves forward, then he stops and stares at her.

'A basketball hoop?' asks Stella. 'I just got one and I've been waiting for someone to come along and show me how it's done. You want to come see? When I was a kid, you know, I always wanted a basketball hoop, we were like, Mom, *please*! Can we . . .' And Stella chatters on and Loreen's son goes off outside with her quite happily and I'm left wondering, when did Stella buy a basketball hoop and from where and why?

'She's lovely, isn't she?' asks Loreen as Stella goes out.

'Yes,' I say, but I'm wondering if Stella bought the hoop for Dylan to play with, if she thought she and Dylan could play with it together, if she already had some plan that he would spend the night with us and be here the next day to play hoop. 'So what was weird about your morning?' I ask Loreen. 'You want juice?' I open the fridge, take out a carton and pour her a glass. Then I stand with my back against the

430

counter because this way I can see out into the yard where Stella is.

'Oh please sit down!' says Loreen. 'You're making me nervous, standing there like that.' She begins to bite away at the skin around her fingers like she used to as a kid. 'I thought you'd know what to do,' she says, 'because you always know what to do.'

'I do?' I'm not really listening; I'm still looking at Stella, still thinking about the hoop.

'Something really weird happened this morning, Karen, something really really weird.' Loreen stops biting at her fingers and she pulls her chair back a little from the table so she can look out into the yard as well.

'Go on.' I'm listening now because Loreen sounds odd, and I realise she's picking the skin around her finger not because she's worried but because she's excited.

'Well,' she says, 'this journalist turned up at my place, he was just standing there when me and Dwaine came out, and I was like, "Oh my God!"' Loreen laughs, pulls her chair back in towards the table and leans forward. 'He wanted to know if I knew Ashley.'

I stare at her. 'What do you mean?'

'The weird thing was, he knew who I was, he knew my name, said was it right I went to school with Ashley. I mean, that is a bit weird, isn't it?' She looks at me like she wants me to agree. 'So I wasn't going to say anything but Dwaine pipes up that yes, we know Ashley, and then the journalist offers me money. I mean a *lot* of money.' Loreen lowers her voice although the door to the yard is closed, I don't think Stella and Dwaine can hear us. 'He offered me

431

thousands and thousands, Karen. He said, "Name your price," so I said, "Oh, two hundred thousand," and he said, "Fine." Ha! Two hundred thousand pounds! I could *buy* a flat with that!'

'I don't get it,' I tell her. 'Why does he want to know about Ashley?'

'Because of Donny Green, of course! Karen, he's mega famous, come on, you've been here long enough, you know that. You were the one who saw that picture in the paper of him and Ashley, remember? He said they want to build up a picture of her, as she's his new girlfriend, find out what she's like, you know, do a profile. He really wanted any old pictures as well. I thought he was a bit loopy to begin with but he showed me his ID and I was thinking, well, two hundred thousand pounds . . .'

'Loreen!' I stare at her. 'You can't be serious.'

Loreen looks embarrassed. 'I'm only joking.'

'What paper is he from?'

Loreen grimaces. 'The *Sunday Post*. You know, the one she and Bel had that argument about.'

'But what could you give him for two hundred grand? Are you sure he even has that sort of money?'

'I do have pictures,' says Loreen, and again she pulls her chair back from the table and looks out towards the yard. We both listen; we can hear Dwaine shouting something and then the thud thud of a basketball and Stella yelling, 'Way to go!'

'Pictures?' I ask. 'Of what?'

'Well,' Loreen hesitates. 'Of when we were kids. Since I moved into my new flat I've found loads of old stuff, loads

432

of old things Mum's kept. There's some pictures from Portugal as well . . .'

'From when we were sixteen?'

'Yeah, there's some of Ashley in that bikini she used to have, that halter neck, the red and white one?'

'Loreen,' I say, because I don't remember what goddam bikini Ashley wore over fifteen years ago, 'you can't give pictures of Ashley to a journalist. You can't *sell* him pictures.'

'This one picture,' says Loreen, not answering me, 'is of Ashley and a boy.'

'Ashley was always with a boy!' I laugh.

'But it was the one I fancied,' says Loreen, and she sits up stiffly in her chair. 'You remember those German boys we met at the bar on the beach? The last day of the holiday? And me and Bel fancied the black-haired one, you know, the really good-looking one, the one in Bermuda shorts? Ashley *knew* I fancied him and she said, she *told* me, he fancied me too, and I sat there like an idiot on the beach saying, "Ooh! Let's go and find them, where are they staying?"'

I stare at Loreen. I have only a very vague memory of any boys in Portugal, and I wonder if this is a hurt she's been holding close to her all this time. I wonder if she can really be this angry over a boy from when we were sixteen, or is it nothing to do with the boy and all to do with Ashley? Because of all of us Loreen always let Ashley get away with anything, she never even seemed to notice when Ashley was mean, and if she did then she was right there ready to defend her.

'And of course he didn't fancy me,' says Loreen, 'and it was Ashley that went off with him. They got off together, on

433

the cliff. They were half-naked, they might even have been having sex.'

'How do you know that?'

'It's in the photo!'

'But how did you get a photo of that?'

'It must have been Bel,' says Loreen, like she's given this some thought. 'Who else took pictures but Bel? Did you have a camera then?'

'No.'

'No, nor did I.'

'Loreen,' I say, 'get rid of the photo, you don't want to keep a picture like that.'

'You think so?' Loreen doesn't sound convinced.

'Yes, destroy it, you can't keep a goddam picture of people having sex! I mean, Loreen, that belongs to whoever it is in that picture, right? It's not for you to sell, and if you keep it then I guess you might be tempted and you can't do that.'

'Can't I?' Loreen asks, and I'm surprised because this doesn't sound like Loreen at all, this doesn't sound like the girl who always wanted to go along with everyone else, who always wanted everyone to be happy, who always did everything she could to make us all get along.

'Or give it back to Bel,' I say, 'if it's her picture, if she's the one who took it, then give it back to her because I guess it belongs to her, right? Or give it to Ashley. Loreen, you *have* to give it to Ashley because it's a picture of her, she's the one who should have it. You have told her, haven't you, about the journalist?'

'Do you know what else I found, Karen?' says Loreen, like she hasn't even heard my question. 'It's funny, isn't it, the way

434

you think you remember how something or someone was? I mean, you have a really good idea of someone and then you find something that makes you wonder if you even remember yourself. I found some old diaries,' she says. 'I found a diary from when I was sixteen, and do you know what, I'd written that Ashley was a cunt.' She looks at me, as if waiting for something, as if she wants to me to say either, how could you? Or yes, Ashley was a cunt.

'Mum!' shouts Dwaine, and he comes running into the kitchen and Stella says they need water and Dwaine runs to Loreen and says he wants to go on the picnic now.

'We'll talk later,' I say, seeing Loreen is torn, she wants to keep talking about the photo and the journalist and Ashley and when we were sixteen, but she has to go and be a mom now. 'Don't do anything silly,' I say.

Loreen nods but I don't think she's really listening to me.

'Come on, Mum,' says Dwaine again.

I walk them to the door and we hug on the steps. 'We have to get together again, all of us, before I go,' I tell Loreen.

'Yeah,' she says, disinterestedly, 'of course.'

Chapter Forty-Six

DUDU

I remember when the girls were little and they each wanted a cat, and they wanted and they dreamed and they begged for a cat, and then Ashley's father bought her one. It was a Siamese cat with silky grey hair and it eyed the girls gloomily when they wanted to play with it. Still, all the girls were jealous of Ashley whose father agreed to get her a cat.

I bend down and scoop up my own little kitty cat. She is sleeping on my chair, making it warm with her body, and I shouldn't really disturb her but I am here after all this time, back in England in my own house on a Sunday morning, and I want the feel of her. But my little kitty cat is no longer a kitten, she is a proud independent cat, and now she is punishing me for abandoning her for so long. As I stroke her head she turns to nip me on the finger and then she leaps out of my arms and goes to sit on the rug in the middle of the room and she sits there with her hip bones up, like a chicken roosting upon her eggs.

So I leave her to be and I go into my kitchen to make some tea and to listen to the radio. What was I thinking of to have been gone for so long? The very first thing they are talking about this peaceful Sunday morning is my old friend Piano

Man. It is said he is living and attending university in Switzerland now, where he studies French literature, and the people on the radio are discussing him, for it seems some reporters have tracked him down to where he lives. This must have happened some weeks ago, it must have happened while I was away, but they are saying that now they know the reason the man lost himself. It was over a shattered love affair. He had met a man and the love affair went wrong and so he travelled to England and he tried to kill himself and when that failed he just pretended not to know who he was.

They say my friend Piano Man has refused all requests to be interviewed since he has remembered who he is and where he is from and started life again. Well of course he has! I tell the radio. Why are they so surprised that he doesn't want to talk about his failed love affair and his suicide attempt? The reporters must have been following him around where he now lives for they seem to know what he spends his time doing, which poetry he loves, which bar he has his coffee in. They say he is often seen carrying bottles of red wine into his rooms in the evenings; this is what his neighbours say and I wonder that these neighbours can't keep these things to themselves when asked by reporters about my friend Piano Man.

I must have fallen asleep right in my chair in the kitchen with my cat on the rug watching me, because now I see it is past lunchtime and Loreen and my little grandsons will be on their way. I get up slowly, my leg is paining me today, but I want to go through my bags, which are still in the hall where I left them this morning when I arrived from the airport, and find all the things I have brought home for my little grandsons.

Then there is a knock and I know they are here already and I open my front door and I stand back because normally my little grandson Dwaine runs when the door is opened, normally he runs right into my house as if it were a play park full of things for him to play with. But today he is standing still on the doorstep with his mother.

'Hello, Dwaine,' I tell him. 'And where is your brother Anthony?'

'Hello, Nan,' says Dwaine, and he hides his head against his mother's handbag.

'Oh come on!' laughs Loreen. 'That's not a very convincing shy act, Dwaine. You've been talking about Nan all morning, yelling at me, "When are we going to see Nan?"' Loreen throws her arms around me. 'So home at last!' she says. 'You look great, Mum.' And she holds me by the shoulders, her head back, looking at me. And you look very tired, my child, is what I want to say.

Now Dwaine wakes up and he shouts, 'Hurrah!' And off he runs into my house because he has remembered I am his nan and this is my home so it is his home as well.

We sit in my kitchen, Loreen and me, and we talk about my trip and the family in Botswana and the weather here and the snow I missed in February and Dwaine's new teacher and a visit from social services that I don't quite understand, and then I see there is something else my little Loreen wants to talk about.

'Dwaine,' she says, putting her arm around her son, 'go and see if you can find kitty cat.'

'OK, Mum!' says Dwaine, and he runs off and I can hear him calling in his sweet little boy voice.

'Where is Anthony?' I ask.

'Football practice,' says Loreen. 'Mum, listen, I've got to tell you, the weirdest thing happened yesterday.' She puts her hands around her coffee cup, her fingertips touching. 'This man turned up, a journalist, wanting to know if I knew Ashley.'

'If you knew who?' I get up, fetch my biscuit tin from the cupboard, open it and put it on the table.

'Ashley, Mum.' Loreen sounds impatient and I remember this voice as a child, when she would be telling me a long story about something that had happened at school and we would be crossing a busy road and I would have shopping in my hands and she would get impatient because she thought I was not listening to her. 'I'm saying, Mum, that a journalist came round yesterday morning asking me about Ashley. And . . .' she waits to see she has my attention. 'And he offered me money for whatever I could tell him.'

'For whatever you could tell him about what?' I begin to take out the packets in my biscuit tin and look to see which ones are most out of date and which can still be eaten.

'About Ashley!' says Loreen. 'She's a celeb now, Mum. She's going out with Donny Green, you know, the pop star, the one Dwaine loves.'

'Why would anyone want to know anything about Ashley?' I look at Loreen, offer her a biscuit.

'Mum, I've just said, she's going out with Donny Green! They want to do a piece about her, so the journalist wanted to know about her. And, get this, he offered me two *hundred* thousand pounds.'

'You're saying a journalist offered you two hundred

439

thousand pounds?' I put the lid back on the biscuit tin and push it down hard so it makes a snapping noise.

'That's right,' says Loreen with a smile. 'So I said yes and here's the cheque.' Loreen reaches into her handbag, which she has hung over the back of her chair, and brings out nothing and she laughs, she is playing with me.

'She always wanted you harm, that girl,' I say, sitting down at the table opposite my daughter who looks so tired.

'What?' Loreen has opened the packet of biscuits and she has a digestive in her right hand.

'She always wanted you harm,' I say again.

'Don't be silly,' says Loreen, taking a bite of the digestive. She chews it slowly; she doesn't eat it as hurriedly as she normally would.

I frown at her because I am not being silly, and I push a plate towards her to catch the biscuit crumbs that are falling from my daughter's mouth. 'She was always meddling with you girls and causing problems between you.'

'No she wasn't,' says Loreen mildly.

'Yes, she was,' I tell her, 'right from the start. I remember that first day of primary school, the way you girls all stood in line together. I remember that day as clear as anything . . .'

Loreen groans, finishes her biscuit and takes another.

'Ashley always liked being the centre of attention,' I tell her, 'and that day, that very first day of primary school, she told the teacher Bel was pushing in and because of that Bel was taken to the back of the line and it was then she started to bleed.'

'What?' asks Loreen. 'I don't remember that. What do you mean, bleed?'

440

'From the nose,' I say.

'Oh,' Loreen takes a third biscuit, 'a nose bleed.'

'It was a very bad nose bleed,' I tell her, because I don't like the way she is being dismissive of this. 'It spoilt Bel's first day and that wasn't fair because all the children were pushing in that day. Bel got told off and getting told off on your first day of school isn't nice, is it, Loreen? And I remember Ashley's birthday party the year you girls all turned seven, the careless way she took your present, the present you had taken so long to choose, and the way she left it lying on the floor.'

Loreen smiles. 'And was I really traumatised by that, Mum?'

I ignore her because she is being stubborn now. 'I remember that time she came over for tea,' I continue. 'She was your first school friend to come over for tea and you were so excited about it, Loreen, and you so wanted your friend to have a good time, and yet the moment she came in she started with all those questions of hers and she made you feel you lacked things . . .'

'Mum, she was just a kid.'

'Yes,' I tell Loreen. 'She was just a kid. And she was the one who forced you to play mummies and daddies.'

'She what?'

'I came into the room, your little bedroom, and there she was half-naked, squirming away on top of you.'

Loreen laughs, but I do not because now I am thinking of that day the teacher Miss Pond told me that my Loreen would never be clever like Ashley, and what a wrong, hurtful thing that was to say, and how, even now, I cannot tell my daughter this. And I think of the nativity play and how

441

Ashley was the Virgin Mary and my little Loreen was a tree, they made my poor child be a tree! And I think of the day of my accident, that day in Brighton. And then I stop because I am overtired, this is too much remembering and I am upsetting myself. We are both quiet for a moment and I can hear the news beginning on my radio and the tick tick of the clock on the wall.

'Her family were always really nice to me, though,' says Loreen, taking a fourth biscuit, and she looks up at me with her face as hopeful as it was as a child when she told me she'd made a new friend or when she asked if she were allowed to go on a school trip.

'Were they?' I ask.

'What do you mean, were they?'

'Were they kind to you, or were they entertained by you?' I stand up and go to my radio and turn the volume down because my head is beginning to hurt and I haven't travelled halfway across the world to quarrel with my own child. But still I cannot stop myself; I want my Loreen to see her friend for what she was. 'She was a very controlling little girl, Ashley Brown, she played you girls off against each other all the time, and she made you miserable, Loreen, she really did.' I look at Loreen and she is watching me keenly now. 'Do you remember when you went to Portugal?' I ask, and Loreen nods quickly, so quickly she must have been thinking of this herself, and then she puts her head down and she studies her coffee cup as if she has not seen a coffee cup before. 'Do you remember how first she said one of you could go and then she said not, and then she chose another and you were eaten up with the worry of it all?'

442

'No I wasn't,' says Loreen. She is still protesting, but not as much as before.

'Yes you were, you would lie awake with the worry of it all. And she made you lie . . . Yes she did! She made you lie to her father and say she had stayed with you when in fact she was running off with that little boyfriend she had back then and . . .' I turn my head to the left because that is where Loreen is looking and I see Dwaine is no longer upstairs looking for the cat, he is standing by the doorway to the kitchen inspecting something he has in his hands, only he is not really studying what he has in his hands, he has made himself very quiet so he can listen to us, that clever little boy.

'So now she is a pop star?' I ask.

'She's not the pop star, Mum,' says Loreen, and her voice is annoyed again. 'She's going out with a pop star.'

'My mum *knows* Donny Green,' says Dwaine, coming into the kitchen, sidling up to his mother.

'What sort of life is that, a pop star?' I ask, filling up the kettle again and turning it on.

'I don't know,' says Loreen, standing up. I begin to speak but Loreen puts her hand up and I remind myself that she is a teacher and that this is how, perhaps, she responds to an unruly child in class. 'So, anyway, what do you think I should do?' she asks. 'Karen says I shouldn't have anything to do with the journalist.'

I look at Loreen. So she has had this conversation already, she has not come to me, her mother, to ask what she should do, she is asking everyone she can think of. 'And what about Bel?' I ask, and I smile because Bel always makes me smile. 'What does she say?'

Chapter Forty-Seven

BEL

Shit, I'm glad it's Sunday. I'm glad I'm walking and not in my car. It seems like I live in my car. But today it's Sunday, my fun day, and I'm going to look at some cameras. That's why I'm in this game, so I can buy cameras and take snaps and earn a living from doing what I do and love best. I turn left off Gower Street, even though I was going to go right to Tottenham Court Road, but something is making me walk this way. I reach Gordon Square and stop by a fig tree next to three old-fashioned red phone boxes. I remember this tree. I slip my camera off my shoulder. There is something about a fig tree right in the middle of London, it looks exotic here. I like the way the leaves look soft, almost hairy, even from a distance, and I want to frame the tree, to snap it in such a way that someone else could feel the soft hairiness of the leaves.

Then I remember another tree. I remember all those years ago when I was in Portugal and seeing a fig tree for the first time, the four of us together, at Ashley's parents' house. And the only reason I was there was because Loreen said she wouldn't go without me, and then because Ashley gave me the money. We were sixteen; sixteen and I'd never been abroad or seen a fig tree before. I had my first SLR. I took pictures of the fishing boats. I stood on the cliff and took pictures of the dragonflies mating. And here I am, at the age of thirty-four, on an empty London street on an empty London Sunday, and I'm a snapper. I'm a snapper who follows celebs. And I've been put on watch outside Ashley's boyfriend's house. How did things come to this?

But nothing happened last night, nothing at all. I left Mum's and went on my watch at Donny Green's in Notting Hill. His place is set well back from the road on a gravel driveway with some sort of conversion at the front. I could have sat opposite it, there were no parking wardens about, but I didn't. Instead I parked my car as far from the house as I could and hunched myself down on the seat and waited. Then, two hours later, I was pulled off the plot. I don't know why the desk keeps on doing this. Sometimes I think they have no idea what their snappers are doing, we're like manic little chess pieces they move around London at will.

But today it's Sunday. I'm not working. I'm free. It's sunny and the birds are out. I walk on and for a second I can't work out what I'm doing or where I'm going. Then I know where I'm going. I'm going to Tavistock Square.

I can't believe I used to work around here. It seems so long ago now. I pass the green front of the Tavistock Hotel and see a sign for offices to let. I come to the British Medical Association building with its odd round windows. I pass the house with the plaque that says Dickens used to live here. I see a street cleaning truck and then a sightseeing red double-decker bus taking a route down Bedford Way. On the top deck tourists sit in colourful t-shirts, cagoules wrapped loosely round their necks. They must have been warned

445

about the English weather, they must have been told it might rain. I watch the bus and I think, does the guide point to the square as the tourists pass and say, 'And this is where the bomb went off'? I feel shivery. I put my camera bag over my shoulder and squeeze my fingers into my palms to make them warm. I'm here. This is where I was just after the bomb went off. I can see how the street was when we came down from the office, the mayhem, the screams and the running and the air full of glass. But there is no one here today, nothing but parked cars and a couple of pigeons flying in a skittery manner down onto the pavement. I cross the road and walk past the park and see the tip of the stone that was put up in memory of conscientious objectors. There is still no sign of what happened here. In the park there must be a memorial now, but out here there is nothing. Just a Sunday afternoon in Tavistock Square.

I see three men in green uniforms inside the park. Do council park people work on a Sunday? The men look up as I pass and I stare at them; I want to see some memory of what happened here on their faces. What is it like working here in this park? But the men are just looking up because someone is walking by. Their faces show nothing. I turn and see two women coming out of a building. Are they at work on a Sunday too? I look at their faces closely, searching for something. What am I expecting? Horror? Fear?

I can see the fear on the faces of the people that day. I can see Jodie screaming as the security man herded us out. I can see the woman on the street who thought she had lost her little girl, the man with the Halloween blood on his face, the woman in the sari being led away. I try to move my mind past

446

that, to what happened next, try to lose that feeling that everyone feared what would happen next. Can't people still feel that feeling? Tavistock Square feels haunted to me.

What did I do after the bomb went off? I left the square. I walked all the way to Mum's. And that was when I met Glen. That was the day I went out with him for the first time. And look at me now. Nearly two years later and I'm a snapper and the people I work for are after Ashley's boyfriend.

I'm on the other side of the square, still searching for some sign of what happened here, but there is no sign, no sign at all. I turn, head back to Gordon Square, to Gower Street, to Tottenham Court Road and the camera shops. I have all afternoon to look at cameras and then this evening I have my date. Shit, I sound like Jodie from the office. How many times did I have to listen to her on a Monday morning, telling us all about her date on Saturday night? And now I have one, the date Loreen set up for me. She's mad. And so am I for agreeing. But it's Sunday and I can do what I want. Today is my day off and so is tomorrow.

I haven't bought a thing. I had a good look at the cameras, but I resisted. For the first time in my life I'm saving money not spending it, but now I'm home too early and I don't want to be here, getting ready for a date. I'm deliberately not going to get ready. I'm going to go just like this. I put the TV on, settle down in the chair with a packet of Polos, just as the phone rings. I almost don't answer it, it could be for one of my housemates and they're all out, but I pick it up anyway.

'Hi hon, it's Loreen!'

'Hiya.' I lean forward, turn the sound down on the TV. I know what she's going to say.

'All ready for tonight?'

'Not really.' I pick up the handset and walk to the kitchen. I'm hungry. I think there's a piece of pepperoni pizza in the fridge left over from last night. 'How are the boys? How's your mum, is she back from Botswana?'

'I've just come from hers and she's fine, although she's a bit odd. I think it's because she just arrived this morning so she's still a bit spacey.' Loreen pauses, I can hear the sound of traffic, she must be walking down the road, perhaps she's got the boys with her. 'I'll tell you about it in a minute,' she says, 'and we need to meet up because I've got to tell you about the weirdest thing that happened yesterday, but first, what are you wearing tonight?'

'What I've got on.'

'Oh come on, Bel! It's a date, wear something nice. Wear that white top I gave you for your birthday.'

'Loreen, you're sounding like my mum.'

'I think you two will get on great,' says Loreen. Again she pauses, perhaps she's crossing the road or telling the boys to do or not do something. 'I mean, think what you've got in common. He says he's really into photography, you're both about the same age, you're both in the same part of London. You have to text me the minute you get there and tell me what he's like, OK?'

I sigh. I don't want to go on a date any more, I'd rather stay home and eat cold pizza and watch telly. 'What's his name again?'

'Raymond. It's quite a nice name,' says Loreen, 'quite steady. Two syllable names are like that.'

I open the fridge, search around for the slice of pepperoni pizza. 'What did you tell him my name was? You didn't use my real name, right?'

'No, of course not. I called you Mabel.'

'What?'

'I said your name was Mabel.'

'Why?'

'I thought it was a nice name,' says Loreen, sounding offended.

'A nice name? *Mabel?*'

'Well it's not that different from Bel, is it? Ma*bel*. And I didn't put you're thirty-five.'

'Because I'm not thirty-five.' I find the pizza box, take it out of the fridge.

'Well you pretty much are. I put thirty-two.'

'Anything else I should know?'

'No, that's it,' Loreen giggles. 'Text me when you get there, OK?'

Shit, I'm late. It's eight-thirty and I was supposed to be here half an hour ago. I walk into the pub and survey the place. I'm good at surveying. I can't be on a street any more without taking in number plates, checking to see who is going where and doing what, who is bringing attention to themselves, who is avoiding it. I've come into the pub from a cobbled side street entrance where people are sitting outside in the evening sun, and inside I'm surprised that the bar feels light and airy. I see a blackboard with a long list of real ales written in white

449

chalk, another with today's special: steak and kidney pie with sweet potato mash. I'm hungry; I always seem to be hungry.

I look around the tables and at the people sitting on black leather sofas. I can't help it, I'm wondering if there are any celebs in here. On my right, a few tables down, is a fireplace with a library of books and magazines on the shelves beside it. In front of me is the bar and its wooden surface gleams even from here, and there are bowls on the counter and I wonder what sort of nuts they have in here and if they're free. But I'm supposed to be looking for a man, a man as described by Loreen, and as Loreen doesn't describe people the way I do, because she will always pick on someone's good points, I don't know what I'm going to find. I'm looking for a thirty-seven-year-old, tall, black, good-looking man, and he'll be wearing a yellow shirt. A yellow shirt? Why?

I see a man at a small round table on my left where the bar is less crowded. He has a Sunday newspaper, an *Independent*, propped up against an unlit candle and there's a big glass of red wine in front of him. He's black, he looks about my age and he's not bad-looking, in fact he's very nice-looking. It could be him; he's wearing a shirt the colour of faded mustard. I start walking towards the bar when the man looks up, a little expectant. I don't stare at him or look at him directly, but I can see him doing this, sense the way he is turning. Then he goes back to his newspaper and for a crazy second I think the newspaper could be a prop, he could be an undercover journo using it to hide behind. I've been in this game too long. I hear the bar door open and shut behind me and the man looks up again. Then he sees me and he raises his eyebrows like he's asking if I am me, if I am who he thinks I

450

am. I put my hand up, give a smile. This is him. My heart beats rapidly as I walk over, like suddenly he's the only person in the bar.

'Mabel?' he asks.

What? Shit, that's me. I'm supposed to be Mabel. 'Yes,' I say. 'Hi . . .' I'm so thrown that I've forgotten his name so I just put out my hand.

'Raymond,' he says, and he gets halfway out of his chair. 'But everyone calls me Ray.' I like the way he looks at me, it's a direct look, like he has nothing to hide. And he's not looking me up and down, he's looking at my face, and I'm looking at his, and I see he has two faint curved lines around his mouth that he's got from smiling. So he's a happy person. That's good. His hair is short and his forehead is smooth and his lips are so beautiful I want to kiss them.

'I'm sorry I'm late,' I say. I'm about to make up a reason for this when he smiles and says, 'No prob,' and he says it so easily that I don't feel the need to make up anything after all. 'Actually, it's Bel.'

'Sorry?'

'My name's actually Bel.'

'Oh,' he says. 'So Mabel is your alias?'

I laugh because this is quite funny. 'This is strange, isn't it?' I ask, pulling out a chair and sitting down.

'Is it?' Ray looks a bit worried.

'I mean, it's fine,' I say quickly. 'It's just a bit strange, you know, meeting someone like this.' I take my jacket off and put it on the back of the chair. I get my wallet out of my pocket. 'Wine?' I ask, looking at his glass, which is nearly empty.

451

'I'll get it,' he says. 'What would you like?'

I don't like fighting over who is getting what, but he's standing up now so I'll let him. I can see he's taller than me, and when I look down I see the tips of his trainers are wet like he just ran through a field. He's wearing jeans and a leather belt and as he stands his mustard-coloured shirt rises up a little so I see the two lines of muscle that lead down to his pelvis. I look away, hoping he hasn't seen me looking at this, that he doesn't know the thought that just flashed into my head, and quickly I say, 'I'll have red wine too.'

'A bottle?' he asks.

'Why not.' We smile at each other and I think, this could be fun. So I settle back in my chair, have another look around. There's a woman by the jukebox, she's laughing with a friend, and then she puts in her money and the song begins to play. It's Duran Duran, 'Girls on Film'. I hate this song but I can't help it, I feel mushy. It makes me think of being young, of being a teenager, of falling in love.

Ray comes back with a bottle and a glass and sits down.

'Hope this is OK,' he says, and he shows me the bottle. I nod that it's fine, as if I know anything about wine. He pours and looks up and smiles again, and for the second before we clink glasses I find myself staring right into the blackness of his eyes. But there is something odd about all of this, it's not just the oddness of meeting a man I don't know in a pub, a man that Loreen has arranged for me, it's something else, something I can't put my finger on. My phone buzzes and I flick it open under the table. It's a message from Loreen. *What's he like?!XXX*

'So . . .' I say. I'm not sure what Loreen has said about me or whether he even knows Loreen set this up. 'So . . .' I say, because he's waiting for me to finish what I've started, 'you're into photography?'

'That's right,' he says, and he gives a laugh and it sounds exactly like someone I know but I can't think who. 'I used to be a photographer.'

'What, press?'

He looks surprised. 'Yeah.'

'Who did you work for?'

'Oh just about everyone. Now I'm on the desk.'

I take a drink of wine and it fills me up and makes me feel red and warm. But now I feel even more that there's something wrong here, there is something wrong with this picture. It's the way he said 'desk'. He said 'desk' the way I say 'desk', the way only someone in the game says 'desk'.

'For who?' I ask.

'I'll tell you if you don't hold it against me,' Ray smiles. It's a nice smile, a sexy smile, but he doesn't have to tell me because I already know.

Chapter Forty-Eight

KAREN

I wonder if Stella's really asleep or if she's just pretending as she lies next to me on the bed on this warm Sunday evening. A breeze blows through the open window and the thin white drapes shiver. 'Mmm, it's so hot,' Stella murmurs and she pushes away at the sheet. 'Good evening,' she looks at me and smiles and there's a crease below her eye from where she's been lying on the pillow, 'I love waking up to you.' We have been in bed since this afternoon and it feels odd to wake up now and find it's nearly dark when instead it feels like it should be morning. I put my arm around her and feel her breast soft against my arm, and I know I should just leave things as they are but I can't.

'Why did you leave him?' I hear the words sharp in the air and I know I have broken the mood, I have spoilt everything.

'Oh honey,' Stella sighs, and she moves away a little and I smell a light lemony scent from the conditioner she put on her hair this morning. 'There's no one thing that made me leave him, it just built up over the years, but you know it's because I never loved him, not really, not like I love you.'

I take my arm away from her. 'Love!' I laugh, and I can

hear my voice, so dismissive and so desperate. 'What does that mean?'

Stella rolls onto her side and props herself up with her elbow. She looks disappointed. 'It means I want to be with you.'

'With or without children?' I ask, and my heart is racing.

'How do children figure in this?' Stella sits up on the bed.

'Well that's why, isn't it? That's why you left him, that's why you left *Nick*,' I say, 'because you always wanted kids and he didn't.'

'What makes you say that?'

'Look,' I say, and I wish I hadn't because I sound like I'm talking to a work colleague or a student or someone who doesn't mean that much to me, and not to Stella, the woman I have loved since the day I found her in the kitchen of Professor Greer's house eating corn chips from a bowl. 'Look at the way you've been with Dylan.'

Stella smiles. 'He's such a sweet kid.'

'Yes, but you really *want* him, don't you?' I say. 'I mean, you really want to look after him because you really want a little boy, that's what you said when you first got here, that you always wanted a little boy.'

Stella looks confused, like she can't ever remember saying this. 'I think it's a bit late for that,' she says at last, and she looks hurt and I want to put my arm around her again and pull her up towards me. 'Dylan needed help, honey, I just wanted to give him some help. You've been struggling with this on your own and it's really upset you and no one wanted to get involved, you've been trying to get your neighbours involved and they wouldn't, and I just wanted to help out.'

'But you bought the hoop,' I say, and I can hear how ridiculous this sounds.

Stella laughs. 'The hoop? I just wanted something for him to play with.' She gets up from the bed and I look with longing at the smoothness of her back as she takes my thin black gown and puts it on.

'You mean you don't want children?'

Stella turns and looks at me and she appears to think about my question that is so insistent. 'I did,' she says, as she ties the gown around herself. 'Yes, I did, I really, really did. But Nick never felt the time was right. And I just waited, I guess, I just hung on in there and waited for him to change.'

I look at her, feel a stab of anger when she says his name, even though there is no reason for her not to, even though I'm the one who started this. 'But why didn't you tell me, how long have we known each other that you couldn't tell me?'

'Because, Karen, you've never wanted children, you always made that clear to me, so why would I tell you that I stayed with Nick because I wanted a baby, or that I left him because he didn't want a baby, when that's something you don't want? Don't you think that would have been kind of cruel?'

'But,' I say, and I can see Stella is fighting to control herself now; she wants to move away, to leave the room and to have this over with. 'But if you left him because you wanted a baby then that's still what you want!'

'No, honey, because I'm with you and that's something that belongs in the past. Now it's something that maybe I could have had once, and never did.'

'Have you contacted him?'

Stella looks amused. 'Why would I want to do that?'

I lift up my head as she bends towards me and her lips find mine and I close my eyes and my body feels as if it's swimming.

We are sitting out in my yard and we can hear the sounds of neighbours having a barbecue, see smoke rising from a back garden a few houses away, we can hear the pop as a bottle of champagne is opened, a bang as a glass door closes, and then a child laughing hysterically.

'Are you looking forward to going back?' I ask Stella as a bunch of party balloons float into the air over my yard.

'In some ways, yes. I like England but . . . hey!' She holds up her hands and laughs. 'Not so much that I want to stay here.'

I pick up my peppermint tea and sip it. 'I'd like to see everyone before we leave,' I tell her. 'Loreen was real odd yesterday, wasn't she? I'm going to call her, maybe she can get everyone together, what night should we go?'

'You go, honey,' says Stella. 'They're your friends, you'll be easier there without me.'

I feel happy this morning, from the moment I wake I feel lightness inside. Stella is not here, she is downstairs fixing breakfast and I can hear coffee beans in the grinder and the rattle of the grill pan being opened and laid with bread. I go downstairs and open the drapes in my living room and let in the sun. I hear a squeak as my front gate opens and as I look out I see a woman and a little girl coming up my path. The girl stops halfway and she bends to look at the two tomato plants I have set out near the gate and she rubs her fingers against the leaves and then sniffs them and offers her hand for her mom to sniff too. Then the mom takes the girl's hand and holds her tightly, she's almost pulling her up the rest of the path, and her face looks worried like she's making herself do something she doesn't really want to do. Then I realise; this is the woman and the little girl who used to live upstairs. I let the drapes fall back into place before they see me; I hear a key in the front door and then it is silent. I can't help myself, I want to know why they're back.

'Hi!' I say, opening my door.

'Oh!' The woman looks startled. She has a parcel in her hand and she's just about to put it down on the shelf in the hallway.

'I'm Karen,' I say. 'You used to live upstairs?'

The woman turns to me, her eyes weary, and I think she's going to ask why this is any business of mine, but instead she sighs and puts the parcel on the shelf and her hands fall by her side. 'Yes, I thought I remembered you.'

'That's for my brother,' says the girl seriously, reaching up on tip toe to touch the parcel.

'Well,' says the mom, 'more like your step-brother.'

I smile at the little girl; she is wearing a pale blue t-shirt with the words *Hello summer!*.

'Do you see Dylan much?' asks the woman lightly, so lightly that I know this is not a casual question, this is important to her.

'No. Not really. But I do hear him.'

'What do you hear?' asks the woman anxiously, and then she seems to remember her little girl is standing there next to

458

her and she says, 'Sweetheart? Go and get the rest of the things from the car, OK?'

The little girl looks at me and then at her mother and for a moment I don't think she will leave us, but then she does and we stand there not speaking until the gate squeaks open again and the little girl goes to the car.

'What have you heard?' asks the woman, and her arms are folded tightly now across her stomach.

'Oh, shouting, banging, things falling down . . .' I stop because this sounds lame and I wonder whether I should tell her the other things I've seen and heard. 'He shouts at him, and he curses a lot. Sometimes he locks him out of the apartment. I think that's what happened on Friday night, because Dylan stayed with us.'

The woman stares at the carpet in the hallway and when she looks up again her eyes are full of tears. 'Has anyone . . . been round? From social services?'

'I don't think so.'

'Well they're supposed to, that's supposed to be the deal.'

'And I've seen bruises,' I tell her. 'I don't know how he got them but I rang . . .'

'That's why we left,' says the woman, and she's holding herself so tightly that I wonder if this is why she sounds so breathless now.

I think of the time she and the little girl lived upstairs, how there was another life going on that I knew nothing about. I think of the night they moved in, how the sounds of domesticity from upstairs soothed me as I sat on my living-room floor writing up my notes, and now I know what was really going on up there.

'But I couldn't take Dylan with me,' says the woman. 'His dad has custody, we're not married or anything. His dad's got a social worker; he's been warned that if it happens again they'll take Dylan into care. I'll ring him this afternoon but maybe, if you hear anything, could you let me know?'

'Of course,' I say, and I wait while she gets out a pen and piece of paper and writes down her phone number.

'And could you make sure he gets this?' she asks, and she smiles and pats the parcel on the shelf. 'Dylan always wanted one of these.' The little girl comes rushing in then and she's carrying a jumble of parcels, smaller than the one on the shelf, and her mom takes them from her.

'Oh well,' she says to me. 'That's that then.'

When the bell rings a few moments later I rush for the door, perhaps the two of them have come back, perhaps there is more she wants to tell me. And I forgot to tell her I'm leaving, that if something happens upstairs I won't be here to hear it or to let Dylan in or to call her. But when I open the door it's my mom who is standing there. I look past her, peer over her shoulder, at the pathway and the bins and the two tomato plants, to see where my sister Romana is.

'Karen!' says Mom, as if she's been waiting for a long time for me to let her in. She looks pale and her hair, I realise, is totally white. When did this happen, when did my mom's hair go white? 'Is this a bad time?' She attempts a laugh.

'Where's Romana?' I ask. 'What's wrong?'

'Does something have to be wrong?'

'No,' I say cautiously, and I hold the door back while Mom comes in. I see she has a small green umbrella in case it rains, which it won't on a day like this, but Mom has always been prepared for the worst. Just like me. For a moment I feel like doing something daring and out of character and completely surprising, but I don't, I just lead her in.

'It's a big house,' she says.

I don't answer her, because is this how it is going to be? My mom comes to visit me, alone, and we are not going to have a conversation, we are going to talk small talk and then she will leave again? I lead her into the kitchen, which is empty, Stella must have gone upstairs, maybe she knows my mom is here. Then I hear the sound of water: she's having a shower.

'How's Dad?' I ask as Mom sits down.

'Your father's fine.' She smiles. 'But Romana's gone.'

I stare at her. 'What do you mean, gone?' I feel a prick of panic. 'Gone where?'

'To America.'

'Hell,' I mutter, and I put the coffee and the milk and the sugar and two cups on the table and I slam them down because why does Romana have to go to America? That is what I did, I went to America, and I made a life for myself. Why does she have to go there as well?

'She got made redundant, Karen,' says Mom, 'so she's using the money to travel. I'm worried about her really, because Romana could never look after herself, not like you.'

'Romana always knew how to look after herself!' I object. 'And she has always had you wrapped round her goddam finger.'

A flicker of pain passes over Mom's face. 'Well it hasn't been easy and you always were the strong one, Karen . . .'

'No I wasn't!'

461

'. . . the independent one. You always knew what you wanted and you could look after yourself, so I didn't worry as much.'

'You didn't even come to graduation!' I say, and then I wish I hadn't because this was years ago; I didn't think I cared so much about this.

'This is lovely coffee,' says Mom.

I watch while she drinks it and I can see it's too bitter for her, but she won't say this, she will just keep on drinking this bitter coffee and never say she can't bear the goddam taste.

'I suppose I was a bit overprotective,' she says.

'Just a tad!' I say, but I can't help laughing now.

'It wasn't easy, you know, Karen, having a child like Romana.' Mom laughs as well and I feel a little guilty that we are talking about my little sister like this, but it's a guiltiness that I like, it feels pleasant to me.

Mom puts the cup down and looks round the kitchen. 'Is your . . .?' She stops, but I know what it is she wants to ask.

'Is my girlfriend here, Mom? Is that what you're asking? Is Stella, my girlfriend, my partner, here?'

'Yes, that's it,' says Mom mildly. 'I'd like to meet her.'

Chapter Forty-Nine

BEL

Shit shit shit. I got off with Ray from the desk. That's the first thing I think when I open my eyes: I had sex with Ray from the desk. I roll over in bed and throw the quilt off because it's too hot. What's that sound? It's driving me mad. It's my phone. I'm not going to answer it, it's Monday morning, my day off. My head is pounding. I can taste brandy in my mouth. Why did I drink brandy?

I hope it's not him. I hope it is him. 'Yeah?' I get the phone.

'Good morning, Bell!' It's Pete on the desk. What's he doing ringing me on a Monday morning? Shit, don't give me work, not today, not on a Monday. I hardly ever get a shift on a Monday. I hold the phone hard against my head. 'Are you available, Bel?' asks Pete, ever polite.

'Yeah,' I say, because it's force of habit. Then I sit up in bed, does Pete know? Does he know about me and Ray? Is that why he's ringing me first thing on a Monday morning, because he knows what happened last night? I can't hear any sign of it in his voice. I try to picture Pete; all along I've had a clear idea of him in my head. His posh voice, always with a tinge of sarcasm. I see him as blond, thin, a long haughty nose. The sort of man who wears v-neck jumpers over checked shirts. But I could be completely wrong, like I was completely wrong about Ray. All this time I've been dealing with Ray, week in and week out, and I had a picture of him in my head and I got him completely wrong. Of course we never had much of a conversation. I answered the phone, he sent me somewhere. We never actually talked to each other, never discussed anything other than the job I was on, but I had a picture of him, and he was nothing like that. I thought Ray was ex-army, with all his military talk, all the *Operation this* and *Stand down, Bel.* I'm sure Glen once said Ray was ex-army. I pictured him as a beefy middle-aged white man with a preference for camouflage jackets. But all that talk is just a front; it's just a persona Ray adopts to help him deal with the day-to-day crap of being on the pictures desk at the *Sunday Post*. He's not like that at all, it's just the way he deals with this game we're in, because he'd like to be out there taking snaps too, only he got into debt even worse than me and had to sell his cameras.

I laugh out loud, thinking about what he said last night, how he tried to keep working as a snapper without any cameras, how for three months he kept on turning up at jobs and begging frames off other snappers until the humiliation became too much. And now he's a deskman and he doesn't want to do it any more, he doesn't want to be in this game any more, just like me, just like Glen. So I might have got it all wrong with Pete as well. Maybe he's nothing like he sounds; maybe he's adopted some persona too. And how do they picture me? I never asked Ray about this.

'You're not going to like it,' says Pete, and I sit up even

more, try to focus, 'but it's our old friend Donny Green again.'

I chuck the phone on the bed. Shit. Why are they putting so much time and effort into Donny Green? What has he done and why are they after him? I get up fast, pull on yesterday's clothes, get downstairs and brew some coffee. There's a dull pain in my head where my brain should be. Half an hour later I load my gear into my car and leave. I'm just going to get the job done. I'll get to the plot, ring the desk, then I'll go and get some breakfast. I'm halfway to Donny Green's place in Notting Hill, my mouth is dry and my fingers are shaky, when I suddenly think, did I turn the cooker off? I made my coffee, I turned off the gas, I drank my coffee and left. But what if I didn't turn it off? I did, I can hear the little click, see the dial as I turned it until it pointed to off when my coffee was done. But what if I didn't, what if I've left the gas on, really low? Something could fall, like a tea cloth, and ignite and start burning and that would be it, the kitchen and the house up in flames. I can't turn round now, I can't go back and check. I know I turned it off. But what if I didn't? I haven't had enough sleep. I had too much to drink last night. I should have said no when the desk rang. I shouldn't have answered the phone at all. But I did and here I am and it's all happening again because today I don't have the strength to fight it. How long have I been fighting this? Most of my life.

I try to think of something else, to redirect my mind. I think of last night. When did we leave the gastro pub? Midnight? Then we went to Ray's because he asked and I thought, why not? Sometimes you've just got to take something when it's offered to you. I pull into a petrol station, fill up, buy some chewing gum. My thighs ache. I can smell Ray on my hair. When I lay there in his bed last night, in a room as full of junk as my own car, I was totally at peace. And then I got the urge to move on. I was awake. It was three, perhaps four, in the morning. It was that time when even London is still. One half of me wanted to stay, the other half wanted to go, but for no good reason other than that's what I always want to do. Why do I always have to move on just when I'm happy? I didn't mean to run away, I didn't even want to run away. I wanted to stay there with Ray and that's what frightened me.

I get back in my car. I'm going to have to get hold of Ashley. They are after Donny Green and they're not going to stop until they have him. And what if Ashley's there, at Donny Green's place in Notting Hill today, and she sees me? How would I explain that? What if Ashley sees me with an SLR round my neck, doorstepping her boyfriend. What would I say then?

I pick up my phone to ring Ashley, but then I think, what does she do on a Monday morning? I don't know what she'll be doing. Taking her girls to school? But don't they go to boarding school? And hasn't she got an au pair to do that? Will she be going to work, what time does she go to work? I don't know what normal people do any more because I'm a snapper and I don't live a normal life. But then nor does Ashley, because she's going out with Donny Green. I scroll through my address book, trying to find her number. I can't remember the last time I rang her, perhaps last year when we met at her parents' place. Her phone goes straight onto answer machine so I leave a message. *Ashley, it's Bel, I really need to talk to you, call me back, please.* I sit for a moment, wonder if I sounded urgent enough. I almost expect her to ring me straight back because it's clear I need to speak to her; I never call and leave a message like this. But my phone stays silent.

I drive off. I can't think straight today. I don't want to go to Donny Green's, not if Ashley might be there. I need food. I need a fry-up like Mum makes.

Mum's doormat has gone, the one that said WELCOME and GOODBYE. Instead there is a new doormat in the shape of a hairy brown squirrel. Mum opens the door dressed in her gym gear. 'Oh it's you,' she says.

'Smells of bacon,' I say, walking down the hallway, my mouth watering. I picture crispy bacon sinking into thick white bread all sodden with butter. Something is different about Mum's hallway; for once it's light in here. I see a little strip lamp fixed above the pictures I took of Mum like a 1950s film star all those years ago at art school. When did she get round to doing that? It must be Glen, I think, who did that. I get into Mum's kitchen and there he is; I can just see the top of his white-haired head over a newspaper. The table is covered in Sunday newspapers and he's turning the pages, studying the pictures. When I walk in he looks up. Shit, I hope he hasn't heard about me and Ray from the desk.

'Alright, Bel?'

'Fine,' I say. 'Only I'm working on a Monday!'

Glen shakes his head sympathetically, picks up his coffee cup.

'It's my day off!' I say. 'In two years I can count the number of times they've put me on a job on a Monday on one finger!'

'You should have said no, mate.' Glen drinks his coffee, puts the cup down. Mum's fur ball of a dog comes trotting into the kitchen and tries to leap up on Glen's lap. 'Hello, girl,' he says, patting it. 'Good girl.'

'No!' Mum yells, but it's too late, the dog lets out a torrent of wee on the kitchen floor.

'I know, I know,' I tell Glen as Mum takes a mop out of the cupboard. 'I wasn't thinking when I answered the phone.' I look round the kitchen; it seems lighter in here too. The plants! The plants have gone! It's like they finally burst through the glass and made a bid for freedom. Mum must have put them all outside.

'You look rough, did you have a late night?' she asks. 'Glen, how many eggs do you want with this?'

'Yeah,' I say. 'I had a late night.'

Mum perks up, turns towards me with a spatula in her hand. 'Anyone I know?'

'No.' I steal a look at Glen but he's leafing through the papers again. 'I'm sick of this,' I say.

'Who are you on?' asks Glen, and I think, he can't help it, he can't help but be interested even if he says he's not working for the *Sunday Post* any more.

'Donny fucking Green,' I tell him.

'Language!' says Mum.

'They keep putting me on him,' I tell Glen, 'and then pulling me off again.'

'Donny Green?' says Mum, her voice shrill. 'You mean the pop star, Donny Green?' She looks at me and then at Glen. 'I wouldn't kick him out of my bed if I were ten years younger.'

468

Glen looks at Mum, raises an eyebrow.

'OK,' she says, laughing. 'If I were twenty years younger.'

'What's the story with him anyway?' I ask as Mum starts frying the eggs. I can't wait until the bacon's done. 'Is he having it off with someone?'

'Not quite,' says Glen, and he sighs, lays the newspaper down on the table. 'It's young girls, see, he contacts them up on the Internet and what he actually does is . . .' Glen hesitates. 'He takes photos of himself, pleasuring himself, if you see what I mean. So this one girl, only sixteen, has all these emails of Donny Green's . . .' Glen coughs, '. . . cock.'

Mum makes an annoyed sound; I can hear oil popping in the pan. I sit down abruptly at the table, thinking of that day at Heathrow following Prince Harry. This was the story Glen was talking about then, the girl and the pop star, the one whose mother found the pictures on her daughter's computer. 'So you've been on it too?' I ask.

'Quite a few times,' says Glen. 'His place, his mother's, his brother's. And the girlfriend's. Nice place in Hampstead.'

'Oh?' I ask, like it's nothing to me. 'Hampstead? When was that?' I think of when Glen said never to tell him if I knew anyone famous, so should I tell him now or not? Because it's Ashley he's talking about, it must be.

'Last December.' Glen sighs. 'Pathetic, isn't it? I mean, what does he have? Money, fame, nice house, record deal, nice clothes, fast cars, pretty girlfriend . . . And what does he do in his spare time? Take snaps of his cock.'

Mum makes an annoyed sound again.

'They've been sitting on this story for a while now, Bel, this has been going on for months, so I'm surprised no one else

469

has it. If one of these girls has gone to the press, then some-one else must have. I've a feeling a few papers have been sitting on this because it's common knowledge Donny Green's not the squeaky-clean celeb he pretends to be. And there's not much going on at the moment, is there? Anything happening in the world of politics at the moment? Naah, we've only just got a new Prime Minister.' Glen gives his high girl's giggle and takes the plate Mum hands him piled high with fried bread, eggs and bacon.

An hour later I'm on my way to Donny Green's because I have to, because the desk will ring and I won't be there. I pull onto his road, feeling queasy now; the fry-up has made me feel worse. I'm thinking about Ray last night and if I'll see him again, and I'm thinking about Ashley and I just want to drive off somewhere and not stop. Why hasn't she answered my message? I park up and pick up my phone, send her a text that it's urgent, and just as I send it my mobile rings. It's her, I think, and my fingers start to tremble and I don't know if it's the brandy I drank or the lack of sleep or the fact I've got to tell Ashley now and she'll kill me.

'Hello, Bel,' says Pete. 'Anything happening?'

'Nothing, this is a dead plot,' I say, relieved I'm actually here and can say that. Donny Green's driveway is empty, there's no car here. It's a hot day but none of the windows are open. There are flyers sticking out of the letter box. I check the street, I don't recognise any of the cars, no other paps are here.

'We're moving you on, actually,' says Pete.

Again? They're moving me on again? 'Where?' I ask, grab-bing a pen and a piece of paper, and I think it's going to be Macca, it's going to be Ant and Dec.

'We're not sure of the exact number, Bel . . .' says Pete. 'It's an estate in Highgate. Holly Lodge. Just get there and sit tight for the time being, OK?'

'Fine,' I say, because I know exactly where Holly Lodge is.

I get to Swains Lane and drive up towards Holly Lodge; whistling to myself because whatever story I'm on I can pop in and see Loreen later. That's good. That cheers me up. The hill is steep and the cars in front of me are driving slowly like they almost can't make it. I pass Highgate cemetery, see a canopy of tall, thin trees and thick oval gravestones yellow with age. I pass two roads leading into the Holly Lodge estate and then I come to the road where Loreen lives. And then I remember, you can't get in this way, there's a white gate across the road and it's locked. So I turn round, go down the hill and enter from the other side, from the bottom of Swains Lane. And then I think, why are they sending me here? My mind's a mess; I don't even know what job I'm on. My phone rings and I expect it's the desk, but it's Glen. 'You OK, Bel?' he asks.

'Yeah, fine, why?'

'Just checking. You seem a little overworked to me.'

'No, I'm fine.'

'You on Donny then?'

'No,' I laugh. 'Now I'm on some plot at Holly Lodge, Highgate.'

'I know it well,' says Glen. 'Traitor's Hill.'

'Traitors what?'

'That was where the gunpowder men were supposed to have sat when they blew up the Houses of Parliament. What story are you on?'

471

'They haven't told me,' I say.

'Oh, one of those,' laughs Glen. 'But Bel, take it easy, OK?'

I drive halfway down Loreen's road, park next to the grass verge that leads up to the five-storey mansion blocks. There are at least six blocks on this road; there are hundreds of flats here. The outside walls look newly painted. I haven't been here for a while, I've forgotten what a strange estate this is, so high up, so grandly handsome on the outside like some mock Tudor stately home.

My car windows are open and I can hear doves in the trees, the faint hum of a lawn mower, the metal jangle of a wind chime on a balcony. The pavement is covered in fallen white blossom, like chewing gum stomped into the ground. This is a good spot, there's only one way to get onto this street and that's from behind me, and there's only one way to get into any of the flats and that's from the front. I root around in my car, looking for some Polos because I still feel queasy.

A recycling truck drives past, filled to the brim, then a smart red Ferrari. I sink down a little on my seat and watch because the Ferrari looks very out of place here. It parks just two bays ahead of me and the door opens and the driver, a woman, gets out. Shit. She gets out gracefully, straightens down a white skirt, adjusts a pair of massive shades. She's holding a huge handbag in one hand and her phone in the other, I can just see its shiny blue case. She shuts the car door, sets the alarm, then she walks up the steps between the grass verges. So she's around, so Ashley's around, and she hasn't been answering my calls. She must be coming to see Loreen.

I didn't know Ashley visits Loreen. Loreen said she hadn't heard from Ashley in a long time. I look at my watch. It's almost dinnertime, Loreen will be at work. What is Ashley doing here, visiting Loreen at dinnertime on a Monday? And how come Ashley's visiting Loreen when she can't even return my calls?

I watch as Ashley walks across the pavement, up the steps to the walkway that leads to the double black front door of the mansion block. She presses a buzzer on the pad to her left, speaks into the intercom, and a moment later she pushes open the door and goes in. I look in my rear-view mirror and I know that Hillman, I know that car. Fred from the *Mirror* has just pulled up. I watch while he parks a few bays in front of me as well. Shit. So this is it, I'm no longer on Donny Green. It's Ashley I'm on now.

Chapter Fifty

DUDU

'Dear Victor, I hope you are well.' I stop and put my pen down upon the table. I am writing a letter and I do not know what to say to my late husband's brother. I do not know if I should write in English or in Setswana, although I suspect he would prefer English, and I do not know what I want to say to him either. I want to thank him, of course, for his hospitality during my stay, and I would like to extend an invitation to his family if they should ever find themselves in England.

I pick up the pen, it is a very beautiful pen. I bought it in a shop in Johannesburg airport and it is imbedded with glittery jewels the colour of jelly. I study the pen, lay it back on the table again, because if I extend an invitation then perhaps Victor Kudumane will see it as an opportunity to send out his last-born child Dorcus and I do not want that. I am an ungrateful old woman, I think, how can I not want a member of my own family coming to stay with me? Perhaps, I think with a smile, I am turning into my daughter, wanting to live alone with her boys and not with me, her mother, and for the first time that I can ever remember, I am happy and I am grateful to live alone.

The radio is on, but turned very low. My cat is not here,

she continues to pretend to abandon me like I abandoned her. I am alone and I close my eyes and think of my trip home, and I picture myself on the summit of Dimawe Hill surveying the land below. My little grandson Dwaine would like that walk, I think, opening my eyes; he would like to walk up high among the tea bushes and the rocks and see a snake perhaps, he would like that. And I would tell him stories of the old days and the battles of the past and even Anthony would like that, for I remember his excitement at school when the children were learning about Shaka Zulu. And I would take both Dwaine and Anthony to see the rock paintings, I would show them my favourites, the three giraffe all facing the same direction, and I would show them the deep dark cave where Mma Sechele hid. This seems very obvious to me now, sitting here in my kitchen on a sunny Monday lunchtime. I will take my grandsons with me, why did I not think of that before?

Then I remember that I did, I thought of it the day I arrived in Gaborone when I came out of the airport and saw the statues of the animals, the elephant and the two zebras, so lifelike amid the cacti and the aloe and the cars. But then I forgot, I became overwhelmed with the way my country had changed. I forgot about my idea of bringing the boys to Botswana; instead I thought there was no place for me there any more and so I made my false goodbyes that day on Dimawe Hill like the foolish old woman that I am.

I will tell Dwaine about my idea when I collect him from school this afternoon, and I will suggest that the boys' father contributes to their fares instead of giving them all those silly expensive toys at Christmas; he can pay for them to go to

475

Africa instead. But I will pay for my Loreen, for she deserves a holiday.

I stand up, gather my gloves and a jug of water, my shears and a small rug, I am going to do some work in my front garden. I have not spent time in my front garden for a long time. I open my door and as I do I think that there was a time when people did sit in their front gardens, on deckchairs perhaps, with tea or squash on a table, a plate of biscuits, a newspaper. In the first years I lived in England that was how it was: people would sit in their front gardens and call out to their neighbours or people who were passing, 'Nice day, isn't it?' 'On the way to church?' 'That's a lot of shopping you've got there, having a party?' Now people's front gardens are all paved over and if there is space they have a car parked there, just like my neighbour on my left and most of the houses opposite. People prefer to sit in their back gardens now, for these are more private spaces, and they like to make them more private still by erecting walls and fences just as I have done in mine.

I put my front door on the latch, walk down my path inspecting my plants, stopping to admire my roses with fresh, soft petals as yellow as the sun. Then I look out onto the street to see if anyone is around, for although people no longer sit in their front gardens, if they do come out to weed perhaps or to water their plants or to clean their windows, then it is like they are saying, I'm here, in public, you can talk to me.

I put out the rug on the small patch of grass that is in the middle of my front garden and kneel on it and begin to weed around a clump of London pride, a strange plant that has spread from my neighbour's rockery on the right. The star-shaped flowers are as ornate as a lady's brooch, sticking up in a solitary fashion from the chunky green leaves. As I am weeding a woman walks by with a little girl and she stops and says, 'Oh what beautiful roses!' Then they walk on and I look around my front garden again and think how these are all English plants: roses and pansies and geraniums and London pride, and I wonder why I do not plant the flowers and the trees I know from Africa. Cacti perhaps and aloe, bougainvillea and even a palm tree, for I have seen palm trees now in people's front gardens in London, which was never the case in the past. I think of the other plants we had when I was a child in Africa, and I think of taking my grandsons to Botswana and whether my Loreen will let me pay for her to go.

She should take that money, I think, as I finish my patch of weeding and move my rug a little nearer to the short brick wall that surrounds my front garden. This seems very obvious to me now; she should take that money that silly journalist was offering her because what would she tell those reporters about her friend Ashley? It would not be anything bad, for my Loreen always sees the best in people. There may be some stories she could tell, but she never will, because Loreen has always seen in Ashley something that I do not believe was ever there. Loreen saw a yellow-haired girl that she wanted to be her friend; I saw a girl who had no loyalty and who made others lie. 'Rise above it,' I hear my late husband's voice in my head, and I smile because I haven't heard that voice of his for a very long time. Where have you been, I ask him.

I move my rug once more, my weeding is almost over, and then I hear a purring noise and my clever little cat has come and found me in my front garden and she comes up to me and nips me, only in a kindly way as she might a kitten. I will ask Loreen this afternoon when I collect my little grandson from school and take him home, what she intends to do about this journalist of hers. And I will ask her, as I did yesterday, what her friend Bel thinks about this, for Bel was never as easily led as my little Loreen, my little girl who was like two fishes swimming in different directions. Bel was never impressed by Ashley the way my Loreen was, instead from that very first day at primary school those two saw each other as rivals, and I think of the birthday party that day Ashley turned seven and how I watched the girls playing musical chairs and how, after each little girl had been knocked out, only two remained, Bel and Ashley squared up to each other like little bulls.

478

Chapter Fifty-One

BEL

Shit. Here we go again. I get out of the car, lock some of my gear in the boot, check it, unlock it, lock it, check it again. If anyone saw me doing this they'd think I was mad. I am mad. The fact that I'm here and Ashley is here and I'm on Ashley and she's visiting Loreen is making me mad. But at least I'm on my own; at least they haven't sent a journo to meet me.

I see Fred from the *Mirror* lounging in his car just ahead of me. He seems half-asleep. I wonder how much he knows? Does he know the whole story with Donny Green? What has his desk told him? If he's been sent here it must be to watch Ashley, because why else would he be here, but if I go up and ring Loreen's bell now, then what's Fred going to think? I've got to make him think there's nothing happening; he's going to have to leave before I go in.

'Hiya,' I say, stopping at Fred's car.

'Alright, mate,' says Fred, winding down the window. 'What's up?'

'Nothing,' I say with a groan. 'I've been here for hours, it's a dead plot. I'm going to give it five minutes and then shove off.'

'Righto,' says Fred with a smile. 'I fancy something to eat myself.'

I walk back to my car, wait five minutes and pull off, giving Fred a wave as I pass. I go down to Swains Lane, drive parallel with the Heath, then ten minutes later I make my way back. Fred's gone.

I walk up the steps to the mansion's front door, stop at the sign that says no hawkers, no ball games, no dogs. There are dozens of doorbells in the pad to my left and for a second I can't think which number Loreen lives at. Then I press the bell for number 48. The intercom buzzes into life. So she's there, Loreen's at home.

'Hi,' I say, 'it's Bel.' My voice doesn't sound normal and I can't hear what Loreen says because the intercom makes everything distorted, but the front door clicks and I push it open. The hallway is huge, it's like walking into my old primary school; naked thick brick walls, echoey and cold to the touch. There's a pile of flyers on the floor and up on a notice board: yoga classes at the community centre, a jumble sale, new dates for rubbish collection. I head for the stairway, just as a dog starts barking frantically from a flat on my right, and I walk up, past a tall, high window with individual panes of bubbled glass, just like we had at primary school. I walk up to the third floor, see how white paint has been torn off the stairway walls in great bald patches, and head down the corridor to Loreen's, passing flat doors made of thick green metal like a prison.

At first the corridor seems silent, then I can hear signs of life: a TV, a child shouting, someone throwing a ball against a wall. I get to Loreen's door and there's a '4' and an '8' in blue on two white ceramic tiles like you get abroad. I wonder when Loreen got these. I knock on the door; I don't know who's going to open it.

'Hi hon,' Loreen says. She has a piece of bunched-up toilet roll to her nose. She looks worried. 'I didn't know you were coming over.'

'Sorry,' I say. 'You ill?'

'Yeah, I'm off sick, there's no one in the world that gets as many colds as a teacher.' Loreen sighs, she looks rough. I'm waiting for her to move back and let me in or for Ashley to come up behind her. 'Aren't you working today or something?' Loreen asks.

'I am, I am working.' I can hear how crazy I sound. 'Can I come in?'

'Yeah, yeah, of course.' Loreen hasn't laughed once since she opened the door and that's not like her, that's not like her at all. She turns quickly so that we're both jammed together in the hallway and then she walks ahead. Why does she want to get ahead of me? I look left, into her bathroom, then right into one of the boy's rooms, and then we get to the front room. There's a bunch of roses in a vase on a wooden table. There's nothing else on the table but a pile of old photographs.

'Sorry, it's a mess in here.' Loreen squats down, begins sliding the photos off the table and into her hand, quickly, like she really has to tidy things up. Why would she apologise to me about mess? I've known her most of my life, she knows I don't care about mess any more than she does.

'Let's have a look,' I say, holding my hand out for the photos.

481

'Oh, they're old rubbish.' Loreen shuffles the pictures in her hands like a mismatched set of cards, but she does it clumsily and a few of the photos fall back onto the table. I pick them up. These are really old; they're square-shaped and the images are faded black and white. These are photos from our school days. Here's Karen on a trip, waiting in front of a school coach, pulling a silly face, she looks about twelve. And here's Loreen sitting on a train platform eating chips; I remember the coat she's wearing, it had fake fur around the collar, she used to love that coat. Here's a woman who looks a little familiar; perhaps she's an old teacher of ours because she's sitting in a classroom at a tiny table covered in books. And here's a photo that's different from the rest, this isn't square, this was taken with an SLR. My heart gives a leap. Shit. This is Ashley in Portugal. I remember taking this photo, standing up on the cliff over the sea, looking down. I remember the very second I took it, the boy and the girl up against the cliff and then when the girl turned I saw it was Ashley. I haven't seen this photo for years; I thought it got lost somewhere along the way. How come Loreen has it?

'Mrs Greenrod,' says Loreen. She takes the pictures from me, puts them in a pile with the one of the woman at the tiny classroom table on top.

'Who?' I sit down on the sofa, pretend I haven't just seen the photo of Ashley and the German boy up against the cliff because it's confused me, because Loreen is obviously trying to hide it, because I have other things to deal with right now, like where Ashley is. She came in here a good twenty minutes ago. Is she in Loreen's bedroom? Is she in the kitchen?

'You know, Mrs Greenrod, from primary school.' Loreen

shows me the picture again, the woman sitting at the tiny school table covered with books. 'She was the one we all loved.'

'We did?'

'Yeah, Bel, we adored her, she was really, really lovely. Remember that day we went to visit her, after she'd left and got married and had a kid? And she lived in that awful house and the baby was screaming, remember? And she stood there and said, "Girls, never get married." That's what she said! I was devastated by that.'

'Where's Ashley?' I get up from the sofa, feeling jittery. I don't remember visiting Mrs Greenrod or a screaming baby.

'What?' Loreen looks confused.

'I thought Ashley was here.'

'How did you know that?'

I shrug. 'Where is she?'

'I don't know. She rang the bell, I buzzed her in . . . I thought you were her when I opened the door. She phoned earlier, she sounded really upset.'

We both think about this, about Ashley being upset, and I get a quick, lurching feeling of jealousy because Ashley won't return my calls, but when she needs to talk to someone she comes to Loreen. 'I've got to tell you something,' I say, and it sounds so silly that at last Loreen smiles.

'D'you want some tea?'

'Yes, but in a minute. Loreen . . .'

'Oh!' says Loreen, her hand dramatically to her mouth. 'How did it go?'

'How did what go?'

'The date.'

'The date?' I laugh. I can't believe Loreen wants to know about my date.

'Come on, Bel! With Raymond. How did it go last night? You never texted me back. Was he nice?'

'Yeah,' I say, 'he was nice. But the thing is, I already know him.'

'You don't!'

'Yeah, he works on the pictures desk.'

'The what?'

I put my hands between my legs, squeeze on them tight. 'Shit, Loreen, don't be annoyed, OK, but I've got to tell you something, about what I've been doing. I feel really crap about this but I'm not at the film production place, I don't work there any more, I haven't done for ages. I'm a snapper, that's what I do now. I take photos for the *Sunday Post*.'

'You didn't tell me!' Loreen looks really hurt. I don't think she's taking in what I'm telling her, she's only taking in that I didn't tell her something.

'No, because I didn't know if I could make it, I didn't want to tell anyone in case it never worked out. But then they started using my pictures, then I started getting work, and now, well . . .'

'Now you work for the *Sunday Post*?'

I hang my head a little, but when I look up Loreen is beaming. 'So who have you done? Anyone famous? Anyone I would know?'

'Lots,' I say.

'Oooh,' says Loreen, and I can't believe she's not angrier with me. 'Do you know . . .?'

'Do I know who?'

'Oh it doesn't matter,' she says, as there's a sharp knock on the door. 'No one rang the buzzer,' she says, looking puzzled. I watch her walk along her hallway, sniffing. Then I hear the door open and Loreen saying, 'Hi, hon,' and a faint sound of bracelets. Ashley comes into the front room and her cheeks tighten when she sees me.

'Bel,' she says, like she's trying not to be surprised, but she looks back at Loreen with a look that says, you didn't tell me Bel would be here.

'D'you want tea?' asks Loreen.

'Whatever,' says Ashley, and she unwinds a white scarf, something made of material so flimsy that it actually floats in the air as she throws it onto the sofa. 'I got completely lost,' she says. 'I went up to the fifth floor, I thought you lived on the fifth floor.' She puts down her handbag and sighs as Loreen goes off to make the tea. 'I suppose she's told you?'

'About?' I don't want to give anything away but I'm wondering what Loreen knows that I don't know.

Ashley narrows her eyes at me. 'She has told you, hasn't she?'

'Told me what?'

'About Donny.'

'No,' I say. 'What about Donny?'

'He cheated on me.' Ashley's eyes flick to mine, like she wants to challenge me in some way, like I'm the one to blame.

Loreen comes in with the tea and she gives me a pointed look as she stands there holding the mugs. What? I want to say. What have I done?

'Bel is working for the *Sunday Post*,' Loreen says, putting down the mugs. I stare at her. Why is she telling Ashley this? It's up to me to tell Ashley this.

'What?' Ashley sounds dull.

'Bel works for the *Sunday Post*.'

'Oh come on!' laughs Ashley. She picks up her tea, begins to drink, and then she realises me and Loreen are looking at her, waiting. 'You don't? How could you possibly work for a paper like that?'

'Well you read it!'

'I do not!' Ashley puts down her tea, stares at it. Then she looks at me. 'What the fuck are *you* doing working for the *Sunday Post*?'

That annoys me, it annoys me the way Ashley says that, like she expects me to say I open the post or make the tea. 'I'm a snapper,' I say. 'A photographer.'

'So,' she says, and she does that smile that makes her face both beautiful and scary, 'that's why there are photographers outside my house. You were the one who put them on to me, were you?'

Chapter Fifty-Two

We're still sitting here in Loreen's front room like everything is normal, like every Monday Ashley and me pop round like this. Only it isn't normal at all and neither of us pops round like this, at least I haven't for a long time. We used to, though, there used to be a time when we spent most of our lives popping round to each other's, and when we weren't doing that we were ringing each other. There was a time when we knew just about everything going on in each other's lives, the interesting things and the boring things, arguments with parents, fancying someone and not being fancied back, exams and homework, who said what and why, everything. But that ended a long time ago. Now I see Ashley maybe once every six months. Now I don't see Karen for years.

Ashley is still staring at her tea; I drink mine although it's too hot. My head is beginning to clear. I go to the balcony door and look out: there's a couple of dead plants, a wind chime nailed to the wall, broken plastic toys, a deflated football. I open the door and in the distance I can hear the sound of a school bell and the shouts of children, a faint wave of happy noise. School must be over for the day. I didn't realise it was that late.

'Sweet?' says Loreen, coming in from the kitchen, carrying a big glass jar like the ones that used to be in the windows and on the shelves of sweet shops. I come away from the balcony as she takes off the rubber-ringed glass lid and offers me the jar. I put my hand in and feel around with my fingers and pull out a handful of jelly babies. 'Ashley?' Loreen asks, walking over, offering the jar.

Ashley stares at her. 'Not hungry,' she says.

I've already put the jelly babies in my mouth, Loreen is already sucking on her sweet, and we look at each other because we both feel bad now, sucking away like this. I think maybe she's forgiven me for not telling her I'm a snapper, now that she's told Ashley.

'So what exactly happened?' asks Loreen, and she pushes the sweet to one side of her mouth. 'Do you love him?'

'Of course I don't love him,' Ashley says. 'How could I?' We watch as Ashley gets a little stick of lip balm out of her giant handbag and begins to apply it to her lips, softly, rolling it back and forth until her lips shine. Then she tosses the lip balm back into her bag.

'But I thought you two seemed really happy together,' says Loreen. 'So what exactly did he do?'

'He slept with someone,' Ashley snaps. 'What is there to tell? He just came home one night, he's been staying with me because the press have been hounding him . . . and he was incredibly upset.'

'Mmm,' says Loreen.

'Shit,' I say, looking at the two of them on the sofa. 'He's a shit. I thought that the minute I met him.'

Ashley turns sharply. 'Yes, he didn't like you either.'

Loreen giggles.

'What do you mean?' My mouth feels sticky; the jelly babies are lining my teeth like soft, sweet plastic.

'Well,' says Ashley, 'that evening you all came round he said you kept on looking at him.'

'What! I wasn't looking at him, he was the one looking at me!'

'He liked you, though,' says Ashley, and she smiles at Loreen.

'Did he?' Loreen looks pleased.

'Oh for fuck's sake,' I say.

'Anyway, go on,' says Loreen. 'He came home one night and . . .'

Ashley bends down and unzips her boots. I see she's not wearing tights or socks, her feet are naked and her toenails are painted a perfect pink. 'He said he wanted me to be the first to know, that if it got out then the press,' Ashley scowls at me, 'would be all over it. He said he didn't actually *do* anything with this tart who picked him up. He said he thought it was a set-up because the press are always after him, that she put something in his drink.'

'Yeah, right,' I say. So she doesn't know, Ashley doesn't know the whole story at all, but this must be why Fred was here; whoever's slept with Donny Green has sold their story to the *Mirror*. Maybe the *Post* knows this too. I go back to the glass doors and step out onto the balcony. There's a stream of people below, mothers with children fresh from school; two girls are on scooters, several of the women have buggies. The children are straggling all over the pavement, running, skipping, being kids. I keep watching, I like the way the children move, the way they invade each other's space, the way they run into each other and then fly apart again. Then I see Fred from the *Mirror*. So he's come back, he's parked just where he was before.

I get closer to the edge of the balcony, look at the neighbouring mansion to my right: it has a neat red roof and a stack of chimney pots, small like children's fingers. The sky is going grey now. It's just suddenly going grey and all the colour is fading like the world just turned into a negative. I can smell the wet slate smell of rain in the air. I look at the London skyline in the distance between the mansion blocks on the other side of the road. I can see the Eye like a metal bracelet someone has tossed in the air and it's landed among the solid fat blocks of offices and flats and high-rise buildings. Behind the Eye it's misty, and it could almost be that the city ends right there and there is something else, sea perhaps, just after. I wish that was true, that there really was sea out there.

I look down at the street, at a lamp post curved like a question mark on top, a lone plane tree with flat wide leaves, two cars nose to nose on the street, so close it's as if they are talking to each other. Then my phone beeps and I quiver. It's getting cold out here. It's a text from Ray. *Last night was great, hope we do it again.* I put my head down and smile. I wish I'd stayed there with him, I wish I'd never left and gone home and answered the call from Pete on the desk and been sent on Donny Green on a Monday morning. If I hadn't, if I'd stayed with Ray for even just a while, if I hadn't had the urge to move on, I wouldn't have answered my phone and then I wouldn't have ended up here. My phone rings and I know who it's going to be. Shit. I close the balcony door with a rattle and put the phone tight to my head.

'What's going on, Bel?' It's Pete on the desk.

'Nothing's happening at all.' I make myself yawn. 'Looks

like a dead plot to me. I'm just going to pull off for a wee, if that's alright with you.'

Pete laughs. 'Please yourself, I believe we're going to move you on anyway. I'll get back to you in a bit.'

I flip my phone shut and step off the balcony and back into the room.

'What were you doing out there?' asks Ashley. Then she flinches at the sound of Loreen's buzzer. 'Who's that?'

'I don't know,' says Loreen. 'Should I answer it? Do you not want me to? Do you think *he'd* come *here*?'

'He might. He might have followed me. We had a screaming row this morning.'

'That was when I texted you,' I tell Ashley.

'Did you?' says Ashley, carelessly.

I feel a surge of anger that she didn't return my calls. If she had then I would have told her everything. My messages were urgent, she must have realised that, but she couldn't be bothered to reply. The buzzer goes again and we watch Loreen go into the hallway and speak into the intercom. 'It's Mum,' she calls back to us. 'I forgot, she's bringing Dwaine back.'

I sit down on the arm of the sofa. Next to me Ashley is looking intently at her phone, deleting things furiously.

'Mum!' We both look up; we can hear Dwaine yelling excitedly in the hallway. 'And Wendy said I had to go on the traffic lights because I was talking too much and *interrupting*, but guess what, Mum? She forgot at the end of the day and I never went on the traffic lights and Jayden was really *annoyed*, Mum, and he said . . .' Dwaine stops in his tracks. He has run all the way along the hallway and now he's come to

491

the doorway and seen us in his front room and he's just frozen. He hangs his head a little and squeezes himself against the doorframe.

'Hi Dwaine,' I say. 'Want to see my camera?' I take my compact out of my pocket and hold it up and he comes forward, shuffling his legs like an old man.

'Hello, my dears,' says Loreen's mum, coming into the room behind Dwaine. She's wearing a lot of clothes for what has been such a warm day: a soft pink scarf, a coat belted tightly in the middle, a thick skirt that has a flutter of grass caught on the sides. She doesn't rush into the room, she moves slowly, carefully, because this is the way Loreen's mum has always moved. Dudu never hurried like the rest of our mums, she never tore around like my mum. She walked slowly, as if she had a purpose, as if she enjoyed the journey as much as she enjoyed where it was that she was going. I bend slightly to kiss her on each cheek, try to remember the last time I saw her. She seems to have got smaller; I don't remember Dudu being so short. Instead I remember when she was taller than me and she would bend to do up my coat or stroke my hair. 'Bel, my dear,' she smiles, 'I haven't seen you for a long time. Aren't you tall? Shall we close that door because it's getting chilly now, isn't it? How about some tea?'

'Mum!' Loreen shouts from the kitchen. 'I'm doing it, OK?'

'And Ashley,' says Dudu. 'How are you, my dear?'

Ashley gets up; she looks a bit reluctant but she offers her cheeks for Dudu to kiss. 'You look very lovely,' Dudu says to Ashley, and she says it in a way that it doesn't sound like a compliment at all and it makes me smile and with a rush of memory I think of how Loreen's mum was always on my side, whenever there were fights between us she was always on my side. Why was she so good to me, what was there about me as a child that made her do that?

'Out the way, Nan!' says Dwaine. He has run out of the room and is trying to get back in again.

Dudu laughs, a laugh that says she is annoyed, not amused. 'How can you talk to me like that?' she asks Dwaine. 'In Africa a child would never be allowed to . . .' but then she tails off, she just puts out her hand and rests it on Dwaine's head and her eyes look far away and she seems totally lost for a moment. I think about how Loreen said her mum was acting oddly since she came back from Botswana yesterday, and then I think how Loreen's mother was always talking about *where I come from* and *back home in Africa* and how it made me feel there was another world out there. And I thought I was going to find that other world, and here I am, still here.

Dudu keeps her hand on Dwaine's head but her eyes are bright again now. 'I brought you some biscuits,' she calls to Loreen, and she puts her bag down on the table and riffles through it and brings out two packets of biscuits and a news-paper. She tips the newspaper onto the table and I pick it up and see it's folded at the horoscope page. Dudu sees me look-ing at this and she laughs. 'It's a load of old nonsense, my dear, I don't know why I ever read these things. What are you, Bel? Libra?'

I nod, impressed that Loreen's mother remembers my birthday.

'Well it says here . . .'

'I don't want to know,' I say.

Dudu smiles at me. 'This is a day when everything will come together for you. That's nice, isn't it?'

I smile; Dudu is just like Loreen, always looking on the bright side of things.

'Ashley, my dear, what sign are you? Leo?'

Ashley looks at Dudu and she seems transfixed. 'I don't believe in horoscopes,' she says.

'No, my dear,' says Dudu, and she holds Ashley's gaze until Ashley looks away, 'nor do I.'

Chapter Fifty-Three

Shit. I wish I wasn't here. I wish I wasn't here in Loreen's front room. Dudu is laying out biscuits on a plate like nothing is going on, but she knows something is going on because she stops for a second and looks up at me and her expression is strange; it's like she wants to smile and has decided she can't. When there's a knock on the door I hear Loreen shout out warningly from the kitchen, 'Dwaine! You're not to open the door on your own!' But Dwaine is already rushing down the hallway and I hear the click of a latch and the door opening.

'Hello,' says a man's voice. 'Remember me?' I can't hear Dwaine reply, but I can hear the man ask, 'Is your mother in?'

'Yes,' says Dwaine. 'She's here with her friends . . .'

'Dwaine!' shouts Loreen. 'What did I tell you?' She sounds so alarmed that I come to the hallway to see what's going on and I catch sight of the man at the front door. Shit. I know him. I know that overeager face and that ill-fitting suit. It's Brian, the boy journo from the Heathrow job. How did he get in here? He hasn't seen me yet and he mustn't see me. I throw myself into Loreen's bedroom, leave the door ajar. He might not know I'm here; as long as his desk hasn't spoken to mine, then Brian won't know I'm on this job too. I told Pete I was going off for a wee and he said that was fine, they were moving me on anyway, so he doesn't know I'm still here

495

either. I can see clearly through the crack in the door as Brian comes into Loreen's flat; he's moving so quickly down the hallway it's like he's been given thirty-five seconds to get in or else. I know he must have been sent to find Ashley, but why did he just say to Dwaine, *Remember me?*

'Ladies,' says Brian when he gets to the front room. I can just see the side of his face; he's so excited he's sweating because he's just seen Ashley sitting there on the sofa. He must think this is his lucky day.

But Loreen's come after him now and she touches him on the shoulder. 'Excuse me,' she says angrily, 'but I didn't let you in.' Brian tries to step forward, to get into the front room, but Loreen grabs his arm and holds on.

'Ashley Brown!' Brian shouts in desperation. 'Any comment?'

'Who the hell was that?' asks Ashley as me and Loreen come back into the front room.

'I believe that must have been a reporter,' says Dudu. 'He has been sniffing around here asking my little Loreen what she knows about you, my dear, because you are a pop star now.'

'Mum!' says Loreen. 'I told you!'

'I always thought Loreen would be famous, you know, Ashley.'

'Mum!'

'That was what I was told by a fortune-teller one day on Hampstead Heath and do you know what? I really believed it,' Dudu chuckles to herself. 'But Ashley, my dear, you're the famous one now, aren't you?'

'What do you mean, he's been asking about me?' Ashley looks furiously at Loreen. 'When was this?'

'Saturday,' says Loreen.

'What, he came here? But how does he know we know each other?'

Loreen shrugs. 'I don't know, he just said he was from the *Sunday Post* and he wanted to ask your old friends what you were like. He said they were doing a profile of you because of Donny Green.'

'Because of Donny?' asks Ashley. 'You mean he wanted to write about me because he knew about Donny and that tart more likely. I can't believe you would do this to me, Loreen.'

I expect Loreen to look stricken but her face is oddly defiant. 'And what is it you think I did?'

Ashley wasn't expecting this response. She sits up on the sofa, leans forward. 'You didn't talk to him, did you?'

'No,' says Loreen, 'I didn't. Although I could do with the money.' She looks at Ashley, at her expensive clothes, her expensive handbag, her expensive boots left lying on the floor.

Dudu starts eating a biscuit, gives one to Dwaine when he runs back into the room. He takes it, crams it in his mouth, runs out again.

'Mum!' says Loreen. 'He won't eat his dinner.'

'What money?' asks Ashley. 'What did you mean, you could do with the money? Don't tell me he was offering you money to tell stories about your old friend!'

'Well he was,' says Loreen. 'He offered a lot, actually.'

'And don't tell me you considered it, did you, Loreen? Did you? Did you consider selling stories about one of your oldest friends to a fucking journalist from the *Sunday Post*!'

Ashley stands up, her face is flushed and she sounds like she's going to explode. I've never seen her so out of control before. 'And what would you have told him, Loreen? How could you anyway? How could you do that? Do you know what I'd do if someone came round asking about you?'

'Well they're not going to do that, are they?' snaps Loreen.

'What I would do if someone came round asking about you,' continues Ashley, 'is I would tell them to fuck off because we're friends, aren't we, and friends don't do this.'

'I'm going to make tea,' says Dudu as Dwaine comes back in, slower now because he's weighted down with a pile of books. He doesn't make it to the table in time, instead the books drop and he says, 'These are my mum's when she was little like me.'

I crouch down on the floor and pick up the books. They're the old girly annuals Loreen used to read. The covers are garish, it's like they used to use brighter tones than they do now. I pick up a *Blue Peter* annual and open it and the pages smell chalky. Inside the pictures are carelessly cropped and without sufficient contrast; they didn't have Photoshop back then. I pick up *Look-in*, turn the glossy pages, stare at the cut-outs of band members, which for some reason have been tinted green or blue. And then I pick up *Oh Boy!* and this one I really remember. I can see Loreen and Karen now, in Loreen's room, or in the classroom, or in a newsagent's, or on the beach at Portugal, their heads together, reading *Oh Boy!*. It's like a tabloid on the front. *It's best for Boys! Look good all over! Great pin-ups! In gorgeous colour! Fantastic true-life photo stories! Star special!!* That's seven exclamation marks and I haven't even opened it.

498

'Where did you get all these from?' I ask.

Loreen crouches down on the floor next to me. She's deliberately turning her back on Ashley who is still standing there, furious, waiting for a response to her outburst about what friends should and shouldn't do. 'Mum's been saving them for me. Oh my God, how we used to read this stuff!'

'We?' I ask.

Loreen laughs. 'OK, me.' It's the first time she's laughed since I arrived. She takes the *Oh Boy!* annual and begins to turn it around in her hands like she's holding something precious, she doesn't open it, she just turns it around in her hands. 'I feel like I'm holding my sixteen-year-old self,' she says softly. 'You know what it was? You know why I always loved these magazines so much? It was like they promised something, like they promised us a sense of growing up, of possibilities, of what our futures would be. And yet they didn't promise anything at all, did they? Apart from how to get a boy.' Loreen tosses the *Oh Boy!* annual across the floor. 'That's why I've given up dating, because I'm sick and tired of trying to find someone, of trying to get someone to fancy me, like me, marry me.' She laughs, only bitterly now. 'It's pretty sad to think you can waste your whole life, isn't it?'

'Loreen,' I object, because I can't bear to hear her talk like this. 'You haven't wasted your whole life, don't say something like that. Look at you: you've got your boys, your flat, your job, your mum. It's more than I've got! What have I got? A house that's not even mine that's falling apart, a job that's like a non-stop fucking car crash, a—'

'Can I draw on it, Mum?' asks Dwaine as he picks up the

499

Oh Boy! annual from the floor, and when Loreen nods he rushes out and comes back in with a big bag of pens and crayons. Dwaine sits down on the floor and opens the annual; he stops at a double-page spread titled '*A good girl's guide to gossip*' and he starts scribbling earnestly on a photo of a boy and a girl locked in a kiss in a doorway.

'Where did you dig these out from?' asks Ashley. Her voice is calmer now but then I see she's not looking at the annuals, she's standing by Loreen's shelf, the one above the table. She's found the photos I saw when I first came in; Loreen must have put them there. Ashley holds them up, starts walking round the room. 'That was on that school trip to France in the second year,' she says. 'And that's Mrs Greenrod from primary school!' She laughs, and it's a light, happy laugh, like she's not angry with Loreen or me any more. 'Where did you get this from?' she stops, and her face has gone tight. She holds up a photo and I see which one it is, it's the photo of her and the boy in Portugal, and I realise it's exactly the sort of snap the *Sunday Post* would love, because it's got that snatched quality. It's not posed, it's not really even in focus. The people don't know they're being watched. It's a private moment.

'Oh Christ,' Ashley whispers, looking at the photo, her face stricken. Then she squints her eyes and frowns. 'I remember that bikini.' For a moment her face softens as she looks at her young self in her red and white spotted bikini. 'I look quite good,' she says.

'You always looked good,' says Loreen. 'And you knew it.'

'No,' says Ashley slowly like she hasn't even heard Loreen. 'I mean I never knew that, I never knew that I looked OK, I

500

always thought, you know, I hated my body. That was why . . .' Ashley stops talking, studies the picture again.

Me and Loreen don't know what to say. We all wanted a body like Ashley's, everyone at school wanted a body like Ashley's, how could she not have been happy with that? But I watch her still looking at the photo and the expression on her face is as if she is looking at something awful, like it's something she'd rather forget. And I think good, because I want her to feel guilt that she got off with the boy me and Loreen fancied, that she lied to Loreen, that she got what she wanted like she always got what she wanted.

'But who *took* it?' she asks. 'Loreen? Who took this picture? Look, you can see, someone is looking down on me, they've taken it from above. It wasn't you, was it?'

Loreen looks at me and I shrug. Ashley knows already, she knows because I remember her laughing and looking up and seeing me with my camera in my hands, and I remember how I ran along the cliff top back to the house. She made me feel I'd done something wrong, but it was her who had done something wrong. And I hid the film, pushed it deep inside my suitcase, and then I'd checked it and I'd checked it and I'd checked it again. She knew I took the photo because that was why Ashley had been so angry that night, the last night of our holiday, that was why she had touched her blood to mine when Loreen made us cut our thumbs, and that was why she told me never to tell. And I didn't tell because I didn't want Loreen hurt; I didn't want her upset just because Ashley got off with some boy. And how could I tell on Ashley anyway, when she was the one who'd given me the money to go to her parents' house in Portugal?

501

'You know it was me,' I say.

'Do I?' Ashley looks startled. 'How would I have known that?'

'Because,' I say, and I get up from the floor. 'Because you saw me and you said that was what the pact meant, that we never tell.'

'Never tell what?'

'Ashley!' How can she still be lying after all this time? 'We did the pact and I asked what it meant and you looked me in the eye and said it means we never tell.'

'Oh come on!' Ashley laughs. 'I was just saying that, it didn't mean anything!'

She looks at the picture again, but then she seems to realise something and when she speaks now her voice is gritted like she's on the edge of tears. 'But what have you got this out for?' she asks Loreen. 'What were you going to do, give this to that journalist?'

'No,' says Loreen.

Ashley stares at her, wanting more.

'Karen said not to.'

'You asked Karen!'

'Well I didn't know what to do.'

'You could have asked me!' Ashley sits down, still holding the picture. 'It's my picture!'

'Well it's a picture *of* you,' I say.

Ashley scowls at me. 'What do you mean, a picture *of* me, it's mine! Even if I didn't know you were taking it, it's mine because it's of me.'

I'm about to contradict her, but she's turned back to Loreen now. 'If someone came round and asked about you,' she tells her, 'that's what I would have done, I would have called you at once! I would have asked you what you thought.'

'You're not the easiest person to ask things you know, Ashley,' says Loreen.

'What do you mean, I'm not the easiest person to ask things?' Ashley looks affronted.

'Well you're not, there's a lot of things you don't talk about.'

'Like what?'

Loreen's face is worried, like she's said too much, like she's started something and now she doesn't know what to do. 'Like your father . . . after your parents split . . . like your divorce . . . you know, you never talk about all those things. I could have rung, I was meaning to, it only happened on Saturday, but whenever I call you're not around.'

Ashley stares at Loreen. She gets her lip balm out again and rubs it angrily on her lips. 'What did he offer you then, if you told him about me?'

'Thousands. Two hundred thousand pounds.'

'Oh come on!' For a second Ashley looks pleased, and then she looks afraid. 'But why would they offer you that much just because my *boyfriend* cheated on me? It's hardly headline news, is it?'

'It is if it's Donny Green,' I say, and I take a deep breath because now is the time, I can't let this go on any more. 'Ashley, if you're going out with a celeb then you're fair game, you know that's how they see it. But it's more than that, it's more than just cheating. I don't know what this whole story is that Donny's told you, but do you want me to tell you what I know?'

503

'That would be nice,' she says icily, flipping the lip balm back into her handbag.

Now I'm angry, why does Ashley always have to blame me? It's not my fault, I haven't done anything wrong. I look over at the balcony door, I want to escape, I want to get out. I wonder why Loreen's mum is spending so long in the kitchen making tea. I can hear a radio playing and I think she's settled herself down in there so as not to be in here with us. 'It's worse than you think,' I tell Ashley. 'It's not just that Donny Green cheated on you, it's what else he's been doing.'

'Like what?' asks Loreen.

'Yes do tell us, Bel,' says Ashley nastily.

'He's been taking photos of himself, naked, masturbating.'

'Oh come on!' laughs Ashley.

Loreen is staring at me, her hand to her mouth.

'Then he sends them to young girls on the Internet. A mother of one of the girls found them; she went to the *Sunday Post*. As you do.' I attempt a laugh, but then I see how Ashley is slumped against the sofa, see a muscle in her face twitch, like she's trying to regain the composure she lost just now and is about to lose again. She doesn't want to believe me and she hates it that I'm the one telling her this, but she does believe me because she sees it's true. I sense her humiliation, see it in the way she's hugging herself. 'I didn't know anything about this, Ashley.' I sit down next to her on the sofa, I want to tell her how sorry I am but I know she doesn't want to hear this. 'It was months ago, they've had these pictures for something like six months. So whatever Donny's told you about the woman he's just slept with, the timing isn't right, this is something that's been going on for a long time.'

'When you say "girl", do you mean a *girl*?' asks Ashley.

'Yes, I mean a girl. She's sixteen. Just like you were in that photo.'

'I feel sick.' Ashley leans forward and puts her head in her hands like she's on a plane and she's just been told to adopt the crash position.

505

Chapter Fifty-Four

I'm on the balcony, looking, waiting. It's dusk now and under the grey sweeping sky the mansion blocks opposite look ominous. On the street below two men are standing under the weak white light of the curved-topped streetlamp, chatting. I watch them, wondering what they're talking about, and then I recognise one, it's beanie man. So it's not just Fred from the *Mirror*, there are others here too. I can't see if Brian is still around, but there's another pap at the far end of the street, I recognise his car, and then another, loitering on the road.

I jerk back on the balcony as the two men under the streetlamp look up. I see them scan Loreen's mansion block, then they turn and look at the block opposite. Beanie man is gesturing at the roof. I look over as well, see that the middle part of the roof is flat and there's a banister, so there must be steps leading up there. Is beanie man thinking of going up there to take snaps; is that why he's pointing it out?

I turn round on the balcony, look through the door into Loreen's flat and at the light and the warmth inside. I can hear a tap being turned on in Loreen's kitchen and a lid put on a pot and through the open window I can smell garlic frying in the pan. Karen's here, she arrived an hour ago, and now she's cooking. I hope she's making something with meat.

It starts to rain, a gentle spray, and I put my compact away in my pocket. I move to the edge of the balcony again and look down at the waiting paps. But I can't concentrate now because I'm getting that urge, the urge to check. I want to know that my camera is in my pocket, even though I just put it there myself. I want to feel it, to know it's solid in my pocket and safe. But I know that if I touch it once I'll have to touch it again because this is it, it's happening again, and so I grip the balcony railing, focus myself on what's down below, force myself to look at the road, the streetlamp, the two paps chatting. Then I see that I'm doing what I always do, I'm trying to avoid the thoughts, the thoughts that tell me to do something. Because if I give in to the thoughts then I've failed, because that's what it is, I fight it and I fight it and then every time I check something, I've failed. It doesn't matter if it's the boot of my car, the dial on top of the cooker, or my camera in my pocket, if I give in to the impulse then I've failed. But what if I don't avoid this thought, what if I face it; face the fear that if I don't check my camera then it will fall and break, face the fear that things aren't safe, that things can't be controlled, that nothing has any guarantee.

I picture my camera on the ground, smashed and broken, and as I do the strangest thing happens, the urge to check that it's still here in my pocket begins to fade, softly like steam into the air. I hold onto the railing, deliberately bring the thought back into my head again, bring it right up close in my mind and look at it, think about it. I feel as if I am opening myself up to something dangerous, because the impulse to check is something that has always been hidden, it's been hidden away in my mind and I've hidden it away from anyone else, but if I bring the thought out, look at it, examine it, then it fades. Why have I never worked this out before? I feel I'm

507

on the tip of discovering something enormous and life shattering, then my phone rings.

'Bel, it's Mum.'

'Hi Mum.' I cradle my phone between my shoulder and my ear, try to protect it from the rain.

'You OK?'

'Yeah, I'm OK.'

'You working?' asks Mum.

'Yeah, well, sort of.'

'Glen said for you to take care. You seem very tired at the moment, Bel, and very . . . agitated. I was thinking . . .' Mum pauses.

'You were thinking?' I prompt.

'Yes, you know what we were talking about the other day, with your brothers?'

'Mmm,' I say, and feel a twinge of anxiety. I can't hear Mum that well and I don't know why she's starting a conversation like this when I'm standing out on a balcony in the rain.

'Bel, are you there?'

'Yes, I'm here.'

'Well,' says Mum. 'You know what your brother Rich was saying, about it running in families?'

'It? What do you mean, *it*?'

'What I'm trying to tell you, Bel, is I struggled with that.'

I hold the phone even tighter; I can hear blood hammering in my ears. 'You struggled with what?'

Mum sighs like I'm being difficult. I hear a faint click; perhaps she's turning the electric kettle on. 'I was like you, that's what I'm saying, always checking things, you know. When

508

you were born, just after you were born in fact, I used to wash my hands, oh I don't know, a hundred times a day. But even before that, Bel, I had things, you know, little rituals like your brother was saying, where I had to do things in a certain way, count to three when I came down the stairs, that sort of thing. All perfectly normal!' Mum laughs but I don't join in. I just think, three, why did she count things to three? 'I learned to manage it I suppose,' says Mum, 'that's what I'm trying to tell you. So I started collecting things instead.'

I picture Mum in her kitchen surrounded by her latest collection, the squirrels. I think of the years of collecting sheep, of her recent interest in monkeys, of all the collections over all of the years, and suddenly I see Mum's collections for what they are, they're childish. They are just like me when I was a kid, putting my unwanted dolls in a row, having my crayons all lined up, having everything just right under my bed. Mum arranges her collections with just the same sort of obsessiveness I used to do.

'I think taking pictures is your way of managing it,' says Mum.

'Oh.' I don't know what to say, this conversation is so sudden and so odd. Mum is telling me something she's never told me before and I'm torn between understanding and anger. Anger that she could have told me this before, because if she had then maybe I wouldn't have felt so alone with my craziness; understanding because when she tried to stop me when I was a kid, when I wanted my plaits just right or I wanted to stand on a certain spot on the playground floor, she was so upset because all that time she had it too.

'Is it raining where you are, Bel?'

'Yeah, a bit.'

'And you know Sharon opposite?'

'Yes.'

'Well her son's the same, he's only ten, and he's been seeing someone.'

I don't answer. Has Mum been telling people about me then, about my checking? I feel furious for a second but then I think, it's not a secret, it's not something I need to keep to myself any more. I want to think about this, about what Mum's just told me, I want to try and understand it and live with it, and I'm about to ask her who her neighbour's son has been seeing when I hear the balcony door open behind me.

'Bel!' Loreen says. 'Food's ready.'

Chapter Fifty-Five

I come back inside to find Karen in Loreen's front room laying the table, efficiently removing the roses and the photos, putting down dishes and glasses. 'What's up?' she asks. I know she's asking about Ashley but I shake my head, I can't tell her now. I wonder where Ashley is anyway; she must have gone to the loo. 'Fine,' Karen says, annoyed. 'Take these.' She gives me a handful of forks and walks off. Then she comes back with a big steaming earthenware dish of sauce and Ashley is behind her holding a giant saucepan of spaghetti. Karen tells me to get the salt and pepper from the kitchen and the Parmesan cheese, and then she calls everyone to eat.

'Mum says she's going to eat in the kitchen,' says Loreen, coming in with a bottle of wine, 'with Dwaine. He's exhausted, he should have eaten ages ago but he's too excited with everyone here.'

We sit down around the table and Karen dishes out the food, Loreen pours the wine. 'Not for me,' I say, putting my hand over my glass because I need to focus, I need my head to be clear.

'Ashley?' asks Karen. 'Are you OK?' Ashley's taken the bottle from Loreen and she's pouring wine into her glass, only her glass is full and she's still pouring. She sees us watching her, gives a blank smile. She doesn't speak; I haven't heard her say anything since Karen arrived. Then she turns because someone is at the doorway.

'Hi Anthony,' says Loreen to her son. 'Good football practice?'

Anthony looks at us sitting around the table, me and Ashley, Loreen and Karen. He's wearing a white football kit and his trainers are caked with mud. He makes a face of disgust. 'You're talking with your mouth full, Mum,' he tells Loreen. 'That's so embarrassing.' Loreen closes her mouth quickly, then she opens it again, opening it wide to show him what she has inside and we all start laughing.

'Anthony!' Loreen's mum calls from the kitchen. 'Come in here and eat with us, my dear. Then afterwards I can read you a story.'

'I'm not a kid,' he scowls, but I see him walk into the kitchen, moving slowly like his grandmother does.

'Isn't this nice?' asks Loreen with a soppy smile. 'When was the last time we were all together like this? We've never been at mine like this, have we?'

Loreen is right; it is nice, with the rain outside and the food and the warmth inside, and the fact we are sitting here together. And I want to pretend it's all OK, that Ashley's not cracking up, that I'm not in a flat with a herd of paps outside just waiting to snap one of my oldest friends. I look at Ashley sitting opposite me at the table, her head is down, she's not eating and she's not drinking, she's just sitting there and there is something drained about her, like she's lost all her energy and all her colour. I know it's been a long time since I really thought of her as my friend. But she is, because we go way back, we go all the way back to primary school and we spent

512

our childhoods together, we spent our teens together, and if Ashley is hurting now over Donny Green then I need to be on her side.

'It takes a long time to grow an old friend,' says Karen.

We all look at her. 'That's nice,' says Loreen. 'Who said that?'

Karen laughs. 'Hell, I've no idea, I just read it somewhere once.'

'But that's it, isn't it?' Loreen's eyes are shining. 'That's what friendship is about, isn't it? It's not something that comes quickly, well it can come quickly, you can make a friend just like that, but real friends, old friends, take a long time to grow, don't they?'

Ashley gets up from the table, she hasn't eaten a thing, and she goes and sits on the floor. She takes a small jar out of her enormous handbag, opens it and picks out a little white pad and begins cleaning the pink varnish off her toes.

'When are you going back to California?' Loreen asks Karen brightly, like she hasn't noticed Ashley has just left the table.

'Wednesday,' says Karen, staring at Ashley sitting on the floor, still wondering what's going on.

'I wish we'd seen more of Stella,' says Loreen.

'We'll be back,' Karen smiles. 'Maybe next summer, if everything works out.'

'What do you mean?' asks Loreen, because she's heard the note of uncertainty in Karen's voice and Karen never sounds uncertain about things.

Karen sighs, holds up the pan of spaghetti to see if anyone wants any more and when we all shake our heads she says, 'Stella wants a baby.'

'Shit,' I say. 'But you don't, do you?'

Karen looks at me as if wondering how I can ask this question. 'What do you think?'

Loreen leans over the table, lays her hand on Karen's arm. 'But if she does and you don't,' she says, and her voice is soft, worried, 'then what will you do?'

'Sometimes you can do things for someone you love, you know?' Still Karen sounds uncertain. 'And sometimes you can't.'

'But you'll come back?' I ask.

Karen smiles. 'Stella thought we could try and rent the same apartment, although I wouldn't want to really, with everything that's been happening upstairs.' She picks up the plates, starts stacking them on top of each other.

'What's been happening upstairs?' I ask.

'I haven't told you?'

'No.'

'I thought I had,' Karen sighs. 'There's this big guy up there. He's real creepy, from the first minute I saw him I thought he was creepy. It's just him and his boy, Dylan, and he's been yelling at him, swearing, you know? So it's gotten worse, we've seen the boy with bruises. Stella even let him in one night and he slept at ours. And you know what?' Karen's voice is angry now, as she slams a final plate on the pile. 'Everyone in the goddam street knows about this! We can all hear it and no one will get involved.' She stops, sniffs the air. 'Can anyone smell burning?'

We all sniff the air as well. 'No,' says Loreen, 'I can't smell anything.'

'I've tried, you know,' says Karen, 'I've really tried. I've rung the council, talked to social services, I've written to them as well and they just didn't seem interested.'

'For fuck's sake!' says Loreen, and we all stare at her because she never swears like this. 'They're quick enough to come running round here and check on me!'

'What?' asks Karen.

'I had a child protection officer come round here last year,' says Loreen. She nods because we're all looking at her like this can't be true, even Ashley has stopped painting her nails and is paying attention now. 'Because, get this, Dwaine drew a willy and gave it to his teacher! So they sent this bloke round to question me. The school didn't even tell me, they just referred it straight to social services!'

'You're kidding,' I laugh. 'You didn't tell me.'

'No, really, he came round, suit and all, and questioned me, was I a single parent, did I live in a council flat, did I let Dwaine watch *sexually explicit* things on the TV? He even wanted to know if I had boyfriends come round!'

'Nosy bastard,' says Ashley.

'Well,' I tell her, 'we're all nosy bastards, aren't we?'

'We are?' asks Ashley, putting away her nail polish, screwing the lid of the bottle as tight as it can go.

'Haven't you noticed?' I ask. 'Haven't you noticed how you open up any newspaper, any magazine, turn on any TV programme, and there are pictures of people doing all sorts of private things? That's what I do for a living, for fuck's sake. Just look at *Big Brother*, look at all these "reality" shows which invite us to sneak up on people, see them doing private things, watch them kiss, take a shower, even have a fucking shit!'

515

Loreen giggles and pours herself more wine.

'We're constantly being encouraged to be nosy bastards, aren't we?' I ask. 'What about the little girl who went missing in Portugal?'

'Oh God,' says Loreen, and she puts down her glass.

'We've seen just about every aspect of her family's life, haven't we? It's like we are spoon-fed their grief, and everyone has an opinion on what happened, don't they? Every newspaper, every radio show, it's full of people saying what the parents should and shouldn't have done . . .'

'But,' says Karen, and she nods at me, she sees what I'm getting at, 'when it's our own goddam neighbour, when we actually *could* get involved and *do* something then people just don't want to know. I know they say it's up to social services, I get that, but what about our responsibility? Why can't my neighbours just tell this big guy upstairs, we know what you're doing and it's not right and it has to stop? He must know that we know, that we can hear all this going on and because we do nothing then it's like we're saying, fine, you go ahead, buddy, and beat up that little boy.' Karen stands up, the dishes in her hand. She heads for the kitchen and almost trips over Dwaine who is on the carpet, scribbling away. I think he's drawing on one of Loreen's old annuals, but when I get up to have a look I see it's a new magazine and that Dwaine is drawing a big felt-tipped willy on a photo of Donny Green. Ashley gets up too and comes over and when she sees what Dwaine has done she starts laughing. 'You'll have to make it smaller than that, babe!'

'Mum!' Anthony shouts urgently from the kitchen. 'Mum!'

Loreen leaps up from the table. 'What is it?' she yells, she

516

must sense something is really wrong. 'Oh my God!' I hear her shout, and as I rush to the kitchen doorway I see Dudu fanning frantically at a pan on the stove, the blue of the gas mixing with the red of the flames, and the more she fans the higher, more intense the flames grow. Loreen darts for the stove, turns off the gas, grabs the towel from her mother, runs with it to the sink and turns on the tap. Then she flings the sodden towel over the pan. Dudu watches, her face looks trembly. 'Are you OK?' Loreen asks.

Dudu opens her mouth to speak but nothing comes out.

'Mum, what happened?' Still Dudu doesn't say anything. Loreen looks round the kitchen, trying to find someone who will tell her what happened if her mother can't.

'Nan fell asleep,' says Anthony. He looks down at the floor, like he's ashamed of this. 'I was in my room. She was going to make us hot chocolate.'

'Did you? Mum? Did you fall asleep? With a pan on the stove?'

'Ah, my little Loreen . . .' says Dudu.

I see Loreen tense, her fingers ball up briefly into two fists and then she releases them again. 'Not quite so little any more, Mum, hey?' She pats her mum on the hand, takes her gently to a chair and gets her to sit down. 'She's fine,' she tells her boys, 'Nan's fine, she's just a bit tired and she's going to go and have a rest on your bed, OK, Dwaine? You take her, OK?'

'OK, Mum!' Dwaine comes forward very self-importantly and takes his nan by the hand and she gets up with a soft groan and he leads her out of the kitchen.

'She's not herself,' says Loreen, her voice a whisper as she watches her son lead her mum out of the room. 'Since she

517

came back from Botswana . . . I don't know what happened there, but it's shaken her. I think maybe she found out things weren't as she remembered them, that things change and she doesn't know what to think about that. Because you know Mum,' Loreen laughs, 'always living in the past.'

Loreen has gone to give Dwaine a bath, Anthony is in his room and Dudu is resting. I'm alone in the kitchen when Karen comes in with the rest of the dishes. She closes the door behind her. 'So what *is* going on?' she asks. 'Ashley is goddam weird tonight. It feels like we're all goddam weird tonight.' She turns on the tap, fills up the kitchen sink with water, hands me a tea towel, and I just stand there because I don't know where to start.

'It's Donny Green,' I tell her. 'You know, Ashley's boyfriend?'

Karen nods, pulls that face she used to pull to make us all laugh.

'He's been cheating on her, she just found out, that's why she's come round here. That's why I came round too. You're not going to believe this, but the *Sunday Post* sent me here earlier to take photographs of her. They sent a journo too.'

'Go on,' says Karen, pouring washing-up liquid into the sink, agitating the water with her hands.

I laugh at how casual she sounds. 'Aren't you surprised?'

'That he cheated on her? Not really.'

'No, I mean what I just told you, that I'm a photographer, and for a paper like that.'

'Well,' says Karen, 'I'm not surprised you're a photographer.'

We stand in silence for a moment, and then Karen starts washing the plates. 'Ashley's furious with me,' I tell her. 'That's why she's not saying much. Because I knew about Donny cheating before she did. And she's furious with Loreen because she let this journo in and he offered her money. She found these old photos that Loreen dug out, one's of Ashley in Portugal with this boy . . .'

Karen nods, and I remember that she already knows this.

'She's blaming me when I didn't know anything about it.'

'Oh well, you and Ashley.'

'Me and Ashley what?'

Karen just smiles and starts stacking the washed dishes on the drying rack.

'So,' says Loreen, opening the kitchen door, 'what are we going to do?'

Karen turns, surprised. 'Why?' she asks. 'What do you think we should do?'

Loreen doesn't answer, she just shouts, 'Ashley!', and then she waits until Ashley comes into the kitchen and then she closes the door and tells us all to sit at the tiny table like we're her class and she's going to tell us what we need to do today.

We sit down and Loreen is the only one left standing. 'You have to get him here,' she tells Ashley. 'It's obvious, isn't it? You tell him to come here, tell Donny you want to hear his side of the story or something, it doesn't matter what, just get him here. And then you,' she points at me and she looks so like a teacher that for a second I think she's going to say I failed a test, that I didn't try hard enough, that I didn't hand my homework in on time, 'you, Bel, take the picture.'

519

Chapter Fifty-Six

I'm back on the balcony again. The rain has stopped and the air feels cooler, cleaner, than it did before. I'm standing with my phone in my hands texting Ray because I want to see him, I want to tell him I'm sorry I ran out on him last night, that given the chance I wouldn't do it again. I send my message off into space and Ray texts back at once and I like that, I like that he doesn't play games. I put my phone away, think what would happen if I wasn't a snapper any more, if Ray wasn't on the desk any more, if we could get together and maybe live a different sort of life. But then, I think, you need money for that.

I look back into Loreen's front room and the way the door frames the people inside is so perfect I want to take a snap. Karen is crouched down in front of the telly and at first I think she's adjusting the sound, but then I see she's sorting through Loreen's old girly annuals. Dudu is on the sofa, reading a book to Anthony, and he's sitting there, still in the football kit he came in in, still in his trainers encrusted with mud, and he's shoulder to shoulder with his nan, listening to her read the book. In the middle of the room Ashley's still sitting on the floor, but now she's putting nail varnish on Dwaine's toes and his little boy face is furrowed in concentration. He's had a bath and he looks sweet in his stripy pyjamas. Ashley finishes one foot and Dwaine inspects it, then he wriggles his toes and he shouts something; he's probably asking his mum to come and have a look. Ashley smiles at him, then she takes her phone out of her handbag, checks it, and even from out here I can see her face tightening. So I know what's happened, she's got a reply.

I turn my attention back to the street below. I've been out here watching for a long time, waiting. And then it happens. A Bentley convertible appears, black and sleek like it's just come out of a showroom. I watch it drive up the street, hear the wetness of the road as it pulls up outside Loreen's mansion block and parks behind Ashley's Ferrari. At once Fred from the *Mirror* gets out of his Hillman, beanie man comes running, the dildo of his long lens bouncing against his chest. I can see Brian and two paps close behind.

The Bentley parks and I watch as the driver's door opens and Donny Green gets out. I can see his shaggy blond hair, the blueness of his shirt, the whiteness of his trousers. Who the hell wears white trousers? He's looking at something in his hand, a mobile perhaps, and he's still studying it as he starts up the steps between the grass verges that lead up to the pavement. Two girls ride by on mountain bikes and one of them screeches to a halt when they see the Bentley and then Donny Green. They stare, nudge each other, then one shouts out, 'Donny!' and she shouts it in a mocking way, like girls at school teasing a male teacher, a young one who thinks everyone fancies him.

Donny Green waves to the girls, casually, not really looking, because he's used to this sort of attention. He doesn't even seem phased by the fact there's a pack of paps out there. But he doesn't notice beanie man, not until he's halfway up

521

the steps to the pavement. By then it's too late. Beanie man has leapt in front of him, his SLR in his hands. Donny Green tries to dodge, to turn his face away, but beanie man is right there, on a higher step, flashing him up. The two girls on bikes have been joined by others now; people have come out of the flats to watch, some have their mobile phones out, trying to catch a snap of the action. I peer down over the balcony, watching. I want Donny Green to make it up here, I don't want him to run away from beanie man and the rest of the paps, because we're waiting for him. I don't know if Loreen's plan is going to work, but I've rung Glen and everything is in place.

Donny Green gets to the top step and he reaches the pavement and still beanie man is ahead of him, running backwards up the next flight of steps that lead to the mansion's front door. And then on the very top step, beanie man trips; one minute he's running backwards snapping Donny Green, the next he's stumbled and fallen, something flies out of his pocket and hits the black metal railing, and he's lying there, face-down across the step, his left hand outstretched. Donny Green keeps on walking and I see him lift his foot and bring it right down on beanie man's hand. I wait for beanie man to leap up, to shout out, to clutch his hand and drop his SLR. But beanie man doesn't get up, he doesn't even seem to protest. He just swivels on the steps and points his camera up and starts taking photos of Donny Green standing on his hand.

Then the balcony door opens behind me and Loreen is standing there. 'Are you ready?'

I come into the front room, look around. It's all been

cleared up, there's no sign of the meal we had earlier, you'd never know four women had been eating in here. Dwaine's crayons have gone and the girly annuals are stacked neatly in the cabinet under the TV. The overhead light is off, the table has been wiped; the only things on it are two red candles which give the room a warm, cosy glow. The TV is off and there is the faint sound of music from Loreen's CD player on the shelf, the shelf where the old photos still are.

'Is it OK?' Ashley asks, and I see what she's done; she's made it feel romantic in here. I almost laugh, because this is what Ashley does, she's an interior designer, and I think of that day Jodie in the office was reading the *Sunday Post*, reading all about Donny Green and his new house in Notting Hill, and I know now that's how Ashley must have met him, she must have been designing his house.

'Very nice,' I tell her. Ashley sits down on the arm of the sofa and crosses her legs at the ankles. She looks totally calm, but the bracelets on her arm jangle a little and that's how I know she's shaking.

'You get it,' I say when the buzzer goes.

Ashley goes into the hallway and I follow. I pass Loreen's bedroom and look into the kitchen. Dudu is sitting at the table. She has a cup of tea in front of her but her eyes are closed. I check there is nothing on the stove and then I close the door. I look into Dwaine's room. Loreen is sitting on his bed. 'Sleep,' she urges him as the buzzer goes again. 'Right now, go to sleep.' She pulls up the duvet, tucks her son in.

'But Mum!' says Dwaine.

'Chocolate!' Loreen whispers. 'Chocolate in the morning if you go straight to sleep now, OK?'

Dwaine beams and snuggles down and Loreen waves that I can shut the door because she's in charge now; this is all her idea and more than anything in the world I want it to work. I pop my head into Anthony's room; he's sitting on his bed, playing on a Nintendo. Karen sits next to him on a chair, leafing through a magazine, and she raises her eyebrows at me like she's asking, is this how you want it? I close Anthony's door as well, then I run back along the hallway to Loreen's bedroom where I hid when Brian the overeager boy journo came round earlier. It's a good spot; through the door, open just a crack, I can look down the hallway to the front door, I can see Ashley's just about to reach it. She pulls open the door and he's standing there, Mr hot-shit pop star Donny Green in his white trousers, with an expression on his face that even from here I can see is fake.

'Babe!' he says, and he throws open his arms. For a second Ashley is undecided, I can see her body make a quick sudden motion like she's going to go towards him and fall into his arms, but then she doesn't, she grips her arms by her side, she manages to stay where she is. 'Babe,' Donny Green says again. Ashley turns and lets him follow her down Loreen's hallway and into the front room. He doesn't seem to question whose flat he's just come into or why no one else is here, he just follows Ashley and all the way he's talking, quietly, urgently, 'Babe, I'm so sorry, it was a set-up, they've been hounding me, you know how it is, it will never happen again . . .'

I watch him from the doorway and I think, get him out, Ashley, get him out and onto the balcony like I told you. I can't do it in here, this is Loreen's flat, it's private property, get him outside in public and we'll have our snap. But do it quickly, before the other paps know you're out there, because right now they're all on short lenses so they won't be able to snap the balcony anyway. I rush across Loreen's darkened bedroom to the window, pull aside the blind and look down at the road. There's a group of people right outside the mansion block on the pavement, standing close, talking, laughing, like they're having a party. In front of them, on the grass verges, I count ten paps. I see Fred from the *Mirror*, Sam from the *Express*, and for a moment I think I see broadsheet Jimmy too. But where's beanie man? Then I see him, he's standing at the doors to the mansion block opposite and he's ringing the buzzer. He's going for the roof, I think, he's going to try and snap Loreen's flat from the roof, and my heart lurches as he pushes at the double door because someone has let him in and because if he gets to the roof he'll have a clear view of the balcony.

I rush back to Loreen's bedroom door, peer out to where Ashley and Donny Green are in the front room. But I can't see them, I can only just hear their voices. I have to take a risk, so I step out of Loreen's bedroom, stand in the doorway to the front room. Donny Green has his back to me, but Ashley sees me at once. I have my SLR in my hands and I signal to her, she has to get him outside. Ashley's face shows no sign that I'm here, she just smiles at Donny Green. 'Babe,' she says, 'I know, it's OK,' and she takes his hand in hers and leads him to the balcony and I'm there in a flash. I start snapping at once, ten frames, and I know with my first one that I've got it, the moment that Ashley lifts her face to Donny Green as if to kiss him, and instead a spray of spit hits his manicured cheek and she slaps him, hard, across the face. And I get the moment he realises this, as he turns to find me right here hosing him down, and I run backwards into the room. 'Hey! Bitch!' he yells. But I don't care because I got it and I know no one else got that snap but me.

Chapter Fifty-Seven

ASHLEY

My therapist has asked me to think of boundaries and so I indulge her and I lean back in my chair and I envisage emerald green fields rolling out before me on a summer's day and rows of picket fences neatly dividing the land. Here is the boundary fence that separates my working life from my life as a mother and here is the boundary fence that separates me from my ex-husband and here is the . . . Only I don't think she quite means this. What she means is setting boundaries for myself, so that I don't hurtle headlong into the sort of drama from which I have just pulled myself, only half intact, still hurting. However she doesn't know yet, I think, what has brought me here.

I like my therapist's room; its design is at once homely and businesslike. The wooden blinds at the window are the colour of pecan and the shade of the wood is complemented both by an elegant writing desk, behind which my therapist sits, and the chair I have chosen which has simple rounded lines like that of a sea shell. The scent in the room is a subtle jasmine, and I have noted three ceramic bowls of pot pourri placed at strategic intervals on the bookshelves lining the far wall. On my therapist's desk is a framed photograph turned towards her and which I am assuming is of her family: a husband, perhaps, or a lover, a child or two, perhaps even a grandchild. She wears a black cardigan, a classic Dior with a round neck and tulle trim along the arms, and around her neck is a pendant, the silver bright and clean against the black of her cardigan, the stone inside as mauve as a sunset at the coast. She does not look like the sort of person who reads the *Sunday Post*, although you can never tell.

I appreciate being in here; I want to stay in here as long as I can, although I no longer feel so horribly trapped if I am out on the street or at home. It's only recently that the photographers have stopped shadowing me, and now, at last, when I emerge from my house in the morning there is no one there waiting for my girls and me. Doorstepping, Bel has told me they call it, although given the opportunity I think these photographers would hurl themselves right through my front door. But I am old news now. I am a nobody again and I am glad it is over, that if I sit on a park bench with a boyfriend there will be no one to snap me and put it in the *Sun*. I am glad that when I go out to a bar I don't have to keep looking round, ever fearful, wondering if someone is waiting to catch me again.

When I went round to Loreen's last month, as I walked up the stairs in her monstrously cold block of flats in such a daze that I went to the wrong floor, I thought I'd made a dreadful mistake. I was appalled to find Bel waiting there and I thought Loreen had betrayed me, that when I had rung her in my distress, she had in turn rung Bel. But of course she hadn't, it was just my latent paranoia.

And then Loreen's mother arrived, and if there is one

person who has never liked me then it is Loreen's mother. I always knew, with a child's instinct, that she didn't like me, perhaps it was because she always seemed to catch me at my worst, like the day she came into Loreen's bedroom and found me instructing Loreen on the finer points of inter-course, which I had gleaned from my father's *Joy of Sex* and which I had witnessed once or twice while standing outside my parents' bedroom door early in the morning. How hor-rified Loreen's mother had been then, how I had been forced to lie and say it had been Loreen's idea, although I could see her mother didn't believe a word of it. I can date Dudu's dislike of me from that day and it was a dislike that was so intense that, years later, when she got hit by the car in Brighton, it was me she blamed. And yet it was Bel who suggested we go and find Dudu hidden away in that for-tune-teller's place on the seafront and I was just, for once, agreeing with her.

I stayed at Loreen's flat, however, even after Dudu arrived, and I stayed while we had our miserable meal and while the others shared stories from their lives, everyone discussing and commenting except for me. It was relief in the end when Loreen told me what to do. So I texted Donny and I gave him Loreen's address and I led him into Loreen's living room and all the while I tried not to hear him, as he apologised, as he pleaded. And then he relaxed because he thought it was just the two of us and naturally he thought that I would for-give him, as I had twice before. He called me 'babe' and said, 'They're fucking stalking me outside,' and I smiled at him so sweetly and led him to the balcony and that was when Bel snapped him, that is what she calls it, snapping, as if she were a piranha fish, the very moment I spat at Donny Green and slapped his handsome face with the back of my hand.

The very next morning the picture was everywhere, in every paper, on every newsstand. It was an exclusive and that's what Bel wanted. I don't think she could believe it at first, that I was willing to agree to Loreen's plan, but when you have been humiliated like that there are very few options left and the best option in my opinion is revenge. I took the vengeance for myself of course, I am well aware of my selfish tendencies, but I also did it for Bel because that was the picture she wanted, she knew exactly what she wanted. And I provided her with that moment and that photograph because then she would like me, it's as simple as that.

My therapist has decided I have said something of interest for she opens a notebook on her writing desk and she jots down a few words, quickly, like a doctor writing a prescription. But I am far more interested in the conclusion I have just come to, that I have spent my entire life attempting to persuade Bel to like me. And the only reason for that is that Bel has simply never cared. She has never cared whether I like her or not because Bel can do without me, and that fascinates me so much that I want her to care, I want to *make* her care. I used to tell tales on Bel when we started school; I thought that was what you were supposed to do, be honest and tell the truth. So if I saw Bel pushing in the dinner queue or writing rude words on the blackboard or stealing a grape from the harvest assembly then, at once, I told a teacher. It took me a long time to realise this was not telling the truth, this was telling tales.

Still, I tried to get her to like me, and yet the only way I knew how to do this was to try and buy her. I promised her things like my father promised me things – holidays and trips to Harrods and new clothes – I wanted to get her interest and to keep her interest. I said she couldn't come to Portugal when we were sixteen because I thought that would *make* her want to come, and then I said she could, and I gave her the money because I thought she would like me for that. I stole the money over a period of several weeks, starting with the crisp ten-pound notes left out in white envelopes on the hall shelf for my parents' cleaning lady. The year before last I gave her a white gold necklace for her birthday and that didn't make her like me either. But now perhaps she will.

Bel sold the picture and so she has the money to travel like she always wanted to, Loreen has the money she needs so much, Karen has donated her share to a children's charity, which is very like her, and I'm spending mine in therapy, which is very like me. I could have gone to therapy before, of course – I could have gone at just about any point in the last fifteen years – but there is something very sweet about going now.

I laugh suddenly and my therapist glances at me in a disapproving manner, but I can't believe Donny seriously intends to sue the agency that bought Bel's photograph. He has said it was an invasion of his privacy – dear God, the ego of the man – but as Bel has pointed out, he couldn't very well expect privacy standing outside on a balcony when he knew full well the paparazzi and his fans were out there. And what of the pictures he sent of himself, the ones he emailed to those poor girls on the Internet? Was he not already invading his own privacy, and theirs, with those? And what of my privacy, had he not violated that? Bel has told me he wants to sue her for breach of confidence, which I find amusing in a dreadful sort of way, for it was my confidence that he breached, not hers.

Bel left three weeks ago with her new man Ray, and she may be halfway around the world by now. I will call her when I leave here, when my session is over, and I will call Karen too because she and her girlfriend are back in California. And I will tell Loreen what they say when we meet tomorrow for a civilised drink, and she will tell me all about her date because she says she thinks this is it, he's the one, although she hasn't told me where she met him yet.

'Tell me about your daughters,' says the therapist, because I have not been very forthcoming on the topic of boundaries and have obviously said nothing else worth writing down. So I do, I tell her about their ages and their likes and dislikes and their school and their au pair Afina who is Romanian and very good. 'Tell me,' she says. 'Do you have fun with them?'

'Oh yes,' I say at once. 'I often take them to the cinema, the theatre, museums. Amy has piano lessons and Mia has a tutor for her . . .' And then as the therapist sits there blinking at me, twirling the pendant round her neck in a most irritating fashion, I hear myself and I realise, I am my father. This was his idea of parenthood. He wanted me to do well, to succeed, and he would be furious if I didn't succeed, if someone dared to do better than me, especially if it was Bel, and that was another reason why I wanted her to like me, because as far as my father was concerned she was my rival. It didn't matter if it were a party game or a prize at school, I was to win, I was to beat Bel. I remember the day we left primary school and Bel got a prize and I did not and all the way home my father ranted, *You've got everything, Ashley, how could you not get a prize with all the extra tuition you get, are you sure you didn't get a prize, how on earth did Bel Lavender get a prize and not you . . .*

My father was the most competitive person I have ever met in my life. I think of sports day when he would instruct me on warm-up exercises, ensure my laces were properly tied, that I drank water and would not become dehydrated, and then he stood on the sidelines and he shouted, *Go on, Ashley, you can do it, go on, faster, faster, watch out for Bel behind you!* He shouted so loud and so furiously that other parents actually put their hands over their ears.

And yet while my father apparently wanted the best for me, he did not actually want to spend time with me. If I wanted to draw a picture or make a house out of a cardboard box, then I simply didn't engage him any more. And by the time I was old enough to ask, to demand even, that he spend time with me, to realise that this was what was missing, he had left. If you are abandoned once then you expect it to happen again, and of course it did. It happened with my first boyfriend Steve, it happened with Jay B, it happened with the girls' father, it happened with Donny Green. What is wrong with me that I'm so unloved?

I think of mentioning this to my therapist – of telling her about Steve and Jay B and my ex-husband and Donny Green – but she will probably make the startlingly astute observation that the men in my life have been replicates of my father. Why has it always been like this? Everything I have ever done has been in terms of my relationship with a man.

When Donny cheated on me the first time it seemed so

expected, when I heard him in his bathroom that dreadful night of the bombs, speaking on his phone, speaking softly to his PA, saying, 'I'm dying to see you as well, babe.' Bel and Loreen were at a bar in Soho that evening, a bar just a stone's throw from my office where I ran away from Donny and sobbed half the night until the au pair rang and asked when I was coming home. I knew they wouldn't even notice I wasn't there. I would have added nothing to their evening; they were better off without me.

And when Donny cheated on me again, I simply hid myself away. I stopped even answering calls from Loreen, because if you despise yourself then what are you going to say to your friends? But when it happened a third time, and when he told me the press knew, then that was too much.

The session is over but I would like to stay here another hour or more if I could. I write out the cheque and I pick up my handbag and then I stop in the corridor, which has a carpet that is stained but serviceable like a hotel. I go through my bag and I take out the picture Loreen has given me, and I look at myself in my red and white bikini and then I look at him. I can feel the touch of that German boy, the way he cornered me on the cliff as I was going back to the house to join Bel, and the way he ran up behind me when I didn't even know he was there. I didn't want him to touch me, but I thought, if I allow this, then he will let me go, and he wanted me and I could never resist a boy who wanted me. Bel never mentioned what had happened, that she'd seen me; she never told me she'd taken a photograph. When we touched our thumbs and made our pact and I said 'never tell', it didn't mean a thing. I'm staggered that Bel ever thought it did. I stand in my therapist's corridor and I tear the picture, it's not as easy as I expected, there is a glossy layer to it that takes a while, but I manage and I shred it into little pieces and I put them tidily in the waste bin that has been so kindly provided and I walk out of my therapist's building and I take out my phone to call my friends.

Acknowledgements

Many thanks to the following people who helped me while I was writing this book:

The snappers who freely shared their experiences, but who would rather not be named. Anya Reid for a conversation that started things off. Peter Dale, Professor Emeritus at The University of California, Davis, for his patience over my haphazard memories of Davis and for correcting my academic mistakes. Bonty Botumile for help with my fading Setswana. Tricky for letting me poke around her balcony. Chris Demetriou for teaching assistance. Linda Macpherson, lecturer in law at Heriot Watt University, for her very helpful guide to photographers' rights in the UK and for her discussions on privacy, a vague and ever changing area of law. Thanks also to Professor Eric Barendt, Goodman Professor of Media Law at University College London.

I read the following books while researching this novel:
Watching the English, by Kate Fox
Paparazzi, by Peter Howe
Mr Paparazzi, by Darryn Lyons
The boy who couldn't stop washing – the experience and treatment of Obsessive-Compulsive Disorder, by Dr Judith Rapoport
Accidental IT Girl, by Libby Street